Callie,
  I hope you'll enjoy this
"road trip."
  Thanks!

Bound for Ebenezer

Glinda McKinney

Glinda McKinney

glindamckinney@att.net

The photograph on the cover of
BOUND FOR EBENEZER
is of the historic Massey House
in Victorian Village, Memphis, Tennessee.
It was built in 1846
and is now being used as headquarters for
the City Beautiful Commission.
Much appreciation and many thanks go to
Scott Blake, President of VictorianVillageInc.
for his time and advice,
and also to **Monty Shane**, who photographed
the Colonial Revival house especially for this book.

Also by Glinda McKinney
(First printing, The Painted Lady of Shallot,
pen name Jeannie McKinney)

The Ladies of Shallot

When a young woman sells her father's masterpiece to remain in her home, consequences await.

Unable to handle the notoriety of being depicted somewhat mystically while a young girl in her father's paintings, which initiated her mother's jealousy, Crystal Bell has almost become a recluse as an adult.

When Crystal mistakenly delivers a copy of the painting, the buyer's retribution forces dangerous decisions on her. She must deal with three men who want her, give refuge to a young mixed-race family, learn about a secret that changes her entire life, accept new relationships with her mother as well as elderly Sarah in the mansion next door,
and fight for her very life.

To Gerald, my help and sustainer in all things. You made this book possible.

To Patty Duncan, my first time reader, many time editor, counselor, literary adviser, steadfast supporter, friend, and author of Ellen's Eye and Detour to Dallas.

To JUDGE McKINNEY for technical aspects of this book.
To HAILEY McKINNEY for formatting the book for print.
To LIZZY McKINNEY for designing the cover color and text.
To JACQUIE McKINNEY and TUCKER McKINNEY for the author photo.

Thank you Carol Tomlinson and Beth Patterson for reading this manuscript.
Your suggestions were so much appreciated and made the book better.
Any errors this book contains are the fault of the author.
To Jerrie Moffat for an East Tennessee book signing.
Long live Bookstop Plus in Bartlett! To readers and friends who came to my book
signings for The Ladies of Shallot and bought it for
your friends also and gave me such good reports and reviews.
To Phyllis Sheehy for writing its first review, a five star one at that.
To all who asked for a sequel to The Ladies of Shallot, as well as encouraging me to get
Bound for Ebenezer published. I wish I could name you all!
Again, Dear God, let anyone instrumental in its creation have reason to be proud of
this book that attains to literary fiction, and let all who read it be at the very least
content with their time invested in it.

PROLOGUE

FOR a summer afternoon, early July if he calculated correctly, it was comfortably cool, especially on the bench in the shade of the tree. The tree probably wasn't over seventy feet tall, but its lowest branches had long since gotten high enough to swing out over the low roof of the old brick building, probably originally a blacksmith shop, that was now painted white and had a gas pump out front. Although it had been years since his class on southern trees, he thought this one was a red oak because of its long leaves and small acorns with just a little cap almost like a beret. This variety didn't grow in Mississippi, but he'd seen forests of them in Kentucky.

The breeze stirred it, making a siren song that would lull him to sleep if he didn't move soon, although he'd slept well last night. Hadn't even taken one of the pills the doctor gave him for his leg. His bed was a pile of hay, but the dark had surrounded him like a barrel, and he'd felt reassured about his eye under the patch stretched around his temples, because his uninjured eye couldn't see in the blackness either.

Although not as quiet as last night, it was so peaceful now, just a work-day conversation between the two men inside and tools clinking occasionally under a suspended car. He was tired from the walking this morning. His body felt like one big sore muscle. But he still didn't regret his decision. He stretched his leg out as much as he could in the canvas brace with the staves in it that covered his khaki trouser leg, and rested his arm hanging in the drab olive sling against his chest. He'd just relax and rest here a while more...

PART I

BATTLE IN ELAH VALLEY

And Saul and the men of Israel were gathered together and pitched
by the valley of Elah, and set the battle in array against the Philistines.
First Samuel 7: 2
Holy Bible
1 King James Version
set forth 1611 A.D.

ONE

S hep snapped awake. A woman in a black shroud turned her legs to slide out of a long black car. She looked at him and pitied him at first, but then smiled. She walked to him and sat next to him on the bench. She put her arm through his and leaned her head on his shoulder.

What? Instantly he became aware that he had been asleep in a vacant place in his mind that hadn't even let any memories in, and he didn't know where he was, but that he had been wakened, and not by explosions. No. Not tanks and machine guns. It had only been the smooth sound of an engine that did not have to strain to carry its load, unlike the army vehicles that he had grown accustomed to. But it was more like a recruit driving it who didn't know yet how to handle the vehicle.

He did a double-take, if only with the one seeing eye it could be called that. Damn. In his hallucination of waking, he had imagined what he wanted to see happen, he supposed. Because in fact, a woman was sliding out of the car. But she didn't come to him.

She wasn't in a shroud either, but dressed in black high heel shoes, a strap around the ankle peeking out of loose-fitting dark gray slacks as she stretched her legs to the ground. A white short-sleeve blouse was tucked in. She was like a magazine advertisement of a female who was taking advantage of freedoms the war was bringing, no matter who she was. She lifted a chauffeur's cap, revealing thick black hair in long, smooth curls. And no matter what else she was, she was young and he couldn't deny, beautiful.

He almost wondered if he could still be dreaming. The huge black Cadillac LaSalle was preposterous in this backwoods, like an emperor's carriage would be in a hinterland. It was a '40 or '41 he'd guess, by far the nicest vehicle he'd seen since he'd been on the road. Probably would have been even if the automobile factories hadn't converted to build war machines. The little group inside was exhibited like a framed photograph behind the expansive windshield. And if that wasn't revealing enough, you only had to look through one of the six side windows or large rear window.

Why in Heaven's name did it come to this wide spot in a dirt road in a Kentucky valley hidden between two hills? This unincorporated community hadn't even felt the need to identify itself with a welcome sign. They didn't expect, probably didn't even want, any strangers. Especially such as the little group lighting on the place in front of their eyes.

The license plate on the front bumper said the car had started in Washington, D. C., the very place he had begun his odyssey. Was that some kind of God's irony? Certainly this was not its destination any more than it was his, or any more than a steer would deliberately run into the slaughterhouse gate. Could it be they were having car trouble?

And how did the young woman get a job driving the damn car, if she couldn't do any better than she'd done pulling in here? It had crunched to a not exactly smooth stop on the gravel in front, even with its hydraulic brakes, even a bit of grinding of gears as she shifted too early.

He should have been used to strange sights by now after serving the past two years in Uncle Sam's army, but this beat all. The car might as well have been pasted with a banner identifying it as Trouble. The dust wasn't settled and already the talk between the two men inside the cluttered little gas station had stopped, their conversation hanging like balloons over cartoon characters.

They were already in aggravated mode, having been kicking the bald tires of an old pick-up parked in the shade not far from where he sat, when Shep had limped up about half an hour ago. After a few minutes the two men had gone inside discussing a dirty Ford sedan that was suspended over the work pit, and owned by the hefty man in tan pants. Shep's glance at the impotent car had put him in mind of a behemoth pig blackened and ash-blown, being removed from its burial cooking by the black workers on his place down in the delta.

The two men's voices had floated out the open window of the small building with the careless assurance that their viewpoint was the only relevant one, as they calculated the cost of rebuilding the car's transmission, versus simply adding oil and taking it up to Ohio to sell. "Damn Yankees deserve it," the big man had avowed, ignoring the reality of Kentucky's loyalty to the Union in the 1860's. "And don't forget ole' Jeff Davis was ours," said the petite man, who had introduced himself to Shep as Mr. White, owner of the station. Shep wondered if that was to counter the fact, apparently troublesome to them, that Lincoln was theirs, too.

"Fed'ral gov'ment got no right telling states how to run their business," the big man had added.

Sure, this war was different, they had concluded. Had to join the Yankees in this one, like in the Great War. Shep wondered if maybe they'd added that for his benefit as a soldier; he wasn't certain.

"Reckon it's true about the Jew-killing?" Mr. White had asked, raising his voice enough that Shep had realized he was to answer. "Papers say so," he had replied, without opinion in his voice. Not going to get anything started. Just rest in the shade, enjoy a cold drink, be on his way in a few minutes.

"Now that would be one to ponder out back over your catalogue in the mornin'," the big man had stated, accepting no opinion of someone he didn't know, directing his theorizing back to Mr. White. But loud enough to show he didn't really care if Shep heard.

And the voices had never tired of the subject, reaching him even now as he snapped awake: "And what if Hitler was to say after the Jews and Polaks comes the Ni – !"

Shep could practically see their hackles rising as the two men had given up their diatribe to witness the black apparition descending upon them.

All things considered, it might not be such a strange sight in certain sections of Washington, Shep thought. But around here, just like where he was headed, you just didn't see this.

A fine car, led as if in flight by the winged goddess of a hood ornament.

And three Negroes as its occupants.

And, "Parking in front pretty as you please!" according to Mr. White, accompanied by the other man's exasperated, "What the hell is that?!"

TWO

They'd accepted Shep as an unusual though worthy wayfarer, being an injured soldier hitchhiking home. No more questions to him than would be a friendly inquiry of any stranger – of their own kind, that is to say white, as opposed to a trio as unlikely as Martians in a flying saucer. Where was he coming from, where'd he seen action, where was he heading now; and they had accepted it when he'd answered a hospital in D.C., a little place in Italy they wouldn't have heard of, and a little place in Mississippi they wouldn't have heard of either. His way of practicing more of what he'd learned lately about giving as little information as possible, like that was all there was to it.

So here he sat on this bench, his Double Cola from the low red cooler filled with ice and melted ice, making a ring on the plank. He had been astonished that the drink was still being made in its twelve ounce size considering the sugar rationing. He swigged the last couple of ounces as he watched the scene unfold, the talk floating about like smoke which you don't notice since you're not alert, until you see the actual flames.

Even the mechanic buried under the fettered Ford stretched up to see what the arrival was that could have smothered the incendiary talk. For a moment the mechanic looked like a circus strongman supporting a car on his head. He wiped his face with a rag and rested his chin on the board floor ending at the pit wall.

But in spite of wearing the driver's hat and doing the driving, the young woman wasn't the chauffeur, and that answered one question, at least. It was her incompetent driving and not car trouble. Because through the other front door came a very big, very black man, probably in his late fifties. He was dressed in a black double-breasted chauffeur's uniform with tall black boots that would rival any goose-stepper's you'd see in the newsreels at the pictures. He stomped his feet, bringing up fine dust as he fastened his top button in spite of the heat. Looked like he'd been napping for a while and needed to get his circulation going.

He grabbed the chrome handle just behind his and swung the door open toward the rear and extended his arm inside. A frail old lady emerged leaning on it. She was probably eighty-five if a day, only a white lace collar and frizzy white hair relieving her wrinkled grey-blackness. She was as small next to him as a sparrow to an eagle.

Damn. Hadn't they ever been out of the Negro section in D.C.? They looked to be sophisticated, but they obviously knew nothing of what was just two states removed. He – she – certainly didn't pull up in front in a car that cost every bit of fifteen hundred dollars, probably more than the station owner would clear in a few years. And she damn sure didn't get out and look around like she wanted to buy the place, instead of going to the side and waiting for service at the own good time of the mechanic. You just keep on, don't you, he said silently to her, hoping she'd impossibly hear his warning, hoping it was that and not an admonition.

They must have gotten lost at the detour a few miles back where the bridge had been washed out, just like he did, coming from the same place. He knew why he was here at this moment. His leg had been throbbing, as he had not seen nearly as many vehicles as he had counted on – to hitch a few miles at intervals to relieve his walking – when he was offered a ride on a farm wagon that had let him off a mile or so east. The farmer had told him a service station was down the road where he could rest and get a cold drink. He had figured he could eventually intersect the state route he wanted, if this was actually the road he thought it was on his map, folded now inside his small duffle. And he didn't even feel a stranger in this place not too different from where he was returning. That's why he knew what was going to happen.

THREE

The mechanic crawled out of the pit into the silent commotion. The Charles Atlas look-alike clutched a wrench, his arm bulging out of his undershirt that the sleeves had been roughly cut out of.

Shep's money was on the chauffeur, even against the wrench, because of sheer size. Had she purposely looked for and hired Jack's giant? Maybe she thought she would encounter trouble along the way. No. Her entire persona showed she didn't expect this. How could she be so ignorant?

The two men inside the office all but collided in the doorway, the door propped open by a brick; but Mr. White, in dark blue work pants and white short-sleeved shirt with cigarettes, matchbook, air pressure gauge, pencil, and a worksheet stuffed in its pockets, gave over to the other man.

Gaddamn. Lot to learn about being observant. How could he not have noticed earlier? The big man's tan pants could be called uniform khakis, and he wore a white shirt with the sleeves rolled up, his black tie loosened for the summer heat. Looking inside Shep saw flung over a chair a brown jacket which he would bet had a badge pinned to it. The big man walked back to the chair and returned to the door fastening a pistol and holster around his large middle, shuffling it until he got it comfortable.

The mechanic stepped forward and looked toward the office. There would be a shotgun inside. But he must have decided the three of them could prevail. Yes, White and company would checkmate the black players.

But this wasn't any of his business. Not his fight. Hell, even the U.S. Army said he couldn't fight now, and they didn't say that easy. He had to agree he wouldn't be any good in a brawl, with his braced leg and slinged arm. And even with only one blue eye to see with for the present, maybe forever, he could see this situation well and good.

"The hell you think you doin'?" the lawman said to neither the young woman nor the big man, but more to the car, still taking it and the whole situation in, his right hand resting on his pistol.

"Girl, you can't drive a car like that," Mr. White added, apparently distrusting his own vision, maybe like God had said to the bumble bee about its flying ability.

The young woman had the good sense, if not the good sense to be afraid, to not answer, but she didn't shrink back. Big mistake. Was she from another country?

"Where'd you get that car?" the lawman asked.

She did take a step back at that, hearing the disregard for whatever answer she'd give. The chauffeur stepped back, too, and settled the little old woman back into the back seat and rolled her window the rest of the way down to allow in a little more air. Surprise. Shep wouldn't have thought he'd back down. Oh. He wasn't. He turned and started walking toward the front of the car. Just where was this other planet they were from?

Shep reached for his duffle. He had orders to get home, get as fit as possible, and get back. There was no rushing timetable, and taking this snail's trail was exactly what he wanted; but no room in that scenario for treading into this land mine, waiting for the hovering step that might hurl them all into jail.

Repeating the lawman's question, but speaking to the chauffeur, the mechanic said, "The hell you think you're doin'?" It seemed he thought only one thing other than size held sway in a situation like this, and that was color. His, if it was his own habitat.

The young woman put her hand on her driver's arm and he stopped. "We don't want any trouble," she said.

What must have seemed reasonable to her was another big mistake. Just keep on if you want to set off that explosion and see what real trouble is, Missey, Shep thought. You should have said, Mister we won't cause no trouble, and said it like you were already guilty of doing it and you were sorry about it and wouldn't he please not hold you responsible. A lot of intent in one statement but he'd heard it said just that way.

God. His mind was telling him to leave down the road, but his body wasn't budging. Was he going to have to do something, something about this thing that he didn't have any business doing?

"Sir... we ..." the woman started then stopped, maybe nothing but the grace of God giving her the good sense to be intimidated. Then the devil of pride got her hackles up. "We need to buy gas."

Shep looked at the windshield. Incredible. A Red C Sticker on it stuck out like a big sore thumb. Plenty of gas coupons with that one, reserved for doctors, mail carriers, ministers and a few others. Mr. White wouldn't like that either.

"And if you could give us directions ..."

Damn. Goddam. He wanted to grab her arm and tell her to stop, ask who did she think she was, Queen of the Black Cadillac? She was no foreign diplomat's daughter nor had no sugar daddy in government - not a far stretch with her looks if that's what she wanted - or she'd have that unrestricted "X" gasoline sticker paving her way. Maybe she was the pampered daughter or wife of a doctor or influential preacher in the Negro section of D.C. Or even the owner of a business where people owed him favors; he could have finagled a red sticker that way.

"Don't think you'll go anywhere for a while," the lawman said, satisfaction oozing with his words. "We got to find out whose car that is." Envy spilled from his eyes, covering the   vehicle like molasses over a biscuit. He unsnapped his holster.

Damn! Nothing Shep could do to keep this unknown spot in the road from becoming home to a bloodletting. The best he could hope for was that these people would give up their car and get their story out and the whole country would find out about it when other things besides the war became important again.

Just then the lawman noticed her gas sticker, and it was permission for all he'd hoped for. "Get the shotgun!" he yelled to the mechanic. "Look at that," he said to Mr. White, pointing to the windshield. "Them red stickers, lot of them are counterfeit!"

Her driver curled his fists and his mouth and his eyes and his back.

Good God. Was he going to have to do something? He didn't know what it could be. But the army didn't release a man just because he couldn't fight physically. They patched the man and tested him and evaluated him. Then they trained him to improvise and handle situations like this or worse. The Army had a lot of gaddamn expectations! What's more, they'd all assumed it would be his own life at stake, and not in his own damn country!

"Whitey, get the keys out the car. Can't belong to them. Bound to've stole it." The lawman said it like the verdict was already in.

The driver's face registered his contempt for that accusation and he stepped forward. The young woman stepped between the two men.

Shep felt as if he'd been hit between the eyes. Her mistakes had gotten worse as they stacked up, but her courage could not be questioned.

"The car belongs to me. The title and registration are in the box. But I think we should leave now," she said, making a move to turn.

The lawman would say those papers would be fakes, too.

"Just try it," the lawman said, hope in his I dare you attitude. "Fakes. Prob'ly got counterfeit money, too. Got to keep it for evidence. Gonna have to confiscate that fine automobile, too. May not ever know who it belongs to." He stroked his chin and drools of expectation could almost be seen as he reached a conclusion to his dilemma. "Don't matter," he said, glancing toward the station. "We got plenty of rope in there, Whitey? Think we'll have a party tonight."

Good God. He couldn't mean it like it sounded.

"We can get together," said the mechanic.

In 1944 in the middle of Kentucky? But they'd had a star in the Confederate flag, too, regardless of their failed vote. But, no, this wasn't a state's version of justice. This was individual hatred and old grudges this trio had nothing to do with. And more than that, greed. Envy and a chance to satisfy it. A man's character will out. Somebody said that. Long time ago.

The young woman's face changed to show something, not fear –he didn't think fear lived in her - not even anger, maybe the survival instinct. She looked at the car, possibly trying to calculate how quickly they could get in and get it started. Then reality caught up with her. They'd never make it in time.

FOUR

"Hello, there," Shep said, hobbling into the line of fire. Something had to be done, and goddamn his luck he was the only one available to do it. Every nerve was prickling the message that this particular war had been going on too long and he couldn't win it.

Nobody knew who the recipient of his greeting was, but it got everyone's attention. The three white men had forgotten all about him, looking at him as if he were a worm that had turned up in their nice peach, and the interlopers had not even noticed him, judging from their shocked faces, wondering if this was yet another contention.

"Who you talking to?" Mr. White said.

"They're here for me." Where *that* came from he didn't know.

The woman and her colossus looked at him as if he were saying he was Zeus and this was his chariot.

"What does that mean?" the lawman said, "Here for you."

"Just what I said."

"Mister, you must've been bad injured in the head, too!" Mr. White said. Shep noted without surprise that he'd dropped the Lieutenant title he'd used earlier.

"Why the hell'd they come here for you?" the lawman said.

"I believe that's my wife's maid and chauffeur. Come to meet me. I'm a Lieutenant in the U. S. Army, headed home on medical leave. Nothing unusual about this in the delta."

"That don't shed no light." The lawman shifted to address his two cohorts without taking his eyes from Shep. "Boys, we just may have an imposter. This ain't no Southern boy."

The mechanic's shotgun pointed at Shep's chest.

The men would probably remember his name because they'd never had a wounded soldier hitchhiking through here. So, keep as much of the truth as you can. Always best. But especially in a situation where you could get yourself tripped up under interrogation, he'd learned. "I'm Shep Haddon," he said to the woman, turning sideways to look at her and to narrow the target for the mechanic. "Are you in Kentucky at the direction of Dorthea Haddon, to meet her husband?"

If she didn't have the quick wit to play along, or the sense of self-survival that he thought had kicked in a minute ago, the fight would start, shooting would follow. Any survivors would be in the sheriff's car headed to jail. The Cadillac would be a thing of their past. That would be their best case scenario. Worst case, the three of them would be introduced to a bunch of white-robers deep in the woods about midnight, like the lawman had alluded to a few minutes ago. And the other men hadn't so much as twitched a brow at it.

And when Shep saw the light of day again – he didn't think they'd have the guts to hang a U.S. Army officer – he'd wind up in a court martial for interfering with the law on some trumped up charge, nobody believing this preposterous tale without any bodies, the car sold to black marketers. And Captain Boyd would be saying you call that handling a situation?

"Here for you?" she said, her tone indicating she'd never seen him before in her life.

"Maybe you didn't expect such a broken-down soldier."

"No, I didn't expect someone like you," she said, perhaps because it was easy enough to agree about his physical condition. "But we couldn't have met at a better place."

"If they're here for you, why didn't anybody know it?" said the lawman.

"Guess I was dozing over there. Worn out from walking. Didn't pay any attention to what was going on. Wouldn't have recognized them if I had. She's hired new help since I've been gone. They didn't see me. You had them pretty busy here."

"Now you tell me what you're tryin' to do, soldier," said the Law, wavering, wondering if he had jumped the gun.

"I don't think I owe an explanation." He'd better come up with one, though. "I guess I didn't admit to my wife how I'd changed. How bandaged up I'd be. They wouldn't have thought it was me if they'd noticed me. Guess it all does look a little unusual."

"Don't it, though."

"My wife insisted she was going to send a car for me."

"You too good for the bus?"

"Too constricting on my leg. Doctor said walking is good for my rehabilitation." He headed off the next question. "Couldn't get train reservations to anywhere." Trading on sympathy, but this warranted it.

"Well, how'd they find you here? Elahvale ain't exactly on the beaten path," Mr. White said.

The lawman looked to see that the mechanic still had everything covered.

"They got lost like I did. You heard the girl ask for directions." And it would have to be at a place named after a Biblical battlefield, wouldn't it? If the young woman didn't have enough inherent feeling about the place not to bristle at his calling her "girl," this was a lost cause. "Anyway, my wife said they'd be waiting in Louisville. We anywhere close?"

"Just missed by seventy mile."

"Then we're lucky all around, I guess. This walking got old."

"Sounds sort of strange to me," said the lawman. "Why there?"

"A Negro hotel there. Good place for them to wait. About half way from D.C. for me." Major slip. Had they noticed the license plates?

"Ain't this out the way to Mis'sippi? Looks like goin' down through Virginia n' Tennessee'd be your best bet," said Mr. White.

Now that's a question he could answer easy enough. "I had a ride to Charleston."

"Why a company like this?" said the law.

"Guess Rufus here could have made the trip on his own? Probably had to have somebody to read maps, keep him from driving up to Detroit or Chicago. Maybe deciding to stay there." He looked at the young woman. "That right?"

She nodded.

He saw something different in her attitude toward him from a moment ago. Speculating as to why he was doing this for them. A brave soldier, saving their lives?

"Well, why ain't your wife with 'em? She so anxious about you."

"Five thousand acres of cotton don't run itself," he said.

"Well." The lawman gave a quick look to Mr. White, to gage his reaction.

"Just where'd you say you're from?" Mr. White said.

He'd better say now, and be truthful. The man could make a phone call to check it out. "Little town called Shepperton." Then he added, "Mississippi," in case the man thought to quiz the young woman.

"And who's the ole mammy in the back seat?" the lawman asked, after Shep recognized that he was registering and considering that Shep's hometown just might have been named after his family.

"That's about all the questions I'm going to answer."

Just then the door opened and the old lady turned herself to the outside and stretched to reach ground. She'd put on a small black hat with some netting that covered her face. Rufus, as the driver was now known, hustled over to help her. When she was on her own two feet on the ground, she looked up at Shep.

"You've only lost one eye," she said, in an authoritative voice. "Don't pretend you didn't see me. Embarrassed of your old mammy."

Now he hoped his surprise didn't show. "No ma'am. I'd never be embarrassed of that." And that was the truth.

She pulled the netting up from her face and said, "Do you think I'd let these two fetch you without me?"

"No ma'am," he said. "I should have known my old mammy would want to come meet me." And that was the truth, too.

"You get over here and let me look at you." She pulled a white hankie from her sleeve at her wrist and dabbed her eyes.

"Good God," he muttered, limping to her.

"Walkin' all over the country like this. Uniform's got all dusty. Shoes need polishin'."

He automatically brushed at his olive drab pants leg, for the first time noticing just how right she was, and holding his cap in his hand hanging from his sling, polished the brass on the cap with the sleeve of his good arm. She'd turned into a drill sergeant.

"Praise God we've found each other." She reached up, barely could touch the epaulets on his shoulders so tiny and stooped was she.

He found himself bending awkwardly and receiving a hug stronger than he could have imagined her capable of, and looked down to see a tear hung in both her eyes. She could have been his old mammy, except that Thula'd been gone to her well-earned reward fifteen years.

"What happened to you?" she asked. "What did you suffer to make you do this?"

He knew the others, the white men, were meant to think she was talking about his walking home. He understood she meant what could he have undergone that would make him get involved in their trouble. Strangers. Black strangers in a white man's world. He wasn't sure. Maybe it was something she could not imagine, and that he hadn't considered earlier. What a man learns when he's dodging war's death, and what fearful questions latch on when he's the one spared. She stared into his good eye, the one he was certain showed the uncertainties that lurked within.

"So you one of them plantation owners, huh?" said the lawman, and Shep felt himself moving up the ladder in the man's estimation.

"Grayson Farms. On the river." Only half-way from being true.

"High cotton, huh. Still live like before the war. You know the war I'm meanin'," the lawman said with a satisfaction that said he might not get his compensation, but it was enough to know that here was a man still living the life. He tucked his pistol into its holster and shuffled it around behind from his bulging stomach until it settled in its accustomed spot. He turned to the other two men. "Some folks still know how to live," he said, then turned back to Shep. "All right. OK. Fight the good fight."

"Better put that shotgun up before it accidentally goes off," Mr. White said to his helper.

"Won't be no accident," said the mechanic, taking it inside.

"We'll need the gasoline, a tank full if you can spare it," Shep said. And we'll need a whole lot of luck so you won't think about where the license plates are from.

FIVE

"Got your book?" Mr. White asked.

The driver came forward removing the gasoline ration book from his inside breast pocket. Mr. White took it and pulled out coupons.

"Fifteen gallons. Fifteen cent a gallon. That'll be $2.25." The young woman pulled a leather wallet from her black alligator skin purse and thumbed through a thickness of money to extract a ten and handed it to him. Mr. White snapped the crisp bill between his fingers, deciding to forego any more questions. He unrolled a cylinder of bills he took from his pants pocket and put the ten on the outside and methodically flipped a five and two ones from the top and fished three quarters from his pocket.

He gave the bills and change to Shep. Shep had paid ten cents a gallon yesterday, putting as much gas in an old man's car as he and his coupons allowed, when he got out at the gas station where they would part company after riding about thirty miles with him, and now he toyed with the idea of asking Mr. White for the extra five cents a gallon he had charged. But maybe it cost more to get it delivered here in the middle of nowhere. At any rate, no sign announced the price. The locals would know the going rate. But most importantly, Mr. White knew they could afford to pay and they couldn't afford to make a scene about the overcharge.

"I'd relieve her of the rest of that stack," Mr. White told Shep.

Rufus gave Shep a look that said just try.

Shep handed the money to her. "My wife will require a strict accounting," he said to the station owner. And that would have been an understatement if he hadn't made this whole thing up about Dorthea sending them. But now he thought he might not have been far off the mark; she would have sent a car out of exasperation if the thought had even occurred to her that he was already out of the hospital, walking and hitching home. The farm had that coveted blue unlimited sticker for agriculture, each coupon worth five gallons. They'd had their own gas pump before the war, and he was certain she'd managed to keep it replenished. Dorthea wouldn't have called it hoarding. She had an X sticker for her car. Her cousin William Grayson was in the U. S. House and had arranged it. At any rate, she would have managed to get him transported home if he had only told her. And if he would have let her.

The mechanic washed the windshield and even polished the grill, giving an extra swipe to the insignia scrawled across it, enjoying servicing the fine car in spite of his reservations. Shep wondered what Mr. White and the law would think the proper seating would be for him. Rufus had quickly installed the old lady in the back seat and the young woman had stood by her door, and maybe reading Shep's mind, said, "I'll sit in back. If you don't mind being up front."

Much of the seat and floorboard were packed, not cluttered, but space utilized, with boxes of varying sizes. Provisions for the trip? Contraband of some kind? Probably not. Being so conspicuous, they would be unlikely candidates for the black market.

Rufus helped the young woman in, settled himself in and started the car. Over the smooth hum of the engine, Shep heard the mechanic say, "Look here, Whitey," as he stepped back from washing the rear window and finally looked at the license plate mounted on the center of the trunk. "This car ain't from Mis'sippi." Rufus accelerated and Shep said to him, "Slow, like nothing's not true," and waved out the window as Rufus made the circle onto the road.

"It's from District of Columbia!" Mr. White yelled.

"Stop that car, if you know what's good for you!" the lawman called.

"The very reason we're leaving!" the young woman said with the indignity of a guest being thrown out for no reason she would acknowledge.

The lawman ran after them, trying to get his pistol out of its holster, still shifted around toward his back, yelling to the mechanic, "Git that car off that ramp!"

"Got just two quarts of oil!" the mechanic yelled.

The truck's flats kept it out of the chase. It couldn't have caught them, anyway, Shep thought, and as they rounded the bend said, "Now! Put on the speed."

"Hold your hat!" Rufus said.

A few minutes later when it became clear the law was not hot on their bumper the old lady said, "I had hoped some things were changed."

Shep turned to look at her just as the young woman put her hand inside her large rather flattish rectangular pocketbook.

"I thank you for what you did back there," she said. "That couldn't have been easy. Coming up with a story like that. Stepping into our fight. And I hope you don't live to regret it." Then she withdrew a pistol from her purse, and he was no longer the high-minded soldier to her. "But maybe you have a weapon and think you can take our car and money when we can stop and put you out."

Good God. Who were these crazy people? What was their business? Maybe she could have handled all this without his interference.

"Angelene, put that pistol away," said the old lady. "This man's not going to try to harm us. I looked him in the eyes."

Shep felt she said eyes rather than calling attention to his patched one.

"I guess he'd be too smart, anyway," Angelene said, halfway shrugging, maybe having thought it over.

Shep understood what she didn't say, that the driver could take him in one blow, the shape he was in.

The old lady looked at Shep and tilted her head toward the driver. "His name's Walter."

"Pleased to meet you, Lt. Haddon," said Walter with a nod. "Walter Smith."

Angelene put the pistol in her purse and gave the clasp a snap.

That was the end of that. Good. Dorthea would have been humiliated and scandalized, no matter how she lived her life, if she should ever learn that her husband was killed by a Negress in a black Cadillac on the back roads of Kentucky, with the law hot on their trail. What explanation would she have come up with to make it acceptable?

"Then, Mr. Lieutenant Haddon. What did you have in mind?"

Angelene's voice was rich, a little southern in it, like a southern Negro school teacher, who maybe had been schooled up north. But she was no school marm. Again he wondered just who he'd gotten himself mixed up with.

"I didn't have time for a master plan," he said. "But I figure we better stay together at least until we get well away. Out of Kentucky, probably."

"You're probably right."

"Yeah. We don't have time to stop and put him out," said Walter, grinning sideways at Shep. "That white man may want us more than he loves his car."

Walter was gliding the car around the dirt road's curves in the low hilly country as naturally and easily as a kid licking an ice cream cone.

"He'll probably be reasonable, take time to put oil in," Shep said, hoping but not believing.

"He'll follow us," Angelene said.

"No way he can catch us," Walter said. "If I know which way I'm heading."

"If you have a map we might plot a course."

"They're in the box on the floor to your right," Angelene said.

So that's what he had been bracing his leg against. He bent to get it.

"It's in your way."

"It'll do," he said, noting that she didn't actually point out his stiffly braced leg, angled awkwardly in its attempt to fit. He picked up the top map, Kentucky. Under it Tennessee. They were headed south – they'd know what to expect at a backwoods gas station if they had already been down and were headed back to D.C. He unfolded Kentucky, then folded it to show the large middle section of the state. A crossroad looked to be intersecting about a mile ahead if they were where he thought they were. As they approached it, he looked to his right down the road and caught sight of a black car speeding as if trying to outrun its own dust storm just as Angelene said, "Look!" and pointed to the car.

He glanced back at the map. Damn! The road must be a shortcut to where they were now from where they'd just left! "Show me what Detroit's finest can do!" he told Walter. The car shot forward like it had been waiting to do this since it left the assembly line.

One of his rides had told him Kentucky had been busy road- building the last few years. He hoped her maps were up-to-date. Should be another intersection, gravel road, about five miles ahead. But he wouldn't wager on it. Not a gambler. Well, just what would he call this whole situation? Necessity.

The black Ford was falling further behind.

Her body turned on the seat so she could watch out the rear window, Angelene finally said, "Is that smoke?"

"Steam, smoke, from a locked-up motor!" said Walter, his eyes darting again to the rear-view mirror.

The lawman must have been angry out of his mind not to have taken the time to fill it back up with oil.

"Thank you, Lord," the old lady said, her hands folded under her chin.

"I'd say thanks to Cadillac Motor Company, and Walter's driving," Angelene said.

"I praise God for that, too." The old lady's voice cracked with emotion.

Shep felt let down that blessing wasn't being invoked for him, too, as well as feeling he shouldn't be claiming any credit. He was irritated at himself for even thinking such a thing, and blamed it on the stress of running from the law with three strangers. Three strangers not his race, admit it.

"And for a certain soldier who may think he has to live up to his name," Angelene said, after possibly having thought about the irony.

He was thoroughly aggravated at her, now, and even more with himself, maybe for thinking he had to do something back at the station. He opened his mouth but decided not to comment. What could he say? He didn't know that answer. But God knew he'd been accused of it before.

SIX

No one spoke for a while. They seemed to be going against type, content to drive on the course he had set for them for the present, mostly north, slightly west, he thought, with few people to note their traverse. But backwoods people usually weren't too ready to get in somebody else's business and talk to the law, even if they saw a strange sight. These people whose car he now lolled in apparently thought their time together would be so brief no further discussion or introductions were necessary. Glancing across his left shoulder he saw that the old lady had dropped off to sleep.

It would help if he knew where the trio was headed and if it was imperative they waste no time. But he'd been schooled in gentlemanly restraint all his younger life, and it wasn't easy to overcome. And didn't they owe it to him to at least say what the hell direction they were headed? But "Where are you headed?" was allowed even of the strangest stranger, even if they weren't thrown together in this twisted travel, and damn well necessary, even if they didn't want to reveal anything about themselves.

"Where are *you* going?" she shot back when he asked.

"A little town you've never heard of in the Mississippi delta. Shepperton. Like I told them back there."

After a nice long silence, she said, "Maybe around two hundred miles south of Memphis? Not too far from Vicksburg?"

"Yes." Now how would she know that? Shepperton was only a depot stop, a couple of gas stations and general stores, and whatever it took to sustain about two hundred people. Could she have investigated train accommodations and noted it?

"I am the navigator, Mr. Haddon. You got that right in your timely fabrication."

There she was the schoolteacher again.

"And you're walking there," she added with mild sarcasm.

"I hate to admit it, but I wasn't planning to walk the entire way. Planned on my thumb helping out."

Walter laughed.

He had even started thinking about taking a bus part of the way. Not as gaddamnn tough as he'd thought he was. But he hadn't caved in so far. Every time he thought of it, he remembered why he was walking. But back to the subject at hand. He was going to have to drag it out of her. "So you're headed south, New Orleans perhaps?"

"That's right," she answered without skipping a beat. He noticed Walter catch her eye in the rearview mirror.

They could continue north to Indiana, cut across the river, and go down through Missouri and Arkansas. Cross back over in Memphis. The sheriff probably wouldn't be eager to report them, at least in Indiana, explain even his version of what had happened and how they'd gotten away.

"Family there?"

"No. A vacation. And you? That plantation exist? Your wife really there?"

He nodded. "And no doubt she would have sent a car for me if she knew I was coming home ... walking ..."

"True devotion," Angelene said so quickly he wondered if she believed it could be true. "But you wanted to surprise her."

"Yes." Neither true, actually. He was rehabbing his leg, actually, as he had said earlier. But more than that, walking took a hell of a lot longer to get there than riding on wheels. And that's what he wanted.

Walter slowed the car's horsepower, downshifting on the sharp curves and rough gravel patches which sometimes took over from the packed dirt.

The old lady roused and he heard whispers between Angelene and her. "Walter, I believe we'll have to look for another station," Angelene said.

"There won't be a – " Shep started, but Walter gave him a sideways glance and he realized nature was calling the party.

Damn. Didn't they know they wouldn't have been allowed to use the restroom back there in any case? The restrooms, though around back and entered from the outside, always had "Whites Only" painted on the door, if the need was felt that it wasn't just naturally understood. Maybe they'd have been allowed to use the little outhouse that was probably still out back. Must've lucked up until now. He'd noticed some places in his travels northward that had facilities marked for both races, and even some that made no distinction. Or, it was possible that they had managed to seek their kind out until today's little hitch.

"Look. Could I suggest we slow down a little and watch for a place to pull off the road? To take care of your needs." Not the comforts of home, but it couldn't be helped. "The car might not be noticed a little distance from the road even if someone came by." He didn't want to say, if the lawman finds another car to come after us in.

Angelene pushed her fist against the seat between her and the door, but agreed that was the smart thing to do.

It was well after eight o'clock, the country's ground inhabitants reverberating sounds from Babel. Now they would be a little less conspicuous, although they'd not met one vehicle in an hour, according to Walter. The old lady had dropped off to sleep after their stop, and so had he. Hunger pangs had woken him. He hadn't eaten in he didn't remember when. It was well past time to think about what they were going to do for the night. Angelene would assume they could pull up to any hotel in any two stoplight town, and be granted a room just because they had money. Only trouble with that theory was those towns were non-existent and there wouldn't be any hotels, especially for them. Most travelers were wise to make sure they were in a big town to sleep. Anyway, if there were rooms to let in Kentucky, they couldn't show their faces at them with the law having undoubtedly put out the word in his own state. On the other hand, she had the car title and they had broken no laws. Not that he knew of.

They were maybe in the center of Kentucky, and Walter had been driving the speed allowed. He'd heard Walter say earlier, "Think we're back where we were an hour ago," but he'd decided to let Miss Mapreader handle it and hadn't roused himself. Just who the hell were they? How did she come by all this wealth? What would they be doing here if they were going from D. C. to New Orleans? She must not be much of a map reader after all. But then, he hadn't taken the straightest shot, either.

"Hungry?" Angelene said.

In the faint light of the last night of the late moon's decline now invading the car, he looked back at her and saw a smile as brief as a shooting star.

"Angelene, that wasn't polite," the old lady said.

"That's all right. Soldiers are always hungry. Forgot to dig into my rations today." And just to satisfy his curiosity for once, he turned and asked Angelene, "And did you have arrangements for food and shelter tonight?"

"Yes, I made reservations."

Huh? Yes? And was it at a hotel that would have accepted them on sight? He hoped she couldn't see his surprise, with his face in the shadows. Her face in the shadowy interior reminded him of the rich hot cocoa Thula had put him to bed with on cold winter nights. He could see the creamy whites surrounding the golden brown of her eyes and another shooting star smile, and realized she liked to get the better of him. Wouldn't you think she'd laugh because she was happy she wasn't rotting in jail about now? Or worse?

"You're surprised," she said, laughing just a little laugh and a sarcastic one at that. But nevertheless, he thought he'd like to hear her laugh again, on some happy occasion.

"Can you blame me," he said, laughing a little himself, "for getting the idea you thought you were on a Sunday drive in the nation's capital?"

"I tried to tell Angelene how it would be," said the old lady, informing him but reiterating it to Angelene. "She's never been out much. It's time we introduced ourselves, too. I'm Farissa Johnston."

"How do you do," he said, nodding.

"I'm Angelene's great grandmother. I'm ninety-four to my belief."

"Mama Gran," said Angelene, "Mr. Lieutenant Haddon probably doesn't want to know that much about us. Or need to know, no longer than we'll be together. We're only helping each other out like civilized people of the same country. Good Samaritans all."

"Then we wouldn't be Samaritans," Mama Gran said.

"I suppose you're right. Wouldn't one of us have to be from here? God forbid."

He almost felt her shudder.

"It's nice to make your acquaintance, Mrs. Johnston," he said. "Please call me Shep. I would care to know whatever you want to tell me, but I don't want to make Miss ... Johnston? uncomfortable."

"Miss," said Mama Gran. "I was not afforded the privilege of marrying."

Her voice had the sound of the south. She had been a slave? God. 1944 now, ninety-four years ago would have been 1850 – eleven years before the war started; when the war ended in 1865, she would have been ...

"Mrs.," said Angelene.

"I beg your pardon?" said Shep. Could she be contradicting her grandmother?

"I'm Mrs. Midnight," Angelene said. "I do apologize for not introducing ourselves earlier. Since we had the benefit of knowing your name."

"I'm pleased to meet you," he said. Good God. What kind of name was that? Was she telling the truth? She did not extend her ringless hand. She had taken off her leather driving gloves when they'd left White and Company, and they lay on the purse on the seat between her and Mama Gran. He wondered where Mr. Midnight was. Was she joining him in New Orleans?

"I'm relieved to hear you had made arrangements for the night," he said, wondering if that could be relevant now.

"I'm not as naive as Mama Gran let you think. Last night we rested comfortably in a small hotel in West Virginia. From where are you traveling?"

Again, the correct phrasing, sounding a little stilted in this circumstance. Was she making sure he understood she was not uneducated? "Washington, actually, as I said at our inquisition."

"Where was the fighting you got so beat up in?" said Walter. "If you don't mind talking 'bout it."

"It's all right. Italy. Salerno. Then up in the mountains."

"Was it General Patton's army?"

"Clark. Fifth Army. And a few others."

"Were you in Walter Reed Hospital?" said Mama Gran. Her voice sounded Southern slow now, and crackled with sympathy and age.

"Yes. First I was e-vacked to a ship. Taken to Spain, later flown to D.C."

"Don't even fly me to heaven," said Mama Gran.

Shep laughed. "Walter flew this car."

"Yessuh, thirty-five's been mighty hard to hold to the rest of the time," Walter said, chuckling.

He saw the smile set in Walter's profile as Walter let him know that he ordinarily tried to keep to the decreed gas-saving speed limit.

"I don't know what we'll do now," Angelene said.

SEVEN

S he hadn't exactly asked his opinion, but he said, "I wonder if we shouldn't just try to get out of Kentucky. I think if we keep going in this direction, we'll get to Indiana eventually."

"Yes, that might be the wise thing. But that's farther north."

So she was in a hurry. And going definitely south. "I need to study the map again. I'll need some light." His was in his bag in the trunk.

"There's a big flashlight in the top box on the seat. I'm sorry not to have thought to put the floor box back here. Walter wouldn't move them for himself, when I drove. I hope you haven't been too uncomfortable."

"Not at all." He got the flashlight from a polished wooden cask about the size of a shoebox that was stacked and strapped on a larger box on the seat. As he had wagered this long walk on doing, the leg was getting stronger every day, but the healing still hurt.

"I don't know if Mama Gran can ride much longer."

He noticed the old lady didn't bother to refute that.

"Look," he said, just as they passed an almost grown-over drive. "If Walter could back up to that place we just passed, I'll check the maps."

A house sitting about a quarter mile from the road was crumpled down on two sides, the rock chimney standing like its own Stonehenge at the back. Might be a nest of vipers bedded up in it, but the home's human inhabitants had been gone many a year.

The box was stacked with folded maps; he flipped through Virginia, West Virginia, North and South Carolina, Georgia, Florida, Alabama, Kentucky, Tennessee, Mississippi. Louisiana on the bottom. So they had been undecided which way to embark on this trip. Cross the mountains as he did or go down through the eastern states then drive straight west, or even angle across. Any other way and they'd never have crossed paths. For some reason he was glad the other maps had not been used.

Walter turned the car around in case they needed a fast exit. Then he reached for a flashlight under his seat and said he'd look around for "rest areas" and got out.

"Louisville," Angelene said, and gave Shep a wickedly ironic smile, clear in the powerful lantern light.

After a moment he realized she meant the hotel reservations she had made, and just shook his head in mild disbelief. He could only lock his eyes to hers and smile, too, thinking of the ironic turn of events.

After spreading out the Indiana and Kentucky maps and studying them a few minutes, he still wouldn't bet on where they were, but he would guess at least a couple of hours from Indiana, based on a roadsign Walter had seen earlier.

She thought it over a minute.

"Mama Gran's tired. And Walter's been driving since seven this morning. Except long enough for him to rest and me to get us lost."

Mama Gran turned to Shep. "Used up. Need to eat. Need to sleep." She leaned her head against the seat back, looking as if she'd slide down it into a little black silk pile topped with white lace.

He tried to maneuver his leg, thinking to get out and help Walter scout the place, but Walter returned.

"Would you get out some water, Walter?" said Angelene, reaching to brace up Mama Gran.

Walter reached into the box made to fit over the hump in the floorboard that ran from the front to the back and pulled out a jug of water. Angelene reached into her purse and withdrew a silver cup, constructed to collapse flat into itself for storage and stack for use. Mama Gran sipped water, then Angelene had some. Walter pulled a cup similar to a shaving mug from under his seat, poured the last of the water into it, offered it to Shep. He declined, although he had finished his thermos at the earlier stop.

Angelene said, "You'll save us getting thrown in jail, yet refuse to drink after Walter?"

Walter held the mug on his knee and looked at it as if poison fish swam in it.

"Angelene, girl ..." Mama Gran said, then said to Shep, "Go ahead. There's more water in the trunk," then put her hand on the middle of her chest and tilted sideways onto Angelene.

Was the old lady dead? Just like that? At ninety-four, who should be surprised, but he'd gotten the idea she had a while left. Maybe she could stay if she had the will, had something she wanted to do yet, someone she wanted to see ... He'd seen men live in spite of death coveting them. "Mama Gran," he said, realizing he'd used the name settled upon her by Angelene, that it had left his mouth even as his brain put in the conventional order, as he opened his door and got out with effort, almost collapsing on his miserable leg, and pulled Mama Gran's door open. Her head was resting on a pillow in Angelene's lap and Angelene had a handkerchief doused with water, rubbing her face with it. He patted Mama Gran's hand. Walter passed a small bottle over the seat to Angelne. She took the top off and held it under Mama Gran's nose. Smelling salts. She coughed a little and roused.

~ 29 ~

"Tired," she said. "Forever tired."

He was unable to believe in the words he'd like to say to her, that she'd be all right.

Her left arm was still lying like a broken mast, useless against the hull of her chest. Her heart would play out, maybe imminently. He felt himself caught in a curious position, hoping his time with them would be over before he would see the final moments of this old lady who had looked into him, yet he didn't want to soon end his time with this unwise, intriguing party he was thrown into traveling with.

"Maybe we should stay here for the night," he said, just as Angelene said practically the same thing. "See anything threatening around?" he asked Walter.

"Nothing but green," Walter said.

"We brought a store of food," Mama Gran said to Shep. "Eat some when it's offered."

He one-handedly helped Walter gather brush and throw it on the access path from the highway, as Angelene held the flashlight beam close to the ground. His knee didn't bend as he expected it to, didn't guess he'd ever accept reality, and he almost tripped. Angelene reflexively reached out a hand, but let him get steady on his own. Walter took the light and he followed to explore the three-sided house, careful not to wave the beam indiscriminantly into the night.

The interior walls were down, if there had been any, for it was a small place. About like the shacks and sharecropper houses on the farms down home, thought Shep. Though there was no sign of it now, there must have been a porch, essential for churning milk, washing clothes, shelling beans, and sitting on on hot nights, as well as for relieving the crowded rooms any time. The porch was always out front so any company coming or wayfarers passing could be noted. Usually in these houses, at the back door was a stoop with a wire clothesline strung in a rickety pattern from its posts to fence posts in a yard surrounded by cottonfields.

He remembered as a child seeing Thula taking her wicker basket of clothes to the lines, two parallel lines strung neatly in the back yard between posts with crosspieces, with another bracing crosspiece to adjust the line down to pin the wet clothes on, and then up to allow the clothes to flap dry in the wind high above the dusty grass. She'd bring a wet rag to clean the lines of dust and bird droppings before hanging the wash. Sometimes he'd run among the clothes for play and would get a good swat from her.

He'd thought of Thula as older than petrified wood then, and black and wrinkled as he'd figured petrified wood to be, but she wouldn't have been nearly as old as Mama Gran was now. She'd died when he was sixteen, and they'd said she died of old age. Just "give out." But she was only eighty-one. She was in fact the "mammy" that Mama Gran had so accurately accused him of having and the others had so obligingly accepted.

As he moved in the dark, tripping almost to a fall, his weak leg again not responding to his command to dislodge itself from the wild pea vines, Angelene called, "Would you try not to break your good leg? Just come sit with Mama Gran? I'll decide what we need out of the trunk."

He got back to the car and stood against it. He was over wanting to curse his leg for some time now. He'd accepted how lucky he was to still have it. It was already beyond what the Army doctors first envisioned for him.

"Your leg. It's going to be all right."

Mama Gran said it so softly.

"Pardon? Oh, you're asking about my leg, will it be back to normal. They say not quite."

"No. I wasn't asking."

Maybe the old lady fancied herself a fortune teller.

"I'll tell you how I know. I'm not a card reader. But I'm a judge of a man. You'll do what it takes. Even walk across the country to restore its strength. Get it bendable."

He thought about it. "I wonder if I'm only putting off ... Let's say I hope you're a good judge of character." He heard clattering behind them at the trunk. "Let me see if I can at least lift something."

"You only have one working arm," said Angelene, a large basket dangling in her hands.

"You tell it like it is, Mrs. Midnight."

"Angelene, we're in the wilderness, but you don't need to act as if we are," said Mama Gran.

"You're right, Mama Gran. I'm sorry, Lieutenant."

"No apology necessary," he said, uncomfortable even knowing that she had offered one.

"And we've been provided a guide to take us past the places we should fear to tread," said Mama Gran.

"He's a gift from God?" Angelene said, her sarcasm dripping, holding up her lantern, looking him over as her ancestors must have been inspected on the blocks.

"As you see, I'm nobody's answer to a prayer," he said, thoroughly embarrassed, wondering if they had read his earlier thoughts.

She lowered the lantern and turned it to the trunk.

He glanced in the trunk as she searched with her light, remembering to keep the beam focused down. There were boxes and canvas bags and leather suitcases filling every crevice in the trunk among the spare tire and – wait, two spare tires! Just who did they know? This trip hadn't been undertaken without forethought.

"You do have my respect," she finally said, handing him the basket.

Respect. Maybe he could take that. While he was considering telling her he would try to earn it, she spoke.

"And you're the nicest one-legged, one-armed White boy I've ever seen."

"Ange --" Mama Gran started.

But Shep laughed, loving her way of changing the plane of their conversation, then Angelene laughed, too, and he broke his off so he could enjoy hers like he'd thought earlier he would, even though she was laughing at him. Then he laughed again so she wouldn't think he didn't find it humorous.

"Got a nice laugh, too," Mama Gran said.

He heard Angelene's soft "Umhmmm."

"Can't I get some sympathy for this patch?"

"Is there another blue eye under there? Or ..."

He'd been told it might have to come out when it got infected before they could get him into surgery, but thanks to God and Army medics and doctors and half-blind luck, it was still in with possibilities of sight before it. "No parts missing," he said. Keep it light.

"Then no sympathy for the shepherd," she said, and called to Walter as he strode over, "So this is home for tonight?"

Walter said he thought he and Shep could sleep in the ruins and she and Mama Gran could sleep in the car. "I found a place for you and Mama Gran to be alone," he said, lifting and carrying the old lady, with Angelene lighting their footpath, then Walter returned alone. He and Shep went off to another side.

EIGHT

When the women returned, Walter had a soap bar, a large cloth and a jug of water waiting well away from the car. He poured water over their hands and they rubbed the soap between their palms, then he poured water over to rinse. Then Mama Gran dried her hands with a corner of the cloth, and Angelene used a corner, handed him the soap and said "There's a corner for each of you," and poured the water for their ablution.

Angelene made a table out of the hood and served up canned tuna, a hard yellow cheese, large olives which they chewed away from the pits with Walter spitting his into the weeds away from them as if it were a contest, apples, and cornbread muffins, which Mama Gran said she made for the trip because Angelene craved them almost every day. "I'm just a simple girl used to simple food," Angelene said, eating a half in one exaggerated bite.

"I figured as much," Shep said, bringing a big chuckle from Walter.

Wanting to share provisions, Shep got out a K-ration, like he had found necessary to use only once so far on the trip. The women handled the wax coated box, "SUPPER" printed on it, about the size of a small jewelry cask that Dorthea stored her diamond bracelet, necklace and earrings in. He opened it and they lifted the six- ounce flat can with the stamp identifying it as pork, and fondled the cellophane envelope containing applesauce, sniffed at it but wouldn't let him open it. Walter examined the gum, cigarettes, can of alcohol for heating. Angelene lifted the sheets of tissue. "Napkins?" she said, just as she realized they were for more explicit hygiene. Her laugh was a little at her own expense, and a little at the army's, he thought, but he liked hearing it, even when she said, "The Army thinks of everything, does it?" What an under-statement, and she knew nothing of what the army was capable. What would have been her reaction to the army's having decided to include in some provisions a deviously calculated cost-saving. Little packets of practical disease prevention instead of a possible later more expensive and time-consuming cure for its soldiers who hungered for a woman's sexual provender. But she would have probably sarcastically agreed, as he was certain Dorthea would, that if the army had noted a couple of extra little benefits the condoms provided, like also protecting the woman from pregnancy and from disease as well as the warrior, that it was one of their better ideas.

Walter sat on the ground and leaned against the car, his legs stretched in front of him, bracing his plate on his thighs. Mama Gran sat on the side edge of the back seat, her feet dangling out the open door, barely reaching the running board. Angelene sat on the wooden chest laden with foofstuffs that Walter had heaved out of the trunk. Shep sat on his front seat, his braced leg angled out and

~ 33 ~

his other foot resting on the running board, his plate sitting on his slinged-up arm.

Mama Gran ate only enough to keep her alive, he thought, and Walter consumed his food not greedily but befitting such a large man who required large nourishment, in big hunks as if he were feeding a furnace. Angelene ate with enjoyment, from time to time commenting on the good taste of something – how mellow the cheese was, how crisp the apple. Food was the topic of conversation, along with the pleasant night.

As they worked together clearing up, with the lantern covered with a cloth to hold the light down, Walter said, "Don't leave any scraps out, might be bears around."

"Snakes be more like it," said Mama Gran.

Trees were thick on both sides of the road. No space cleared for fields, or more likely it was let to grow over years ago. This space would be taken over by growth completely in another year or two, and when the last sawed wood tumbled down, no walls would hold up the chimney, and without evidence of the fire needed for sustenance, man's intrusion here would be unnoticeable. What had happened to the family that this place had been abandoned by them? He watched Angelene look about.

"Or some more good Kentucky citizens lurking," she said.

Unlike last night, stars on this Kentucky night were out now about as bright as he'd ever seen them. No guns going off in distant skies, no kitchen lights flickering. Not even the flashlight now. Only the moon distantly high. He pointed out a constellation and was required by Angelene to name the others he knew, and tell what he knew about them. She professed not to be able to connect the lines to construct the big picture in her mind. Walter said he never knew there were that many stars in the whole world. Mama Gran said she'd never understood why or how they moved to new places when the seasons changed. Shep had Walter hold an apple up for the sun and he rotated and revolved an olive for the earth and she nodded.

Angelene opened a little case and took some cream from a small jar in it and got a cloth about the size of Dorthea's handkerchiefs from a seemingly unending supply in a canvas bag, having spread the other cloth over the top of the opened door to dry. As he tried to not watch, she stroked Mama Gran's face and then her own. She said, "Never saw your wife do it this way, I bet."

"Sorry, I didn't mean to watch," he said. He didn't say that no, he hadn't seen Dorthea clean her face. She had her own inner sanctum for such, and he wasn't allowed in. He retrieved his duffle bag which Walter had stowed in the trunk at the station and now wondered just how in hell he'd been able to fit it in.

"It's all right," she said good-naturedly. "I don't suppose we can have many privacies ... traveling this way."

In that event, he wanted to say, I'd like to ask a few things about you. But he didn't. He thought about what the women would do for a possible necessity in the night. Hell, he wouldn't put it past them to have a chamber pot tucked away in the trunk's recesses.

But Walter had thought of them. "Whenever you feel the need, give me a holler. I'll walk you over with the flashlight."

"Thanks, Walter," she said, and then, he felt it was to show she could laugh at herself, maybe even a way of exposing that she wasn't as protected as she might have been giving him the idea she was, she said to Shep, "Brought our own k-ration paper."

Mama Gran said, "I've never heard such talk."

Walter didn't even act like he heard her, showing that he knew when to exercise discretion. Angelene had known what she was doing when she hired Walter. Or maybe he'd even been with Mama Gran before Angelene's birth. Shep wondered how old Angelene was. More than twenty-five and less than thirty, he would guess if he was never told.

Angelene put what she wanted for morning on top as Walter busied himself repacking and getting blankets from the trunk and spreading one on each of the seats; there were already small pillows in the car for supporting Mama Gran. Then Walter took a blanket and satchel from the car trunk to the shell-of-a-house. It was so old and dilapidated that Shep thought if it were in Italy they would call it an ancient ruin and research its history. When Walter returned, Angelene said he could escort them and then they'd get to bed.

NINE

S hep treaded carefully in the opposite direction, afterwards to the relic house
with his duffle. He didn't want to go in. In the new darkness and closeness,
it looked like it had been run into by a tank. He knew exactly what that looked
like. He went in and unrolled his sleeping bag on the piece of remaining floor,
which could collapse any day now from the feel of it, and these remaining walls
would crumble into the rubble around it. He saw Walter's flashlight return to the
car and then head out in another direction. A while later Walter shuffled heavily
into the shadowy interior.

"Want a cigarette?" he asked Walter.

"Thanks. She don't allow no smoking in the car."

"Figured," Shep said.

"This sure not like you's use to," Walter said.

Shep sat with his back against what had been a joist of the one inside
dividing wall, bent his good leg and stretched the other out in front. He could
not see the car and the brush-blocked access to the road. Walter clicked off the
battery light. Right now it was pitch, black-tar dark, the moon gone behind the
hills, and clouds had come to cover the stars for intervals. He had watched them
coming in, big and heavy but moving fast, he thought taking their rain to dump
northeast of them. Dark didn't scare him. But the memories that seeped from
his brain, gradually filling the darkness pressing against him did. "This is better
than I'm used to," he answered.

He felt Walter digesting that. "You been sleeping out in the open on
this trip?"

"Yeah." Actually only twice. He didn't want to talk about what he'd
gotten used to in the weeks he was in combat. Many a night – or day – until the
day they'd found it, he and his men would have traded a week's leave, if that
future time were ever to come, for these accommodations. And even this meager
protection. Germans couldn't see through walls. If they didn't suspect somebody
was there, and a place like this would look totally abandoned, they might not
waste ammunition on it. Then that last night, they'd found a little place. Part of
two stone walls and a little bit of roof on a villa well away from Salerno, months
after General Eisenhower had announced the Italian surrender in September. But
the German Army doesn't surrender.

Shep and a corporal with a three-infantryman crew had reached their
advance objective without any resistance and were waiting for Sergeant Regis
and the rest of the platoon a couple of hours behind them, who were waiting for
the main unit. Corporal Kolosky had joked about putting a "V" on a wall with

his face black for his old gang, the Vigilantes. His Polish group had fought the Eyeties, as he called the Italians, for boundaries around a few blocks of the biggest city in America. Said he'd like to go home and tell them he'd beaten them in their native land.

Had the whole country been at war? Shep'd grown up thinking only the Negroes and Whites down south had their little skirmishes.

Kolosky had put himself on first guard and the others had settled in to try to steal a nap if they could get warm enough. He'd always thought of Italy as a warm country. Darkness came. Finally one star broke through thick clouds like a beacon, like the light at the top of the well he'd descended with a rope tied around his chest under his arms, ten years earlier.

He was almost asleep, after wondering what this foreign farm had produced, thinking it was time to sow the winter peas at home, when a rumbling German Tiger came pawing up over a little rise not fifty yards away, two rows of teeth-like front armour giving the tank the appearance of a demonic grin. It wasn't worried about wasting ammo. Its long gun fired and fired, the shells spewing like a mad dog flailing its rabid foam from side to side. Stone walls fell, like the well walls crumbling as he was being pulled up at home those years ago. The roof beat them with two by fours and tiles and water spouts as it fell on them. His gun fell from the cradle of his arms.

Then a surprise. Instead of his and his men's oblivion, the tank broke into parts. It was like a thing he remembered from Dorthea's tenth birthday party. A piñata – that's what it was called – a hollow but strong paper and glue contraption in the shape of a bell, that she had whacked with all her might. The tank had hit a mine. The Tiger tank, thinner armored on the bottom than anywhere else, must have been recently fueled, its tank large because its miles per gallon was so low it had to drink gasoline like an alcoholic. It was an explosion waiting for a lit fuse.

If he and his men had gone past the house, it would have been them triggering the mine, unless the god of war had benignly directed their footsteps. The tank's five man crew was flailed out like candy and toys from Dorthea's piñata. Before Shep knew his arm couldn't grapple his gun out of the growing pool of blood it rested in, to shoot the five mangled men in the name of humanity, or shoot them in the spirit of war's wages, another tank appeared, its cannon of a gun firing indiscriminately, setting off another mine next to the first one, killing their own men as they mowed down his.

He fumbled on the ground until he found two grenades, and not thinking of wells at home or birthdays or the hole through his right side just under his arm, held them against his chest, grateful they were the pineapple grooved and not the old smooth and slippery, as he ran to meet the roaring

Tiger. Its nimble tracks were already carefully and slowly pivoting on a dime to avoid the mine field, its long gun leading its return. He ran after it as it moved slowly to pick out the same path it had come on. He caught up to it without getting mowed down by its machine gun, not understanding why, at last concluding the crew had thought all in the destroyed villa were dead. He trotted along its left side until he was even with its front, so close he could feel the ground shifting and sinking, even though the tank's tracks were extra wide to spread out its unwise weight. As he pulled the round loops at the same time with his left middle and index fingers, left-handed as he was, he curiously noted how hard it was to hold the safety levers secure against the little bombs' sides with his right hand. He let the grenades drop from his right arm just in front of the track and counted, as if he had all the time in the world instead of four seconds before the fuses would light and explode against the tank's side, the Achilles heel of the mammoth.

The rear of the tank caught up with him as he reached the number three in his count and he dove behind it, not even having time to wonder if he would hit the ground or be blown up as the grenades and tanks exploded on the count of four, possibly with a hundred and twenty gallons of fuel just behind the steel plate. He possibly had counted on German planning to save his life. The front to plunge ahead and rear to protect the fuel source were twice the thickness of the ribs. The tank didn't actually disintegrate with the first explosion, but both ends collapsed against the sides like a concertina, rippling with small explosions. Twisted fate let him make the dash almost back to his men.

He felt like he was in his own hellish allegory, and he prayed it led to heaven. Fitting, here in Dante's Italy, going through a hell-war the fourteenth-century poet would not have had words for. The noise and the heat might have compared to that boiling inferno Dante imagined having to trespass on his journey to find heaven, when the other of the Tiger's fuel tanks exploded, hurling parts of the rear steel and nickel plate back, and blowing him to the wall. Kolosky grabbed him as another explosion rocked the first tank, then all he was aware of was something in his eye that made him think a grenade had exploded in it.

And then the black. Like in the well at home. But dark and deep and inescapable as the river Styx, with no pinpoint of light to focus on as there had been in the well. And thinking no, he shouldn't be hurt; why was he hurting so? The falling walls of the well didn't mangle him when he was young and unaware, bringing the boy up.

Shep hadn't known his leg was crushed in three places, hit by the flying stones from the exploded wall so far from home, brought to life again by the second explosion. He thought he was being hit by boulders thrown by demons.

He hadn't known a piece of the tank had sliced his already bloody arm almost off. But all was nothing to the something in his eye, as if a stone were embedded in it. He became aware of a weight on him, heavy but warm and strangely comforting in the swirling pot of pain he knew was carrying him to death. He prayed the journey would be quick, no descending levels of horror such as the poet had to traverse to get to that desired heavenly door.

TEN

But angels, it had to be, transported him back home instead of leaving him to make his way to death. Perhaps this was some kind of reward for his deed that day, bringing the boy up, if in fact it was a good deed. Perhaps remembering was simply a delaying tactic he pulled out of his subconscious soul in reaching that finality. Perhaps he was too weak to face death. He put it off with all his dwindling awareness.

He saw himself out on the tractor plowing under the early spring weeds just before dinner break. He smelled the fresh damp of big clods of earth being turned up, mixed with honeysuckle, and he was so thirsty, as parched as the penitents of Dante's purgatory; he wished for even the one scant swallow of the sweet honeysuckle blossom that grew with abandon on every fence at home. He remembered the shouting and screaming like someone was being eaten alive, and thought it could be on that battleground but knew his mind was still on home that day when he saw Ulys Sealy's wife come running, flailing her arms like she was trying to free them from a thick net. Hearing her shouting, "He in it! He gone drown! My boy!" Seeing himself jump off the tractor and run to meet her, knowing he could run faster than he could go on the slow tractor, in his mind resembling and crawling like the slow Tiger tank, dodging the pines at the edge of the field, and having to go around the drainage ditch. Seeing her turn back when she saw him racing to reach her. Hearing his own shout, "Where?" thinking it was too early in the year for boys to be playing in the creek. He himself was freezing. Seeing her point to the houses then grab her head like it was about to fly off her neck. Puzzling that somehow she looked like Corporal Kolosky.

Racing and losing against time. Others in the house row gathering but seemingly not fathoming what must be done. Himself yelling, "Go to the barn! Bring a rope!" Seeing a part of the well wall, in his mind as tall as the Italian villa wall, had rotted, and caved in as the boy leaned in to bring up the bucket with the pulley and rope. Thinking if this farm was ever under his control ... Thinking of Dorthea and her plans for him ... Ulys, coming home for the noon meal, pulling up in the farm truck then, or was it a truck there in that shredded villa garden in the tank aftermath? Again at home, he saw Ulys assimilating the gist of what had happened, just as the man returned from the barn at a gallop with the rope over his shoulder. The boy's mother kneeling at the edge and crying, "Ulysses! Uly!" and Ulys trying to jump in, with others' arms grasping him from the brink.

Himself giving one rope end to Ulys to tie to the truck while he tied the other end around his own chest under his arms. Feeling Ulys backing the truck as needed, the rope tightening, cutting his breathing; delving darker against the slimy stone sides, and finally feeling the cold water on his ankles, getting colder with full body immersion. Bumping into the floating bucket, wondering that it had managed to stay empty and not fill and sink. As he was sinking, hearing voices echoing to Ulys in the truck, "keep coming, keep on," until he couldn't hear any more, and when he thought he'd burst or drown, feeling the bottom and the small body at the same time. Grabbing an arm, yanking on the rope as his air exploded out of him. Taking in water before the rope became taut and he broke the surface.

Just as that time so long ago on familiar ground, after a few minutes his prayer was answered on that foreign soil, and he felt breath in his lungs and knew he wasn't alone, just before he lost consciousness again. A weight on him was cold and stiff and heavy, but he couldn't have moved it if it had been a feather. He passed out again. Some time later he woke at home again. Only this time he was a deer. The deer carcass he'd stumbled upon in the woods one January when he was a kid – it had been shot and evaded the hunter only to stumble away and keel over and freeze in the field behind his house. Before he succumbed again he thought how quiet it was in the frozen field of home.

He came to at some point on the cold ground of Italy in winter, feeling encased in ice, struggling in another of Dante's circles. Next time he came to he understood where he was. He hadn't gone through all the Italian's damnable infernal levels and made his way to Paradisio. He was fully immersed in the war around him, Fifth Army guns in the distance. He sensed commotion, realized a medic was dosing him and he could see something that looked like a gray blur out of one eye. He could feel the weight was off him by then. Feel the sensation of warming up under wool blankets and a cloud of morphine. Gradually he realized Kolosky was beside him and he made his eye focus, one of the last sights he saw for three weeks. Kolosky, open-eyed but unseeing, his head attached only by a thread, a tendon, to his body. Of the five men, Shep was the only one living to remember it.

The medic told him they'd found Kolosky on top of him where the blast had put him. "You mighty lucky, Suuh," said the rich voice, reminding him of Ulys.

"No, Kolosky was unlucky," Shep said.

"Shrapnel through his neck," said the medic, "then it went into your eye. Don't know if it missed the vitals. Too much swelling."

Then he closed it with gauze, and Shep knew although the medic was trying to be gentle, it felt like he was using the iron threads reserved to close the eyes of the envious, in that hellish dialogue that had so freshly entered his mind. His body told him he was living the nightmare poem, instead of remembering writing a paper on it in college, and he was envious. He wanted to be like Kolosky. Be out of this purgatory he was having to endure. Be already gone to Paradise.

Kolosky's body and blood were what had warmed him at first, and then the cold, the cold ground and Kolosky's cold body, prevented him from losing all his own blood.

When he came to again, the Captain was kneeling by the stretcher. "You do all this? Blow that tank?"

"No. No Sir. Kolosky was on top of me. He did."

The Captain talked to the medic and then said, "Sorry, son, you're guilty. Bandaid says the grenade pins were still ringed on your fingers. Somebody's looking out for you. The private must have been blown on top of you in the explosion. You're gonna get the medal and that's that."

"Kolosky saved my life."

"We'll send his medal to his folks."

Shep told Bandaid to draw a "V" on the tank's crinkled wreckage with some adhesive tape. The medic thought it was a gesture of victory. Then Shep felt a hypodermic in his good arm and as he drifted off, a peaceful blankness claimed him just after he wondered what Dorthea would think of this state of his being, although he'd survived the Italian Inferno; if love was the origin as well as the cure for sin's hell, he knew what Dorthea would do. She would point out his faulty body, just as Beatrice had railed against the love-besotted poet's faults. But the beautiful woman Dante had never attained in life had finally led him on to paradise in his poem. Shep would not count on that from Dorthea.

He had thought about things at home, even the worst that he had endured, that night he suffered his wounds, the chaplain had speculated and the psychiatrist had confirmed, to keep himself alive, although he had thought dying was the way to escape war's fist. Home was the heavenly refuge even in its hard memories. He thought he remembered his last thought that Italian night. Was he spared for a reason?

He hoped he didn't dream tonight, lying on his green army blanket, his lumpy duffle for a pillow, in this falling down world around him. No. A dream would do. A nice dream about something, anything. As long as it was just a dream. He stubbed out the cigarette.

After supper, military training had overcome him and he had suggested he and Walter take turns sleeping, just in case. Angelene heard and said, "In case of what?" "Whatever," he said, "Bears, no-goods. But the last thing we need is a shoot-out. If the law comes upon us and we can't escape, we'll just have to trust the justice system." Angelene had taken charge. Shep would take first watch, Walter second, and her third. Her tone told him not to try to change her mind. He left his pistol in his duffle.

He did his leg and arm exercises, trying not to make too much noise. Walter had gone to sleep quickly but roused himself at the agreed hour while Shep was trying to decide how to explain not waking him.

Gaddamn. They were in their own country and not bothering anybody. He tried to dismiss today's close call as something it wasn't – one in a million, and said just go to sleep and dream if you can. Dream of a woman's body warming you. Lying beside you through the night. All night. A woman who wants to warm you and be warmed by you, and who doesn't expect that you will meet her every expectation simply because she expects you to. Not a woman who never lets you know that she wants you without condition, yet presumes you will fulfill her idea of what her husband should be and do. Not a woman who would make herself absent if you disappointed her. Dream of Angelene if you dare. Let her be your guiding angel. Or whatever you want her to be in your dreams.

ELEVEN

Shep woke with the light and the instantaneous feeling that something wasn't right. He lay very still to get his wits awake. He never considered he was in combat. It wouldn't have been this quiet. Maybe he'd had one of his nightmares and it was lingering.

He looked up and saw Angelene standing a few feet away. She was holding her pistol pointed at him. Wait. This wasn't happening. Not to be believed. He must still be asleep. "Don't move," she said very quietly. Just as he felt – or maybe only heard, as his senses were heightened – the rustling next to him, she fired, and he rolled over a couple of times and into Walter, who had been startled awake and had with speed of a striking copperhead fished a pistol from under his pillow.

The snake, the actual snake that she had shot, twitched a time or two and then rolled over itself. "Goddamn!" Shep said, wishing he could jump up, but it was impossible with his leg so stiff and his arm hurting like hell from rolling on it, and his backbone and legs and whole body quivering like muscadine jelly.

"Damn!" yelled Walter. "Whatta hell's happenin? You shootin' Shep? What for?"

He said it like she could have done it. Didn't like the sound of that.

"Look there," she said to Walter, flicking the pistol toward where the snake lay.

Walter looked and Shep saw that Walter could jump. Faster than any big man still half asleep should be capable of. He was out in one step.

"Hell of a way to wake me up," Shep said, looking at the four foot creature, clothed in perfect greenish camouflage for the trees and country around. Realizing he was glad he'd slept in his uniform. Maybe it had felt at home next to him in his drab olive wools. "It's only a pine snake. Or something like it."

"Well, isn't a snake a snake? Bad? Not that I've ever seen one. Except in the zoo."

Never seen a wild snake? She must never have left concrete. "Happens not. This kind eats other snakes, field mice and such. Not poisonous."

"Oh."

"Has round eyes. Up and down slits are the rough ones."

"Well, I'll be sure to look it in the eyes next time."

He heard Walter and Mama Gran discussing the happening.

"But thanks anyway," he said.

~ 44 ~

"So I didn't save your life? Looks like I still owe you for yesterday," she said.

"I expect it was talk just to scare you."

"You very probably saved our lives."

"Well, I was happy to do whatever I did," he said, hoping he sounded lighthearted. "But I'm getting the feeling you could take care of yourself."

"Maybe so. In my surroundings. I expect so. With an exception."

"That right?" he said, but she didn't say more. It still wasn't polite to ask a lady what she didn't want to tell. But he didn't think any longer that she was the daughter of a preacher man. Maybe the undertaker. She may bring him business. But what would the "exception" be? "The army could use a shooter like you. Where did you learn?"

"My husband taught me."

For fun or necessity? He wanted some answers. "Are you going to him? Or will he be joining you?"

She gave him a long look while she considered her answer. "Yes."

Now what the hell kind of answer was that? He suddenly found himself not caring too much about a lot of what shouldn't be done by a gentleman. But before he could ask just where the hell are you going and why in God's name are you going there, Walter came up, leading Mama Gran for a look, and said, "How you know that devil was here?"

"I was getting the coffee ready to put on. Saw it slide right in here. Didn't know which of you it would be after. I was afraid if I called out you'd think I needed help. I didn't know what you'd do ..."

"You did the right thing," Shep said, looking around at the hills almost surrounding them. He wondered if anyone lived close, if anyone was traveling, if anyone could have heard the shot.

"There's been no traffic all night," Angelene said, understanding his unspoken concerns. "No lights coming on anywhere I could see."

A whole new light on things. She'd been awake all night. Afraid of locals or wilderness? Or didn't trust his and Walter's watch? No, he didn't think any of those would keep her awake. Just a worrier?

"I'm a light sleeper," she said.

A small pot of coffee was perking on a grate set over a small twig fire. Angeline picked up the dried towel from the night before and with water from the jug and a little soap, they followed the same cleansing procedure as the night before. He pondered the singularity and common-sense of this ritual as Angeline broke out the basket, taking out rolls and jam. She got out a sugar dish and a small can of condensed milk, opened it and poured it into a creamer. Was there a complete set of china in that basket?

As they sat in their previous spots and ate – Angelene mostly nibbling – and poured boiling coffee into china cups, no saucers, and cooled it with milk, he wondered if they ought to be hurrying. He was getting the little worry like he used to have when his platoon would be on detail. Would the lawman still be pursuing them? Or did he think they were in Indiana by now? Nevertheless Shep swallowed worry down with the breakfast of manna. He was taking his last sip, watching Angelene's head tilted back a little to sip down the bit of milk that was left in the creamer, when he saw the two men coming from behind the house.

They both had shotguns pointed as they walked. They were in worn overalls and faded plaid open-collar shirts and muddy boots. Cockleburs clung to their legs and a blackberry vine full of berries clung and drug from one of the men. They'd taken pains to come upon them unbeknownst. For a minute they didn't say anything. Their look said it all.

"What the hell?" the older of the men began finally.

Shep stood. "Hello there, good morning to you," he said.

The two men looked at each other, thrown for a second. "Hell with good morning!" said the older man, probably the father of the younger.

"Whatchu doin' here?" the younger man asked. Unlike his father, curiosity rather than pure hostility was in his voice.

"We got lost in the night," Shep said. "Came upon this place, figured it was abandoned --"

"Abandoned? Abandoned, hell!" the older one said. "I own this place! Daddy owned it before me! This here's Kentucky. Ain't like down south."

Good to have another real life perspective on the state of Kentucky that said a whole lot about it. A whole lot different from yesterday's perspective. "Glad to know it."

"You can believe it or not! We built a new place on the back forty. But this ain't abandoned! No, sir!"

He was striking out. Think quick. Another test time.

"We didn't see anybody to ask," Angelene said.

"No, sir!" the daddy was still attesting. "Ain't abandoned! Place is mine! Don't want no squatters on it. Dark or white!"

"Whatchu shootin' at?" the younger one asked.

Angelene stepped forward. "Mister," she said to the older one, "seeing as you and I are the same color, I can appreciate what you are feeling. You think this white man here, this soldier in uniform, assumed he had rights to simply camp out on your property without permission and restitution." She gave a look toward Shep that said to the man, "and you weren't wrong about him." "But you should understand the heirarchy of our little group," she added.

"What you sayin', Missy?" asked the young one, watching Angelene as if she were in a movie he didn't understand.

"I'm saying this car is mine."

"Yours? Who the hell are you?" said the older man.

"Angelene Midnight's my name."

"What kinda name's that?" the young man said.

She laughed like Shep had wanted her to yesterday. Genuine and shy and spontaneous. "Angelene's the name my great-grandmama there gave me at birth. Midnight's the name my husband gave me."

Was she telling the truth?

"The man there your husband?" the older one asked, indicating Walter.

"No," Angelene said, "he's like an uncle, but he's actually my employee, my driver."

Walter stepped forward, putting his round black leather chauffer's cap on, and extended his hand. The older one thought it over just a miniscule amount of time, possibly realizing the shotgun wouldn't put Walter down, unless he had deer shot in it, or perhaps deciding to see what was going to naturally come of this morning's discoveries, and held the barrel down and extended his arm. They clasped in a way unseen before by Shep - possibly because the Negroes at his place had always known each other - their forearms lying against each other and arms clasped by each other's hand for a time. "Walter Smith's my name," Walter said with respect. "Arch Tillis," the man said. "This my boy, Archie." Walter and the boy shook hands, then Walter gave over to Angelene again.

Arch looked at Angelene. "Well if he ain't your husband, is this white soldier?" His look said he better not be.

Shep felt Angelene scrutinizing him like Arch was, and he didn't know if it was for the benefit of Arch, or if she was taking the opportunity to actually study him, try to figure out something about him.

"We pitied this soldier, hitch-hiking yesterday afternoon, and gave him a ride with us," she said. "You can see he needs one. He's been in the war, injured all over."

"He the one doin' the shootin?"

"No. I shot a snake. Sorry it was only a pine snake," she said, glancing at Shep. "Or something like one."

"Wasted a bullet on a common snake?" Archie said with a hoot.

"How you own this car?" Arch asked.

"You must have a lot of money," Archie added.

~ 47 ~

Shep didn't like the sound of that. Robbery could be on the young man's mind. Shep's pistol was in his duffle and Angelene's was already back in her purse on the car seat. Walter's gun was already in the car pocket; he'd seen him replace it. God. They had practically an arsenal, but were totally unable to defend themselves.

Again Angelene laughed.

Arch gave his son a look that said don't ask foolish questions. Shep realized that the boy hadn't thought of the possibility of robbing her, and that the father knew it would be possible, for some man, but not him, a man with integrity at stake.

But Angelene had. At least enough to settle the situation amicably for all. "Yes," she said. "I do have a good amount in a bank in Washington, D.C. And I always expect to pay for what I use."

"How'd you get it?" Archie asked, never having such ungentlemanly questions schooled out of his repertoire. "You a movie star for our kind or something?"

Then Angelene laughed again, her usual, sarcastically. "I'll tell you," she said, finally. "I married rich."

Well. Partly answered.

Arch laughed at that. He could understand that. A pretty woman like that could marry the richest man in Kentucky. Black man, anyway, or in Washington or wherever, it was plain to see.

"And I've managed to make some of my own."

Somehow Shep wasn't surprised at that.

"We were to stay in a hotel last night. Would hotel price take care of our sleeping here under your stars? It was a fine night."

Archie's eyes lit up, and Arch was thinking it over. He ought to be hospitable to someone of his own color.

"Walter, pay Mr. Willis $40 for the use of his land."

"You sure you're not hooked up with this white man?" he asked. "He ain't trekkin' you 'cross the country to do his biddin?"

"I have no reason to lie," she said. "I owe nothing to this white man."

Shep understood from that statement she now considered them even in life-saving favors.

Walter took a sleek leather folder from his inside coat pocket and thumbed through to fetch out the two bills.

"No," Arch said. "Won't cost you nothin' for sleepin' here."

"Then take it for your snake I killed. It was good for your land, I gather, rather than harmful."

After a short time of internal deliberation, Arch accepted her decision and her word as final and accepted her money also.

"One other thing you can do for us," she said, nodding at Walter, who thumbed through his bills again and pulled out another twenty. "I'd just as soon no one else knows we were here."

"You in trouble with the law?"

"We've done nothing wrong," she said.

"Well, we don't talk to no law. Go the other way if we see'em comin. Don't need no money for that."

"Anyone else who might come asking, then," she said, and Walter handed him the bill. Arch took it, holding it with the other one, deliberating again, perhaps wondering as Shep did, would someone else come looking for her. But he answered her last question, where in the state were they? With Archie showing his large teeth again in an astonished smile, the two watched as they took their leave.

She walked to the basket and packed it like an efficient soldier assembling his rifle under the watchful eye of his sergeant as Walter moved the branches they'd hidden the pull-off with, and Shep nudged some dirt on the fire.

When he climbed in and looked back to see how Mama Gran had fared through the ordeal, he saw that she had Angelene's pistol in her lap, the barrel pointed at the Misters Willis. He smiled and so did she. Walter and Angelene ducked into the car and they pulled out as Archie examined the bills one last time and tucked them into a pocket on his overall bib.

TWELVE

He found where they were on the map and traced roads leading to Tennessee. "Maybe somebody's trying to tell us we should get out of Kentucky as soon as we can."

"We planned a little side trip," Angelene said.

"A side trip?" He tried not to be exasperated. After yesterday, how could she want to linger in the state?

"As we're now even in owing each other our lives," she added, not overlooking his reluctance which apparently showed in spite of his guard, and rolling her eyes in mock disdain, " – don't bother to thank me – you can make your way in whichever direction you feel the need."

"You don't mind if I thank you for the ride, do you?" Shep said. "Walter, would you pull over?"

"Walter's not stopping," Mama Gran said. "Angelene's going to apologize. And you're going to hold your horses."

"Yes ma'm," they all said in unison and without hesitation at the tone of her voice, as if they had been given orders by a judge. "And we'll head south. I understand the place isn't far from Tennessee. We won't stay long."

It must be some family member, he thought. It would be understandable if she wanted to take a little while for that. Be her last chance.

"I expect the lawman doesn't have the state officers looking for us. He'd never want to explain how he let us get away," she said, intuitively understanding the man's bluster and pride.

"And his motor burning up. He wouldn't want that to get around," Walter said, smiling.

"Probably right," Angelene said.

"Who knows what a man like that will do," Shep said, uselessly, of course; they all knew that. Did he just not want to agree with Angelene? Or did he think he had to be the one who made the decision?

"You two," Mama Gran said, gazing from Angelene to Shep, "are a lot alike. Too much, maybe, to get along for too long a time. But I reckon this trip isn't too long a time. It would behoove you both to think on how you don't just quit a friend, without a real good reason."

"Friend?" Angelene said.

"Saving each other's lives ought to make you friends."

"Mama Gran, you're a lot like my old Thula --." He tried to stop talking before the words could come out. He felt the heat rising up the back of his neck.

"I knew it!" Angelene said, not even trying to hide her self-satisfaction with having him and his privileged southern up-bringing already figured out. When he said nothing, she added, "But I won't hold it against you. It speaks well of you, I think."

"I won't deny that my mother had a lady to help her. My mother was ill most of the time. I don't know how just the two of them managed me." Basically it was his mother managing to help Thula.

"I can hardly take stock in that. You're a perfect gentleman and a Sir Galahad," Angelene said.

"Then they did a better job than they knew," he said, remembering the time he climbed up the kitchen cabinet to get a trinket they'd put out of his reach because he'd done something he shouldn't, he couldn't remember what; but he did remember the cabinet tumbling over as he just managed to fly out of its path, breaking most of the dishes, and an apple pie cooling there. What a mess. And they made him clean it up.

Another time he'd been chasing the dog, who was chasing a chicken, then the rooster got after them all, and he'd run into a wagon loaded with cotton and split his head while looking back at the rooster. Thula had doused his scalp with kerosene and put one stitch in it, pulling the silk thread out a couple of days later. That hurt worse than anything. Up to that point. And once, he'd actually had to defend himself against a little girl; it was no use telling his mother and Thula that she'd taken his pencil and that it was a spanking offense to be in Miss Bank's classroom without one. And that when he'd politely asked for it back, the girl had stabbed him in the hand with the point he'd so painstakingly sharpened with his pocketknife. His mother and Thula made him sit in the kitchen and read to them while they cooked supper and cleaned up the kitchen, for not offering the pencil to Dorthea in the first place. Dorthea had a cruel streak then, which she explained years later as merely a strong sense of self-preservation. Could it have been so long ago he was a boy who would let Dorthea get the best of him even then?

"Tell us about your childhood," Mama Gran said.

A fair enough request from an old lady. He shifted in the seat to look back at Angelene to see what her feelings might be on that subject. "Please do," she said, with enough disinterest that he knew she was interested. "My daddy had a farm in Mississippi. I had a sister, fifteen years older than me. She married a lawyer and moved to Mobile when I was just starting school. I enjoyed visiting her. It was a big old house on Government Street."

"Sounds like a fine place. Big trees and yards to go with the big fine houses?"

Mama Gran wasn't looking for her own raison d'etre to charge him. She was looking for his reasons, his processes that had instilled in him the necessity to do what he did to help them. Or possibly only to satisfy her curiosity. But not to have something to hold against him. Not to put the past on his shoulders. He nodded.

"Is she still there?"

"No ma'm. They lost it in a hurricane several years ago."

"Do you still have the farm?"

There was no shame on him in what happened, but he didn't want to say in front of Angelene. Admit not defeat, for it wasn't of his doing, but something. Loss of pride? But Mama Gran had bestowed friendship on him and Angelene, and he'd wanted to know her, had started trying to figure her out since she had lit in his vision. There was something about the way she didn't know she was thought of as a second-class citizen by many of his race. Instead she acted like she belonged in the world, period. "We lost the farm the same year," he said, realizing that he wanted her to know something of what made him. "Just the house and enough for a garden and cow pasture were saved."

"Um hum," Mama Gran said empathetically. "Lots of folks did. Angelene's daddy, my grandson, lost a business."

During the depression, he figured she meant. But that wasn't his daddy's story. His daddy had one weakness, and it was gambling. But he wouldn't get into his father's personal trials. "Sorry to hear it," he said, wondering if she'd offer more.

"One time he owned a fruit and newsstand in Washington. Could throw an apple and hit the government house."

"Now he'd be doing good business," Angelene said to the window. "Maybe ..." Then she changed her pensive attitude back to the one he knew best. "Newspapers can't put out enough news with your war going on --"

"My war?"

"Angeline, don't be so cynical."

Shep wondered what kind of school education Mama Gran had. Or if she had none but had just kept learning.

"All right, Mama Gran. Anyway, the war, and people wanting food to eat always in a hurry. I think one of these days I'll open a restaurant where people just drive up and the waiter will come to the door and take their order and hand it to them. Eat it on their way."

"It just might work," Shep said, ignoring her familiar sarcasm, and not saying there were in fact such places already in existence.

Walter chuckled. "Be needin' plenty of drivers then, I guess, while they eat their dinners."

"Angelene's just put out, because she got a complaint from a table the other night that the food was taking too long," Mama Gran said.

Well, this was the opening he was looking for. "So you own a restaurant."

"Yes. Well, no. I run one. LaLa's." She smothered pride. "Have you heard of it?"

He regretfully shook his head. Damn. Why hadn't he gotten out to see or do a few things that last week when he could have. Patsy had asked him. But he didn't want to hobble around on crutches.

"Let me see," she said, dropping the subject and reaching for the map. "You said last night we were probably in the middle of the state. That's not far from where we want to go. Hodgenville. A little below Elizabethtown. I think we can stay on this state route."

Hodgenville. He'd heard of that someplace. Who did he know from there? Wait. Of course. "You're going to see Lincoln's birthplace?"

"You have any trouble with that?" Angeline said.

"I'd be proud to see it myself." He couldn't help hoping the lawman was not one to put himself on the table for ridicule, as they had earlier speculated, and had let the matter of their getting away from him drop. Anyway, they were willing to take the chance.

Whether it was the actual cabin the Emancipator was born in or a representation, it looked to be of Biblical age. It would fit in one of Dorthea's double parlors, with her furnishings pushed to one side. No doubt it would fit in Angelene's restaurant. It was unrelievedly stark. To think of a man, much less a man who would father a president, felling the trees, hewing them, stacking them, mudding them ... while hunting food, clearing and planting a garden. Then again, what better work ethic for a man who would be president to inherit? Not with a cadre of slaves, some to build and some to cook and some to plant – then how to explain other presidents?

An audible sob came from Mama Gran. Walter blew his nose on a white handkerchief the size of a baby's diaper. Angelene clenched and un-clinched her fists and cleared her throat. Shep's eyes felt moist, even the patched one. But crying tears was not in him anymore. He prayed his thanks that he was not born to his station when his ancestors were – when this man split the country apart for his principles and fought and died to put it back together.

In a short while Mama Gran turned toward the car and they followed. "Let's go see the other one," she said.

~ 53 ~

He knew who the other one must be. In Mississippi you learned your history. The history of the south. You knew about Ft. Sumpter and Robert E. Lee, the Battle of Vicksburg and Appomattox. And Jefferson Davis, President of the Confederacy. He was born maybe a day's carriage ride from this very place. Another of God's ironies?

THIRTEEN

They stopped at Bowling Green, with Walter showing a deftness for finding the part of town where they would be welcomed. He'd asked Shep, with an inclusive look at Angelene, if they should detour to a "White place" and pick him up later. Shep said he'd stay with the party unless it made them uncomfortable.

He hadn't seen another White face in the diner or gas station. Little black boys stood barefooted in the dirt street and stared at the car. They'd stared at him as he emerged. Angelene said they'd probably never seen a man so beaten up as he was. Maybe never seen a soldier in uniform. He appreciated her attempt to make him feel less conspicuous for at least half the wrong reasons. Walter gave the boys a dollar and said they could wash the car if they would bring several buckets of water and some clean rags to the grassy lot next door, where he'd parked. He'd supervise from the diner and pay them another dollar when they finished.

They had ordered bacon and eggs though it was almost noon. Walter asked where a grocery was and they stopped for fruit and other things to replenish the larder. Ration stamps were not a problem. Many things were not affected, anyway, in the small neighborhood store in the Negro part of town, as much of their stock was home canned and the loaf of bread was homemade. Angelene held each jar up to the light and commented on its beauty like she was at a county fair looking to award the blue ribbon.

After only a short time of reverence to Lincoln, true to their promise, Angelene consulted her maps of Kentucky and Tennessee and they were underway again.

Presently she said, "We'll have to go west on the next highway. We'll go through Logan and Todd Counties. And do you know who we're talking about, Mr. Haddon?"

Shep didn't want to lie. And though he owed them no apology he didn't want to remind them of their differences, of who he was, a White person of the south, educated White in the south, bathed White in the south. And proud to be that person, make no mistake. But it wasn't important to let them know he knew something as trifling as this. But it wasn't trifling to them. He could only imagine their motive for wanting to set foot on a place that gave birth to a man who left his country to lead one that wanted to keep their ancestors in slavery.

"Angelene, why do you not accept this man's truth and friendship?"

"You're right," she said. "He can't help it if he isn't Negro." Then she laughed, and he smiled.

"I shudder to think where we'd be now if you were," she said. "So, help me with this map. I can't tell which county Fairview is in. Mr. Davis still doesn't make things easy for me. It looks right on the line between Todd and Christian Counties. And don't say I need glasses," she said to Mama Gran.

"I'll vouch that you don't," said Shep, "after that marksmanship this morning." He looked at the map and tried not to know that he already knew the man was born in Christian County.

"It's Christian County," Angelene said, squinting and tracing lines with her finger on the map.

"Imagine that. Christian County," Mama Gran said.

No wonder the state had such a hard time making up its mind, Shep thought. The two most pivotal men in the country's bleeding cut, born within a day's carriage ride of each other.

"I don't think I need to see it, anymore," said Mama Gran after a moment of quiet. "I was going to spit on his grave," she told Shep. "I promised myself when I was a lot younger and foolish."

Angelene said, "Are you sure?"

"It wouldn't be befitting a woman of my age, so close to my maker, to do such a thing."

"So you're going to forgive and forget," Angelene said.

"I didn't say that," Mama Gran said. "I won't live that long. Not to forget."

"I'll bet Mr. Haddon knows his history."

He knew but certainly wouldn't say that the man had a memorial obelisk that looked in his history book to be for view from miles around. No need in comparing it to the simple marker at the other birthplace. "I do know, at least I've read, he isn't buried there," Shep said, not failing to notice he was once again Mr. Haddon, not even Lt. Haddon, much less Shep, "so it's inconsequential."

"I didn't say that, either," Mama Gran said with conviction.

No doubt she'd had much more intrusion in her life than what she had alluded to earlier. He felt some of the things that might have happened to her would be unforgivable, no doubt, to any but the strongest. Had she passed the resentment down to Angelene?

"We'll head south, in that case," Angeline said, actually shrugging. "Walter, we'll stay on this road instead of turning west up at the next road."

Shep dozed, and woke to Angelene humming. Not a real tune. But enough to show that all was right in her world for the moment.

"Are you awake? Look at this map. There's a county road several miles ahead. Looks like a shortcut. We could be in Tennessee in time to get a room for the night."

"No reservation?" Shep asked, looking at the map. "This road won't be good, it's just a dotted line. But you're right about it being shorter."

"Walter, it's about five miles ahead. No reservation," she said to Shep, "but Nashville's a big town, isn't it? Lots of hotels?"

"I expect so." Sometimes hotels had back doors and rooms blocked off for Negroes. Maybe that was the case there. She wouldn't take kindly to that but she and Mama Gran could have a comfortable night. Also, with Meharry Medical College for Negroes in Nashville, there might be a nice hotel only for people of her color.

These were people with money. Money talks. But facts were facts. The long ago war had been fought and won by people who wanted to bestow freedoms, hadn't it? He resented the fact that it hadn't settled matters such as this. What if this war turned out to be just as inconclusive?

"You would have gone through Nashville at any rate," she said, drawing a crow-flies-road with her finger across the map, angling southwest from Washington. "Like the man said, there are shorter ways. You know why we came this way."

He nodded. They had bared their souls to him as they expressed their gratefulness and resentment for the two men dead so long ago who had been responsible for so much in their lives. He'd tell them the truth of his journey. Enough of it. "I got a ride from the hospital with a nurse going to Charleston, West Virginia."

She tilted her head a bit. "I thought you wanted to walk." He recognized the skeptical suspicion that she expressed, but he understood that she had seen through his explanation, and knew there was more to it. She knew what it had taken him days to understand.

"I walked from there." Walk away from there was more like it. Away from a longing he had seen and away from a gift of love that would result in disappointment and unfulfillment. But remembering the days following, walking and hitching rides, he knew he had desperately wanted to delay reaching home or he would never have attempted this walk-along, even though the doctor had told him walking would be good for his rehabilitation. He had not told the doctor what he had in mind. He might have been held for psychiatric evaluation. There was a damnable number of miles from D.C. to the delta. And he had underestimated the pain in his leg that the first couple days walking had brought. Only a few days ago had he noticed a lessening of pain and more mobility. He did static exercises sitting in the car, but that wouldn't be enough. He would have to spend hours at night to make up for this sitting.

"Did you actually contemplate walking that distance?"

"Actually, I counted on hitching a lot of rides."

Angelene was quiet; he figured she wanted to say "You're welcome," but restrained herself.

"I do feel better about your mental stability hearing that," she said, and gave him a smile.

Thankfully Patsy had convinced him to accept her offer to ride the first part of the journey. She'd gone into nursing because her father was a doctor, now mostly retired because of a bad heart, and conveniently she had her father's car and gas. She had planned her time off to coincide with Shep's release, he realized, but he had been unable to digest her motive. He'd stayed with her family four days, her parents making him welcome, and daily feeling stronger because of their kindness. Her father had cleaned his eye and given him some hope for it, and had massaged his leg and exercised his arm. He had walked the roads and fields, only an hour the first day, adding an hour a day.

He had stopped denying that Patsy had hoped for the friendly attachment between them to grow. He could see it had been that way from the first as he now looked back on it, although he still could hardly credit it. And maybe he would have let it grow, another time, but it hadn't taken hold. For all the wrong reasons. Sadly, not only because of Dorthea, although he'd told Patsy it was. And not because he wouldn't have found joy next to the pretty and compassionate woman who had taken care of him in the hospital. Not even because he had doubts he could have managed to make her satisfied in his condition.

It had simply not been a thing his being said to do. He would have been taking from her without giving. Ivy on a tree. He had nothing of emotional value he was capable of giving her now. His heart and soul had been surrounded by uncertainty for so long, and then his body of broken things, that it had taken his full concentration to begin the physical healing process. Perhaps it had boiled down to selfishness on his part. Nothing to spare for a needy soul. Dorthea could do without his emotions for as long as it took, if she got all else.

But he had gotten involved in these people's lives. And their emotions. Maybe the inside had started its healing.

FOURTEEN

The land they were traveling just a few miles from the Tennessee line was green with trees and fields. Green roofs were sometimes miles apart. Even the rivers were green. Not like Mississippi mud rivers. The narrow Kentucky highway curved and rose and dropped like a ribbon thrown from a height. So unlike Mississippi soft delta roads, mostly flat and straight.

"Cars ahead," said Walter, slowing as they rounded a long curve.

"Roadblock!" Shep said.

"They're looking for us!" Angelene said. "Turn the car around."

"You're sure? After all," he reminded her, looking over his shoulder at her, "we didn't break any laws. These are state troopers. They'll have respect for the law."

"I've had an example of Kentucky law," she said.

He wouldn't be able to convince her. He had a choice, though. Anybody he knew would say he didn't use what sense he still maintained if he didn't get out now. Why stay in this damned car with these people he still knew next to nothing about. "Nothing behind us, Walter," he said, realizing he'd already made up his mind. "Try to maneuver where we stay mostly behind the traffic in this lane. Out of the line of vision up there. We can even drive back in this lane, stay out of their line of sight, providing no more traffic comes along."

Walter was just finishing backing around in a couple of short turns, a tractor ahead pulling a trailer overflowing with hay helping block the view toward the roadblock, when Angelene said, "Look!"

A state trooper car was coming into view from the way they had come, that they were now facing, blocked their lane, and turned on its flashing lights.

Now things were different, now that they were spotted. If they took off, a chase and gunfire would be inevitable. "We'll have to stop. They might be reasonable if we explain things to them."

"No. They won't."

"Let's see what charges they have, before we get into a chase with state troopers. Nothing more serious should have been called in than wanted for questioning." Captain Boyd would help get to the bottom of this. And if he couldn't, U.S. Representative William Grayson owed him a favor. William had gotten drunk at a frat party one night while Shep was still in high school. William had passed out and woke up throwing up, locked by frat brothers in the Dean's office on the second floor. He'd called Shep to come get him. He'd put a ladder in the truck and drove over seventy miles in an hour, not easy in his old truck. William had climbed down like he was sober. It had never been mentioned again. And it wouldn't be now.

"All right. But don't cut the engine yet, Walter," Angelene said.

"If they take us in, I'll have them contact my Captain."

"That would be too late for me."

What in hell did she mean by that? Was she really wanted? Possibly even by the feds?

The troopers got out, guns drawn.

"They won't believe whatever I say. But you should get out and stay. This could ruin your Army record. And your wife wouldn't like knowing about this."

That might be the smart thing to do. And he had been accused of being smart a time or two. But who was he kidding? He wasn't leaving them to fend for themselves. And he knew whatever charge was against her, it wasn't valid. "I'll do the talking. Walter, if I say 'go' take off."

"They won't shoot with an Army officer in the car," she said, understanding that he was binding himself with them.

Shep thought the opposite. If they thought an Army officer had broken the law, they'd love apprehending him.

A trooper came to each front window. "Keep your hands on the wheel, driver," Walter's lawman said.

"Lt. Haddon?" Shep's patrolman asked.

"Yes, Sir," Shep answered in a friendly manner.

"Are they holding you hostage?"

Goddamn. "No. Nothing at all like that."

"Yeah. What we was told. We're gonna have to take you all in."

"Why would that be?" Shep asked.

"Stolen car. Turned in as stolen in Washington."

Well, damn. Washington? Who would have done that? No chance to talk their way out of that. And anyway, if Washington, D.C. law was in on it, that was a whole new light. "This car's papers are in the pocket. Shows ownership in her name."

"Fakes."

"That so?" He glanced back at Angelene and she shook her head. If he had a choice between believing her or someone he didn't know, it wasn't a choice. "Guess we have no choice," Shep said to the trooper. "Be all right if we follow you in the car?"

The trooper took stock of them. Shep saw him calculating. A disabled soldier, a young Negro woman, an old mammy, and a driver who was hired to do a job, wouldn't want to be in law trouble. What was the alternative, anyway? Call for a paddy wagon?

"Reckon so. Let me radio for the car up there to come on and follow you. We'll lead."

The troopers walked back to the patrol car. They didn't turn their car around, leaving it facing the LaSalle. One leaned in and radioed the car ahead, then they leaned against their car and lit cigarettes to wait for the roadblock to be let down and the light traffic to start moving. They nodded to the driver of a truck that stopped in the lane behind them.

When he thought of the probable outcome of a chase, Shep decided he was going to give it one more try. "I think they'd back down when it's proven the car is yours," he said.

"It wouldn't happen that way."

"We have no choice but to go with them."

"I have no choice but to not go with them. I do want you to get out, though. None of this concerns you."

Damn, what justified trying to escape from state troopers?

"If you stay, maybe they'll listen to you about yesterday, what the sheriff there was trying to do, and you'll be cleared."

But that still left the other charge from D.C. "We go or we stay."

"I can't stay."

She must have a damn good reason. Some kind of trumped up charge. Now just might not be the time to get into it. She believed what she was saying, and he believed her. While he was convincing himself flight was the only alternative, and thinking the time to make a run was now, before the traffic started up, Angelene said, "Walter, take off!"

Walter said, "Hold on!"

The stunned patrolmen froze, then threw their smokes down and took an instant to decide whether to jump in the car or draw and shoot. The driver jumped in and put the car in gear and turned it around as the other one drew his pistol and fired. Then the driver pulled away before realizing he was leaving his partner behind and backed up. By the time he jumped in it was too late to fire again because another car had driven up and was between them, as well as the truck. Shep watched the patrol car from the roadblock meander as if they had not noticed what was happening and finally darting away from the light traffic behind them.

"Oh, Jesus, Mercy on us!" said Mama Gran.

"Anybody hurt?" Shep said.

"Faster!" said Angelene. "We've got to get away from them!"

"We're close to the state line," he said. "That's why they had the road block here. We've got to head south." Sounded strange even to him! But across the state line, things would have to be called in all over again. And again, would these troopers be in a hurry to explain how the quarry evaded them? They might just let it drop. If they didn't apprehend them before they got out of Kentucky, their attitude might be to let it be Tennessee's problem.

They were paralleling a meandering stream, crossing and re-crossing it, going back north. In the distance behind them he caught sight of the state trooper cars before they were lost behind curves. The Cadillac motor probably could outrun them, but they needed to avoid any more of them. "We've got to get going the other way." On the left of the highway ahead was a leaning gray barn, long deserted. "Could you get this cruiser behind that barn?"

Walter slowed to cross a shallow dry ditch and dodged a downed fence to circle the barn and head back the way they came from, and sat idling so close to the back wall of the barn that an elbow could not have stuck out the window.

It'll never work, Shep thought. Be thinking! But behind the barn they heard the sirens get close and fade down the road, then the second car followed.

"Look after us, Jesus!" Mama Gran said.

"Probably all right to go now, Walter," he said.

"Ain't soon enough for me!" Walter said.

"I think the roadblock was almost at the road I found on the map earlier. The shortcut across the line. Let's look for it," Angelene said.

FIFTEEN

They met only two vehicles, slowing at the approach so as not to attract any more attention than the car would by itself, with Angelene and Mama Gran slouching in their seats so as not to be seen. They did not have to speed past a vehicle on their side of the road. They didn't even see a farm wagon in a field. The traffic must have been local and all gone home. They passed the place where the roadblock had been earlier and not a mile ahead was the turn-off, marked by a post bare of a sign, barely visible because of overgrown bushes, obviously not used as a road anymore. It was narrow, only one car wide, packed dirt ruts grown over with grass and a few bushes, which would help disguise their tire tracks. It might end at a river with a washed out bridge. It disappeared into trees.

"Stop when you get in the trees. Let's come back and fluff up those bushes again," Shep said. They had barely returned to the treeline when one of the trooper cars sped by.

After a couple of miles, a tree was down across the path. Shep got out with Walter. They agreed it couldn't be moved.

"We'll have to go around it," Walter told Angelene. "I'll walk around and see if there's a way."

Angelene got water out and Shep didn't ask why she had no choice in giving herself up. That was what she'd said, wasn't it?

Walter came back and gulped down water they offered him and said a shallow streambed with hardly any water in it was off to the side and they could drive down it about a quarter mile then get back up on the dirt road.

The car wanted to mire in the creek bottom a time or two, but rocks lined most of it. When Walter tried to pull out of it and up to the road, the bank was soft, so Shep and Angelene got out and pushed.

"We didn't contribute much manpower," Angelene said, and Shep didn't even think she was ridiculing him, but she glanced his way. "Facts are facts," he said, laughing. "And here it is out of the stream," she said as they got back inside and she opened a bag of crackers and cheese to pass around.

"No contribution too small," Mama Gran said in a presidential tone.

Walter laughed.

Shep said, "Probably was only our weight being out of the car that made the difference, you think?"

"We resent that!" Angelene added, happy, safe, food in hand. Before long the road got a little better, and was eventually packed dirt easily visible in the grass. The trees thinned out. A prosperous farm's two-story white house with red roof was visible as they made a couple of curves. A wooden bridge with no railing was just ahead, the creek now a running stream several feet below.

He heard the lid being lifted from a tin, and Angelene said, "Anybody want a cookie?"

She took one and munched on it when no one else wanted one.

"You should have milk with it," Mama Gran said.

"That would be – what was that!"

"A blowout! Brace yourselves!" Shep said, pushing against the dash with his good arm.

"Hang on!" Walter shouted, manhandling the steering wheel into obeying him and slowing to a stop on the roadside just after they crossed the rattling planks.

Angelene had her arm across Mama Gran, who had slid down the seat into a little lump.

Walter jumped out and jerked open the back door as Shep slid out and opened the other one.

"Mama Gran, are you all right?" Angelene said. "Mama Gran!"

Mama Gran said, "Did the engine explode? Are we drowning?"

"It was a tire. A tire blow-out!" Angelene said as she put her arms around her.

"Tire?"

"We're in the car, Mama Gran."

"Oh. Now, I remember. For a time I thought it was the steamboat." She put her hand on her heart.

"Let's lay her down with a pillow under her head and a couple of them under her feet," Shep said. "Ger her feet higher than her heart." He remembered his mother doing that for Thula her last few months. "It's hot in the car. Maybe we should get her outside."

"Walter, get a blanket to spread out," Angelene said, looking for a likely spot.

"Well, hello there!" they heard. "Almighty!"

They looked toward the voice and saw a tall white woman in blue jeans and a red long-sleeved shirt, just coming from behind a thicket. She wore garden gloves with the tips cut out, heavy brown boots and a large straw hat. When she pushed it back so she could see better, they could see that she was not a woman who could be called pretty, but had kindness in her face. She was probably around fifty. She carried a gallon tin bucket brimming with blackberries. "Is everything all right?" she said.

"I hope so," said Angelene, after a visible jump at being startled.

"Sounded like a shot."

"A blowout, Miss," Walter said.

The berry picker looked at the path the car left. "Damn good driving, getting across that plank bridge!" Then she looked around, taking them all in. "My, you're a surprise. Nothing been on this road in twenty year. And mixed company! Another surprise."

"We're not. That is, we didn't start out together," Angelene said, not defensively, but cautionary-like, possibly not knowing the woman's feelings concerning such as that.

"Yes M'am," Shep said. "They took pity on me, but we've become friends."

"We've helped each other," Angelene said, no longer at odds with herself.

"I'm one who don't censor my talk. As they caution us these days, my loose lips would sink ships," the woman said, and laughed at herself.

"Then you're in exactly the right place to avoid that," said Angelene, and Shep could hardly detect any sarcasm at all.

"Sure are," said Shep. "Good place to be anytime, looks like."

"I'm partial to making friends, too, Army man. Bet you're a Lieutenant. Read a newspaper article about your rank not long ago."

"Yes Ma'am. Lt. Shep Haddon," he said, reaching to meet her outstretched hand. "This is Mrs. Midnight, and Mr. Smith, and our patient is Miss Johnston."

"Glad to meet all of you," she said. "I'm Miss Pearl Jurvis. Call me Pearl."

"We're looking for a spot to let Miss Johnston lie down and rest."

"I know one. See them trees and shrubs at the edge of that pasture yonder? My house is just beyond them. Think you can make it there?" She seemed to be asking Angelene and him. He and Angelene exchanged looks.

"Would you mind telling us where we are?" Shep said. "We got off on this road ..."

"More of a footpath now. Nobody comes to Tennessee from Kentuck on it any more."

"So we're in Tennessee," said Angelene. "Oh! Mama Gran!" just as she roused and dropped her head again in a faint.

"I'll carry her," Walter said, "if we stopping."

"Sure wouldn't be a problem for you," Pearl said, squinting, either from the sun or appraising his size.

"Yes, we'll stop for a bit. Thank you, Miss Jurvis," said Angelene.

"It's shorter through the pasture, take but about five minutes. But you got to wade through the crik. It's wide and shallow there. Might find some big stones to plant your feet on."

"I have salts for her to inhale," Angelene said, reaching into the box.

"She'll feel better when we get her inside, I reckon," Pearl said.

Five brown cows grazed, barely breaking to look at the walkers. "We can walk out here among them?" Angelene said.

"They're gentle as lambs," Pearl said. "But watch your step."

"Nice Jerseys. Lot of good butterfat to sell to the dairy," Shep said.

"Cream might be already separated after that explosion."

He laughed. "It's some work milking that many." He supposed she would realize it was his way of asking if she had others at home.

Pearl shook her head. "You're right. A high school boy comes over here to help every morning. He'll be off to the army next year." She shook her head again in sympathy. "That tire's ruined. Hope you got a sticker to buy another one." She looked back at Angelene. "Bet you do."

Angelene nodded.

Shep took Pearl's bucket to carry. "Fine looking berries."

"Seems like they just won't stop coming in this year," she said, watching Angelene dig her flat shoes out of the trunk.

SIXTEEN

He and Walter returned to the car. Walter opened the trunk and Shep didn't comment on the extra tire that she wasn't supposed to have. By now he knew she had ways to get whatever she needed. Walter took out the jack and one of the spares.

"Want me to help get some boxes out? Be easier to jack the car up since the flat's on the back. Would be for me," Shep said, "but might not matter to you."

Walter laughed. "Be easier on the car, too."

After the tire was changed, they examined the blow-out. "You had your work cut out for you, holding us on that plank bridge. I could put my fist through the hole. Pearl could have heard it at her house." He picked something glinting out of the tire, not even close to the slit. "Look here, Walter."

"Lord Jesus!"

Shep held a bullet, still retaining most of its shape, in his palm. Somebody was looking out for them. It should have blown out the tire the second it hit. They looked at the hole again. The wounded tire looked as if it had been sliced. But there was only a slight indention in the other place, where the bullet had resided, having come to a stop before penetrating the rubber all the way.

"You mean the bullet didn't make it blowout? How the hell that happen?" Walter said.

"Bullets only travel so far. When they reach their last distance, they lose their bite."

They looked at the tire again, the slice about three inches long.

They walked back across the planks and not far down the path were some bottles tossed around, mostly covered by grass. "This did the slicing," Walter said, picking up the jagged remains of a beer bottle.

"May have been Miss Jurvis's helper and some friends back in here partying," Shep said, remembering having done that himself a time or two.

Walter opened up the repair kit, one for the tire and one for the tube, hot and cold patches. He worked on the tube and got it patched. "Won't hold, probably." Then he put his hand through the cut on the tire, and gave up on it. "Miss Pearl can give to the rubber drive." he said.

"Lucky you have an extra," Shep said, feeling it would be all right now to note it. Be more unusual not to mention it.

"Not lucky," Walter said. "Planning ahead is what it is."

So Angelene had planned this trip well in advance. He wondered what the circumstances were, or perhaps only one action, that precipitated the decision to leave whatever her life was. He would bet, and he called himself not a gambling man, that it was not a vacation to meet an alleged husband.

They drove the car around to Pearl's house, the red-roofed one they'd all been watching in the road curves earlier.

They walked up on the wide covered porch. Several clay pots with red geraniums were placed at precise intervals on the wide railing and a pot of ferns hung evenly from the ceiling on each side of the steps.

Angelene held out a glass and said "I got my milk after all." She sat in a wooden rocker, a small bowl of blackberries in her lap. "These are wonderful," she said, offering them. "Try some. Pearl's inside changing. She said she wore those hot clothes to keep thorns from scratching her, and keep chiggers off her arms and legs while she picked the berries."

Pearl, now cool and trim-looking in a print short-sleeve dress and apron, opened the screen door and guided out an elderly gentleman, tall and twisted to one side, in overalls and plaid shirt, leaning on a cane. "This is my daddy, Jobe Jurvis."

"Pleased to meet you," they said but he didn't return a greeting. "He's had a stroke last year. Don't know if he'll ever think right again." She led him to a rocker. "Get the tire fixed? Sit and rest yourselves."

"Walter patched the tube," Shep said, sitting down on the porch edge at the steps, and leaning against the squared column, his braced leg resting down against the steps. "He says you can give the tire to the rubber drive."

"Want me to put it in the barn?" Walter said.

"Appreciate it."

"Heard any war news lately?" Pearl said. "Got a radio in that rolling palace? My battery's out. Won't get one 'til I go to town next week."

Shep and she exchanged looks, and Walter slapped his knee. "Be darn," he said. "We forgot about the war, I guess."

"Guess we've been sort of concerned with other things," Shep said.

"Walter, why don't you see if you can get some news?" Angelene said.

He started the car and played with the dial a few minutes. Finally bits of a song came through.

". . . . made me love you . . .
. . didn't want to do it . . .
. . . .'

"Can't find any news." He turned the knob again until the same station came through again in bits.

"... pictured in my mind . . .

. . . .

... never thought of you . . . .

... you made me . . ."

Then silence.

After a minute while Shep, and he figured all present, imagined they heard the last words of the popular song, Pearl said, "I always liked that song. Guess we're out of range, hills cut off the waves." Then she sang a line or two, "You made me love you, I didn't want to do it ..."

"Thank you again for taking us in," Angelene said when Pearl paused for breath.

"Why, I thank you. It's a good diversion for me on this dull day. I like to get out of my rut, find out about people."

"What are chiggers, Pearl? Are they like thorns?"

Pearl and Shep laughed.

"Not to change the subject," Pearl said, and laughed again. "Chiggers are little insect buggers from hell. They wait on grass to dig in you and itch you 'til you want to cuss."

"She was raised walking on city sidewalks," Mama Gran said, just then appearing inside the door. Walter helped her out to a rocker and stood by her.

Jobe Jurvis said "there" and looked at Walter and then pointed to a rocker and nodded at it.

"Well I'll be," said Pearl. "I guess you folks are the first thing interesting enough to make him care. Now, I want y'all to stay for supper. I've got some leftovers from dinner, and I'll fry some squash, first of the season. Good time to open my last jar of butterbeans from last season. The new ones are not quite filled out yet."

"That's nice, but we couldn't impose," Angelene said.

"You're welcome for the night if you have no plans."

Angelene got up and handed the bowl to Walter and walked to the edge of the porch. She leaned both hands against the waist high railing and looked out at the distance. "Oh, Pearl, if you only knew how unexpected and thoughtful your invitation is."

"I figure I do."

"I'm sorry we can't stay," Angelene said.

"I am too," Pearl said, looking at Shep.

It was an honest invitation, but more than that, more even than an offer of refuge. It was in her voice. She had a problem they could help with if they stayed. He and Angelene looked at each other. It was another acknowledgment that each had become important to the other, that each had a say in whatever concerned them both. It was her ride, but he now owned his part of it.

"Is there a problem?" Shep said.

"Yes, do you need our help with something?" Angelene said, stepping close to Shep.

"It's not no big problem. Not really a problem at all. I just had a thought if Miss Johnston needed a rest, Mr. Smith might help with some haying." She pointed to the side pasture. She looked at Shep and said, "Figured you to be a farm boy, you knew about my cows. Thought you could help him even the way your limbs can't do all you ask of em'. Nathan Dacus just dying to get his skinny self over here to help again this year."

"Does he overcharge?" Angelene said.

"I reckon so. He expects me to marry him if I need him so much."

They laughed with her.

"Guess I will, but I don't want him to think I can't do without him."

Angelene said, "Yes, the upper hand."

Yes. The upper hand could have a way of holding the other one down, or trying to, if the upper hand wasn't too particular. Or the other hand wasn't too guarded. Angelene understood it. Was she the upper hand or was her husband?

Angelene looked at Shep and they agreed they must let Pearl know something of their troubles before accepting her refuge.

"I think we should let you know. We're fugitives," he said.

"Figured as much," Pearl said. "Why else would you be driving that forsaken road? Like I said, hasn't been used since they put in the highway. No sign up anymore. Ain't even on the new maps. It'd be a nice hidden shortcut across the state line."

Well, so much for Angelene's maps being up-to-date. He wondered if she had had some problem acquiring maps. Why would that have been?

"And you don't care?" Angelene said. "We could be dangerous."

Pearl laughed. "I figure I know why they want to apprehend you."

"Tennessee not like Kentucky?" Shep said, resenting he must go along with her as if it were the truth, but not sorry to have it thought of them.

"Laws are no different for the likes of you two down here. But I don't happen to give a care about it." She glanced at her father. "He's the one taught me that. People are people." Her father nodded. "What's more, you'd be a godsend to me, way I look at it. He may have even sent you. Angels, shep ..."

Angelene laughed and shook her head from side to side. "I doubt we're on a mission from God."

"I'm pretty sure it's coincidence," Shep said, laughing, not wanting or needing to give her their story, maybe putting her at liability if it ever came out that she helped them.

"Nobody in a mile to know what I'm up to, anyway," Pearl added. "Just God and Jobe here." She looked at her father and he lifted his chin.

Well, it was all right to stay, he figured. If by some predestined fate the law did show up, they'd just have to give up and go in to be questioned. Get it all straightened out sooner than later.

Angelene looked toward Mama Gran. "I believe in returning good works," Mama Gran said. "And you're the godsend to us, Miss Jurvis."

Then Angelene looked at Walter. "You'd be doing the hard work."

"There's daylight left," he said, "let's get to it."

"Mama Gran could use more rest," Angelene said.

She apparently didn't have a deadline for New Orleans. Or maybe Mama Gran was more important to her than any set date. Or her husband. If there was a husband. Could it be she wasn't married yet, and was a runaway bride? A jilted man could very well have set the law on her if the car was a gift from him, even if it was in her name. Damn. He was grasping at straws. And that was simply not necessary, he knew that now. He could ask her. And she would tell him. He had no doubt of that at this point. But it was a matter now of more than wanting to know about her. He wanted her to tell him all about it. On her own. Her decision. He wanted her to not be able to keep such a secret from him.

"Well look at that," Pearl said, turning to her father, who was lifting his cane toward a large shed and then toward the car. "He thinks you ought to park in the shed so Bert won't see it. Old truck's not there. I've let Bert take it to court his girl. He rides his bicycle over here to do the milking, saves gas. He can't help with the haying, got to help his own daddy. Let me see. He'll be here about four-thirty in the morning. Reckon y'all could manage to still be abed?"

Angelene laughed. "You can count on it," she said.

SEVENTEEN

Walter was in faded overalls with straps stretched to the limit and unbuttoned at the waist, and a long-sleeved plaid shirt that wouldn't button and didn't think of reaching his wrists. Jobe Jurvis had once been a big man, but not like Walter. Shep wore a pair of her daddy's current-sized pants and shirt.

Shep steered the tractor with one hand, fighting to control it. Jobe Jurvis had adjusted the seat for his long length, but Shep sat on a cushion to raise him enough on the seat for his stiff leg not to have to bend when he needed to lift it enough to push the clutch. Walter followed the hay mow attached to the tractor, raking it in stacks as tall as he was. In a little while Angelene ventured out in Pearl's big boots carrying a quart jar of water for them. "She's saving her ice for supper. The ice man doesn't come for two days. She says ice water wouldn't be good for you out here anyway, hot as it is."

Shep judged they had half the field done when they heard a bell clang. "What's that?" Walter said.

"Farm telegraph," Shep said. "Supper time."

Walter helped him disengage the mower.

"Climb on. We'll hurry and put this under its overhang next to the shed before we get our baths." He laughed. "Pearl told me where the creek pools. We're to go and cool off there."

They got there just as Angelene was leaving a couple of towels and their clothes they had rolled up and left at the house when they changed.

"Pearl said there's a watermelon cooling in the water. It's in a net hooked to a post at the edge. You're to bring it. There, I see it! This looks so nice and cool."

Walter was sitting, taking off some rubber boots Pearl had found for him, that were made to be worn over shoes, so had been big enough.

Shep slipped his arm out of his sling and tried straightening it. It didn't come close to straight. He bent and with his good arm started unbuckling his brace and lost his footing. She grabbed out for him and he reached out for her with his now unslung arm. Damn. It worked! It hurt like electric shock, but it worked!

"You've just been looking for pity!" she said, laughing, as Walter jumped up to help but sat down again and said, "Amazing what hard work can heal!"

He shook off her hand and that hurt like hell, too. But it obeyed his command.

"You just hadn't needed it," Angelene said, accepting that he was not refusing her help, but was just disgusted at himself. "Don't come back to the house without it in that sling. I know that hurt." She picked up the sling. "Never mind." She bent and swished it in the creek several times and squeezed the water out. "It'll be dry by morning. And you'll wear it. At least part of the day. Just tuck your arm in your shirt like Napoleon tonight." She walked off laughing, calling, "Hurry, it's getting dark."

After supper they all sat on the porch to eat the watermelon and enjoy the breeze.

"If you don't mind my asking, just how do you two expect to make it?" Pearl said, aiming her voice at Angelene and Shep, both in the swing but well apart, each hovering at an armrest.

"Make it?" Angelene said, her foot braking, forgetting she had gone along with that premise earlier.

Shep started the swinging motion again. "Friends have a way of making it," he said. "We've got to be honest with you."

"We just met, what, two days ago?" she said.

"Seems like you been knowing each other forever," Pearl said. "But you did tell me different at first."

Seems like forever, Shep thought, if that could be possible without knowing a whole lot of basic pertinent facts about each other. "It was just yesterday," he said.

"Course, I'm a romantic person," Pearl said. "That's why Mr. Dacus is so crazy about me."

EIGHTEEN

It was late next evening as they approached the Cumberland River on Gallatin Highway. They'd left Pearl and Jobe late afternoon, and had with them from her a jar of blackberry preserves from yesterday's bounty that Angelene had helped her with, her favorite large dish cloth that she had embroidered with sunflowers and tied up full of biscuits, a watermelon, and her wish that they could be at her wedding.

They finally crossed a skeletal bridge to enter downtown Nashville, and Shep was eager to hear some war news. The radio had been sporadic in the hills, and he'd thought of the low talk he'd heard in the hospital, the build-up of troops in England, going to meet the Germans for the second time. Like the Israelites and the Philistines. Over and over. He'd get news here, for sure. The top of the capitol dome appeared among the tall buildings a few times, depending on their height. The river banks were littered with barges and boats and all the goods they carried, and warehouses that looked a hundred dirty years old. Again, not like Ole Man River. Anything that close on its banks would have been carried away by its roaming water long before that.

The stone and red brick buildings were dark smoky grey, and he thought it was probably from burning fossil fuel with pollution that couldn't rise out of the sunken area the city was in. He could see it was surrounded by low mountains on all sides. The sun was setting on the edge of the city opposite where they were entering.

"Sort of dreary looking," Angelene said.

"Needs a good spring cleaning," Mama Gran said.

Like the kind his mother and Thula had done each year when he was a boy, making him help when they could catch sight of him. They brushed down the outside doors and portals with brooms with old towels tied around them and dipped in soapy water, and had him swab the porch floors with rag mops until the paint was about to come up. The inside suffered even more. They swept down the corners with fresh broom straw they'd sent him to cut out in the field next to the woods, with orders to check for ticks before he came inside. Then they'd tie an armful of the long shafts together with cords to make the flimsy, swishy brooms.

They bathed everything in the kitchen as if it had been playing in mud all winter. They scrubbed the stove with lye soap, and the ice box with baking soda, and ate a biscuit and jelly for breakfast and milk and cornbread and apples for dinner and supper. They washed and hung out to dry all the curtains. They put the heavy drapes over chairs on the porch to air and tied a rope between the "hammock trees" to hang the rugs over, bribing him to beat the winter out of them by letting him use his baseball bat. Pearl's house looked much the same.

But spring had gone by here and left heat and confusion. People were on the streets everywhere in this middle Tennessee town. All things considered it was different from the western-most Tennessee town of Memphis that he was so familiar with; this was much older, the downtown narrow streets laid out before cars, as was the case in Memphis too, of course. But that city's founders, among them none other than future president and Nashville area resident Andrew Jackson, had the foresight and luxury to plan ahead for traffic, even if they thought it would always be horse drawn.

Walter handled the traffic, narrow streets, crowds, changing lights, traffic cops. He'd seen it all before. In multiples. This city would be swallowed by Washington, D.C. And they were lucky once again. This city had its share of fine cars, it being the state capitol, as well as having the Grand Ole Opry and its country music money.

"There's a hotel," Angelene said as they wound up and down streets. "To the left there."

"It's probably booked up," Shep said. And it probably was, but that was beside the point. He was beginning to wonder if she had ever been out of the Negro section of the capital, which must be a world unto itself.

"There's another."

"I don't think they'll have a room either. We probably should drive around a little, see what we'll find," he said, glancing at Walter, trusting Walter's sense of direction getting them to the part of town they would be accommodated in.

"Mama Gran's tired. I think we should try here."

Walter gave him a glance.

"Walter, park here," she said, feeling herself back in her element, he thought.

"There'll be no room for us," Mama Gran said.

"Money talks," Angelene assured her.

It might buy a room in a booked-up hotel. If the right person had the money. Or if it was the right hotel.

Walter parked in one of the reserved spots.

Shep tried to exit and get to the doorman quickly to ask if there was another entrance they should go to, but he moved stiffly and slowly. And the rich car had spurred the doorman to action apparently before he registered who was in the back seat, noticing only Walter and Shep.

He held the door open for Shep, and said, "Good Evening, Sir. Step right inside, rooms available," before finally noticing the party's diversity. "Perhaps there's another entrance," Shep said.

"Only one entrance for you, Suh," he said.

"Try," Angelene said to Shep, finishing on a hopeful, questioning note. "A couple of rooms would do. You and Walter could share?"

Shep, realizing it was too late to start the discussion he should have, hoped he would be wrong, hoped that when he explained who was with him, they had situations such as this accounted for since the war started; or failing that, he would tell Angelene the doorman was mistaken. He let the doorman usher him inside. He crossed the small vestibule and entered the lobby, small also but grand in appearance, and went to the desk. "Hello, Sir," the clerk said to Shep. "Would you like to register?"

"I need two rooms." He and Walter could certainly bunk together again if a miracle happened and they were let to stay.

"Yes, we have two rooms, it being mid-week," the clerk said as Walter appeared next to him. "You've seen action, Lieutenant."

Shep nodded, adjusting his patch, wondering if his injured state could possibly prevail on the clerk's sympathy no matter what their policy. He wondered if his eye would start functioning when he had to use it just as his arm did. But his brain was finally working. He had to tell who the guests would be, get the clarification on where they should be coming in. "I need to ask what your policy is concerning Negro – "

"Sorry, Mr. Shep, Miss Angelene sent me in," Walter said, interrupting. "Miss Johnston getting bad again."

"Your rooms are ready. Your driver can find a room over behind the capitol, little west of it."

"I'll get the ladies," Walter said.

"Wait," Shep said, but Walter had already gone.

The clerk turned the book around so Shep could sign. "I was asking what your arrangement is concerning Negroes," he said. "Do you have a different arrangement?"

"We don't have an arrangement. They're not allowed."

His look said, Why would you ask?

Shep turned around to leave. A huge vase of flowers sat in the middle of the dark round table centered on an oriental rug between him and the door. A couple dressed for a fine dinner stood, maybe waiting for a taxi, and a couple of gentlemen in high-back chairs smoked cigars.

Angelene and Mama Gran were entering, with Walter behind them carrying two suitcases.

The desk clerk grabbed the book and spun it back around and perused it only slightly while he tried to decide what to say. The lady in the lobby stared and one of the smoking gentlemen dropped his cigar and hastily grabbed it out of his lap and dusted the ashes off.

"Lieutenant," the clerk muttered, looking at the book inquisitively, making sure he hadn't registered. "your maids? your maids can't stay here. They'll have to go with your driver."

"They're not my maids," Shep said. "And he's the young lady's driver."

Another couple had entered the lobby and stopped short, and the two women now in the lobby were sizing up Angelene and Mama Gran. Angelene wore tan leather high-heeled pumps, with only a strap around the heel; a dark green skirt fitted to the hips with swingy pleats down one side and a short-sleeved blouse that looked creamy enough to drink, with a necklace of tan and green and pink and yellow stones. The two women were in bright dresses that showed their ample figures and white strappy shoes that made their feet look large.

Angelene's long hair was pulled back in one of the ropey nets that women had taken to wearing.

Mama Gran was in a dress so like yesterday's it was possibly the same one, just as Thula's used to all look alike, although hers were of print cotton. He knew by now Mama Gran's wardrobe was furnished of dresses that wouldn't vary much from this style.

From nowhere a gentleman stood beside him and introduced himself as the assistant manager. The clerk must have buzzed him. "The hotel has a policy," he said. "No Negroes."

"They're with me," Shep said.

"Is she your wife?"

Oh, what the hell. "Yes," he said.

"His wife!" said one of the watching women.

"And her grandmother," Shep added.

The manager thought that over. "I'm sorry," he said, and he could have meant it. He looked at Angelene. "But the management has rules. I have to follow them."

"I'm not his wife," Angelene said, as if she were a crowned princess. "I have money to pay for my room."

A louder gasp came from the two women. "*Not* his wife!" one said. "Must be his ..."

"I'm sorry, Miss," the manager said, this time not so sorry. "It's not my doing. It's hotel policy. Try the Troy over on Robinson."

There were a dozen things he figured Angelene would say, but she only turned Mama Gran toward the door and walked out. She was embarrassed. She hadn't known what would in all probability happen. Had Pearl's color blindness wiped out her memory of how they met? Could it be as he'd suspected, she'd never been out of her kingdom overnight in a public place? Why the hell hadn't he told her about backdoors? He should have embarrassed himself by explaining the facts of life to her rather than put her and Mama Gran through this.

He probably could deck the manager with his good arm and fight the good fight against the clerk, who looked like the willowy type that Dorthea liked to dance and play cards with, but it wouldn't actually change anything. And there was Walter, wanting to help the ladies but waiting to see if he and Shep were going to extract vengeance. They'd both be hauled off to jail. Angelene and Mama Gran would be left on their own, if they weren't arrested, too. Without doubt the D.C. warrant would be found out about. He looked around the room and said to them all in general, "Enjoy your rooms." That sarcasm would no doubt be lost on them.

Walter followed him out. The doorman was helping the women into the car. He looked sad. "You have to make a living," Mama Gran was saying to him.

"The Troy is two blocks over to the left and one down, then go right for several blocks. They'll take care of you."

The manager followed them outside. "We always have a room for an injured soldier."

Shep ignored him and slid with ease into the seat that had become so familiar to him.

Walter parked on the street close to the door that opened directly onto the sidewalk. The Troy, Negro Hotel, said the sign over it. They went inside. The small room was almost filled with the desk and a phone booth. The Negro man behind the desk stared at them. "Are you at the right place?" he asked.

"We were told you could accommodate us," said Shep.

"We can't accommodate you," the desk clerk said. "This is reserved for Negroes."

"Do you mean we can't get rooms?" Angelene said.

"You can. She can. He can." He nodded toward Shep. "He can't."

She looked at Shep.

Shep said, "I think you should stay. I understand."

"He can check in around front. Troy Tower. I'm sure there'll be a room for a soldier," said the clerk.

"No," she said. "We won't stay here."

Mama Gran put her hand to her chest. Angelene put her hand to Mama Gran's wrist. "I can hardly feel her pulse."

"Where is a hospital we can take her to?" Shep said.

"Memorial's closest, but – "

Angelene lost patience and had by now accepted this new world. "Where's one that will take her?"

"West on Broadway. Be a sign where to turn. I regret all this, all this confusion."

Angeline didn't even waste one of her looks on him as she said, "Hurry, Walter."

PART II

THE STONE OF HELP

Then Samuel took a stone, and set it between Mizpeh and Shen,
and called the name of it Ebenezer, saying, Hitherto hath the Lord helped us.
First Samuel 7:12

Holy Bible
King James Version
set forth 1611 A.D.

NINETEEN

At the hospital emergency entrance, Walter skidded the car to a stop and hurried in. Minutes later he returned with a doctor. He carried a brown leather satchel, still not badly scuffed. He hadn't been practicing medicine long.

"I'm Dr. Brighton," he said to Mama Gran as he listened to her heart with a stethoscope and felt her pulse. He took a tiny pill from a vial and placed it under her tongue. "It'll stimulate your heart." He felt her ankles through the thick black stockings. "Badly swollen."

He looked at Angelene for the first time as she spoke. "We've been spending a lot of time in the car for days."

Shep noticed that reaction that erupts when a man wants to impress a woman. A somehow more assertive voice, an almost perceptible stiffening of the spine, a turning of the wheels to impart something to raise his standing – knowledge, opinion, help, and in the right kind of man all without his realization until later and it's done and over. The doctor said, "She's had these spells previously, I'm sure."

Angelene nodded.

"They're getting more frequent, I suppose," the doctor added, and again she nodded. "You're an octagenerian, I expect," he said, addressing his patient once more.

Shep hoped the doctor would not have to explain himself, embarrassing his patient, although for some reason he wouldn't mind if the doctor learned a lesson from it. When Mama Gran said, "No. I'm already in my nineties," he was glad, and called himself petty for thinking such a thing.

"Feeling better, Auntie?" Dr. Brighton addressed Mama Gran as Thula had been called by her family, having had no children of her own. And as they had, he rhymed it with "font" and "say."

Shep figured Mama Gran would manage to rebuke the doctor for being so familiar.

But she gave him a weak smile and nodded. He held her hand between his and said, "I'm glad you are. Would you like us to admit you, Auntie?"

Shep admired the doctor for inquiring of Mama Gran if she wanted to be hospitalized, rather than consulting Angelene, giving the old lady the dignity of deciding her own fate.

"No," Mama Gran said. "I think I'll be all right."

"I'll give you these little pills. You can put one under your tongue when you feel a spell coming on."

Mama Gran sat up with Angelene's help and rested against the seatback.

"They won't cure you. They'll only temporarily respond to an acute manifestation of your chronic cardiac condition – they'll make you feel better," he finished, visibly put out with himself. Then he patted her on the arm and got out of the car.

Angelene got out and shook hands with Dr. Brighton, introducing herself, Mama Gran, and Walter. The doctor introduced himself to Angelene as Lionel Brighton. Shep couldn't help noticing that the doctor and Walter shook hands like any two men he'd ever seen, and not as Walter and Archie had.

Yes, without meaning to, the doctor had impressed Angelene, with his forthright and dignified treatment of Mama Gran, as well as with his final decisive control of his fountain of knowledge and his finding it unnecessary to announce himself to her as "Doctor."

Shep didn't know if Angelene was holding a grudge because of his making it a "mixed party," as Pearl had called them, and all the resulting hotel trouble, but he knew she wouldn't have intentionally left him out of an introduction or a conversation an hour earlier. He thought he felt her indecision. But before she could make his introductions for him, he stepped around the car and introduced himself.

Dr. Brighton was about six feet tall, as he looked directly across into Shep's eye. But if Shep gained back the fifteen pounds he had lost in the last four months, he'd still need about ten or fifteen more to weigh even with the doctor, who was not heavy by any means. The doctor's serious demeanor, seriously short hair as if to deny the crispy curls, round wire-rimmed glasses, standard doctor smockcoat over white shirt, black bowtie, and black pin-striped trousers were an effort to appear more mature than he was, probably no more than twenty-nine or thirty.

Shep felt old next to him. What a difference a couple of years can make. Two war years. Gaddamn. Quitcher bitchin' Kolosky would have said. You're not competing with this black wonderboy.

"Well, you've apparently seen action," the doctor remarked in an appreciative light as they shook hands, Shep trying out his right hand, it having been out of the sling since they left Pearl's. "You've been taken care of well, I trust. Would there be anything I could assist you with?"

Shep shook his head. "No need. I appreciate the offer."

"You're not from here," the doctor said to Angelene.

"No. From Washington, D.C."

"Will you be here for a time?" he said, almost keeping the hopeful note from his voice.

"Only until my great-grandmother is able to travel."

"She probably needs a couple of days not cooped up in the car. She should elevate her legs, walk a little several times a day to get circulation going better, very little salt, enough fluids."

"Fluids?" Angelene said.

"It seems like a contradiction. But fluids, water especially, will help prevent retention."

"Our doctor said drink little."

"I'm surprised she didn't take issue with the doctor. Old aunties know such things."

"I expect she did. But I didn't."

And Mama Gran would have known it would call for more stops along the way, adding more difficulties, Shep thought, remembering the few times she had reluctantly done so.

"Don't blame yourself for this," the doctor said to Angelene, lowering his voice. "It's sad. I wouldn't want to be blunt ... but I expect you've been told, nothing will prevent what's going to happen." He looked in the car at Mama Gran and then back to Angelene. "She knows that."

Angelene took a deep breath and nodded, flaring her nostrils, her wide nose becoming flatter and wider. "Could you recommend a hotel?" she asked, barely flashing her brown eyes toward Shep.

"Umh, well," he said, looking forthrightly at Angelene, then pointedly at Shep. "I can for some of you."

"It's all or none," she said without hesitation.

Shep felt as if he had been awarded another Silver Star. He didn't feel deserving of it now, either. But he was as appreciative of her statement as the Captain's speech recounting his destroying a machine gun emplacement two weeks before the tank encounter. Shep had been crawling around through brush and wild hog wallows and dodging things out to get him all his life. Coming up behind the machine gun emplacement was less involved than sneaking up on a wild boar he'd hunted with the local farmers when he was a boy. But he was embarrassed at the award ceremony while he lay in the hospital. However, the actual award, the Purple Heart, the beautiful purple ribbon with the gold heart outlining the profile of the first Commander in Chief, he felt different about, his heart swelling with pride to have a medal first designed by George Washington as a Badge of Merit. The ribbon denoting it that he wore on his uniform, the medal in his duffle, now had three oak leaf clusters, denoting the three occasions he'd been wounded. But looking around at the men in the ward who had suffered worse than he, actually missing limbs or eyes, or who had been more valorous than he felt he had been kept him in reality. That day he'd only been scared. Of dying, of his men dying. Of coming back a dead failure to Dorthea. That was before he had slain the tank and been afraid to live. He looked at Angelene, only hoping she couldn't know everything he was trying to conceal behind what he tried to project as merely pleased.

"So, you two are married?"

"Yes," she said, nodding.

Shep recognized her soft, wickedly ironic laugh again, with her head tilted back so slightly, no more just a raising of the chin, and a momentary widening of the lips.

Dr. Brighton used his physician's trained face of not reacting to bad news.

But she took pity on him. "We're married, but not to each other."

At that, Dr. Brighton couldn't hide his concern.

She was still holding out that she was married. Perhaps she was. She would tell him the truth soon. Shep tried to make himself do the gentlemanly thing and explain that they were only newly befriended. But he was enjoying the impression the doctor had of their circumstance. Together, one way or the other. And though he had begun to accept feeling that way, it still surprised him that others thought it. But Arch had suspected it yesterday morning. Pearl had presumed they were together. Even the clerk at the hotel had assumed it, but he'd been too concerned for Angelene and Mama Gran to appreciate it then, even to barely more than recognize it. He understood now that he'd accepted that he'd been involved with Angelene since he saw her step out of her car into his dream. But she was only using him now as an accomplice to forestall what she knew was coming from the doctor.

But as he'd known all along, he couldn't let her do it. Mama Gran would be disappointed in him and embarrassed and so would Angelene when she thought it over. And anyone else could see after thinking it over that there wasn't a chance that a woman like her would be drawn into an affair with a crippled, half-blind, battle-fatigued man like him, much less marriage.

"She was kind enough to offer me a ride since we're heading in the same direction."

Angelene covered up something with a pleasant face, but he wasn't sure what. He knew she wasn't thinking that he would not want anyone to believe he would claim a relationship with her. Too much water under the bridge for that. Maybe it was her surprise that his upbringing as a gentleman held sway enough to not claim their situation to be what the doctor thought, as no doubt many men she'd met would have. But she already knew better than that. Did she also know that he would like to claim it? He couldn't be sure what he felt now. Probably what she felt was aggravation that she'd now have to fend off some kind of invitation, if only for dinner, from the doctor. Mama Gran silently pulled her hankie out and wiped at her eyes. Walter busily wiped dust from the windshield with a rag he pulled from under the seat.

"I know the perfect place, then, for everyone," Dr. Brighton said. "And the food is whatever the doctor orders."

"Thank you," Angelene said.

Her attitude was perfect gratitude to anyone who didn't know her as Shep was learning to.

"My shift is over. Wait here until I go in and write this up?"

"Thank you so much for this medical service," she said, reaching in the car for her purse. "Walter will go in with you and settle it." She was already pulling her pocketbook out.

"Wouldn't think of it. It'll take me a few minutes inside, though. I have to make a phone call."

TWENTY

T hey followed the doctor in his car, a black Ford several years old, down the crowded Broadway back toward the river, with a sharp turn east in front of the railroad tracks, onto Lebanon Pike, which was also identified as U. S. Hwy.70, then out into the dark country. Wherever this hotel was, it wasn't in downtown Nashville. Soon a small town with a sign naming it Donelson appeared and then a sign saying The Hermitage ahead.

"There was a Hermitage Hotel. They wouldn't have let us stay there, I suppose. Could this be one out here for our race?" Angelene said with a touch of aggravation.

"I suspect this Hermitage is the home of President Andrew Jackson," Shep said. What the hell did he think he was, a tour guide?

"Well, aren't dead presidents just everywhere down here," Angelene said. "He's the one who marched the Indians out west."

And this must be the Cherokee Indian trail of tears we're on, Shep thought, remembering that it in historical irony passed along their displacer's home. He was not surprised that Angelene had acquired historical knowledge, probably just the tip of her knowledge iceberg. But as with Mama Gran, he was curious. Was it given to her or had she earned it by the hardest?

"If you're not white skinned ..."

Mama Gran said, "Angelene. Shep's been fighting in a place where it's not color that matters. The human race will always find something to divide it."

"I hate to admit I think that'll always be the case," Shep said.

"Oh, water under the bridge," Angelene said too lightly.

"She learned the states and capitals, too," Mama Gran said, allowing a little pride to come through.

"And the multiplication table, and the continents, and left hand from right ..." said Angelene.

"His arm signaling a left turn," Walter said.

"You left me behind with the capitals," Shep said when Angelene did not respond.

"Think we ought to be followin' him down this dark dirt road?" Walter asked. "Looks like a river over on the right."

"He might be leading us to a den of thieves, you think?" said Angelene, apparently not giving any validity to her suggestion.

"Oh, it don't seem likely," Walter answered her. "But he did make a telephone call."

"I suppose reservations are required for rooms, maybe to eat," Angelene answered.

Shep wondered if her establishment was one that required them, as he didn't notice any sarcasm in her statement.

After about a mile, Walter said, "Could be there's a colored folk's town out here. Who knows?"

"It's neither," Mama Gran says. "He's took on Angelene, is all, and he's a kind man. He knows where to take her so she'll be comfortable."

Well, if Mama Gran saw it, Shep wasn't imagining what he felt. He even suspected improbably that the doctor might be taking them home. The doctor must know there wasn't a hotel that would take all of them.

"For all he knows we're a pack of thieves," Angelene said, not denying Mama Gran's take on the doctor's reaction.

"I 'spect he's taking us to his home," said Mama Gran.

After a laugh that bordered on a sarcastic snort, Angelene said, "I believe we are an uncommon entourage for these parts. And he's taking us home?"

"Pearl invited us."

"But she was a white woman. One of us is white."

Shep wondered at her logic, but said nothing. Then she said, "I just can't see a black man inviting a white man into his home."

Rationale based on where she was from, or from her husband's example? If he existed.

"Used to not be unusual for Negroes," Mama Gran said. "Taking your kind of people into your home. Not many places to choose from."

Angelene laughed. "I guess if you're good enough for us, Shep Haddon, you're good enough for him."

"Riding again on your coattails," he said. He tried to imagine offering hospice to someone, some unknown travelers, at the home he shared with Dorthea. And before tonight he never could have imagined being unwelcome at a hotel.

TWENTY-ONE

The doctor turned left onto a narrow rutted road, hard packed dirt that obviously had never seen a gravel truck on it. Bushes and trees lined each side. After about a quarter-mile, a small boulder with words carved in it, "Stone" being the only one he was able to make out, marked a sharp right turn and there was an open field, which became a small lawn when the headlights encompassed it, with a huge hemlock tree on each side of a gravel walk. To the left of the house, which was of stones the size of cooking pots, grew a holly tree, maybe a hundred fifty years old according to its size, probably the same age as the house. A rough log storage building on the right testified to the antiquity of the homestead. For an instant a barn, dilapidated but probably only a hundred years old, was spotlighted when they turned to park in the side yard. All across the front of the house was a screen porch, which lit with pale light from one hanging bulb just then. A black woman in a rose print dress with a white ruffled apron tied around her waist, large for her sex like Walter was for his, her hair a larger version of Lionel's, glided through the screen door.

"You all, hello," she said. "Come in. Come on in before the light draws the mosquitoes. We're close to the river. Come on in, ladies."

Walter carried Mama Gran in and set her in an upholstered chair next to a long couch the woman pointed out in the large front room. The room, plastered walls halfway up and wallpaper with a Chinese scene on top, was as large as Honest Abe's entire home, with one wall a floor to ceiling stone fireplace with bookshelves on both sides. A braided rag rug covered most of the floor's wide pine boards. Comfortable looking chairs with skirted slipcovers were scattered around. Several tables held lace doilies and oil lamps, though the room was lit, not brightly, with an electric ceiling light.

Lionel began introductions. "Mama," he said, "this is Miss Johnston, here, who I told you about. She needs a day or two of looking after and some of your home cooking. This is her great-granddaughter, Angelene Midnight."

"Miss or Mrs.?" his mother asked him. She raised her thick black brows indicating he'd not been informative enough in his introduction, then large ivory teeth broke through in a smile.

"Mrs.," said Angelene.

"This is my mother, Mrs. Rosa Brighton."

Mrs. Brighton was assimilating. "Angelene Midnight. That's a name you wouldn't hear often."

"I've been told that before. Recently. In Kentucky. No one in Washington seems to notice," she said, and laughed. "But I didn't get a choice for either."

"I gave her the first, her husband the last," Mama Gran said.

"Well, I like them both," said Mrs. Brighton. "But, you call me Rose, and I'll call you Angelene if you don't mind?"

"Please do."

"So you are married?" Lionel said. "I thought maybe ..."

"I married Mr. Midnight fifteen years ago," she said. She looked up to the bare light bulb hanging by a long cord from the tall beamed ceiling, a chain hanging to pull, and studied a mosquito that slipped in with them buzzing around it, and dying when Mrs. Brighton noticed and grabbed a flyswatter, not breaking her conversation, commenting, "You would have been very young, then."

Now this was getting interesting. Here were some people who didn't mind asking what they wanted to know. And now he knew she was married.

"Angelene was thirteen when Mr. Midnight wanted to wed her," said Mama Gran. "I tried to make a deal that if he would wait two – "

Angelene stopped her. "Oh, don't go into all that, Mama Gran. It's boring."

Now why would she have to make a deal? He hoped Mrs. Brighton would continue satisfying her curiosity. Did the man have some kind of power over them? Had she married him against her will? Or perhaps Angelene had been mature for her age and thought she wanted to marry, and Mama Gran wisely thought that was too young an age and made them wait. Somehow Shep didn't lean to that conclusion, and, he realized just then, he didn't think they had created a happy marriage. But that could simply be what he wanted to think, because his own marriage experience caused him trouble crediting others as satisfying.

"I disagree," the doctor's mother said, not taking too long thinking it over, adding in a frank but not unkind tone, "I bet there's not a single boring thing about you. But if you'd rather not talk about it, you're my guest." She smiled kindly at both of them. "Lionel says I get lonesome out here all by myself, nobody but the baby to talk to. Anyway, I got to talking before I got introduced to the rest of this not boring party of folks. I am a widow," she said, holding out her hand to Walter, who clasped it in both his rather than giving her a handshake.

The man knew how to meet people as individuals. Another sure thing, noticed by all, including the two of them from the length of time their hands stayed clasped, was the immediate meeting of like minds as well as like bodies.

"And this not boring man?" she said to Shep, after finally turning from Walter.

"Hello, Mrs. Brighton. I'm Shepherd Haddon. It's nice to meet you."

She crinkled her brows but instantly removed her look of surprise or whatever it was. "And you're afflicted with my son's evasiveness. I've never been this close to an army man. What is your rank, Mr. Shepherd Haddon? I don't know what the symbols on your shoulder are, but I bet you're an officer."

"I'm sorry, ma'am. I'm a lieutenant."

"It's all right, I expect you didn't want to be playing yourself up."

Smiling, Shep said, "Lieutenant's not high enough to be humble about."

"Well, from the looks of you, you fought the whole German army."

While Shep was shaking his head in denial, and saying "Not quite!", her son said, "Now how do you know it was the Germans?"

"The little brown men couldn't have done all this," she said. "Not little bullies. Took big bullies to do that."

"You'll embarrass him no end," Angelene said, enjoying his being at a loss as to what to say. Then everyone joined in the laughter.

Shep recognized in Mrs. Brighton a lot of intelligence and self-confidence, enough to give the impression that she was only a jolly housekeeper for her son. She had some gray in her hair, he noticed, as she stepped under the light, and some wrinkles around her near-black eyes and large-lipped mouth, the picture of character; but all in all her features made a pretty face. Some of her looks – and it seemed as well, her character and self-confidence – had been passed down to her son.

"And now I'll satisfy my curiosity," Mama Gran said. "Did I understand you to say you have a baby?"

Shep had wondered if anybody other than himself had heard mention of a baby.

"Joyanne," Lionel said. "Not Mama's. She's my baby. She's five years old."

That aroused even Angelene's curiosity, but she only said "Oh," nodding as if she understood it all. Maybe because she didn't want an exchange of questions. Mama Gran didn't ask more.

"She's asleep now. Doesn't get to see much of her daddy," Mrs. Brighton said, "but it can't be helped."

"The hospital's short of doctors with some off to serve."

"What he won't say, they got them serving as orde'lies!"

"Medics," Lionel said.

"One administered my first treatment. He saved my life," said Shep.

~ 91 ~

"Then praise be to God," said Mrs. Brighton.

"And amen," said Mama Gran. "It was meant to be so he could save ours."

Mrs. Brighton and Lionel looked from Mama Gran to Shep.

"It wasn't like that. But if that's what she thinks happened, the favor was repaid," Shep said.

"I'll get it out of you," Mrs. Brighton said to Walter.

"I'll be real happy to tell you all about it."

"It can all wait," she said. "Lionel, you show the gentlemen around. Their facilities and where they'll stay, and I'll show the ladies where to refresh themselves before we sit down to supper. Let's hurry, it's nine o'clock."

TWENTY-TWO

Their home included a few other rooms. Close to a river, it could have been a way station, an inn for raftsmen or other travelers.

A bathroom was built onto the back of the house, a large room with a wood-burning stove, a white clawfoot tub, an extremely small tiled shower with a curtain to pull and a toilet. "We men will use the outside facility for all but a shower and shave if you don't mind," he said, "in favor of the ladies." He pointed out the path to the outhouse. "I lime it every so often. Stock of sanitary paper. Lantern at the back door." He looked from the dark back to Shep. "Are you able to climb stairs?"

"I'll manage."

"I'll tote our bags up later," Walter said.

Lionel showed them to a hall just outside the kitchen where they'd go up to the room he and Walter would be sharing, just an attic room with two double beds with feather mattresses, he said. "My sister comes for Christmas and her kids sleep up there. It's the only time the beds are used."

As they entered the kitchen, Mrs. Brighton said, "It'll be hot up there this time of year. Those mattresses will make it hotter. Sorry about that. Put both windows up. Get a cross breeze."

"It'll be the Ritz to some places I've put my head," said Walter.

"Same here," Shep said.

Mrs. Brighton said to Shep, "I wouldn't have thought that."

Well, have I been putting on airs? as Thula had said about Dorthea when he brought her home after school one day to help her with physics. "That gal ain't got any sense if she don't understand some of the things you been explaining," she told him that night at supper. "No common sense, either. Had to sit in the dining room. Use more heat and lights. Wouldn't come sit at the kitchen table to spread the books out like you do. Just puttin' on airs, if you ask me." For once, his mother had a different opinion from Thula. "I think it showed her character. She was brought up a certain way and she is serving notice that she intends to live that way." Thula had nodded in agreement then, and they both gave Shep a long look that he'd tried to ignore.

"You're a gentleman brought up by old south ways," Mrs. Brighton said, "no denying it. You shouldn't want to."

"I, uh, well..."

"Brought my son up with as many of them as I could."

"He was talking about where he's seen action, I imagine," Lionel said, proving his mother had done her job well.

"Now he's in a dilemma," Angelene said, having come into the room, Mama Gran leaning on her arm. "He will either have to admit to being a war hero or that he was brought up as a gentleman."

"And neither of them would want to bring attention to themselves," Mama Gran said to Angelene.

"I'm happy to be ranked in the same class as Lionel," Shep said, thankful he'd listened to some of his mother and Thula's practical instructions, and meaning every word he said about Lionel.

Mrs. Brighton beamed. Lionel looked embarrassed.

"The ladies will have what should be Joyanne's room," Loinel finally said to the silence. "But it won't be a problem. She sleeps with Mama."

"Been asleep an hour," Rosa said.

Then Angelene spoke to the new silence. "This is a pleasant kitchen," and Shep found himself looking around to see what she found to her liking, for her voice told her words to be true even if they were spoken at an opportune time in politeness.

The kitchen was as large as the main room, equipped with a woodstove as well as a kerosene cookstove, and an icebox of the type cooled by fifty pound ice blocks delivered by the iceman, as theirs had been when he was a boy, just as Pearl Jurvis's was. A glass-fronted cabinet held blue and white dishes, and open shelves were loaded with large and small bowls and trinkets. A round oak table not crowded with them all around it was on a braided rag rug similar to the one in the living room. Pearl had seated them in her dining room, saying her kitchen wasn't big enough, but he had gotten the feeling she wanted to treat them as honored guests. Here they were family. This is probably where they would be if there had been a dining room.

Water was furnished at Rosa's tin sink by a hand pump which he figured connected to a cistern that collected rainwater. This would be a rocky place to dig a well deep enough for all their water needs. But maybe this close to the river they'd tapped a pocket. From the beams of the high-ceilinged room hung enamel pots of many hues, black skillets of many sizes, flowers and onions drying. Painted plates leaned on wedges nailed to the walls, even a little girl's dress was over a hanger on a nail to dry. Two dishpans, one for washing and one for rinsing, hung on wall pegs. Towels draped from hooks. A black speckled coffeepot on the stove looked like it lived there. The flowered wallpaper on the three smooth walls indicated that the kitchen was added on, the inside wall being the outside wall of the living room. The walls looked old and somewhat smoked, but didn't give the kitchen a dirty look, just much-and-long-used.

He couldn't agree more to its inviting atmosphere. Dorthea's kitchen was equipped with white enamel and stainless steel. If she found a pot left to drain rather than dried and put away, she reminded the cook next day. He'd never felt comfortable even scrambling an egg for himself there.

"Oh, I need to paint it," Mrs. Brighton said, but her tone said it wasn't a priority.

"A large rock was carved with a name as we turned into your road," Angelene said. "Did it name this house?"

"Stone of Help," Mrs. Brighton said. "Some rafters from long ago, maybe a hundred years, were able to get their ropes around it and save themselves when the river was flooding. This house was sort of an inn. The original part."

"That's a nice history for this hospitable house," said Mama Gran.

Her history of the house put Shep to thinking of the stone moved by Samuel to the battlefield to commemorate the Lord's help with the Israelites against the Philistines.

"I wonder if they had in mind Samuel's helping stone," Mama Gran said.

"The one he named Ebenezer. I've often thought that must be it," said Rosa. "Surely the Lord intervened in both battles." Then she gave a big smile to Walter. "Have some more rice and gravy, Mr. Smith."

She'd also boiled diced potatoes, opened a jar of green peas - the glass jar and lid were on the large drain shelf next to the sink, testifying to her having hurriedly added to her already prepared supper. A bowl of sliced onions and cucumber with a sweetened and peppered vinegar dressing over them made his mouth water and pucker at the same time just thinking of it. She lifted fried green tomatoes that looked to be coated with cornmeal instead of flour like they did at home, from a black iron skillet. A small pail with the vegetable peels sat under the sink.

"It was a fine meal," Mama Gran said, shaking her head no to the offer of more, although she had taken only a spoonful of everything.

"I thank you," Mrs. Brighton said, dishing up peach cobbler from a deep pan. Shep wondered at it being so large; she obviously had not been expecting company when she had prepared it.

"This cobbler could be served at a fine restaurant," Angelene said, savoring her first bite.

"Yes, I've been told that," Rosa said without feigning humility. "I take it to all the church dinners. I like to cook. Grew up cooking for five brothers. I still have a hard time with small portions. We have to eat leftovers many times!"

"None for tomorrow," Walter said, as she put the last of the peas and rice and gravy on his plate.

"No, you go on to your room so both of you can get some rest," Mrs. Brighton said after Angelene's offer of help. "Mr. Smith won't mind helping me, I expect."

"I'll bring in the luggage and then we'll get to work," Walter said, as if he meant they'd be dancing the night away.

Shep started to the sink with his plate.

"Three'd just be a crowd," Mrs. Brighton said in a voice filled with anticipation as she took his plate from him and shooed him out.

TWENTY-THREE

Shep sat on the edge of his bed. With effort not to help with his hand he lifted his aching leg and felt himself sink into the feather mattress. Being in the car so long had not been good for his body or his leg. He'd had to turn sideways and drag his braced leg as he hopped up. Damn leg wouldn't bend enough in the brace and the stairwell wasn't wide enough to swing it out. He wouldn't wear it tomorrow when he took a long walk. He'd carry it just in case, and work on getting the leg flexible instead of possibly letting it get stiffer. He wasn't supposed to do that for about another week. Let the bones and muscles mend from the last surgery. He was supposed to stop at the army hospital in Memphis for a few days of rehabilitation, but until today it was feeling strong. And he felt the muscles deteriorating as the bones mended.

The previous walking days had been good for it and he was glad for the pain when he considered what the alternative had almost been. But walking home was out now. He was not going to leave here without Angelene and her dear ones. So he was going to make the time count while here. Why wait until morning? He went to the stairs and took his brace off. There was no rail, so he put his hands against the walls. He forced his leg to bend enough as he swung it out in an arc to the step below. Then he went to the next step. Then the next. He broke out with sweat. He told himself it was the heat in the stairwell as he backed his way up.

He thought over what the discussion was at the table about the war. A big invasion a couple of weeks earlier, Lionel had said, American and British troops storming a beach on the French coast, with thousands of casualties. "Those poor boys' mothers," Rosa had said. That put things in perspective for him for at least a few minutes. Here he was, and in spite of the fleeting wish for oblivion that hellish day, glad, more than glad, to be here.

Seemed like years since he'd peacefully slept several nights in a row. He wouldn't mind a cigarette, although smoking had been against his sports upbringing during school and college so he'd never taken a real liking to it. It might take his mind off things, but one ash on this feather bed would start a bonfire. So he made an effort of emptying his mind and going to sleep. But wasn't emptiness always liable for filling up with something? So instead of his mind accepting that he needed sleep, he reflected on what he'd discovered about himself lately.

He tried to figure what his philosophy of life, if he had one, would be after the life and death battles in Italy and after the actions and choices he had made during this trip. He found that there wasn't much to think about in either case. His philosophy for his future life would be, for some time to come, what his commanding officer told him it was and he thought it a fine gift. He tried not to think about his feelings and actions concerning Angelene. But like all the others he'd seen come into her universe, he was intrigued. At first. Now it was more than that. And tomorrow there would be more, and the next day more.

But he had discovered about himself in Italy and on this trek that what and who he was, and who he would be was so intertwined with Dorthea, that they were like wild grapevines that tangle and cannot be traced back to the root of each. And tonight Dorthea was like his injured leg. She was demanding her due in his concerns.

Without wanting to, he thought about why they'd married. A match made in cotton country heaven on the surface. Two old delta families. He the man with the need and the know-how, she the girl with the looks and the land. She told him in third grade they'd be married. Maybe she admired him for not beating her up when she stole his pencil. It very well could have been instead that she'd seen him as someone she could manage.

She'd never given him any peace since grade school. She'd taunted him on any weakness or failure he'd shown in those years. She'd chastised him for crying when they were about ten, when he almost cut his toe off with the hoe while chopping weeds out of the cotton in the back field. He had left a trail of blood all the way home. His mother had rushed him to the doctor, cutting short the visit to her of Dorthea and her mother, who was dead only a week later. Now that was something to cry about, Dorthea told him, your mother dying, and he told her she was right. Accept it. She had even influenced his right or need to cry over pain or what was thrown him from the universe or God. But maybe there simply hadn't been an occasion that could have wrung tears out of him. After all, boys don't cry, she said. Anyway, what's magic about tears? But he broke her rule. It was Thula's death when he was sixteen. Sitting on the hard bench all night in her little church where she lay waiting for the service the next morning, he cried for himself and the woman he first remembered wiping those tears. He was the son she never had, she was the invested mother he never had. He had wanted to weep on the occasion acceptable to Dorthea when his mother died a few years after his marriage; but his sorrow was more for what she hadn't been able to change, or withstand, in her life. He felt she wouldn't have chosen not to die, and nothing in his power could have changed that. He hadn't felt the need to shed tears when his daddy had died. His daddy hadn't chosen to live, either.

Yes, he'd finally let himself cry when he came out of the medicated haze and it hit home about his men, enough his tears should have washed the infection out of his injured eye. And when he'd written the letters to his men's families he'd been unable to keep the tears from flowing, wiping his face on his pajama sleeve and requiring a new gauze pad over his injured eye. And afterward, he'd somehow felt a little easier about living through it himself, and accepted easier all that he did to stay alive, and was easier with the knowledge that by then he was glad he hadn't died, that he was glad to be alive and that he didn't feel too guilty about it anymore. And it hadn't been only because he knew Dorthea would want him to live, even if it was to prove her point. That even war couldn't kill him if she wasn't ready.

And after he knew he was going to survive, he set about seeing if he could return to the man he had been. The person Dorthea wanted, not just wanted but expected him to be. Maybe tears were magical. Maybe it was just that he wouldn't fail while he still had to prove something to her. Or maybe a man knows when he must shed a tear or risk killing the care for whatever is held holy within himself.

Maybe he should be a man right now and stop thinking of these times that some people might say he hadn't been manly enough through. He honestly didn't know whether Dorthea would be one of them. What he knew about her would take a long time to recall. But he thought what he didn't know about her would take even more time to find out.

Upon any success, as when he'd won the grade school spelling bee after being forced to enter it by his mother, and having the entire dictionary called out to him by Thula, Dorthea reminded him that that was only what was expected of him. In high school she'd been just as demanding. She reminded him her daddy expected him to marry her and that neither her daddy nor she was settling for anything but the best. Well, that had lifted and frightened him. She undoubtedly would be glad her daddy was dead if he showed up at her door the half man he was now. But those years ago her expectations had led him to excel, to show her that he could do better than even she thought he could. Sometimes he'd disliked her for all his hard work she'd been responsible for, but he was just as often flattered that it mattered to her.

Perhaps he would have done his best anyway. His mother expected him to, and he hadn't wanted to do anything to add to her disappointments. But he'd found himself wanting to beat whatever it was Dorthea expected from him. God knew she was responsible for his Valedictory, his school records in basketball and football, the scholarship because of it. There would have been no college without it, because there was no land and no income by then.

It was common knowledge his daddy was a gambler. But how could he have let himself lose everything? Bet it all away, twenty acres here, forty there, without being able to make himself stop. And then true to his only calling – gambling – he'd lost his bet with himself and pulled the trigger. The cards on the table underneath his chest showed the hand. At least he was honorable and paid his debts. His mother had gone to his sister's in Mobile, never to return to Shepperton, not even for his graduation or wedding. Coach George had taken Shep in to finish his senior year.

The man his daddy lost some of his land to was Dorthea's grandfather, Grayson Ellis. Ellis had bought up whatever anyone had to sell. When he produced the signed deed for the rest of it upon Shepherd Haddon, Sr.'s "unfortunate death," he claimed it was for unpaid loans. That was possible. Ellis might have loaned him money to pay gambling debts, and not actually have been the one to win the land on a poker hand or on a horse race or a football score or a political election. It was just as effective and even more: it was legal.

Dorthea went to Mississippi State College for Women. He went to State. In spite of all her constant reminders throughout their growing up, he thought that would be the end of them. He thought he hoped it would be. He certainly didn't think he'd end up marrying into that family no matter what their expectations, if the expectations actually were as Dorthea presented them. They had his land. How could he marry her?

But after football games and for fraternity and sorority parties, they were usually together. Blowing convention to the wind, she'd drive to pick him up in her sporty car. She dated other men, and he dated a few other girls, but it was as if she gave him permission. They should date others for the experience before they married, she said, when she told him about her dates.

Looking back, he realized none of the other girls appealed to him. Perhaps he'd have been more willing to take a role in his future life if he'd actually been convinced at that time he could have one without her. But Dorthea was consistently the most interesting, the most beautiful, the most complicated while trying to appear the least. He'd not felt disappointment when she told him she had set the wedding date, two weeks after college graduation. Their tenth anniversary had passed while he was with Patsy in West Virginia a couple of weeks ago. He hadn't mentioned it, of course. Hell. Maybe he'd had Dorthea on his mind the whole time there.

He'd gone into their marriage not innocent but as pure as a child. Dorthea didn't. He'd expected she wouldn't. Maybe that's why he did. Several times after parties, she'd suggested they spend the night together, but he told her no. He'd like to think his refusal was for all the right reasons. But he wasn't sure. Maybe it was just because that was one thing she couldn't make him do. It could've been fear. Maybe he wasn't sure he'd be better than she thought he'd be.

Her Grandaddy Ellis had made it clear that marrying her wouldn't get his thousand acres back for him, if that's what he was thinking. If the old man hadn't been in a wheelchair, he'd have told him to stand up and fight. He thought he'd earned a more respectable reputation than that, but he also resented the man thinking Dorthea would have to promise a man land to get him to marry her. All the land, their forty-five hundred acres and Shep's thousand they now owned, would be passed down to her and then their children, Ellis said.

So far that hadn't happened – having children. That he knew of. When he went to Mobile to visit his mother before the wedding, because she had responded in formal written form to Dorthea that she would be unable to attend, his sister had told him Dorthea was possessive and content with herself. She didn't think that Dorthea would want children she'd have to share with or make changes in her life for. His mother had told Sissy that she wouldn't hear anything against her future daughter-in-law, and that some women just weren't meant to be mothers. Nor grandmothers. Sissy had required surgery in her early twenties that prevented her ever having children.

Although he wanted children, he'd never insisted, assuming the time would come when Dorthea would want that also. And finally after nine years that time had come, during their last weekend together just before he'd shipped out. Perhaps she'd gotten to thinking what could happen to him. She'd be stunned to know how close he had come to it. But what puzzled him was that of course, if he didn't make it back, she'd certainly marry again, and would have other chances for a child. He'd not written her just how bad his injuries were. And he knew why. It wasn't that he was afraid he would overly worry her. He simply wasn't his best any more. But that old challenge to be more than she figured he could be ... it just wouldn't let him surrender. And he knew that's why he'd set out to walk half way home, hoping against hope it would delay his return until he was no longer what he was now.

It was sure enough hot in the feather mattress in Lionel's attic; his undershirt stuck to him. But through the windows a cool breeze crossed him from time to time. At least it wasn't hot like in the low delta cotton country, where you could spend a whole night waiting for a breeze, and when it struck you it was like it had already blown across fire.

He woke when Walter got in the other bed, but didn't move or look at his watch. A man was entitled to his privacy.

TWENTY-FOUR

They were all walking along the bank high above the Stones River. Although Lionel had said the night before that it was close, he was surprised that it was only maybe a half mile away. Lionel told them that about thirty miles further around the bend a high-casualty Civil War battle had raged. Shep remembered reading about it and the Battle of Franklin in this middle part of Tennessee from his college war history. Of course, the Mississippi battles of Corinth and Vicksburg had taken more volume in his classes. He would like to hear more about the area's history, but Lionel had a different battle on his mind.

When Shep had woken just before dawn this morning, Walter was already downstairs. Shep looked out the attic window and could see no sign of another house, only the huge barn, wood grayed and shrunken. A light in the barn went out and Lionel emerged carrying a milk pail. Shep was surprised because of the barn's condition – any cow stalled in there was in danger of becoming ground meat – but not that Lionel, a doctor and gentleman, had been milking a cow, such humble labor.

Shep rummaged through his duffle at his meager supply of clothes. He pulled out a set of rumpled fatigues and put them on and looked out as darkness faded into the beginnings of sunrise and surveyed the lay of the land. He picked up his brace and put the sling over his neck, but did not slide his arm through. He made his way down the stairs and out of the house, quiet except for the voices of Walter and the Brightons in the kitchen, so low he couldn't understand what they were saying. Like a thief in the night he closed the door behind himself and stopped at the toilet, then headed to the field between the house and the river. A good place to get started again on his rehab.

Less than a couple of hours later he smelled bacon cooking and followed the scent that the men in his platoon had by consensus, while they were reminiscing of home cooking as they ate rations, voted the best smell in the world. Leave women out of the contest, they said. Mrs. Brighton was at the stove and a little girl, five if he correctly remembered Lionel saying, sat at the table nibbling a biscuit. She was brown and shiny as his Sunday shoes back home. She looked up at him as he entered and was possibly on the verge of screaming in surprise, as her eyes widened and her mouth gaped.

"Well, good morning, Miss Joyanne," he said.

Her grandmother turned to watch but said nothing. The girl was as still as if a spell had been cast on her.

"May I introduce myself to you?" he said. She finally nodded, her mouth still open.

"Lieutenant Shepherd Haddon, at your service," he said, and resisted bowing, although he thought any little girl would like that, but held out his hand instead. She looked at the other arm, which he had relented and tucked into the sling a little while earlier, after having found a broken tree limb just the right size for repeated lifting, and had not known when to stop.

Joyanne had been taught to be polite, as she overcame her surprise – fear – and let him take her right hand in his left one. In a second she overcame that stricture of politeness and said as probably any child would, "What happened to you?"

"I'm a soldier. Do you know about them?"

She nodded. "They have guns. There's a war."

"I was in it until recently."

"Did you get shot?"

"No, not really," he said, sitting down and smiling a little. "Mainly, I got run over by a tank. That's sort of like a big truck."

"Couldn't you run fast enough?" she said.

He laughed and so did Mrs. Brighton as she brought him a cup of coffee.

"Why are you here?" Joyanne asked.

"I let her find out things for herself," said Mrs. Brighton. "There's other things she can't do by herself." Then she hugged Joyanne and kissed on her head, and toyed with the thick braid hanging to one side. "But she'll be doing everything before long. Won't you, Baby."

Had the little girl been sick, maybe scarlet fever with its long recuperation?

"Yes ma'am. I'll get a bicycle then," she told Shep.

Just then Angelene came in, surprising Shep. He figured her to be a late morning person when the opportunity presented itself. She was in a short-sleeved royal purple dress with cream colored beads and cream shell buttons and brown strappy high heels. Her hair, still shiny though curlier and somewhat frizzy, was pulled back with a brown satin band. He realized her wardrobe was tailored to the city and to the spring, not to summer in the south, but she didn't look out of place. She looked just right.

He looked at Joyanne to see her reaction. It was worship at first sight. On both parts.

"Well now. Who are you, you beautiful little girl?" Angelene said.

"I'm Joyanne." She looked toward Shep, then back to Angelene. "What are you doing here?"

"I'm getting your daddy to help my grandmother."

"Is she crippled like him?" she said, looking back at Shep.

He had relented and put the brace on, too, mostly for caution after his long walk, afraid of a setback if he wasn't reasonable.

"Honey ..." Mrs. Brighton said.

"It's all right," he said.

"And like me?" she said.

Merciful God.

"Like you?" Angelene said, and the look on her face said more, that she wished she could take it back, that she wanted to grab and hold the little girl and put whatever it took from herself into the child to make her whole.

That was just about what he was feeling, too. What, then, must Lionel and Mrs. Brighton feel every day? And where was the little girl's mother? Last night she had not been mentioned.

"My daddy'll help us all."

Angelene sat down and held Joyanne's hands. "I just know you're right. Do you know what else? I really like your name."

That sat well with Joyanne. "You knew who I was all the time."

"I also like your doll in your room."

Maybe Angelene was a schoolteacher after all. She knew how to be around children.

"What's your name?" Joyanne asked her.

"My name is Angelene."

"But you're not an angel, are you?"

"Wouldn't want to be," she said, shaking her head and smiling. "I'd have to work too hard at it."

"My mama's an angel," Joyanne said.

Angelene looked at Shep. Her eyes said is there no mercy?

"She went to heaven when we fell out of the ride."

Angelene knelt by Joyanne and said, "I'm so sorry."

"It was at the Negro Fair," said Mrs. Brighton. "A year and a half ago. A chain broke."

Angelene hugged Joyanne. "I have a present for you," she said, and pulled a jeweled pin from inside her pocket.

"A star!" said Joyanne. "Can I wear it now, Mammaw?"

"Yes, yes, yes, Baby. Let Miss Angelene put it on you. But you be careful not to lose it." She walked over for a closer look. "That's real, isn't it?"

"Oh, even the middle one's tiny. Not big as the twinkle in her eye." She pinned it on Joyanne's collar.

Walter came in carrying a load of wood and stacked it next to the stove. "Haven't done that since I was a boy about her age," he said, looking immensely satisfied.

"Why not?" Joyanne asked.

"They use that old coal and steam heat up in Washington. I've been there since my daddy run off from Missouri with all of us. Me, my sisters, my mama, her baby brother."

"Why'd he run away?" Joyanne said, concerned. "Wasn't he afraid you'd all get lost?"

"I expect there were scarier things he was leaving," Mrs. Brighton said.

"Was it white people? I'm scared of white people," Joyanne said.

"Why, she's probably never seen one before that she can remember," Mrs. Brighton said to the room at large.

"You're not scared of Mr. Haddon, are you, honey?" said Angelene.

"Is he a white man? I just thought he was hurt like me," Joyanne said.

"The mouths of babes," said Mrs. Brighton, squeezing Joyanne.

"There's good white men," Walter said. "This one here's good even if he was purple."

"Like Angelene's dress?" Joyanne said, giggling.

"Call her Miss Angelene, Baby," said Mrs. Brighton.

Lionel came in dressed in dark blue pants with a crease so precise it was a wonder his knees would bend, and a white shirt that must have been double dipped in the starch bucket and was ironed to a satin finish, and a red and yellow striped bowtie. As he hung his coat over a chairback he said, "Are you having a party? And I wasn't invited?" to his daughter, hugging her.

"You brought me a party, Daddy."

Angelene helped Mrs. Brighton get coffee for everybody and got the dishes from the drainpan to set the table.

"I've already eaten," Lionel said. "I'm going to the hospital early. Today's my half-day off and I'm going to take it." He twisted Joyanne's pigtail and smiled. She grabbed him around the waist. "We'll go on a picnic this afternoon. That ok, Mama?"

"Down by the river," she said. "Have to come back and get inside the screens before the mosquitoes get too bad. So don't be late."

"You gonna fry some chicken?"

"If Mr. Smith will help me wring some necks."

Angelene laughed. "He didn't even finish drying the dishes last night, I noticed."

"He was busy," Mrs. Brighton said.

Later, after Angelene took a plate to Mama Gran, Mrs. Brighton sent Shep and Angelene to the garden to dig radishes and potatoes and onions for potato salad. "You know how to do such as that?" she asked Shep.

"I'm a farm boy," he said. "But this city girl will shoot a rat snake if she sees one."

"Well, shouldn't I shoot a rat snake? Aren't they bad like rats?"

Mrs. Brighton and Shep laughed.

"I don't imagine they're called that because they eat rats?" she said, figuring it out, but laughed, too.

"Can I go with them?" Joyanne asked.

"No, baby. You save your energy for this afternoon. You can sit with Miss Johnston and me out on the porch while I snap the beans."

Angelene appraised Shep in his work-out gear. "I'll go get into some slacks and flat shoes," she said. "Don't tell about that other snake while I'm gone."

"Of course not. That's the kind of thing a person should tell on herself."

"You had a run-in?" Mrs. Brighton said, concerned.

"You should worry about the snake," Shep said.

"Oh, I'll tell about it at the picnic," Angelene said. "In case any are lurking about. They'll be warned."

Now was not the time to tell her that snakes had no ears.

"Miss Angelene's so pretty," Joyanne whispered, looking toward the door she just went through. "Are you married to her?"

"No, Miss Joyanne, I'm not that lucky." He was getting used to the fact that everyone either thought they were married or up to no good with each other. And liking it.

"Maybe she'd marry my daddy."

TWENTY-FIVE

It was satisfying to be in a garden again. He'd grown up helping with the garden. Even plowed the rows behind a horse after he got big enough. He never had to go in the garden after he married. The women – not Dorthea, of course, but other women – did the gardening. The plowing was done by a field hand on the John Deere.

Awkwardly bracing his bum leg on the long-handled three-pronged fork and pushing with his good arm, he attacked a little hill of dirt to snare the potatoes.

She said, "Let me do it." He handed her the fork. She poked through the first potato she dug up. "Are there plenty more where this came from?" she said. "Should be several on each vine," he said, pulling up as she dug.

"We work pretty well together," he said, as he dropped the potatoes in the bucket.

"I thought we have all along," she said.

That was a surprise. Maybe she had considered him a friend all along, even without Mama Gran's prodding.

"This is a nice place to live," Shep said.

"Yes, a good way of life. But where are the restaurants?" She laughed.

"Lionel is crazy about you," he said.

"Not to change the subject at all?" she said, glancing toward the house, where Walter and Mrs. Brighton were sitting on the back porch resting after they had returned from the corn field empty-handed. "Where's the corn?" she asked.

"Still too early here, I expect. Probably not filled out enough."

Mama Gran was still in bed. Walter and Rosa weren't attuned to the garden; their talk was interrupted with laughter and occasional remarks to Joyanne, playing dolls at their feet.

Their rapport was joyous and as natural as it had been instantaneous last night. Shep wondered how they would take it when parting time came, as it inevitably would. He didn't doubt that for an instant. Angelene and hers were fixed on some destination, for some specific reason, just as he was, but it wasn't to meet her husband for a vacation in New Orleans – he would resign from his new assignment if he had concluded wrong about that.

Angelene didn't deny what Shep said about Lionel, just tentatively stuck the fork in another hill.

"He probably hopes you've left your husband, that you'll stay and marry him."

"I have left my husband." She bent and pulled up a nicely eyed potato and brushed a clump of dirt off it.

Shep reacted like a man trained to anticipate surprises, he thought.

"I thought he wouldn't discover it until he got back. Which should have been a couple more days. Enough potatoes?" She pulled a nice red radish that was peeking up from the dirt in the next row and cleanly sliced off the top with the knife Mrs. Brighton had put in the bucket. "What do we do with the tops?"

He hung the green tops over the bucket. "I figure they have a compost heap." He hadn't seen a hog pen, so no hog to eat them. "So ... No looking back?"

"Uh uh." She moved her head from side to side almost unnoticeably.

He pulled up a couple of large onions and raked dirt off. He had been trained in the past month to second-guess, especially civilians in another country, war countries, it could be life or death; but he had for the most part accepted her story for what she wanted him to. But wasn't this a foreign country to her? Shouldn't he have been alert from the first that it might just not be as unusually simple as it appeared? A lot of this was making sense to him now. Tell me the rest of it, don't make me ask, he telegraphed as he watched her select a green bunch of sprigs to pull up.

"Do you like radishes?"

He nodded. She pulled up several more and said "This is probably enough."

She'd felt the need to leave her husband without even telling him. Afraid to tell her husband. Shep felt just as he had when he first met them. She was in danger. "He won't like that you've left."

"No. He won't."

No doubt they'd been taking back roads all along, to make their trail hard to follow. He knew that her husband would follow. And no doubt she'd made reservations at a hotel for whites, hoping they'd have to honor it or that money would talk, as she'd said earlier. That could be why she insisted on last night's tableau at the hotel. Her husband wouldn't have even thought to look for her there.

"Lionel's hospitality ... it was a godsend. Though we can't tarry here any longer than it takes for Mama Gran to be able to travel. When we leave, you should go your separate way – "

He stopped her with a look.

"Of course you won't ..." She dropped down on her knees and sat back on her heels. "No," she repeated, "he won't like it."

By the hardest he managed to get down, settling a little away from her in the sun-warm dry, soft earth between the rows, and stretched his injured leg as far as it would, and then rubbed it and tried to bend it. "Tell me about it?" he said, understanding and accepting that she wanted to, but also realizing that she wanted the comfort of having him ask her. She couldn't have any doubt he wanted to know all, every last thing about her.

"So you removed your brace."

"It was time." Maybe his leg would be like his arm, come to life when he needed it. And that might be sooner than he had thought.

"After I tell you, you may feel differently about me."

"You know better than that."

"Where was your leg injured?"

"In Italy."

"Is that somewhere around the knee?" she said, continuing his silly joke.

He laughed. "All over," he said, cringing. "And it's starting to cramp."

"Would it help if I massaged it?" she said as he winced and put his hand at the calf and rubbed. She scooted over and moved his hand out of the way and rubbed the calf muscle. Her hand was gentle through the rough material as the fish that had swum around his young legs in the Gulf when he visited Sissy, compared to the pawing fingers of the male Army therapist that he had grown accustomed to. But it sent shock waves up his leg to his thigh and he willed it to stop there.

"He's the corner market owner. The Negro drinking hall owner. The Negro vote-deliverer, job-dispenser, loan-maker. The Negro undertaker. You understand what I'm saying about him?"

For a man who had just bragged on himself to himself, he had not seen that coming. "He's the one a Negro better not cross."

"And I did."

"But you're his wife. He won't hurt you." Stupid to say, because he knew different, but he was trying to make her feel better some way.

"He'll kill me." She off-handedly waved away a wasp. "He'll kill Walter. He'll kill Mama Gran."

He didn't refute what she was saying now, though he wanted to again, with assurance. But he knew the type of man she was saying her husband was. Like the head of the Italian mafia that Private Lucio had talked about, and that he knew plenty about now, after his informative classes. And after fifteen years of marriage, Angelene should know her husband. Like he knew Dorthea and she knew him.

But Dorthea didn't know him as well as she probably thought. She wouldn't guess that he had agreed to a new job before he left the hospital, going to classes with a dozen other men in various stages of recovery, reading manuals, listening to lecturers, memorizing German phrases, practicing making a bomb and diffusing one, and learning ways to find a man and secretly trail a man and kill a man on a city street. She'd suggested he ask exemption for his agricultural contribution to the war effort. He told her he knew that was a vital part, but when he reminded her that the draft pool in their county was small, and somebody would have to go in his place, she had simply nodded and turned away. He was surprised she took it so well; she would be inconvenienced no end. Maybe things he thought he already knew about Dorthea weren't sure things.

And obviously, Angelene's husband hadn't known her so well, if he thought threat of death would keep her. But Shep trusted Angelene to know what her husband was capable of.

She looked at a potato piled on the others in the bucket as if its eyes were returning her stare. "I never thought about it before. Where are the seeds?"

He laughed. "The eyes have it," he said. "You let a potato go to seed. Make lots of eyes and sprouts, cut the pieces off and plant them."

"I don't know any of these things."

"I don't know how to run a restaurant."

"If you're with us when he reaches us, he'll kill you. He'll try." She looked at his leg and his arm and then his eye. "He'll think it will be easy." Then she laughed like she had the first day he knew her. Sarcastically. "Yeah, he'll try."

Was she saying she had confidence in him, though broken, limping, seeing only half what he should see?

"You think he's already found out about you leaving?"

"Yes. Somebody noticed and called him. Otherwise, the car would not have been reported stolen. He pays a police officer for favors. So I'm advising you again to part company with us when we leave here."

He laughed. At himself. So much for self-macho.

"But I don't suppose you will."

Ah. Well. "Why did you leave him? Did you not love him any more?"

"You white gentleman," she said.

"No need to insult me."

She smiled as he did, and said, "You have no notion. Negro Washington's its own world. You see how ... uninformed ... I've been about many things."

And wasn't that what he'd been saying to himself all this time? But still he hadn't understood its ramifications.

"Its boss is boss of his world. He's not above bringing himself some business. That's my husband. The Undertaker. He gets what he wants."

"And he wanted you when you were thirteen ..." Mama Gran said she'd made a deal with him. Tried to make a deal. "He obviously didn't boss Mama Gran."

"She had something he wanted. He knew it would be better for him if he got me on her good graces. She couldn't figure out anything else to do. Besides, he was respected, if not respectable. He would have lost something ... some kind of standing if he had killed her. Since she didn't have a choice, she tried to make the best of it. But he would only wait a few months, until my birthday."

If he wanted her that much, he shouldn't want to hurt her. He wanted to say it to comfort her. But he realized now who she was and that she was telling him what he might could have been figuring out the last few days if he had only let himself. Her husband would hurt her, would try to kill her, if he found her. He would think he had to set an example, no exceptions, even his own wife.

"Everybody will know I left him. I didn't tell anyone, but he'll have to ask around when he gets home from Chicago. So he won't have a choice. He'll have to show he's still boss. Besides, he told me he'd do it if I ever left him."

"Did you try to leave him before?"

She shook her head no. "He never went out of town before. He had to know I would try someday. You keep somebody under glass, they'll try to break it."

"When did you start to hate him?"

"When did I not?"

He had to know all. Not just because he wanted to know. But he had to so he could start formulating some plan, some kind of maneuvers to avoid what must be coming.

"Why was he out of town?'

"To take some classes. On new undertaking procedures. That's one thing he does by the book. Guess he'll plan to use them on me."

"You children there," Rosa called out to them. "You don't have to dig every last potato!" She laughed, and so did Walter.

"We'd better get back to the house," Angelene said.

"You're right. But I've got to know everything so we can make plans."

"I don't know if anything will help."

"The US Army didn't teach us to give up without a fight."

"You knew that before you got in the Army."

He liked that she thought that.

She extended her hand and he took it, accepting her help to right himself. It was the first time they had touched, skin to skin. This was the first time they had been alone. Would they have touched earlier if they'd had a chance? Her unpainted nails were the lightest of brown with the palest of pink half moons at the base and tip. Her fingers were long and strong. Her arm muscles pressed against her sleeve as she gave him her strength. But her palm was soft against his fingers and he was aware that she was looking at their hands as he was. Her hand was covered with sprinkles of dirt, lighter than her skin. His hand was covered with the same sprinkles, darker than his skin. But their hands fit like gloves.

"There's no need to let the Brightons know. Is there? I don't want them to worry."

"We'll walk down to the river after everyone gets to sleep tonight. I'll wait for you by the car. OK?"

She looked at his leg and he said, "I haven't been walking enough lately. I've ended up with a ride, you know."

"I don't feel guilty," she said.

TWENTY-SIX

Rosa scrubbed the potatoes with a brush at the kitchen sink and put them in a large pot to boil, while she and Angelene sat at the kitchen table to slice the radishes and cut up a jar of homemade dill pickles. Mrs. Brighton dropped a dozen eggs in the pot with the potatoes and said that was enough for the potato salad, but she should go out and gather eggs soon.

"I'll get them," Walter said.

"Can I get them, Mammaw?" said Joyanne, putting down a book she was looking through, seated at a small table against the wall.

"No, you should rest ..." her grandmother said, hesitating, obviously not wanting to stymie the little girl with the injunction she'd used earlier, nor wanting to deny her anything. "You can't climb ... Oh, Honey, you can't reach the top nests," Mrs. Brighton finally said with reluctance.

"I'll help her," Shep said.

Angelene looked at him with the question, how are you going to do that? "Tell you what," she said, "We'll both go and help. Will that be all right, Mrs. Brighton?"

"Yes," she said, smiling at Joyanne. "She knows where the nests are. Her Daddy takes her when he can."

"Up there, way up there," Joyanne said, pointing to yet another nest up a ladder.

Angelene climbed up and backed down looking suspiciously at an egg in her hand. "This feels hard as a rock," she said, and Joyanne laughed and laughed and Shep chimed in.

"What? What's the matter? What is it?"

"That's a nest egg!" Joyanne said.

"I know about nest eggs. The money kind," said Angelene, twirling it around like she was a jeweler examining a large pearl.

Shep laughed. "Where do you think that idea came from? This encourages the chicken to lay more eggs. Increase their capital."

"You mean they don't just know to do it?" She said, climbing back up with it.

Joyanne laughed again. "She's stubborn, that chicken! It helps her."

Angelene replaced the ceramic egg, then came back down and handed Shep the basket of white and brown-shelled eggs. She stooped to swoop Joyanne up.

"I could walk all the way," Joyanne said, leaning on her padded crutches.

"Honey, do your daddy and grandmother know?" Angelene said.

"They're afraid I'll fall."

Angelene looked at Shep.

"Your daddy and grandmother know best," Angelene said, looking at Shep for confirmation.

He wondered. His doctors had cautioned him to wait, always wait, and he had until he could wait no longer and then he had put his foot on the floor and had been surprised that his leg didn't collapse. And his doctors had smiled and said we thought it might take   a few more days, but sometimes the body knows best. Just listen to it, be reasonable. Maybe Joyanne knew, her body knew that it was time. But maybe Lionel knew. Her grandmother might be over-protective, but Lionel, he would do what his professional knowledge said was best, and Shep didn't question that.

He put his hand on her shoulder. "How far do you sometimes walk?" Joyanne had gotten around, hobbling on her crutches, looking for the nests.

She was thinking it over. Then she started crying.

Angelene knelt and hugged her.

"I can't," Joyanne said. "I can't walk."

She didn't mean Lionel and Rosa wouldn't agree to it. "Are you a little bit afraid?" he said. "Afraid you'll fall?"

She nodded.

"I think you'll know when its time to try."

"Did you?"

"I finally realized I wanted to, enough to fall trying if I had to."

Angelene took her pocket square out and wiped Joyanne's face. "Did you ever hear what they say about a long walk?" She looked up at Shep, then back at Joyanne. "That it starts with one step?"

"One step," Joyanne said, and nodded.

"You'll know when to take it."

TWENTY-SEVEN

S hep wished the boys in his unit could be there to smell the chicken frying in the black deep-sided skillet. They would have agreed with him that it was even more mouth-watering than bacon. Rosa had soaked it in buttermilk, then dredged it in salt-and-pepper-seasoned flour and laid it in an inch of bacon grease and lard heated to a sizzle when flour was sprinkled in the pan. He could taste that frying chicken all the way out in the woods where he was picking his way through, his method of limbering as well as strengthening the leg.

Rosa wouldn't hear of Angelene or Shep helping in the chicken business, so they had sat on the back porch with Joyanne, watching the pleasure Walter took in the chicken killing, almost the before-history-of-time satisfaction of the man as hunter. Another thing he hadn't done since he was a boy, Walter said.

Shep saw the interest with which Angelene watched the rural food provision and preparation, heard her gasp and shiver when Walter had chopped their heads off on the stump left for that purpose. Joyanne had given her a hug, and said, "They didn't feel a thing." Angelene must have been accustomed to seeing the product about ready for cooking. He wondered about her restaurant. Was it one that would have welcomed him? Was it hers alone? She hadn't mentioned it in her husband's vast interests earlier.

She was helping Mrs. Brighton skin the boiled red potatoes and peel the hard-boiled eggs when he left for his walk after being shooed out of the kitchen.

He tried to concentrate on what pertinent things he should ask when he met with Angelene tonight, think of plans and alternate plans. And convince himself that it might be a matter of winging it. But he found that walking in the woods required concentration to work on his agility, and he let random thoughts intrude of being alone with Angelene this afternoon, and of the revelations. How could a woman live fifteen years with a man she hated? What had been the catalyst for her flight?

He ventured deeper into the trees and relieved himself and thought of Dorthea, of their last time in each other's company, when she joined him in New York for a week before he shipped out. On their first day together she had walked in on him urinating. It was a new plateau for them. Neither had ventured into that intimacy before. He had given no indication that he was aware of her presence, and she made no move or sound. She had stood there like a scientist observing a wild creature in its habitat. Seconds later, she'd turned and left without speaking, but it was as if some carnal nature had taken her over. She didn't wait for night, the usual time she had thought appropriate for their encounters, no matter which one started them, and had invited him into the bedroom minutes later, undressing as he lay fully clothed on the bed watching. Then she'd unzipped him, not waiting for his clothes to come off, yanked one pants leg down and pulled him through the placket of his army shorts, and opened herself to him with an emotion he'd never known her to. They had lain there afterward until they dropped to sleep, her head on his shoulder, her arm and leg across him. When he awoke with her hand on him, he found himself growing again, and she had actually sighed in her sleep. He moved to put his mouth on her breast and she pushed into him, moaning, and tightened her hand on him. He stretched to open the drawer in the bedside table to get the little envelope, even though she had not been concerned enough to wait for him to use it an hour earlier. But this time she said "No," into his ear and pulled him onto her.

He spied a small limb on the ground next to a hickory tree, not yet decaying, a little longer than he was tall, as he exited the woods. He picked it up and examined it. Good piece of straight hardwood, good walking-stick material. He didn't want a walking stick. He took out his pocket knife and gashed out the smaller limbs and whittled a smooth place about a foot from the top for his hand. No. He didn't want one. But he needed one in this rough terrain. Maybe it wouldn't be giving in to have a little thing to lean on for a time since he had discarded his brace.

But his memory of Dorthea's visit to him that time was now in full swing, and he gave in to it. When he had greeted her at Penn Station, she emerged from the subterranean steps like the Greek goddess Persephone's triumphant return from Hell, and entered the hall that was more like a palace than a mere place to embark from a train, hardly glancing at the ornate carvings and columns and steel spans and glass arched ceiling. She was even more beautiful than he remembered, if that was possible. Yes, beautiful enough for Hades to have coveted and stolen. The epitome of breeding in dress and action. Nothing flashy; he couldn't help notice a few men slyly following her with their eyes, as if they knew being obvious wouldn't be necessary and wouldn't be appreciated. Yes, she noticed. But as usual, as if she hadn't noticed, she'd walked and talked and laughed as if it were only for him.

At times that week, he had noticed something in her eyes, a worry or sadness, and he had been touched to think she was concerned about his leaving for dangerous fronts unknown. Not that he ever thought she didn't care what happened to him. It merely was that before, he was her husband and therefore, nothing should happen to him.

~ 116 ~

She had missed him, though she didn't say it. And he'd missed her, God knew. They made love every day – usually at her time and bidding as was their routine at home. Everything must be as she wanted it so she could be her best and enjoy herself. Attractive surroundings. Soft bed. The room comfortably cool if it was summer or toasty warm if it was winter. Her entering the room in a peignoir, but letting it come off easily. Don't muss the hair too much. She wasn't prudish; she wanted hands and lips all over her. And she always wanted the protection between them. Until New York, when she'd tossed the unopened package in the trash can after his attempt to reach it that first day.

For a few months he wondered if she had returned home pregnant. He had asked only once in his writing, when enough time had passed for her to know, and had gotten no answer. If she was she'd tell him when she wanted him to know. It would be no different from anything else in their history together.

They hadn't even made love on their wedding night. She said she wanted to rest after all the partying, didn't want to be tired their first time together. He took it as her expressing her control and he wasn't much surprised, as she'd always, with the one exception of being unable to get him to bed before their marriage, had things her way. And he had not expected their life together to be any different.

After their morning wedding and festivities – the side lawn covered with a dance floor and a pavilion built over it for the occasion, the house overflowing with a hundred guests the church couldn't accommodate for the ceremony – the hundred who had packed in tight to hear the "I do's", wondering if she really would – they drove to Memphis to the Peabody Hotel. They ate a late supper and sat in the lobby listening to the piano being played by someone she knew, a handsome, lanky man Shep remembered that she'd driven all over the south to hear play. Shep commented that they should have gotten him to play at their wedding and reception, but she didn't answer, just sipped her Champagne and a few minutes later said they should go up to their rooms. Connecting rooms, he'd found out when they'd gone up earlier with their luggage.

She had changed the reservation he had made a month earlier. He could go along with her in most things; he was easy-going, perhaps passive about some things, but a man doesn't reserve a two bedroom suite for a honeymoon. But he kissed her on the cheek when she said goodnight and watched as she went through the door to her room. He had wished he had a good book, then thought cards, solitaire would be better – it would give him something to do while he whiled away time and finalized in his heart and soul and psyche that yes, this was his life, and he had agreed to it long ago. He reminded himself that he had known all his life how she was; the wedding night rejection was of course her retribution for his having turned down her invitation to sleep together while they were in college, so he went to sleep and didn't give it another thought.

The next day they walked downtown Memphis; watched the Mississippi tumble by from Confederate Park overlooking the River, the western boundary of the city. As she examined a piece of jewelry or hat in a store window, he stood by her side, wondering how she would feel about him, no longer a challenge. She was and always would be a challenge, he thought, but nevertheless, he felt more secure around her knowing his future with her had actually started. After a late dinner in the hotel restaurant, they danced at the rooftop lounge, the Skyway, until midnight. But she apparently didn't tire. She started on him in the elevator after the only other passenger got off at the first floor going down.

In the few seconds it took getting down to the fourth floor, theirs, her roaming hands had stiffened him to discomfort. But she recovered her decorum before the doors opened. She could not take a chance that someone would see. By the time he had the door to the sitting room unlocked and they stumbled inside, her hand was inside his zipper and she was moaning through her tongued kiss. But by damn, something in him rebelled.

He decided that this time, this first time, she wasn't going to pull all the strings. He wanted to sleep with her. God only knew the self-control he'd exercised at her invitations. And he was going to be good, not like a first timer, but better than she expected, or die in the effort. But it was now going to be when he wanted it. When she let him draw breath, he said, "Long day. I'm so sleepy. That last drink must have done it. Mind waiting until tomorrow?"

She threw her handbag across the room, knocking over a vase of flowers on the table in front of the couch. Watching the water spread and soak into the rug as if it had never been there, as if it had never escaped its vessel, she said, "It's fine with me," and entered her room as if she had not just lost control for the first time.

He didn't think he had slept that peacefully since high school. In the morning he woke with her on top of him, her blonde hair tickling his face and her lips locked to one of his nipples. Her light green negligee, exactly the color of her eyes, was getting tangled around her as she squirmed and pulled off his pajama bottoms, the only thing he'd slept in, and when she turned around one breast was pouring over her plunging top; she'd bared it for him. He'd seen it before, he'd not been above that and touching and feeling and various explorings on their dates, but now that he knew he didn't have to hold back, he wanted to grab it and stare at it and cover it with his mouth at the same time. Her hand was making him stand up and he was in danger of coming out of this first time like a school boy. Which could be her intent. This was a test. And he intended to keep his word to himself.

He'd closed his eyes and thought of a day in high school when she had coolly reached across the aisle and taken his History test answer sheet, each multiple choice answer marked correctly, off his desk and replaced it with hers, half finished and mostly wrong, with only enough time to erase and change names. It was the only failure he'd had, and he found the memory of that day was enough to slow down his need for her in that morning bed, and allow him to proceed in a somewhat more mature manner.

There'd been no more rebellions or trickery or paybacks with their life in bed.

And from the start they made a good pair in the other aspects of their life as well. She had no suggestions and found no fault with his running the farm operation and finances, although he thought she could have done it herself even then, if she hadn't married. Or if she had married anyone else. He didn't forget he was hand-selected for a number of reasons. Sure, he was who she said she wanted. But he was experienced and degreed in cotton and everything agriculture. Anyway, she didn't want to be bothered with mundane chores and responsibilities.

While he did not what was expected of him, but what he expected of himself, she would sometimes drive down to the coast for some sun and a little illegal gambling, or over to Hot Springs for massages and mineral baths, or up to Memphis for more shopping. At home, she committeed and entertained and fund-raised and remodeled and continually saw that the house, built in 1870, the original having been burned during the Union trip down the Mississippi River, was kept in tip-top shape.

It was all just about what he had anticipated, and he had been content, at the very least, and maybe she was, too. He knew she still had her friendship with the piano virtuoso. Some of her trips were to see him play, and she made no secret of it. If anything else, anything of an intimate nature, was going on with the man, she gave no indication of it, and he didn't suspect it. Their private life, she still the only woman he'd ever known sexually, more that contented him. He never contemplated anything else. His hands were never pushed away, his lips were never denied their desire, his body never rejected when he initiated. And if he hadn't satisfied her, she'd have informed him of that, to be sure. She still believed in getting what she wanted.

He thought of Patsy, of what she had wanted from him. He thought she had felt sorry for him while he was under her nursing care. She told him while he was at her farm, a family farm with a history of a small cash crop of tobacco, a farm that would have been lost even on his family's last forty acres, that no, she didn't feel sorry for him. That rather, she felt everything a woman can feel for a man. Hell, she couldn't have. He couldn't even use a bedpan without the orderly's assistance for the first two weeks she had known him. Couldn't see to feed himself at first, both eyes bandaged. She would cut up his food and feed him like he was her child.

He wouldn't have gone home with her if he had known all she felt, if he could have really believed it. He thought in the beginning it was friendship, respect, maybe even something like puppy love or hero worship – she was in attendance when he was presented his medals. She wasn't asking him to leave his wife. Unless he wasn't happy in his marriage and wanted to. She wasn't asking him for a long-term affair and commitment. It was simply that she had not felt for any man what she did for him. Just give her what he felt in his heart for the time he was there and then move on if he must.

Her ex-fiancé had been killed at Pearl Harbor. She had met him when she was in nursing school and he had enlisted because she wouldn't marry him. "You feel guilty, then," Shep had said, trying to sound light-hearted, "and want to make it up to some broken guy a long way from home." She shook her head. "No. I would have felt guilty if I were left a grieving widow, grieving because I had cheated him of love he deserved." He wondered at her reasoning, but who was he to say things that might put second thoughts in her now reconciled heart.

They had been in the tobacco barn, her explaining the curing process. Not since her grandfather's time had bundles dried in racks in the vented barn and then over fires to extract the last vestige of moisture, before selling them in North Carolina. Her father was against tobacco use.

But as Patsy answered his questions with the words of someone longing for the good times of a day gone by, he smelled, or perhaps it was still ingrained in the very structure, the smoke from burning maple wood and the pungent tobacco that she talked about. It scented his nostrils like lit pipes full of rich shreds in some old minaret city. He saw the draped leaves of fading greens and rich browns dappled with sun, imagined dancing girl's scarves, instead of country neighbors come for the tobacco curing party, with homemade cider and corn boiling in a black iron kettle and fiddles and songs of the Blue Ridge Mountains.

Here was a woman bloomed in a different climate, watching her father save lives, and investing her life to do the same, instead of growing up watching her family grasp at any acre of land to be had by legal means or otherwise, telling him she wanted him and loved him without asking for a thing in return; yes, it seemed like a secret, rich, foreign world to be grabbed with both hands.

Was he tempted? Was he so tempted he refused to admit even an inkling of longing for her? He did, in fact, feel most of the things about her that he had thought were her feelings about him. She was a hero, deserving respect for her work with injuries that would sicken a lot of people just to see. Her sweet disposition would inspire many men to love her even without her pretty physical features. The men who could manage it turned their head to follow her progress down the ward, not bothering to hide their interest, knowing she would gladly allow them those few moments of pleasure at her expense. Did he use the excuse of his injuries to save himself from breaking vows to Dorthea? Maybe. But the one thing he was sure of, even if the other reasons hadn't existed, was that here was a woman who deserved a man who felt about her the way she did about him. And he wasn't naïve enough to believe that simply being married and contented prevented a man from wanting another woman like that. Well, hell, it was Biblical. But in spite of all he felt about Patsy, it wasn't like that. It wasn't enough.

Now, as he walked this field, already feeling a new encouragement in his injured limbs, and after being around a woman unlike any he had ever imagined, he knew the difference in wanting. And what would save him this time? She would. Angelene would. Because she would not think of him as he did her, gradually becoming unable to keep it from seeping out of something inside his chest, like his good eye crying, weeping, draining in sympathy with the blind eye.

Angelene saw things in black and white. Not their colors, though of course she would see them realistically as what they were, her Negro and him ... not, or possibly him White and her not. But real realities. Their backgrounds. Their ancestries. Their currentcies, as in current situations. His marriage. The state of her marriage and her life. Their future was determined in spite of the fact that she was fleeing her marriage. Mama Gran, who looked and saw and knew and understood them both, had christened them friends. But Pearl, with an outsider's perspective, had seen something else. He wondered what Rosa saw. He thought, though, that where men and women and passion were concerned, she saw only Walter.

TWENTY-EIGHT

Mama Gran sat in the shade, nodding in a kitchen chair with a tieback cushion that Walter had loaded into the trunk of the LaSalle, along with the picnic supplies, driving it and her and Mrs. Brighton and Joyanne down to the high bank overlooking the carved out, swiftly flowing Stones River. Rosa had glowed in the front seat next to Walter, and he had obviously never enjoyed chauffeuring anyone around as much, as Angelene pointed out to her, not taking any offense, but happy for them.

Angelene had walked between Lionel and Shep, Shep glad for the tall walking stick as it gave him something to concentrate on other than their conversation.

"That's a good idea," Lionel said. "Just don't get to depending on it."

"What? Oh, the walking stick."

"You've been carving on it."

"Whittling's what we call it in Mississippi," Shep said. Old men and cripples sit around and do it, he wanted to add, but didn't. He'd shaved it and carved random shapes – a pitcher neck and spout where his hand gripped it, and had started carving a snake entwined on it.

"Think you can do without it a few steps?" Lionel said, laughing, holding out his hand for it.

Shep handed it to him, knowing something of his "feel sorry for me" thoughts must have shown on his face.

"This is pretty," Angelene said, and Lionel passed it to her to examine. "Oh! A snake!" she said, realizing what the carving was and flung it, but Lionel darted his hand out and caught it, laughing. "It's good work," he said.

"Still a work in progress," Shep said, and Lionel nodded, looking at his leg, and said "Improving daily." Shep hadn't realized he was talking about his injury, but Lionel had seen through his thoughts. "It would need some coats of varnish if it were going to be used for long."

"You won't need it for long," Lionel said.

Lionel had arrived home only an hour later than he had said he would, and his mother had praised him for it. She had warned them that he couldn't turn down someone needing medical care, and they said they were grateful for that, as they had received a sample of it only last night. "So this husband of yours," Lionel said to Angelene, accepting that Shep was not to be excluded from his inquiring and conversation, "is in Washington?"

"He was in Chicago when I left Washington."

"Is he to join you at your destination?"

"I do expect him," she said, barely concealing the irony.

"You're not happy about that," Lionel had said, looking to Shep and receiving confirmation with his silence.

"I don't mind you knowing about it, too," she said to Lionel after only a slight hesitation, "except that I think you might be ..." she considered a moment, "uncomfortable. No, anxious about it all. Worried. And reluctant to see us go. And insist on offering your help on any problem I might encounter, for which there can be no help."

Man, she cut to the chase. She was letting Lionel know she had seen inside him and understood he was loopy about her, but that whatever happened she had to go through with her plan and settle any problem herself. Whatever Lionel said next would probably determine how she felt about him, if not now, for a future time when her present had been settled.

"You've looked through me," he said. "I'm bare to you."

Shep waited for more. For Lionel to mess up his chances with her. But there were no more words from Lionel. Lionel had seen clearly in only a few short hours who Angelene was. Her own person now, and he didn't even know her circumstances, that she had in realty been property for fifteen years. Now she was a woman who had some decisions made that were not to be rearranged.

Shep watched Angelene concentrate on her feet in their brown loafers meeting the uneven ground of clumpy grass, white clover and yellow dandelions and rocks. She nodded solemnly, accepting that Lionel would do whatever it took, even back off while fearing she might be in desperate straits, taking her word without question, to have a chance with her. He believed she had made plans to the best of her ability and therefore they were well-laid plans.

Shep had slowed down a little, letting them think he thought they believed it was because of his leg. "Catch you there," he said, watching them move ahead of him, not their speed but his slowing allowing their separation. Lionel had earned that consideration.

Mrs. Brighton's picnic was as palate-pleasing in its homestyle way as the New York eateries had been in their high style, when he and Dorthea had sampled their fare last June. The fried chicken was as good as it had smelled while cooking. Angelene said all the chopped hardboiled eggs smoothed the potato salad out so the onions and pickles gave it extra crunch. Rosa opened a jar of green tomato relish which Angelene tried on the last of her cornbread muffins that she had insisted on contributing. She also brought Pearl's biscuits and blackberry preserves. Rosa said, "I've never tasted white people's food." She sampled them, then said like a taster at cannery, "Very good. Biscuits just hearty enough to support the preserves. The blackberries not overcooked, and just sweet enough."

They all turned to watch Joyanne trying to chase a butterfly flitting around her like it knew she couldn't catch it.

"I've sometimes thought I'd like to open a little place," said Mrs. Brighton. "Joyanne ... she'll be in school in a couple of years."

Joyanne laughed at first and then seemed to become frustrated. Suddenly she threw one of her crutches to the side and hobbled on one. Lionel jumped from the blanket he was sitting on but caught himself and didn't dash to her. Mrs. Brighton stopped a small cry in her throat before it became an admonishment to be careful. Angelene leaned toward her like she was watching a racehorse straining for the finish line. Even the butterfly cooperated, landing on a low tree branch, teasing until she reached it and put her free hand out toward it, and then flapping away. Joyanne lurched about laughing, not realizing what she had done, until a look of fright came across her face and she stood like a spell had cast her into stone.

The grown-ups were silent, as if they were afraid to speak to her and crack her into pieces.

"Come here, Child," Mama Gran said, perhaps having been awakened by the silence.

Joyanne cast unsure glances around for her other crutch. Lionel looked at Mama Gran and then sat back down, even as his daughter looked to him for help. Then Joyanne looked at her mammaw, who was being restrained on her small folding chair by the feather touch of Walter's fingertips, as he sat next to her on a sturdy stool made of three maple turned legs topped by a slice of log, probably left over from the making of the log storage house.

Angelene got up and went to Joyanne.

Mama Gran didn't challenge her, perhaps understanding what Angelene would do or say.

"Does it hurt, Honey?"

Joyanne considered as she looked at her legs then shook her head.

"Then I'll walk with you. If you start to fall, I'll catch you."

"Hold my hand," Joyanne said, wiping a tear that suddenly rolled down her face, leaning on the crutch and looking about for the other one as if it were a life raft in the sea of grass.

Angelene knelt and hugged her and it was obvious she fought the urge to carry her wherever she might want to go. But she only slid a white lace-trimmed handkerchief from her blouse pocket and dabbed at Joyanne's face.

"I'm not scared," Joyanne said.

"Of course you're not," said Angelene. "It just took you by surprise. You're happy, aren't you?"

Joyanne nodded.

Angelene straightened and held out her hand. "If you really need me, I'll help."

Joyanne reached up but did not touch Angelene's hand.

Mama Gran reached out to Joyanne; it was as if sparks jetted from her knotty fingers to energize the little butterfly chaser. Joyanne let go of her fear of failure, left Angelene's hand and with the one crutch walked slowly at first, gained speed, and at the end of her journey leaned into Mama Gran's lap. Mama Gran stroked Joyanne's head a time or two, and nodded at Angelene with a look of somber understanding. Of what, Shep didn't know.

Angelene curled up at Mama Gran's feet and leaned her head against Joyanne's head. Mama Gran held Joyanne's hand and then took her granddaughter's hand in her other one. It was like a priest's benediction, joining two people in some kind of bond. Now, Shep was pretty sure he knew what was passing from the old woman who had seen almost a century's worth of life and the young woman she was leaving soon. It was her understanding of what could be for the future of the little girl.

Then movement and noise from the others broke free of the paralysis and silence that had thrilled them. Mrs. Brighton let out a wail that ended in "my baby!" and Lionel stood and reached for his handkerchief. He took off his glasses and wiped them and then his eyes. Walter rose to help Mrs. Brighton from her perch and said, "Your grandbaby's gonna be all right, Rosa. Mama Gran said so."

TWENTY-NINE

Shep was leaning against the car under the big oak in shadows made by the bright moon when Angelene came from around the house, hardly visible in brown slacks and blouse, silent in her loafers. She jumped a little when he stepped from the covering of the tree, even though she knew he would be there. She had seemed tense, preoccupied, since the picnic.

Earlier, Walter and Rosa had gone to the barn for the milking, leaving Lionel sitting in an easy chair holding Joyanne, reading to her, and Angelene getting Mama Gran a bath and settled in her room ready for the night. Shep had showered before the picnic, and he had hoped he wasn't using too much hot water as it needle-pricked his back and made him appreciate anew a simple thing. Later, sitting with Lionel in the living room and reading the newspaper that Lionel had brought home in the afternoon, they heard the water running through the pipes for Angelene's bath. She wasn't worried, probably hadn't thought, that their water heater might not be too efficient. He figured they got water from the well with an electric pump, just as he did at home.

"Turn to the last section. Page five," Lionel said when the water shut off, as if waiting for it to stop.

Their assault on the hotel was news. The gist of the report was as it actually happened, with a little indignation thrown in. He replayed the scene; no, he had not signed his name. But Midnight would already know it from his paid informant, after the incident with the Kentucky Highway Patrol.

Although Joyanne had dropped off to sleep, Lionel still sat holding her. "I wondered when she'd try," he said, looking at the crutches lying on the floor next to the chair. "Beginning to think she wouldn't ever want to even let one crutch go."

Joyanne had said her daddy allowed her only so many steps. "Guess she was scared," Shep said. But not afraid to fall. "Afraid to fail."

"I think so. I told her I thought she'd know. I think part of it was she didn't want to be independent, maybe. Maybe be able to go where one of us wasn't there with her. She's still got the accident, the night it happened, all the confusion and screaming and pain on her mind. Might take a lot longer to get over it."

Lionel had done what probably not many fathers in his position could have accomplished, Shep felt, and told him so.

"She's been my guiding light. What she's had to endure ..." He cleared his throat, then said, pointing to Shep's leg, "I suspect your doctors held you back."

"Oh, I went right along with them. Afraid of rushing things. Afraid to chance it. Until I was afraid it'd never make it back."

"Maybe it was fear that made you decide. But children. I don't know. I think their little bodies can heal faster. But their minds have to go along with it. And can't a doctor convince them if they're not ready to lose their fear."

They could hear Walter and Rosa in the kitchen, tending the milk and putting things away, laughing and talking in soft phrases meant only for themselves.

"Mama wants to protect her. Tries not to. But she doesn't go one step farther than the doctor in me says is probably the thing to do. She figures by helping her develop mentally as quick as possible that would help her know when."

Shep thought of the morning in the kitchen. "You both do what you think is best. Apparently it's working."

Angelene came in, smelling like good soap and dressed in brown. Her hair was no longer smooth, and she didn't have it tucked into the thick netting like today. It was pulled tightly back with a scarf around it at the neck, but it had grown in volume and was in frizzy curls. Dorthea would have brushed into submission one hair that freed itself. Sometimes she used a comb or pin to hold back one side. He saw nothing wrong with either. Both knew how to make their hair an asset. Angelene saw that he had noticed her hair, but said nothing.

Lionel had noticed her from head to foot. "Come into my parlor," he said. "Queen Angelene."

She smiled and sat on the small couch. "I don't think I ever played princess and castles before this afternoon," she said.

"And why not?" said Lionel. "Were you a real princess?"

She laughed. The sarcastic one Shep remembered from the day they met. "I guess fantasies just weren't for me."

"No, you're above that. You see things for what they are."

Rosa and Walter came in then, like a pair matched by an engineer. Rosa said, "You're real, all right. And I believe you all were sent here by the Almighty. Can't help but believe it. Look at my baby there."

She walked to Lionel's chair and touched Joyanne's arm. "Runnin' around this afternoon. Chasin' butterflies. Butterflies!" Then she kissed Lionel on the head.

For the rest of the evening, Angelene had been restless in some way. Maybe she believed what Rosa said and was uncomfortable with it. Perhaps she didn't, but didn't want to dispute this woman who had bid them enter and make her home their own.

So now Angelene and he walked toward the river, basically the same path they'd taken in the afternoon with Lionel.

"They're all taking too much for granted," she finally said. "Even Mama Gran."

"This afternoon?" he said, thinking of her and Joyanne at Mama Gran's feet.

"Yes."

He didn't offer any of the endless possibilities that might be the basis for that feeling she had. That she didn't say. That they wanted too much. Rosa and Walter were as good together as anyone he'd ever seen. It was a relaxed reliance of each on the other and a willingness to accept any generosity, and perhaps any sacrifice one wanted to make that they felt necessary for the other. And if they reunited after their coming separaton, it would be just as good between them. Sometimes couples fell into that slot. Not his parents, not Dorthea's parents. Ulys and his wife, yes, back in the houses, even with their son dependent on them for his every care. And Sissy and her husband, through losing their family home and being childless and providing refuge for his mother. He would leave Dorthea and himself out of the comparison. Theirs was what? A fact of their life? What they both wanted? But not to be compared with anyone else for better or worse.

And here was Lionel wanting Angelene for his wife, enough to sacrifice his desire to help her, and put his faith in her competence, or at least accept her decision that she believed she could take care of her problem, if that bettered their chance of a life together.

And the little girl. She wanted Angelene for her mother. Angelene already felt like a mother to her. And this afternoon, what Mama Gran had done. He saw it for what it was. Mama Gran's tying them together almost spiritually.

"What they don't understand, but will accept, is that I have to go. We have to go. It's not a choice we can make. And you, too. Though they'd even keep you," she added, laughing a little.

"It would be easy to think this could be a haven for you," he said.

"If I told them why, they'd no doubt think that was all the more reason for me to stay."

"I can understand why they feel as they do. If you hadn't told me this afternoon."

"He won't give up until he finds me."

"We did make the local newspaper."

Her step halted a little as did her voice. "He may have connections here. If he found me here, they'd all be in danger."

What kind of meanness must be in this man that frightened her so much? Frightened a woman who would face down a sheriff who talked as if he were a KKKer, hold her own with Arch, a man of her race who had wanted a reason to harm her, be willing to risk her life running from state troopers, and march into a ritzy hotel where she wasn't wanted.

"Could we be traced here?"

He thought back to the hotel. They didn't register at the hotel where they were sent. At the hospital, Lionel didn't fill out papers, and presumably had not told anyone about the incident. They were well east of Nashville, and he would expect them to be going west and south. And he wouldn't be expecting them to stop along the way. "No, I don't think so," he said, giving her his reasoning.

"He must have found out I left, because no one else would have turned my car in as stolen."

"Does he have an idea where you'll be going?"

"Yes, I expect so. But I left a map in a drawer with New York circled on it. Maybe he'll fall for that."

But her voice told him he wouldn't.

"But you're still going right where Midnight expects you to be. Make it easy on him." Putting a name on the man made him seem more real. She noticed, glancing his way for an instant.

"I hope to be waiting for him. If so, I'll have the advantage."

In spite of the walking stick, Shep tripped on a stump – watching her instead of where he was putting all three limbs – and she grabbed out to steady him. Then something scurried out of their way and she grabbed out for him again and laughed. "It's the unknowns that spook me. I know him. I'm not saying I'm not afraid. I am because I do know him. I only hope to get him before he gets me. I won't be asking questions or talking it over. So now, what do you think?"

God. She was talking a gunfight? Shooting on sight? He trusted her accuracy. He trusted her reasons. He trusted her. "I hope it works." What were the delays doing to her plans? He wished she was instead going to catch a boat to South America even if she was there the rest of her days and he were never to see her again.

They reached the picnic spot. "Let's go closer to the river. Sit on that big rock." Stones protruded everywhere, some huge as small boulders and others barely cropping up from the land. Suppose that's what gave the river its name, Lieutenant? he asked himself.

This was a deep river run, but he could imagine it up to the banks. Too many rivers around this area, draining into one another for that not to happen.

The moon was overhead with not many shadows by then, allowing them to see the dark water. They listened to the night insects and the subtle noises of the river flowing over its stony bottom. He'd read of the rivers in Tennessee being dammed for electricity, and no doubt that's what lit the lights in Lionel's sturdy home. He hoped this river ran by Lionel and his family like this forever. He'd like to come back to this little piece of what was right with the world someday and know what had transpired as a result of this party's sojourn here.

"What are you thinking of?" she said.

"Electricity?"

She laughed. "You're still too much a gentleman to ask," she finally said.

"And I thought I was only being considerate."

"My point is made," she said lightly but not sarcastically, "but I really don't object to gentlemen."

She reached for his hand and he knew she trusted him as he did her.

He stopped before they got too close to the bank and prodded around with his stick on the spot surrounding the low outcropping rock to make sure it wasn't a resting place for a wild critter. "This place ought to do."

She backed against the rock and lifted herself up to sit cross-legged, her hands on her thighs, outlined against the night like an Indian chief deliberating. He stretched and tried to sit facing her, but one arm wouldn't quite lift what the other wouldn't manage, the healing leg hanging, his foot resting on a small outcropping rock.

"The moonlight view of the river is beautiful. Here, let me help you get up here."

"I may need help to get down."

"Oh, I won't desert you. I'll help when we start back home."

They were both silent a minute thinking that over. Home. She didn't say "the house" or "back." She had said "home."

"I meant, to the house."

"Of course."

She shifted and reached down for him. "Like we've been helping each other. And will. For as long as, well, as long as we need to."

"For only that long?"

She looked at him considering, then out at the powerful river. "As long as we even imagine we need to. All right?"

"Deal."

THIRTY

She was looking around up in the heavens but didn't say anything else. Her eyes reflected the heavenly bodies' light. A nice wind kept mosquitoes away, but it was past their worst biting time, dusk, anyway.

"The doctor said I couldn't have another baby," she said, like she didn't know whether she would have wanted to or not.

Shep felt like he was coming in on the middle of the story. God. What happened to her child?

"At fourteen, a girl's body ... It just isn't ready. And she's not ready to do what a man like that ... a man like that, requires. To ... to ... make himself ... He didn't go to anyone else. Didn't want anyone else to kinow. That's why he agreed to marry me."

He felt ice go through his veins, and knew that one day he would kill a man named like the black darkness that must be in his heart. At least, he would try.

"Sometimes, I tried Mama Gran's advice. To prevent."

In the way of boy talk to make them seem men, his friends and he had discussed all they'd heard about preventives that the Negro women used. Chewing certain leaves, tea made from particular roots, even burying toads or bones under the floor. None of them had even acknowledged they knew that their mothers or sisters or future wives might have the same concern. Dorthea had had a meeting of her farm women after a girl bled to death at fifteen, her folks waiting too late to let Dorthea know to call the doctor. She told them that coating their inner parts with lard was what her mammy said worked. She wrote him about it several months ago. Had babies and giving birth been on her mind? What could Mama Gran's method have been? As for Dorthea personally, she had trusted only the one method. And it wasn't lard. Nor abstinence.

"He wouldn't ... protect me ... from the first."

He'd like to touch Angelene's hand, but he got the idea she didn't want sympathy. This was part of her telling of why she couldn't stay any longer up there in the night with the funeral maker. As for himself, he was getting eager to see the man.

"But," she became silent and shook her head, then finished. "I mostly didn't get a chance."

He wanted to divine which road the bastard would be travelling so he could meet him in the middle of it and send him to hell on a bullet. Fifteen years of life with him. He had married her to use her. She had never known a man's caring and tenderness.

"Do you have children?" Angelene said into his silence and the night.

"No." Should he add, none that he knew of? But it wouldn't be funny to Angelene, and it wasn't a joke with Dorthea and him. Didn't he owe Angelene the truth? She was revealing her truths to him. "There is a chance." How to say this to Angelene? Without betraying Dorthea, his wife, no matter whatever had or had not passed between them. "She apparently ... wanted to ... or rather didn't want to prevent it ... the last time we were together. But she hasn't told me that she was pregnant. Or not."

"You white people. Are you that different from us?"

"I don't think so. It's Dorthea and me, I expect."

"Maybe she wouldn't want you to worry."

Now there was a thought. "It was about a year ago."

"So here you are, walking home in a hurry ..."

"It's a complicated marriage."

A bat flew by and he felt the brush of air from its wings. "What was that?" she said.

"Just a bat."

She flailed her arms around her head but didn't utter a sound.

"It won't hurt you. It's looking for insects."

"Well ... Shoo! I'm too big for you!" she said to the air already empty of bats.

"You don't scare easily."

"Maybe not. I like to think not." She nodded in agreement with herself. "But I know when to run."

"Tell me what made you run."

"My baby came early, I was home by myself. That was before he let Mama Gran move in. She convinced him I might die. She never left. Your mother ever live with you?"

"No. She lived with my sister and her husband." Dorthea's grandfather and father had lived with them until their deaths. Or more accurately, he and Dorthea had lived with them. Three generations also sometimes lived together in the workers' houses on the farm. Same on some white or black sharecropper places.

"In Mobile," she said. "That's on the water, sort of like Washington, isn't it?"

"Not a bad comparison." She was trying to sidetrack herself, maybe unconsciously.

"How did your family come to be in Washington?"

"Mama Gran was brought there as a young woman. Forced to go. Lady's maid."

"The war would have been over by then."

"Didn't matter. You know that."

"All that, and nothing settled."

"But she managed to get away and get lost in the black community. Cleaned hotel kitchens at night. Got to work and make some money for herself." She laughed but her sarcasm returned. "You didn't know I look on the sunny side, did you?"

"You should know. About my family, we fought for the south. They didn't even try to say it was for state's rights."

"Oh, I figured that. Slave-owners for sure. But don't hold yourself responsible. You wouldn't do it. Not now. Who knows, back then, well, who knows."

"Faint praise," he said, "but I'll take it." When she didn't say more, he said, "So Mama Gran stayed in Washington? Met a man up there?"

"Yes. And no. She saved her money and went back to Mississippi. Rode the rivers down, cooking on the boats. She went to get her daughter."

She paused to let that sink in.

"My grandmother. Mana Gran's man had been run over by a horse and wagon before she even knew she was pregnant. She had to leave her daughter, just about five, when she was forced to go away with her former owner. The woman found a family in Vicksburg to take Mama Gran's little girl. Not on a plantation. A restaurant in town. But by the time Mama Gran returned years later, they wouldn't let her daughter go. They wouldn't even take money for her. She was fourteen and pregnant with the owner's son's baby. The son was from the owner and a slave woman he had."

"So ... you're ..." he didn't want to say it, he felt guilty in absentia, assuming Mama Gran's daughter had been taken advantage of, "you're part White?"

"No. Actually not. No reason for you to feel bad, even if that had been the case."

She actually patted his hand. "The owner was black. A freed slave. I'm pretty sure it wasn't lawful at the time he was set free, down there, but nevertheless. I think his food was so good they didn't care."

Shep knew there had been some Negroes who were free and who had owned slaves, as ironic as that was.

"How somebody this color," she looked at her hand, "could do that, have a slave for himself, but he did. When Mama Gran returned, they let her stay and work in the kitchen until her daughter's baby was born. It was a boy. He lived to be my father. And my grandmother died during the birth."

That's why Mama Gran was so worried about Angelene getting married so young, of course. She knew death was waiting to happen in such a circumstance. He shifted and stared at Angelene, feeling even his eye behind the patch wanting to see. "I'm sorry all that happened to your family. It must make you sad to tell."

"It's all right. Reminds me that good or bad to anybody can come from either color."

"Your mother, did she, did you get to know her?"

"She died from influenza before I started walking."

What kept her a woman of flesh and blood when she had to be made of steel to survive?

"Mama Gran is who made me. She's determined. She managed to steal her grandson and run back to Washington. They never found her. She had told them she had been living in Chicago. She had memorized some of their recipes, and copied some of them. So she got a job in a restaurant kitchen, learning the basics."

That should have been the end of it, then. Of them and the south. Shouldn't it? Wouldn't it have been better for them, Angelene and Mama Gran and Walter to have run to New York? Or actually get out of the country? "Why are you going back south?"

"Mama Gran's determination. Back then she was afraid to stay there long enough to see her daughter, my Grandmother Tillie, buried. She left money for the undertaker to bury her in a cemetery for Negroes. She thought the father, not the man who was my grandfather, but his father, the former slave – would put her in some unmarked grave in the pauper's graveyard, not wanting to spend the money. The undertaker was to go to him and say Mama Gran had paid enough to take care of it."

Angelene stood and looked around, rubbing her neck, not like she was through with the telling, only like she needed a break from it. "It's sort of spooky being out in this big open space."

He shifted around for a more comfortable position and only then realized his good leg had fallen asleep and began to stretch and rub it.

"Now, if that was your bad leg, I'd rub it again," Angelene said. "But I'm not going to spoil you."

"Then sit here and I'll massage your neck."

She hesitated but settled in, her back to him.

He hesitated before spreading his fingertips on her neck, and moved them up to the base of her scalp and back down. She shuddered and he touched with a little more pressure, realizing he had been involuntarily touching her lightly, a lover's touch. He moved his fingers down to her shoulders and rubbed professionally, as had been done to him in the hospital. He felt her breaths get deep and heard her inhale.

"Today is the only time I've been touched by another man, except the doctor who delivered my baby."

Could she really mean that? He waited for the inevitable "touched by a white man." But no. She didn't add that.

"Until I shook hands with Lionel at the hospital. Somehow, I just thought I should."

What had made her feel the need?

"I like it."

"You like it?" That simple. She liked being touched by him. Or simply by another man?

She laughed the way he liked her to. "Silly! I like this massaging. Oooh, it feels like heaven!"

"You know how to take a man down!" he said, laughing in turn.

THIRTY-ONE

Climbing up the stairs, shifting and lifting his leg out as far as he could before the bend, he realized that his walking today had done much good, even though it was sore and might cramp any minute. He felt this might be the turning point. His arm was getting stronger as he exercised daily. He was now also following suggestions Lionel gave him, newly developed by the armed forces, as well continuing those suggested by Patsy's father.

Walter didn't appear to be awake. He didn't suppose Walter would think Angelene would have done anything out of character, even in a meeting with him under cover of night. He would probably know Angelene was filling him in on her history and wanted to keep Lionel ignorant of the danger she faced. Shep felt Lionel might have been unable to keep his former promise and try to stop her or try to go with her if he knew the extent of her danger.

Angelene couldn't help but know Shep wanted to be the one she told her deepest troubles to. Be the one she needed to help her. He hoped he could be up to the task. It wouldn't be from lack of trying.

The Funeral Maker would be formidable if he was anything like Angelene revealed. But could she know the full extent of her husband's capabilities? Shep suspected he was even more than she knew. Only if her husband intended her to know, perhaps to keep the fear in her, keep her from entertaining notions of life without him, would he have made her aware of all his transgressions. At any rate, what she knew was enough.

He had hired Walter several years ago, not only as her driver but as her keeper. Walter wasn't a man without a conscience. He'd collected his pay from Midnight, earning it loyally, not having to inform on Angelene or restrain her because she had done nothing to report on. Until a month ago, when Angelene asked him if he would like to be her employee. He'd cast his lot with her. She paid him his salary now. His money from Midnight since then was in an envelope in his room above the garage, to be found by Midnight on his return, and all the implications that went with the unspent money. Walter was a traitor to him, now on his list.

Mama Gran's health had worsened in the last few months and Angelene had finally accepted that her grandmother wouldn't live forever. "What can I do, Mama Gran?" she had asked. Mama Gran said, "There is no potion to make me better. But there is something. A thing that will make me rest easier under that pile."

"I'll do whatever you want, Mama Gran," she had said, crossing her heart like she had done as a child, even as she had done when Mama Gran asked her if she could marry Midnight.

"We had no choice when he wanted you, child," Mama Gran had said. "Your Daddy dead. Killed by Midnight the mortician. I thought Midnight only wanted your daddy's restaurant when he kept raising the fees so high your daddy couldn't pay."

Angelene had said it with such straightforwardness that it was obvious she was covering emotion when she told him about that, still sitting on the rock, having gradually leaned back against him until they both became aware of their closeness. She had stiffened and broken the touch. He let her move, he would not restrain her, but had then loosely encircled her. "You've been touched now. It doesn't have to hurt." He knew that she had been hurt when Midnight touched her. Maybe every time he touched her.

She leaned back and turned her face into his neck.

"You're as gentle as Mama Gran," she said, some of her sarcasm making a comeback, and allowed him to put his mind back on why they were there.

So the part about her daddy having a fruit and newspaper stand was made up? It had had the ring of truth to it, even Angelene's resentment. He probably began with a small stand. It couldn't have been easy to get a restaurant started. He had probably borrowed money from Midnight when he wanted to expand.

He rubbed her arm and nuzzled his chin in her softly wiry hair. "Tell me everything."

"How could I have done it, married him, if I'd known? So Mama Gran kept it from me. After a while, the restaurant wasn't enough for Midnight and she knew it was me he was after. She knew she'd be dead by his hand and I'd have to live with him without her. Probably not as his wife. So she kept it from me."

Mama Gran had done what she had to. One more time.

"Mama Gran had taught her grandson what she learned at LaBelle. They started making a few specialties and selling them from the fruitstand. It went well until the stand had to close because they were violating an ordinance. Midnight had turned them in to the authorities they found out later. They decided to open a restaurant. They went to Midnight for help, and from then on he owned them."

Everyone in her family had been enslaved by someone.

"Who was I that Mercer Midnight was so set on me? I barely had my permanent teeth in! Hadn't been bleeding but six months. Just little nubbins for breasts!" She grabbed a handful of hair and closed her fist around it. "Enough hair it could have been split three ways. You see how it is now, just a few days out of the shop!"

He had leaned against her hair a little more, liking the strong thickness of it. Mercer Midnight had seen what she'd be in a few years. And meanwhile he had a child to do with what he would. She was probably very lucky that he had agreed to marry instead of just taking what he wanted. What did Mama Gran have over him?

"I believe Mama Gran convinced him she'd manage to kill me if he didn't marry me. If he just took me home. But she maintains that's what he wanted all along. If he hadn't wanted marriage, he could have severed it any time."

"Of course he would want it legal. A man like that tries for a little respectability." He wants to build trust in the community: See, I'm a family man like you. "He knows he can rule only by fear or iron-handedness. But he eventually tries to fool himself." Also, she'd be less likely to run, married.

"After a few years he saw I could cook reasonably well – Mama Gran taught me like she did my daddy. He said he was going to let me run LaLa's. I would have had no choice. But I wanted to do it. Oh, mercy, to be out of the house every day. Talk to people, not just learn about them in books. Me tell a few people how to do something or what to do. Be back in my daddy's restaurant. I tried not to let him know how much I wanted it, and loved it.

"I kept the books, and knew he'd never let me keep much money for myself from it. Even though it was actually mine and Mama Gran's restaurant. So I had a double set of books. I managed to keep an extra cook on the accounts he saw, and found a couple of white suppliers who would do kick-backs. Also, when I catered, I padded it. I don't know, he may have known about it and let me have my fun, knowing he could stop it any time. I like to think he didn't know.

"They came from all over D.C. to eat there. I've even fed a few congressmen and their wives. They called me Mrs. Midnight, asked me to their tables."

He'd been in her city for months. I wish I had gone there, he wanted to tell her, but wishes weren't for grown men. And now he saw a little of why she wasn't ready for this real world where diplomacy isn't a way of life.

"I told Mama Gran I'd do whatever she wanted. And do you know what it was? She wanted me to leave him! She wanted me to run away then, not wait until she was dead. She was afraid I'd lose courage to go after she was dead. I told her no. I would not leave her there. We would go together. She knew I'd say that." She laughed. "She had her alternative ready." She laughed again, softly, but he felt her back move against his ribs in her excitement at remembering. "She wanted me to take her back home. Down to Mississippi and leave her at some boarding house if she was still alive. She wanted me to go on to New Orleans and get on a ship. She feels she abandoned her daughter when she was forced to go north, and then again when Tillie died. She wants to see her daughter's grave. See if she got what she paid for. And if it's there, she wants to be buried there, next to her daughter. And she didn't want Midnight touching her body, burying her. Even to put her next to my daddy."

And as he gently rubbed Angelene's shoulder, she whispered, "This alone would have gotten me killed. He warned me the day we married. Not one touch."

He had touched women since his wedding day. Not many. A few dance partners at charity balls. Hand shakes if they held out their hands at introductions. Patsy. He'd held her, even kissed her. The number paled against the men Dorthea had touched, that he knew she had touched. Hell, she kissed piano-man Josh Sommers on the mouth every time she saw him. "That must have been hard to avoid," he said.

"Not at all. I never wanted to touch another man."

He'd leave it unsaid. Until Lionel. She'd taken his hand at the hospital.

She put her hand over his, her long fingers curving under his. Her smooth, rounded fingernails dug into his palm. "And I never wanted to be touched by another man."

But she wanted his touch. He had to concentrate on something to make his blood rise to his brain. Dorthea, what she'd have done if he'd come home unfit to do his duty by her. But that didn't get things under control as quickly as he'd hoped. Because his brain knew he'd have managed by sheer willpower, a magician levitating, to have come through as Dorthea expected. Or he'd have never returned home. Simple as that.

"Hey, southern gentleman, what's going on?"

She didn't mind. Her voice told him that. In fact, it made her happy. So he had only laughed, too.

They let the moment pass without further comment, just thinking and enjoying the freedom of touching in the darkness, alone, their bodies comfortably separated by a few layers of clothing, knowing somehow that they understood each other's needs for the present. And that this warm and welcome man-woman contact was all the present required.

In a few minutes he said with regret, "I know you don't want anyone to notice we're both missing."

He felt her nod yes against his shoulder. "I didn't want Lionel and his mother to know what I'm up against. They would want to help."

~ 139 ~

It was his turn to nod.

"And I didn't want to just take you aside and have private conversations. How would that have been in their own house?"

"You were right about it. To do it this way."

"I think I knew, when we met, when you rescued us – yes, you did," she said, turning and putting her finger at his lips when he started to deny it. "I understand about things now that I had been told but had never seen. Anyway, I think I knew then that I'd be spilling all this out to you."

R osa was wearing a dark maroon dress and Joyanne was in a frilly light blue dress with white socks and black patent leather shoes when he entered the kitchen next morning after his hike through the woods. "Thank you," he said as Rosa poured his coffee, "and good morning to both you ladies in your pretty dresses."

Joyanne said, "We're going to church." She giggled a minute then said, "We don't wear our best dresses except on Sunday."

"Is it Sunday?" said Angelene, entering dressed as usual, which meant she could leave without much adjusting for church or anywhere else. She wore a dress the color of the darkest red that leaves turned on the trees at home in late fall, with a lacy triangle of white over each shoulder that contrasted so much with the dark dress it looked like fresh snowfall. Her hair was in a bun with several black combs and clips, allowing pearl earrings to show. She moved softly in the same shoes she wore the first day he saw her, to hug Joyanne. "Well. Are you going to a ball?" she asked, hugging her.

"Not to a ball! To church. We're all going!"

"Oh. Church?" She looked at Rosa. "I don't know if Mama Gran will feel like it. She didn't sleep well. I'll have to stay here with her."

Angelene must have been up with her much of the night, and he saw a tiredness in her eyes. But he felt a gratefulness in her voice that she'd get to miss church.

"Oh, she's going, too. She told me yesterday she wants to go."

Angelene didn't conceal her look of curiosity.

"She seems to think she doesn't have long to ..." Rosa stopped, glancing at Joyanne.

"I want to talk to the Lord in His own house again," said Mama Gran, coming into the kitchen, supported by Walter, who had on black pants and a white shirt and flowered tie. "And I want to listen to Him there."

"Would you prefer your plate in your room, so you can rest until we go?" said Rosa.

"I like to be at a table with good people. It fortifies my soul. I'll get rest soon enough."

"Then everyone sit down. Breakfast is ready," Rosa said.

The smell of buttermilk biscuits floated around the kitchen when she opened the oven door. She turned the biscuits out of a square blackened iron pan into a bowl. Walter stirred gravy in a black skillet and Rosa examined it and poured a little milk in and set the pan on a folded cloth on the table. "Keeps it hot longer," she said, looking at Angelene. "No fresh eggs yet today. Who wants oatmeal?" she asked, picking up a stewpot, dishing some into several small bowls.

Angelene selected two for her and Mama Gran and embellished them with sugar and milk. That was all they ate, and Rosa asked them once if they cared for something else, then accepted that not everyone wanted a hearty breakfast every morning. "Glad to see you eat," she said to Shep as she buttered a biscuit for Joyanne to eat with her oatmeal.

"The army doesn't know how to make milk gravy," he said. "I'd never turn this down."

When Rosa poured more coffee, Angelene looked at the small gold watch on her wrist.

"There's no hurry. We've got plenty of time," Mrs. Brighton assured the group.

Shep had gone to church a time or two with Thula when he was little and his mother was too sick on Sunday morning to attend her church. She had gone through times when she didn't seem able to make herself get dressed and leave the house, just looking sadly at Shep when he tried to get her to let him go for the doctor. According to Sissy, she suffered those bouts, becoming longer-lasting and more intense, until the end. Her despondency seemed to feed on itself instead of diminishing, as he thought the natural order of it should be in the mourning process over his father and the loss of their land so long ago.

"Won't have to leave until eleven. Lionel will be back from early rounds by then. Church is just down the road a couple of miles.

"I can't say that I've been to church in some time," Angelene said.

Joyanne turned to look. "Doesn't your mammaw make you go?"

"Now, Joyanne," said Rosa.

"Child," said Mama Gran, "nothing would have made me happier than to take this girl to church every Sunday."

"Don't you enjoy going?" Angelene asked Joyanne.

Joyanne nodded and said, "I like to see the other girls. I like the piano, and all the yelling."

"Shouts of joy," her grandmother said. "I can't wait to hear the shoutin' when we ride up in this big car, Walter driving us right up to the door – if that's all right with you, Angelene?"

"That's exactly the way we'll do it," Angelene said.

Shep wondered where he'd be at the noon hour. He had no objections to going, if that's what his hosts wanted. But going to their church now might not be the simple proposition it had been when he was a small boy.

As it turned out, it was.

And it wasn't even a tight squeeze in the Cadillac for all of them, Mrs. Brighton and him in the front with Walter, and Mama Gran, Lionel and Angelene in the backseat, Joyanne in Angelene's lap. The car shone like new. Walter had washed it the day before with water he dipped from the barrel that collected rainwater at the back gutter of the house, and dried it with old sheets Rosa provided.

It was like a big party where everyone crowded to see the honoree as they parked at the front of the small church. The unpainted wood building had a single door in front, a plain glass window on each side. Within was a simple pulpit and two benches at the front for the choir, with the scarred upright piano opposite them. It differed from Thula's church in that hers was painted white and had a steeple of sorts with a bell that was rung each Sunday morning at eleven, to let all know it was time to head to worship. Few there had clocks or watches. Thula's had no piano or choir and singing from memory was everyone's responsibility. A few hymnals were scattered around here, and one was handed him as he sat on the bench with Angelene between him and Lionel. He felt it was a politeness rather than an insinuation that he wouldn't know the songs.

After all the greetings were done, with the four of them being introduced to all there, and when no one had entered in about five minutes, the preacher, Brother Polk, raised his hand and started singing "Take Me To Calvary," and everyone joined in, swaying and clapping, the piano notes riveting the voices to the ceiling. "Page one hundred fourteen," Brother Polk inserted, noticing that two, Angelene and Shep, weren't singing. Surely everyone else in the little citadel of faith was contributing, according to the volume.

After about an hour and a half had gone by, his leg was refusing to accept its inability to stretch about. As much as he was enjoying the preaching of the Old Testament quotes and the New Testament stories that fulfilled those prophecies, and the amens that acknowledged that Brother Polk was testifying as befitted a holy interpreter, he had to use all his concentration on keeping his leg from stiffening into a cramp by shuffling it back and forth. Lionel apparently realized his predicament.

At the next break, when Brother Polk looked down to refresh his memory from his mostly unused notes, Lionel said, "Amen and Amen, Brother Polk." Other amens chorused and Brother Polk said, "Have I done my job? Have I *done* my job?" More amens. "Sinners saved!" from the back. "Jesus be the

Praise!" responded the preacher. A hallelujah. Shep wouldn't have minded seconding that.

"Hand around the plate!" came from the back. "Preacher can't live on the good book alone!" somebody else said to laughter and the piano started up another chant of a song.

There was precious little, a few dollars and some change, in the plate when it reached them, about half-way back. Lionel put in a ten dollar bill that he had taken out of his inside breast pocket. Angelene had folded up a twenty dollar bill, apparently trying to be unobtrusive, and dropped it in. But it didn't go unnoticed. "Amen, Sister!" said one of the many faces trained on her instead of the choir singing and clapping with the piano.

Shep had put a couple of twenties at the ready in his right pants pocket and fives in his left pants pocket and tens in the rim of his hat before leaving the house. He wanted a selection because he knew he was going to make it a point to notice what Lionel put in so he could follow suit. He would not even think of putting in more than Lionel, in fact would rather not put in any than have anyone there, and he didn't fool himself, all eyes were on them, think he was outdoing Lionel. "Amen for ten," came a happy chorus.

After the plate was brought forward, Brother Polk said, "Come to the alter, Brother. Come to the alter, Sister! Pray at the feet of Jesus!"

The piano encouraged, and the two little girls, probably eight or nine years old, who had sat with Joyanne, Mrs. Brighton, Walter, and Mama Gran toward the front moved into the aisle clapping and stepping to the music. Joyanne stood up, not having her crutch, as her daddy had carried her in, and holding onto the back of the bench in front of her, stepped out into the aisle. The two little girls stilled so suddenly their dresses swirled without them. Mrs. Brighton stopped her hands in mid-air and her praise in mid-note. Mama Gran's head was still bowed in prayer, her hands under her chin.

Lionel, in their row a few behind, seated next to the aisle, was poised like the safety man in a high wire act. Angelene stared, rubbed her hands together with the intensity of Lady Macbeth. Within a few seconds the church was silent except for the slight tapping sound that came from Joyanne's and her friends' hands clapping, as their Sunday shoes bore them down the aisle to stand at Brother Polk's feet.

"Praise Jesus! Praise His Name!" shouted Brother Polk. "The age of miracles is alive! Praise God! Sweet Jesus!" He opened his arms as if to enclose the entire room.

Joyanne abruptly became aware of what she had done and the stillness surrounding her and looked back toward her family. For a moment she was the picture of uncertainty, then Angelene unclasped her hands and clapped them together, moving her head in sync with the girls, urging Joyanne on. Joyanne smiled and began her little clapping again, and soon the congregants were singing and swaying and a couple of the white-clothed elder ladies swooning, needing to be steadied by their concerned companions.

Maybe it was a miracle. Yes, it probably was. Miracles still happened. Wasn't the fact that he was still breathing, much less growing in strength and flexibility every day proof of that? God. He suddenly felt like yanking off the patch that blocked his eye and seeing. Jesus made the blind see. But the doctor had cautioned him, instructed him sternly, not to take off the patch except in the dark to cleanse it with the bottle he carried in his duffle, and that he must go to the army hospital in Memphis for the grand unveiling. Until then when he had the patch off to cleanse his eye, he must not cover his good eye and try to make the clouds and shadows form into shapes through the closed lid of his injured eye. Everything happens in its own time. Even miracles. Be patient.

Brother Polk raised his arms and spread them, gradually lowering them in indication for quiet, then stepped to Joyanne, who by then like the sisters in white was beginning to weaken, and picked her up, holding her up under both arms, facing the audience like an offering. "Yes, in spite of doubt," he said almost regretfully, "sweet Jesus came to us today." Then he turned Joyanne and held her in the crook of one arm, just as a child Shep had always pictured Jesus doing, holding a child safely in the crook of His arm, but not himself. Not his sister. Not Dorthea. Some child he didn't know. Now he could put a face on the child.

Brother Polk spoke to Joyanne, softly and tenderly rather than in his sinning and salvation tones, but in the stillness all heard. "Do you know what has happened, Baby Sister?"

She shook her head as if she had done something wrong.

"You have shown us Jesus's presence here today." He looked around the room.

"Did He bring presents?" Joyanne asked, looking a little hopeful.

Everyone laughed. "Yes, Baby Sister. And you are it. You are the gift. And you received the gift. You are healed by the grace of Jesus and," here he looked at Lionel, "and some God-given help from medical science. Can there still be a doubter here? Doubter, open your heart to miracles and love."

Hallelujahs and praise filled the room.

"I say, can there still be any doubter here?" Brother Polk repeated, his voice warming again, rising in challenge. He got heartfelt amens and praises of belief.

Lionel walked to the front and Joyanne reached out to him. He took her and her little hug was enough to squeeze tears from him. Rosa moved to them

~ 145 ~

and they stood knotted as the other believers at last began to go through the doors to the world around them.

Throughout it all Mama Gran had remained seated and praying. Brother Polk sat down by her and she glanced at Walter, who then moved to wait at the other end of the bench.

Angelene tucked her purse under her arm and adjusted her little pillbox of a hat, watching almost impatiently, he thought. Was she a doubter? The doubter Brother Polk had so earnestly inquired of?

THIRTY-THREE

"Anybody hungry, get yourself a biscuit and some buttermilk," Lionel said as they returned home. "Tide yourself over. I tell Mama she's got to rest on Sundays."

"My boy does the cooking," she bragged, hugging him.

"Not much to it," he said. "I got some hickory wood chips under a grate outside. Over there in the shade." He pointed to the big pecan tree, where a large black outdoor pot sat. He lit kindling in it and smoke began to puff up. "I'll put some pork chops on it when it starts glowing, and some corn in the shucks. Still not filled out too good, but enough."

Amazing what a couple of days of summer could do, but still early up here for good corn, Shep thought. At home they would build a fire with hickory in an old metal drum in front of the houses, let it simmer down, then brace a rack over it and throw chicken or rabbit or pork hind leg, or even possum over it in the winter. Whatever it was smelled like heaven while all the kids milled around waiting for it to get to the crispy skin and easy pulling-off-the-bone stage. Since he'd been overseeing, he'd told them to slaughter a hog for holidays. They sent the tenderloin to the house and he felt bad that they returned the best part, but Dorthea said that it showed they still knew who was responsible for their daily bread. He hoped she'd continued the new tradition on this year's Fourth.

A cool breeze wafted through the shaded valley between the tree and the house. Lionel and Walter carried the wooden table covered by oilcloth from the back porch and chairs from the kitchen. Rosa brought crisp pickled okra from her store of canned goods and a plate of sweet potato slices fried in bacon fat to go with the chops and corn.

"My grill cook couldn't do any better," said Angelene, gnawing on a pork chop bone after having sliced off and eaten what she could.

Lionel beamed and forked another one to her plate. "Tomorrow night I'll do a couple of chickens if Walter'll help Mama with the wringing and plucking again."

Angelene didn't respond, but exchanged a glance with Rosa. Rosa said, "It'll just be the three of us tomorrow night, Son." So that's what the women had been discussing earlier in the afternoon when Shep returned from his walk. He knew it had to be as soon as Mama Gran could travel, and she was noticeably better, even had a happier countenance after this morning's pilgrimage.

"Thought I was the doctor," Lionel said. "I haven't examined my patient today." He took a long drink of tea, the jagged pieces of ice, chopped with the icepick from the fifty pound block in the bottom of the icebox, clanking against the sides of the glass. Then he said, "She can travel. No need to check her." He smiled reassuringly at Mama Gran. "More than one miracle happening around here."

Joyanne stopped nibbling at her okra as she figured out what was being discussed. She hustled to Angelene. Angelene scooted her chair out enough and pulled her up on her knee. "I'll come back," she said. That was enough to satisfy Joyanne. She got up and haltingly chased a robin which had been inching closer to the gathering as if daring someone to challenge it.

They moved inside after picking up their dishes and leavings and Walter went to do the milking. Rosa shooed everyone else out of the kitchen except Joyanne, who sat with a coloring book and crayons. Shep and Lionel settled down in the living room with the checkerboard while Angelene helped Mama Gran get to bed, though it was very early, not yet evening. Shep obeyed Angelene's indication to him to stay when she came into the room later and sat down to look through a family album. But after Lionel's game had fallen apart and Shep had three kings roving at will and hating to take advantage of Lionel even in a no-bet checker game, because she was leaving him in the morning, Shep stood and said he was going to sit on the porch.

He could hear them discussing the photos. "My daddy, Paulus," and a minute later, "That is Beverly," and Angelene's "She was beautiful," and Lionel clearing his throat several times.

Shep stepped inside and said he needed to get a little more walking done. "Just as well you took that brace off again," said Lionel. "I expect you wore it out."

He took his stick which was leaning in the corner, and walked under the waning moon down the road until the church was in sight, sore and tired and hot when he got back. He quietly sat in a chair on the porch, because the swing squeaked a little and he didn't want to wake Joyanne, in the room just inside the other end of the porch.

"You're right," he heard Angelene's voice say through the open window of the living room. The light had gone out as he walked up and he'd assumed they had gone to their rooms. They must have started out of the room but gotten into a delayed conversation. "Walter has found his place in the world."

"So he'll return," Lionel said.

Shep cautiously stood and walked to the steps and down them but he heard a little more.

"There's no doubt he wants to," Angelene said.

"You ... I ..." Lionel said, as Shep reached out-of-hearing range.

Walter had the luggage loaded. He carried Joyanne and a cardboard box that Rosa had filled with sliced ham and a jar each of bread and butter pickles and peaches. Rosa, Mama Gran leaning on her arm, arrived at the car where Shep waited. Angelene had been outside but had hurried back in after fiddling with the tortoiseshell comb she had secured her ever-thickening hair back with. But it was still in place when she returned. However, the silver and jade bracelet was missing from her wrist. No doubt she'd left it as a parting gift for Rosa.

He was sure she was in the quandary he was. How to show even a token amount of thanks for the care and generosity bestowed upon them. He'd gone into Joyanne's room and left a ribbon on her pillow, with a note explaining it was for bravery. If anyone ever deserved it she did. He'd left Rosa one of the two jeweled hairpins he'd bought from the artisan's tray being passed around in the ward at the hospital in Spain where he'd spent a few weeks. He hadn't been able to see it there, but the Red Cross worker's word that they were elegant had proven true. Dorthea might even have liked them, but now, if she didn't want to wear them she had an excuse because there was only one for her.

Lionel was already gone, had left for the hospital a couple of hours earlier. Shep had come down early to tell him goodbye and shake his hand in thanks. Later he had stood his walking stick, which he had decorated with vines instead of a snake after second thought, realizing he could not duplicate the physician's staff with serpent, against the wall outside Lionel's room.

Rosa helped Mama Gran settle in the back seat, then went to stand by Joyanne as Walter arranged the box in the trunk, already packed like a ship's hold, including another box of food items Walter had gone to the neighborhood store and purchased. Rosa and Walter were quiet except when Joyanne required some response. They apparently had settled things earlier, too, and were satisfied with it, as they had moved comfortably together, fitting and re-arranging the goods.

Angelene hadn't exited her room until Lionel had left. All, whatever the conclusion they had come to, had been said last night.

THIRTY-FOUR

"We'll probably be in Memphis before dark," Angelene said, drawing a line on the map with her finger, after they'd gotten through Nashville.

"If we don't have any more detours," said Walter.

The two-lane road wound through mountains, actually foothills of the Cumberlands, not high to someone who wasn't accustomed to mostly flat delta land. He'd flown over higher in Europe, high enough to give him pause, and ridden over higher going from Washington to Patsy's farm in West Virginia. This time of year they were thickly green and at times nothing was in sight other than trees. They met only a few cars and log trucks, the logs extending ten feet behind the trailers, almost dragging the ground with their red flag tied on to warn drivers.

Walter knew his driving, and gave it his full attention. Mama Gran was nodding off when Shep glanced back. Angelene was staring out her window as if nothing was there except space.

"Hold on!" Walter suddenly shouted. "Lord Amighty! Hold on!"

Shep wheeled his gaze back to the front. A log truck was descending toward them just out of its bend about a football field's length ahead, its brakes shooting sparks. The cab was sideways, and that's what saved their lives when the load shifted and a chain broke. Walter fought the car to a stop, as far to the side as possible, with nowhere to go to dodge, a steep bank rising on their right and a steep bank falling on their left and no chance of outrunning it in reverse.

The truck careened faster than it could have gone under engine power, the cab still sideways, the whole thing hurtling toward them like a snorting beast. Then the cab straightened and the bed began to angle sideways, swiping at saplings close to the road, then straightened again. Suddenly the whole thing came to a stop, almost as if it were aimed at stopping at that point exactly, managed from the Herculean effort of the driver, the front of the driver side against the front bumper of the Cadillac toward the edge of Walter's side.

"Godamighty!" yelled Walter, managing to cross his arms over his face. "No!" screamed Angelene, throwing herself on Mama Gran. Shep thought "What the Hell!" but heard himself utter "Good God!" barely getting it out before the rig stopped.

The next instant, as the driver must have been congratulating himself and thanks was forming in their minds, he gave them a glance, looking even more surprised through his thick glasses hanging crookedly on his nose, then closed his eyes in eternity as the top log, a southern pine forty feet long, came loose and shot as if from a flume into the truck cab, spearing the driver, bolting him against the truck. Another pierced the truck's hood, missing the engine like a needle finding the hole in a button, stabbing through into the ground blocking Walter's door. A third, like a javelin, hurtled itself one end down, lodging in the road between the truck bed and the cab, acting as a brace for the rest of the logs as they slid against each other around the bed like gargantuan pick-up-sticks dropped by a giant, broken chains dangling.

Shep rolled his window down. "We'll have to get out the windows on this side! No room to open the door!" He didn't yell the obvious, hurry! more logs could come tumbling any second.

"Mama Gran!" Angelene said, shaking her shoulder.

Shep rolled his window down and pulled himself out, with Walter pushing, barely enough room to move against the mountainside. He made room for Walter, whose door was blocked by the log, hurrying behind him. There was only room for one of them there, so he backed away to let Walter help Mama Gran out and then he helped Angelene as best he could. Walter was already climbing up the bank with Mama Gran's petite body. He and Angelene helped each other up and they roused Mama Gran. There was no reason to hurry back for the heroic driver.

The logs were groaning, as if they would all tumble. "Let's get Angelene and Mama Gran on up the hill," Shep said. "Then we've got to flag traffic before there's a pileup."

"What in God's name happened?" said Angelene as they again helped each other farther up the steep incline. Walter was again carrying Mama Gran.

"His brakes failed. Load of logs like that builds up momentum," said Shep.

"The driver?"

"Didn't make it. How he got it stopped we'll never know."

"We're all right," she said, her shaking voice relaying just the opposite. "Go on and do what you have to."

They found some red flags on the seat next to the driver.

Shep took a couple of the flags and worked his way around the wreck downhill, and Walter went uphill.

It was late afternoon and the wreck was still being cleared. Walter had been reluctantly exonerated. All in the car had been required to show their identification. They must be recorded as witnesses, the officer said. It was determined that the truck had exceeded its load limit, causing brake failure. Much contemplation had gone into the cleanup of the wreckage. Wreckers had wended their way from both directions.

But how to get the precarious pile cleaned up and relieve the driver of his heavy burden and relayed to his hometown twenty miles back, had concerned them for some time. Finally, Shep suggested a tow truck be parked in front of the cab and roped to trees on both sides to prevent slipping. Another tow truck could use its winch to lift the logs from the back, with less risk of the top logs rolling downhill and injuring anyone.

But first the Cadillac would have to be moved. He said, "Walter, would you let me -" but Walter didn't even let him finish. Men who had come to see as well as other traveling men and lawmen put their force against the log which was against Walter's door so he could back down a way and park as far to the side as possible.

The tow trucks arrived and got in place. A log truck was sent from the mill fifteen miles ahead. It required backing in from the nearest place available to turn around in, a quarter mile ahead. Another came from the other way and had been backed up the road for a half mile. No turn around room closer.

Shep looked up the hillside. Angelene and Mama Gran were still on a blanket under a tree. A woman of about thirty was being escorted by the sheriff to the scene. She had brown hair twisted into a knot on top of her head and was dressed in a country woman's clothing, with stout shoes and cotton socks. She stood in her faded dress with a colorful ruffled apron covering most of it, almost as if she had hurriedly grabbed a presentable apron to disguise her old housedress. She got a handful of apron and began to wring it and pushed the sheriff away when he tried to stop her from looking in the truck cab. "Buford," she said, then screamed his name again and gave way, falling into the sheriff.

Angelene hurried down to them and put her arm around the woman's waist. She looked dazedly at Angelene, tried to pull away.

"Now, hon, Miz Bailey," said the sheriff, "you go over there with Miss Midnight and her grammaw."

Mrs. Bailey started to the cab again. "Now, you be good, and go on," he repeated, stabilizing her. "I see Missus Hughes over there." She let Angelene lead her away, with the Sheriff helping. They settled her on the quilt next to Mama Gran and poured her some water.

Another lady, apparently a traveler, climbed up to them, and another.

When Shep looked back again, Angelene motioned him to send Walter to her. Then a representative of the lumber company asked him a question or two. The next time he looked across at the quilted hill, Angelene was kneeling over something, boxes, baskets, lifting something from them — he was astounded as he watched her serving her store of food to stranded travelers. What would this crazy, amazing woman do next?

Next time he glanced that way, Angelene was moving toward him with a cup of water. She asked him to come speak to Mrs. Bailey. "She wants to know what happened." As they made their way up, he heard Mama Gran say, "... if you can't, but at a time of trial, especially in your condition, you get weak."

Mrs. Hughes said, "You're an old lady who has learned a lot with the time given her, I 'spect."

Mama Gran nodded. "I've tried."

"She should eat," Mrs. Hughes said, then turned to Mrs. Bailey. "The baby ... you got to think of it."

Angelene dropped to her knees on the blanket, like her legs were kicked out from under her.

Then it struck him, the apron was to cover up Mrs. Bailey's early stage of pregnancy, which Mama Gran had noticed anyway. Mrs. Bailey watched him maneuver to sit, and looked from him to Angelene, but accepted it for whatever it was. Shep told her about the accident, trying to recount it exactly as he saw it, but using words like "sliding" instead of "careening," "brakes had failed" instead of "brakes smoking," and she cried silently as if it were taking her last effort to understand what had happened; even in the shade and waning daylight, he saw her chest collapse on herself with each sob, as if the maker of disaster had his arms around her ribs squeezing.

Shep understood she wanted all the details. The first letter he'd written to the family of one of his men, he'd been soft and mostly silent in the narrative, thinking being spare with details would spare them pain. He'd gotten a request in a letter from them, wanting to know all the agonizing details. So he knew for some it had to be that way.

But he couldn't leave her without letting her know what he had thought watching the man wrestle the big bull of a truck. Many a man would have jumped from the cab, leaving the truck and anything in its way to mercy's judgment. "He fought it like a bull rider in the rodeo. But he didn't jump off. He was a hero. He did his job and had it won. But," he thought back to when he was spared and hoped his voice wasn't quivering with the sadness and mystery of it all. "But, sometimes it's not what we do." He remembered the surprise in the man Buford's eyes just before he died, realizing he thought he had had the situation licked, and then ... that. That next unexpected bolt to his chest. "It's just not up to us."

Mrs. Bailey nodded, and when Mrs. Hughes handed her a plate, she looked at Mama Gran, who said, "Try a little." Mrs. Bailey picked up a piece of cheese and began to nibble on it.

As darkness began to fall, and he and Walter ate cheese on a piece of bread that Angelene had brought them, Shep became aware of what he'd noticed but hadn't really thought much about, a man wearing a hat with card proclaiming "Press" stuck in it. He had a big black box-camera ever at his face. He would move to a scene and carefully focus his discriminating eye on a minute area – a two-man saw at work; or he'd stand back, even climbing a tree to get the big picture, the truck, the logs, the men.

Now, with light fading, the camera's flash bulbs' shooting star brilliance and ebullition became all the more noticeable, bringing the man's activities to focus in Shep's thoughts. In the worker-ant activity of the clearing up process, the photographer had been just one more doing his part. But now that things were finishing up on the road, Shep noticed the man widening his range to the widow and her comforters on the hillside. He was intrigued by the group, getting several exposures of them, but was drawn back by the sudden commotion at the wreck.

At last the javelin log was being pulled back and Buford's body freed. He was carefully placed on a stretcher and into the ambulance which had come from downhill.

Mrs. Bailey, helped by Angelene and Mrs. Hughes, made her way down to the white open doors at the back of the red-crossed vehicle. Then Mrs. Bailey and Mrs. Hughes got in a trooper's car and followed. The photographer snapped one final picture. Angelene turned away as she realized what was happening, but too late.

Shep went to say good-by to the sheriff.

THIRTY-FIVE

They had been quiet for some time now, back on the road, with darkness all around. The road had descended southwest to rolling, soft hills, no longer mountainous.

The truck bed had at last been hooked to one of the wreckers and the cab to another and hauled away. Food items were cleaned up and everyone finally in their cars, almost reluctantly, as if they didn't want to leave a successful get-together.

The sheriff had held traffic and motioned Walter to pull away first. Traffic poured around both ends of the curve and the parade behind them disappeared before long, leaving them to wonder where all the travelers had dispersed to, as one by one the headlights behind them and the lights they met had gone.

Shep turned around to see what was happening in back. Mama Gran was sleeping, curled up on the seat like a child, her head resting on a pillow in Angelene's lap. Angelene's head reclined on the seatback, but she spoke. "That newspaper photographer. He kept snapping pictures. You'd think he wasn't there to cover the wreck."

She didn't say, snapping pictures of her, but that's what he had done. Guess he didn't often see a woman who looked the way she did, who took charge of a situation like that, by-standing women gladly accepting her suggestions and directions as they wouldn't have at another time and place, and conjuring a meal out of nowhere for them all. She had even started a collection hat handed around for the widow.

Shep had a feeling that would easily make the Nashville paper as one of the so-called "human-interest" stories the news people were looking for these days to counter the war horrors, as they did ten years ago in the depression. She might be right to worry. News traveled even faster these days. And farther. Who knew what press service would pick up a story like that in the midst of a gory tragedy. "I wouldn't be surprised if it makes a paper," he said. But he could give some comfort. "I told the sheriff back there we'd appreciate it if we could keep our privacy. He told me we'd earned that privilege. Said he couldn't keep the pictures out if they chose to use them, but he didn't have to give them our names. Said he'd speak to the ladies."

"Mercer might even know someone around here. Have them on the lookout," she said.

"Probably has people who know people all over the country," said Walter. It was a confirmation, unnecessary, of what Angelene had told him about Midnight, and a confirmation that Walter understood that she had told Shep about her life.

"I should have hidden under a blanket back in the trees," she said with some sarcasm.

"Shouldn't you help the less fortunate?" Mama Gran said softly but forcefully in the darkness. "You're excepted from Jesus's words?"

"Less fortunate?"

"Feeling sorry for yourself won't help. And why start that now?" Mama Gran said.

"You're right."

He could look at the map and find an alternate route. Go on county roads down below the state line, then across Mississippi to the river. Use a lot of backroads. But like in Kentucky, that could bring even more complications and uncertainties. The farther south they went, the more interest and hostility this party would get. Before he could decide, he heard a low knocking, a knock under the hood that would not be ignored. A problem was there as sure as an intruder who would break a door down if you didn't open it for him. "You hear that, Walter?"

Walter cocked his head, and Shep was aware that Mama Gran sat up in the back seat and Angelene leaned forward to listen. "Don't hear it," Walter said.

"A knocking," Angelene said.

"I'll pull over the next wide place," Walter said.

A few minutes later, by the time he found a place, the sound had become a Greek chorus of hisses.

"If it hadn't been night, guess we'd of seen the steam," Walter said. He pulled a mechanic rag from under his seat and lifted the hood, opening up with rear hinges instead of from the sides as on older models.

"What is it?" Angelene asked, joining them.

"Stay back a little," Shep said. "It's a leak in the radiator hose."

"Can you see it over here?" Walter said, using his large flashlight to point it out. Water dripped over the hot metal only to evaporate in a puff, like Indian signals.

"What made it?" Angelene said. For the first time since he'd known her, he heard a little distress in her voice.

Walter moved the flashlight back and forth in a grid pattern. "There," Shep said. "Back a little." Toward the bottom of the radiator core it was apparent water had been seeping from a tiny hole. He continued trailing the light over the radiator up and down. Full sun then total eclipse over the radiator. A thin strip of steel, about the length of a teaspoon handle, with the beginning of a curve on one end, was lodged where the core met the bottom radiator end cap.

"Wait a minute," Walter said and went to his toolbox in the truck and brought back a pair of pliers. Mama Gran was leaning on his arm when he returned. He handed her off to Angelene and pulled the metal out of the radiator and examined it, still holding it with the pliers. "A piece off the truck? Ain't seen nothing like it."

Shep put the rag over the fender for him to lay it on. "It's an earpiece, a steel earpiece off a pair of glasses."

"The truck driver wore glasses!" Angelene said. "Are you saying ...?"

"How did it get in here and do this?" said Walter.

"It broke off and hurled like a spear through the grill when the log hit him." She shuddered as she said it.

"I wouldn't place a bet on that in a million years!" Walter said.

Shep had heard of stranger things happening in battle. This shard of metal finding its way through one of the narrow openings of the grill and crashing into the radiator, yeah, it was one in a million. At least. But million to one odds happened every day on the front. He himself had seen the left shoe on Private Bolton's foot be blown to bits, but not even his little toe was scratched. And look at himself. An odds-defying one, for certain. Only thing really odd to him about this was that it hadn't instead sailed a little higher to come through the windshield and pierce his good eye. "Luck," he said, believing it was more than that.

"You don't think that," Mama Gran said.

"No. I suppose it was providence," he said.

"Yes, Divine providence," Mama Gran said. "Not much luck in anything."

"Well, are we lucky enough for it to last until we can get somewhere?" Angelene said.

"It don't look too bad a leak for now," Walter said. "You know anything about car radiators, Mr. Shep?" he said, rhyming it with gladiators, and bending down to look under the engine for puddles.

Shep had asked that Walter address him only by his name, but Walter had been adamant that he couldn't not use Mr., because he was an employee of Angelene's and she called Shep "plain Shep." Walter didn't call his employer Mrs. Midnight, but did use Miss with her first name. And it was "Miss Mama Gran" most of the time too. So, okay.

Shep bent to look under, too, noticing that his knee bent more today than yesterday, thanks to Lionel's flexibility exercises. He said the army was making discoveries and strides constantly to help the injured boys. And the

~ 157 ~

walking and hill climbing today had been good for it. "I never worked on cars much," he said. "But tractors and farm trucks, I knew very well. Hopefully not much difference." He'd had only a truck in high school and college, and Dorthea's cars were taken care of by the dealer.

"No puddles on the ground," Walter said. "Reckon it's all leaked out?"

"It's probably cool enough to take the cap off and see."

The flashlight bounced on water, but Walter poured in the water that Angelene had left.

"Got any tape in the tool box? Might hold it til we get somewhere."

"Believe I do," Walter said.

It was very early morning, the sun would be up behind them before long to chase them with its superior speed through this low hilly country. Grey barns and houses under large trees close to the road turned up regularly, and from time to time a house, probably newer, with smaller trees sat back a little farther, as if it was finally realized that the traffic was going to be a factor. Few lights were on at the early hour.

He heard rustling in the back seat, and Mama Gran said, "I'm awake," to Angelene. "Don't mind moving if you need to."

Again, her head was on pillows in Angelene's lap, her feet propped up, too, on pillows on the other end of the seat.

At that point, Shep accepted Mama Gran's facts of life. She was going to hold on until she could get to her daughter's burial place.

The few little towns and unincorporated communities they'd come through had been snugly sleeping when they'd passed through in the night. "Bootsville is just a few miles ahead, I think," he said. West Tennessee was well-populated with people of her race and he felt a community would be there where they could find service.

"Will there be a place we could stop?" Angelene asked.

She had accepted their reality by this leg of the journey.

"I believe so," he said.

THIRTY-SIX

W alter seemed to have a sense of where the section of town they needed would be, not that the town was large enough to get too lost in. The streets were still deserted. It wasn't light yet, just on the verge, but Walter pushed in the knob to turn off the headlights. They edged past a couple of streets with some large well-kept houses looking to have been built before the Civil War, and some of the Victorian age. They came to the courthouse, the benches under the trees vacant of elderly men watching the world go by at this early hour. Shep thought they would have found this car and its occupants an interesting interlude in their usual show of cotton wagons and beat-up trucks with drivers they knew on a first-name basis.

Walter made the three-fourths around the square, which was one-way going around it, crossed the railroad tracks on a gravel road past the edge of town, and turned onto the first dirt road past the tracks with several narrow plank or shingle-covered shotgun shacks nesting in very small yards. The familiar smell of country, of fertilized dirt, sprayed cotton, cattle fenced close to the road – not unpleasant to him and perhaps un-noticeable, or if noticed, unpleasant to the others – along with alluring scents of breakfast came seeping into the car, the windows being lowered a little to keep them awake although the night-cool air was still around.

The road was narrow; it would have been a squeeze if another vehicle had met them. But not one was parked anywhere around. At the end was a store that was almost bare of paint it was so patched up. The rays of daylight edged up over the roof just as they stopped. The most faded sign he'd ever seen that was still readable said, "Hosannah Store." A gasoline pump stood like a worn out guard in front of it. Shep wondered where the customers for the gas came from.

Just then an old black man in over-alls opened the wooden door from inside and bent to prop it with a brick, then pushed open the screen door and noticed them as they stopped. He stood staring, one hand hooked in the strap of his faded overalls and the other hand rubbing his chin in wonderment. He opened his mouth to say something but didn't as Walter got out. He repeated his pantomime as Shep climbed stiffly out and nodded and said "Howdy." When Walter opened Angelene's door and she stepped through, the old man said, "Lands amighty." Shep was glad for the old man's sake that Mama Gran was staying put for the time being.

"Good morning to you, sir," Walter said, and the angular old man froze like he was a figure saw-carved from a cypress stump.

Angelene was in no mood for that. "I was wondering," she said as if she were the chairman leading a seminar, "is this a place where we would be welcome for a little while?"

The man nodded slightly.

"We'd like to buy some groceries," she said, nodding, with a question implied.

"Yessum," he said, nodding back.

"We'd like to buy some gasoline, too," she said in the same manner.

"Yessum," he said, still nodding back to her. Then he put his hand to the side of his face in surprise at himself, and said, "Well, I mean no m'am."

"We can't buy any?" she said, and Shep recognized a mighty struggle to keep an attitude out of her voice.

"No'm. We don't have gas here."

She looked at the pump next to him. "You're out?"

"No'm. We can't sell it here."

The screendoor was screeched open and let slam shut by a woman as light-colored as any Negro person Shep had ever seen, and as big around as the rain barrels people in the delta kept under their eaves. "Daddy, who you regalin' out here in the dirt? Oh, I see!" She was wearing what looked like a sheet-dress, pink and green flowered, and was barefooted, her large feet as pink-soled as the flowers in her dress. She had light brown hair in profusion, befitting her size, some corralled in thick pigtails wrapped around her head. "Daddy, you go in and get the stove fired up. Slice some bacon off that slab in the cooler."

She huffed out to them and looked in the car as if she knew there was still another party inside. "Won't you come inside, Old Antee?" she said to Mama Gran, helping her out before Walter could interject himself, but he finished the job. "I been expectin' yall," she said as she herded them toward the store.

"*You* have been expecting *us*?" Angelene said.

"Sorta." The woman smiled with white teeth like clamshells, large enough for a woman her size. It made a blazing sight with her large brown eyes in their sea of white, in her creamy face with no wrinkles, the skin being stretched from all the flesh under. He would guess she was about forty. "You a perty thing," she said, gazing all over Angelene.

Angelene appeared as surprised by her as her daddy had been by them. "You know of us?"

"I see why someone be after you."

Sounded like Midnight had put out the bulletin.

"Mr. Smith, I guess you better pull that luxury automobile into the hay barn. No hay in it. No cow."

Walter looked at Angelene and she nodded. He handed Mama Gran off to her and got in the car.

"Check the nests while you in there. Several on the shelves up to the right, and the woodstack behind the old plow."

"Yes, ma'm"

Man, the army could use her.

"Watch out for the chickensnake. He swallowed a egg yesterday, may not be around today."

"Yes ma'm!"

"I wondered what a angel of midnight might look like. But you be a surprise," she said to Shep, stopping the party in their tracks to look him up and down.

So, Midnight didn't know about him. Or hadn't when he got this word out and about.

"That a Army uniform?"

"I'm a lieutenant." He figured Angelene would comment on her not knowing that, but he saw her deciding not to.

"No need to tell me you name. Better I don't know. No need to ask what happened to you. War. It's still a hellish proposition."

"Yes ma'm," he said, and couldn't help nodding.

"My daddy's daddy'uz in the war down here." She shook her head and crunched her brows. "Went with his old master. Ended up fightin' an' bloodied. For the sake of the south!" She shook her head again. "Well, he said it was his home. Didn't know nothin' else." Resignation stained her voice, but in spite of it there was a pride in it, too. "Got berried as a sojur."

Shep thought of what he could say; she watched him as if expecting a response. "He believed he was defending his home. There's honor in that," he said.

That seemed to suit her. "You from down here?"

"Yes, ma'm." He took her at her word not to give too much information.

She assessed him a second or two, then nodded, and then looked at the car. "Well, you'll be a unknown to him. And a little trouble, too, I s'pect. The car, everybody on this road's seen it by now, and that's okay. Hopefully nobody in town did. If they did, we'll know quick. Sheriff'll be plowin' dust to get here."

They walked through the cluttered store to the rooms in the back. The kitchen was everything Pearl's and Mrs. Brighton's weren't. Small and drab and a dearth of utensils and only a few dishes stacked in an open cupboard, and a few boxes of jars and lids for canning on a chair in a corner. But in cleanliness and neatness, they were alike.

The black iron skillet, big enough for an army mess hall, its inside smooth and gleaming, sat on the commercial-sized kerosene stove. The oval wooden doughbowl about the size of a basketball on the oilcloth-covered table was protected from flies with a checkered dishcloth. A fifty pound floral-printed cloth bag of flour was next to the table in a tin bucket on the floor, tied tightly with a cord. The morning's coffee grounds were in a beat-up dishpan in the white porcelain sink, waiting no doubt for the breakfast scraps to be added to be fed to a hog in a pen out back. The washed percolator basket and stem lay in the drainer next to it. Shelves built into the wall were littered with jars of jelly and green beans and pickles and tomatoes, this year's crop not put up yet. Her daddy was at a small table covered with brown butcher paper by the stove, slicing bacon pieces off the slab she had sent him for.

She poured coffee for them out of the large tin coffeepot warming on the stove burner, and went into the store section and brought back a bottle of milk from the cooler. Then she put on another pot of coffee to perk, and set about making biscuits. She poured flour into the bowl, then looked around and counted, adding two more handfuls as she looked toward Walter coming from the barn, then stirred in salt and baking powder with abandon and formed a depression with her fist in the middle of the pile. Then she spooned out one heap of lard from a waxed cardboard box and dumped it into the flour and finished filling up the hole with milk. "Want some in your coffee?" she asked.

Angelene had been staring at nothing, lost in thought, but when it dawned on her what the woman asked, she said, "You mean you don't know?" and laughed as she took some.

"Had that comin'!" their hostess said. She thrust her hands into the doughbowl, squishing all together into a white sticky mess oozing between her fingers, adding more flour as she worked it into a smooth dough ball that lost its stickiness.

"Were you informed personally that we'd be passing through?" Angelene said. "Or was it a general be on the lookout?"

"Mr. Midnight don't know me from Abraham's goat," she said, pinching off lumps of dough, dipping them in flour, rolling them in her fighter sized palms as lightly as if they were soap bubbles, putting them on a large black square pan.

"I want to thank you for your hospitality, Miss ... Mrs. ..."

"Don't tell me I've not said who I am. Miss Hosannah Brewster."

Shep said, "Pleased to meet you," as he got up and reached down the stewpan hanging on the wall that looked too heavy for her daddy, and that he was eying for the grits in the cloth bag on the table.

"You are kind to take us in," Mama Gran said. "I don't believe you're planning to save us for him."

"Not hardly. I known too many women need to get away from their man. But I do have a plan. If it suits you, Miz. Midnight. I'll tell you about it after breakfast."

"I expect you've got it all laid out in a blueprint," Angelene said, with not a trace of sarcasm.

"I'll take that the way you said it. With no pall meant to fall on my character."

Angelene nodded. "It was a compliment."

"I do plan ahead. I'm a competent person, given what I have to work with. Now, you ladies want to relieve yourself, outhouse out back, behind the barn. Bucket of water and necessaries on the back porch to wash. Don't guess it be like where you from."

"Whatever you have is good enough for us," Angelene said, "and appreciated."

"Gentlemen might just wander out into the trees for their business," she said, as Walter entered and put five eggs into her bowl that already held several.

"We sell kerosene, but got to go to the white station over the tracks to get gas. They say we don't know how to handle the coupons. They just want the business. But nobody much in our part need gas, anyway." Hosannah reached for another of her biscuits and lavished it with butter and apple jelly.

"That might be a problem," Angelene said. "Don't we need some, Walter?"

"We could make it a few more miles."

"Do you know how far we are from Memphis?"

"Well, I never been there," Hosannah said.

"Heard tell it a hunderd miles," her daddy said, carefully pouring a little more coffee into Mama Gran's cup.

Shep didn't dispute the old man, but he thought it was more like forty or fifty. He would check the map when he had a chance. But he had a feeling Miss Hosannah Brewster had an arrangement for their fuel needs, like a quartermaster who must plan ahead.

She considered a moment as she ate her biscuit and buttered another one. Angelene had stared at her own plate much throughout breakfast and Shep wondered if it was so she couldn't keep track of Hosannah's consumption. He hoped that was the cause, and that she wasn't getting exhausted with her flight.

"I rekin I have it taken care of," Hosannah said. A blush came on her light-skinned face. "A man works there, be willing to bring a can here when he comes to eat his cheese and baloney sandwich for dinner."

Shep could see that Angelene was a little surprised that Hosannah had a man, but he didn't think Hosannah noticed it.

"Daddy, you go over there in a while. Say I'm out of kerosene to Mr. Buck."

"But ..." said Angelene, before indicating with a nod that she realized there was more to the plan, that here was a woman who foresaw needs, as she did, a squirrel who stored away.

"Mr. Buck. He don't know Riley puts me a little gasoline in a can when he gets the chance. Few drops here, few drops there." Her nose flared. "Somebody come in here, ole truck on empty, don't have no card, we got to take care of each other. Anyway, he be swappin' out the cans without Mr. Buck knows."

"I wouldn't, I wouldn't want you to get in trouble ..." Angelene said. "I have coupons."

Shep saw her wheels turning. She didn't want to possibly be caught at it and be accused of stealing.

"Mr. Buck get his money. I pay for the kerosene. He charges me double. It be enough to take care of the gasoline I get instead sometimes." Then she gave a sly smile. "You can leave me one or two of them coupons." She listened a second. "Got a customer." She heaved herself up and went to the front.

THIRTY-SEVEN

About noon, Riley pulled up in a wrecker and got out with a five gallon can. He was a slight man, much like Hosannah's father, and looked to be in his late twenties. He stood there until Hosannah appeared and told him to come into the store. He shyly nodded at the group that had been watching him. He waited while she sliced bologna off a long roll, red-rag wrapped, put it between two thick slices of white bread she had slathered with Blue Plate, and topped it with yellow cheese she sliced with a wire off a block. She wasted no motion, used little energy, had it ready and fixings put away in a ritual that would have impressed an army efficiency expert.

She nodded toward the back and Riley took his sandwich on the piece of brown butcher paper to the kitchen. She fished some ice out of the cooler with a slotted spoon, put it in a tall glass and poured tea in it and took it to him. When he apparently was through eating, she followed him to the front door and said, "I see you tonight," and he hurried out.

"Riley say Mr. Buck told him be on the lookout for a black car with a tag from some place 'cept Tennessee. Riley couldn't remember where," Hosanna said when he left. "Said Sheriff Gilroy wants to talk to them if they come this way."

"I don't want to cause you trouble," Angelene said.

"I don't expect no trouble," Hosannah said. She pointed to the front where the gas can was. "Riley say just shy of three gallon in it."

"It'll be more than enough to get us to Memphis," Shep said. "But, Riley's news ..." It meant they should wait around here until night, but he didn't want to bring it up to Hosannah without talking it over with Angelene. He looked at her.

"Are you thinking tonight?" she asked him, and he knew she understood his thought. "But I wouldn't," she added, "unless ..." and he said, "I know," understanding she didn't want to bring a possible hardship on Hosannah, putting them up for the rest of the day. "But she probably already has thought of it," he finished. "Yeah," Angelene said, "probably already something in mind."

Hosannah's body began to shake with laughter. "You two got your own language."

Angelene looked mystified.

But it seemed to him they had grown so dependent – or comfortable – with each other they could sometimes understand what kind of problem or solution the other might be considering. That day at Mr. White's station she had of necessity concluded what he had in mind. Although they might not have been in harmony at that point.

"Now, just how long you two known each other?" Hosannah asked. "Lawd, don't say that's why you broke away from Midnight," she finished to Angelene.

Angelene took it better than she would have on their first day together. She'd have sputtered in utter disgust at the notion. But now she laughed and looked him up and down. She and Hosannah had developed some kind of rapport, a mutual respect, in their like competency. Not Queen Bees exactly. They weren't above getting their hands dirty being worker bees, too.

Hosannah looked him up and down, too, appraising. "Hey, I saw him first," Angelene said, smiling, just as Hosannah laughing, said, "You saw him first."

Angelene laughed. "Ever see a man that embarrassed?"

"He happy, though!" Hosannah said, her body still moving with laughter, like a tablecloth on the line being waved by the wind.

"I'm a poor wounded soldier," Shep said, bracing his hand on his stiff leg and hobbling to a chair. "Can't believe you're making fun of me."

"You should have seen him when I met him," Angelene said. "Braced up, slinged up."

"Wonder what he looks like without a eyepatch?" Hosannah said.

"It may be masking a host of imperfections," said Angelene.

"Hey, I don't have to take this," Shep said, pretending to try to get up.

"Nurses idolize him. And he's practically a braggart," Angelene said. "Got all kinds of ribbons and medals tucked away. Gives them away," she said, smiling at him. She must have seen it on Joyanne's pillow.

"I'll hobble right out if you can't show some respect for these injuries," he said.

"Winning and breaking hearts all over, huh?" said Hosannah. "Well, my Riley boy would be real hurt if he thought I was fancyin' up to this white man. Guess I'll have to leave him to you."

"But I don't get him, either," Angelene said in melodramatic tones, stepping over and putting her hand on his shoulder as if to hold him down. She stood close enough that her leg was against his, and he knew she had felt the need to touch him.

It was the first time she had touched him in the presence of anyone else, and although she was joking and playing along with Hosannah in what appeared to be a rite as natural and familiar to the two women as a responsive reading they both knew, belittling of the whole male race if it came to that, it – the touch – was a milestone that he understood as theirs. His and Angelene's.

Angelene was secretly sharing with him, betraying her partner in the game to say something to him.

He had tried not to think of the night on the rock by the river, when they had touched. He had tried not to want that touch again. Tried not to hope that she would want it so much she would come up with a reason to touch. But he hadn't tried very hard. He'd learned with Patsy that he couldn't make himself feel or not feel emotions, have or not have desires. There were there or they were not.

"Yeah, he would be married," Hosannah said. "Yeah," she added somberly. "And it would be for the best. Seein' he's a man like he is."

"Yeah. Best for everybody," Angelene said.

Hosannah, noticing the bittersweet tone, said, "Think I hear a customer," and migrated into the store.

Angelene moved to sit facing him and surprised herself – he knew, because he was as unexpecting of it as he would have been if a butterfly had lighted on it – by reaching up to touch his eyepatch with her fingertip. Mama Gran had been sure he would see again. He had tried to keep the time for the eye opening at the Army hospital in Memphis put away like a stock certificate in a safe, not to be considered until the date arrived. Now he was eager to keep the appointment and get the bandage off. To know once and for all.

"Does it hurt?" she asked. She traced the strap across his temple and then trailed her hand down his ear. He leaned into her hand and raised his shoulder against it.

"No," he answered without thinking of the pain that wasn't too long in the past, that at first must have been what a caveman felt when the crude spear was shoved into his eye by his enemy, with no hope of quelling the sear.

"So we'll talk to Hosannah about staying until tonight?" she said.

He nodded. "Midnight ok?"

"Midnight," she said, not meaning the darkest hour.

He stretched his arm out to reach around her waist as they both still sat in facing chairs. She leaned forward, putting her forehead to his.

"Angelene," Hosannah called as she approached the door. "Not to be interruptin'. I got some girls here want to see what a city woman look like. You 'meanable?"

Angelene backed away and caught his smile.

Hosannah came inside and said. "It be all right. Nobody here turn you in. One reason, they all afraid to catch attention of the sheriff. But they don't know he like a big old hound dog. Don't want a whole lot to do."

"What about, you know, what Mr. Midnight's offering?"

"I'm the only one you got to worry about talking to that rapscallion. Case you ain't figured, I'm the Mr. Midnight here."

Angelene laughed. "My word. Well, I'm not too surprised."

"Now, about the reward."

"I probably, I might be able to match it."

"Now you look here, Miss Angelene Midnight."

Shep thought Angelene would have figured out that Hosannah probably intended some way to cash in as well as get them out. But Angelene probably hadn't dealt with too many powerful people, even of her own color or gender. "Angelene," he said, "I'll bet Miss Hosannah has a plan for that, too." He put his hand on Angelene's knee and looked at their hostess. "Right?"

"Exactly. Now, I'm realizing more than I did even before you pulled up here in your midnight car, that you need to be away from that black heart. If he kept you under that darkness, prevented you from the recognition of folks that would help you cause it's right, whether they get a due or not."

Shep felt the muscles in Angelene's thigh tighten, and moved his hand to his own knee. She stood, facing Hosannah. "If you live in dirt, you have to keep washing yourself or you'll get dirty. But I was taught better."

"Now, don't be too hard on yourself. Like Mr. Shep said, I got a plan. A plan to profit me somewhat and don't harm you, just like the Good Book says!"

Proverbs something. He'd learned his share of Bible verses for Sunday School. Slightly paraphrased, but he believed he followed her train of thought. "So, you'd like to give Midnight some information, enough to collect?"

Her large face lit with satisfaction that here was a man who understood it wasn't necessary to pass up a gift fairly laid in the palm of her hand.

Angelene had begun to calculate, let her business sense come to the fore. "Of course," she said. "Yes, you should."

"But it can't be no false information," Hosannah said. "After all, he know where to find me after all's said and done." Then she crinkled her eyes and tilted her head at Angelene. "If your intentions don't work out. Whatever they be. But I'm bettin' on you." She patted Angelene's cheek.

"You know we're going at least to Memphis," Shep reminded Hosannah. "He does, too," Shep said, looking at Angelene.

"There's no doubt he knows where I'm going," she said. "Memphis. On to -"

"No, don't say more," said Hosannah, holding up her plump hand, showing her pink palm, so fat-puffed the lines seemed to cut the flesh. "But he doesn't know when you'll be there."

Angelene nodded. "So. If you wait to notify him? Say until tomorrow night?"

"Ought to do. But he'll want proof you was here."

"Yes, before he turns money loose. But he lives by his word. You can bank on what he says he'll do."

Hosannah would understand that was not meant to be a comfort.

She said, "I can understand that. It's so nobody don't cross him."

"I want to repay you for – "

"I'm not doing this for recompense."

"Maybe you should accept something," Shep said. "He would expect you to. And you don't want him to suspect that you're partial to Angelene. You'll need some crisp money to show him."

"I can see the wisdom of that."

Angelene reached for her purse but he put his hand on her shoulder. "I'll take care of this."

She put her hand over his. "I'll leave something personal, then. A scarf?"

Hosannah nodded. "That yellow one with the little flowers you had over your shoulders when you got here. Case he don't really want to take it," she added, "I can see it on me now."

"Then it's settled," said Angelene. "Oh, I guess I'm amenable to seeing the girls now."

"You'll be having a fan club," Shep said.

"I'll just pretend I'm from Hollywood, like Arch Jr. thought," she said, following Hosannah into the store.

THIRTY-EIGHT

"They just didn't seem to fit each other."

"Maybe they see in each other what's lacking in themselves," he said, understanding she meant Hosannah and her young man.

"Yes," she said, "I can see where that can happen. If two can manage to accommodate each other."

Midnight and Angelene couldn't have managed that, he felt her finish without saying. Had he and Dorthea recognized that something in the other filled up a space left by nature? But were they complementary? Or were they destructive to each other, like lava that inhabits a volcano and finally tears its lips to escape?

They were behind the barn, not too far back from the side of the house, plucking a chicken that Hosannah had grabbed by the head and swung like a party noisemaker, its neck going round and round until it was snapped and stretched and its eyes popped when she handed it to him, saying, "May not believe it, but I can't chop the head off one."

Hosannah had already put on a small pot of water to boil over a twig fire outside, and had put one of her aprons on Angelene. It circled and met in the front, and was fastened with a big safety pin. Shep was in his undershirt, having earlier come out of his shirt because of the heat, leaving it on the back of a kitchen chair, and had changed into his sweaty fatigue pants, a dishcloth tucked into his belt. He hadn't done this work since he'd helped Thula when he was seven or eight. He didn't mind. As a farm boy, he wasn't under any illusion about food's origins, even though he'd been out of the direct processing of it for many years. "Saving for a new mattress," Hosahhah said, "so if you don't mind, pluck it before anything else. Don't want blood on the feathers. You can bleed it over there." She pointed to the edge of the yard, well away from the house. "Bury the insides. Shovel's in the barn."

Angelene looked like she would gag.

He plucked the feathers, held it by the feet and made a nice slit in the neck for it to bleed out. Thula had taught him to do that so it wouldn't splatter everywhere.

"I don't know if I'll be able to eat chicken dumplings tonight after this," Angelene said.

"Then don't look while I do the real messy stuff." But she watched as he cut the neck off and pulled out the organs and then did the same at the opposite end. After, he dipped it in the hot water for a few seconds to loosen the rest of the feathers.

They were waiting until midnight to leave, as Hosannah had concluded with them. There was no radiator hose at the station that would fit the car, Riley had said. If there had been, he would have been unable to get it to them without Mr. Buck's knowledge. So he checked the cloth tape and doused it with rubber cement glue, saying he thought it would last until they reached Memphis where they could get a hose.

After the girl fan club had left, neighbors wandered in to see the visitors. Kids had run to the back and peered in the barn to look at the long black car, as had some of the men. "Nobody here turn you in to the law," Hosannah reminded them. "Don't nobody but me know about the Midnight offer. Wouldn't matter anyway. They afraid of Northern folk they color just like they be the law down here. And they don't talk about my business." She had squeezed water out of a dishrag with emphasis. "No sir."

They dropped the feathers on a tarp that Hosannah had spread. She told Angelene when they dried to put them into the burlap bag she sent out with them. Shep cut the tips off the big feathers so they wouldn't be pointed and sharp in her mattress.

"This would make a person cuss," Angelene said, feathers flying anywhere but into the bag, and Shep, laughing and pulling out his pocket knife, said, "Oh I would help, but ..." and used it to pry out a few stubborn pin feathers.

Mama Gran sat on the porch, in back here because of the store being on the front, in a rocker lined with ruffled cushions, a washed feedbag spread over her lap, and chatted with the older women. They had brought kitchen chairs to sit on. Their hair was tied up in head-cloths, floral aprons covered their longish dresses, feet bare or in black oxfords. The contrast in the women and Mama Gran was stark, but respect was mutual.

He watched Angelene as she took in their ritual. They would pull a handful from the bushel basket of green beans that sat among them and nimbly separate one from the bunch to pinch off the ends to drop in a pan at their feet. Soon the beans would all be in that hand, snapped into three or four pieces, then dropped into the pan in their lap. They kept Mama Gran busy by asking her questions about living up with the Yankees.

Walter and Hosannah's daddy had gone out to the cornfield with a bushel burlap bag to gather corn, the first of the season, she had said, a little early because she planted a week early this year, the weather appeared so favorable.

Angelene had looked at the crowded stalks in the field that ended at the road. "Is there only one ear on each stalk? Seems like a lot of plant going to waste."

~ 171 ~

He had laughed. "Field corn will have two, usually. This is sweet corn, for cooking."

"But stalks won't be wasted," Hosannah said. "Used for animal feed."

The sound of a car scattered the children playing in the dusty road.

Shep and Angelene huddled against the back wall of the barn. Shep could see the Sheriff's car through a missing board as it pulled up out front. Dust flew before settling again on the sparse gravel in the parking area. The women became silent.

Hopefully it would take Walter and Hosannah's daddy a while, or if not maybe they'd notice the car in time for Walter to wait it out. But no, there they emerged from the tall corn, Walter's head almost to the top of the sweet corn stalks, bending to hold two corners of the heavy bag, dragging it between two rows. That noise must have kept them from hearing the car. Walter had on his black pants and one of Hosannah's feedsack work shirts. She'd insisted he not wear his white shirt to do the work. He'd changed his boots for other shoes.

"Afternoon, Miss Hosannah," the lawman said as he got out of his car. He had light brown curly hair about the color of Hosannah's, oversized hanging ears, big feet and hands like they forgot to stop growing, long body well rounded in the middle, and a droopy face. Hosannah wasn't wrong to say he was a big old hound dog.

"Afternoon, Sheriff Gilroy," Hosannah said.

"Came by for a souse sandwich," he said.

"You ain't supposed to like that stuff!"

"And put some of them homemade sweet pickles on it like last time."

"Yessir!," she said. "Got me another crock of them cucumbers making in the kitchen right now. Come on in out the sun, Sheriff."

He started toward the store then caught sight of Walter and the old man, who had stopped dead still at the end of the row.

He turned to face them squarely but said not a word. She had him pegged. He wanted a handler, like a hound dog did.

"That my cousin, he on daddy's side, three four down, only got here in the night."

"Ridin' the freight, huh?"

"Jumped off at the bend where it slows. Gonna help bring in the crops," she answered again.

"He's a big 'un," said Sheriff Gilroy.

"Look who's talkin'," she said easily, like they'd had this conversation before.

"Guess it runs in the family," he said.

"Look at us," she said, encompassing them both in open air with her arms.

Angelene's mouth dropped open. "Does that mean ...?" she whispered.

"Sounds like they have a mutual ancestor somewhere back in the line."

"Come on over here, Tavious," she called to Walter.

He slung the bag over his shoulder and strode over.

"Where you ride in from?" Gilroy asked.

"Chicago," she answered for him.

"What's your last name?"

"Turner," she said.

"Have to check it out," Sheriff Gilroy said.

"Go ahead. Won't find no writs or werrents on him. Come on in and get the sanwich or you won't be hungry come supper. And Miss Betty know what you been eatin'!"

Shep wondered if Sheriff Gilroy was in the habit of taking his sandwich to the kitchen like Riley did. He wouldn't miss seeing the shirt, and Shep couldn't see even Hosannah coming up with something plausible to explain it.

It was going to be a while. He and Angelene sat next to each other on the ground, leaning against the back of the barn. The sun blazed on them from the west. Southwest Tennessee was hotter and more humid that Lionel's middle part of the state. The chicken waited in a pan covered with a dishcloth and he wondered if it would be half cooked when they took it in. Flies buzzed around it, and wanted to light on his fingers, freshly finished with the gutting and no time to wash them before Sheriff Gilroy arrived. Angelene waved them away with the back of her hand. A wasp came to join them and she ducked her head against him as he swatted it away. Presently they heard the Sheriff's car start and leave. She still had her head against his shoulder and neither of them moved. He was in yesterday's clothes, sweating, smelling of chicken guts. How could she be next to him? He wanted to touch her arm, touch her face. A mustache of perspiration was above her lip. He wanted to put his tongue on it and take it to his lips. He was as thirsty for that salty drop as he had been for the sweet honeysuckle nectar when he was deliriously dying on that Italian ground months ago. The shade from a tree reached them. At last she said, "I guess we'd better go in," and stood. While he was fumbling to get up, she stretched her hand to him. "No, my hand's so –" She laughed. "And the rest of you smells like a rose? Let me help you."

He found the shovel leaning against the wall inside the barn and dug a spot at least a foot deep and buried the offal and the head, feet and the blood. He cut the chicken into quarters in the dishpan, and they went inside. His shirt was nowhere to be seen. He wondered if the sheriff had confiscated it. Angelene pumped water at the kitchen sink for him to wash his hands and the chicken, and then he took it to the stove to drop in the deep pot of water as Hosannah had instructed him earlier to do, and there wadded up in the pot was his shirt!

"Oh, no!" said Angelene.

"Didn't have no long time to think on it," said Hosannah, swishing in in her side-to-side gait. "I'm wide enough I hid it from him coming in while I wadded it up and threw it in."

"I hate to say it, but it's just what that shirt needed!" said Angelene.

"May be the only thing she hasn't already pointed out to me about my sorry state."

"Well, I'll just pour that water out and put some more in with a little starch!" said Hosannah. "Guess you better get the doodads off it first!"

He laughed, and thought it was lucky that it was the summer khakis made of cotton that he was able to buy before leaving the hospital. Officers purchased their own uniforms, so he hadn't had to wait for an order to be sent down the line. He wasn't sure how the olive drab light wool would have done in a boiling bath.

THIRTY-NINE

The shirt hung stiffly on a line stretched from a porch post to a lone fence post, with no fence remaining. Walter and Mr. Brewster shucked corn in the shade out back, hacking off the worm-eaten ends with large butcher knives. Then Mr. Brewster sharpened a couple of short, thin knives with a file while Walter dipped the ears in a bucket of water and stacked them on a clean cloth about the size of a small tablecloth. Hosannah brought two large dishpans and her father showed Walter how to cut the kernels off. Shep had done it as a boy that way, just like Thula had taught him. Slice the tops of the kernels off all the way around the cob, then another slice all the way around taking the middles, then a third slice to finish up the kernels. Then a spoon was run up all around the cob to take out the pith and all the milk left on the cob.

Shep couldn't help thinking how it would taste after being cooked for a while in a big pot with some butter and cream. But his yearning was also for the days when he did that and other simple but life-replenishing chores. When the hot sun made everything slow down. When the high blue overhead made anything he wanted seem possible, and made him believe it could go on that way forever.

Hosannah's father said cutting corn was too messy for Shep. Walter, his sleeves rolled up and a butcher apron tied high under his arms, stood on the ground at the edge of the porch, the prepared ears to his left, the pan for the cut corn in front of him, the washtub for the shorn cobs at his left foot, making it a rote task such as the army would have been proud of. Shep kept his make-do apron on and got out his pocket knife again, washed it and started slicing. He was already going to have to change clothes before they left. The cobs piled up quickly and the old man dragged them in the tub to a bin by the barn.

By the time they took the last pan of corn in, Hosannah had the rest of the corn coming to boiling in a big stewpot, and was lifting glass jars out of boiling water. When the corn was ready, he watched Angelene help her fill the glass jars with corn and then seal them with lids and rings and put them in the pressure canner to steam. He was almost surprised to see a modern cooker there. Hosannah probably had a plan for recouping its cost, sharing it with the other women. She put the last of the corn on to cook for their supper. She put the green beans in the big cooler in the store, telling the women they'd get them canned tomorrow. The kitchen was as hot as a steam bath. He'd seen it done all his life, but Angelene apparently hadn't, and took interest in it, as if she'd be demonstrating it later. When the time was up, she carefully lifted the jars out of the water to cool on the table, and wiped her face with the big apron. She smiled when Hosannah told her to listen for each lid to ping and indent slightly to insure the seal. "Guess you spent a pretty penny at the stores up there," Hosannah said. "Yes. I don't know if it was harder making that money or doing all this," Angelene said. "That's one!" as a jar lid popped.

"You got nowhere to go," Hosannah said to him. "But we want to talk girl talk. I got to find out the latest fashion!"

"He probably knows more about it than I do! Probably shopped in New York," Angelene said, shooing him out. "How about taking a nap on the porch?" So he did. He was afraid of being seen by someone if he walked. And then he did leg exercises and push-ups, able to put more weight on his arm that so recently had been something he had to practically carry. Time was getting short. His leg was still a challenge.

Presently Hosannah had Angelene call the men in for a supper of corn, green beans, and chicken and dumplings, and some of her pickles the sheriff loved. Supper was their big meal of the day because it took her all day to get a meal cooked, she said, what with running the store and dispensing sandwiches at noontime, and now the canning time. Angelene had forgotten her aversion to the chicken killing, or had worked up an appetite, and asked if all the cooks down south were as good as the ones she had encountered so far. Hosannah graciously said it was extra good because of all the help.

They were on the thin blacktop in the shadow of trees on both sides of the road and crossing over one winding black ditch or creek or narrow river after the other. This close to the Mississippi, all kinds of streams wound their way to flush their silt laden waters into their destination.

They had left Hosannah's at midnight. She sent them on a bypass of the town, through wagon tracks that started behind her store that led to wagon ruts in a pasture, which they would follow to find two twelve-foot long boards, one foot wide-by-two-inch thick to cross the drainage ditch that ran along the road. It was a short cut to a lot of places, she said, or a way to get to the highway if you might not want to go by way of town. Just good it wasn't raining tonight, she added. "That big car would sink the planks into the ditch and get stuck." He and Walter had dragged the planks across the ditch, narrow and all but dry now, but deep and wide enough to keep a car from crossing it, and Shep had guided Walter as he inched the car onto them.

Hosannah had said it would take some good driving to get the car across the boards. But she had accurately assessed Walter's driving skills. And he had done it without headlights, as she had suggested. Shep and Walter had replaced the planks in their location and crossed back on foot.

Now it was a waiting game to see if the radiator would steam them on to Memphis. Mama Gran made as little notice as she could, but they all knew when she reached into her black knit purse and got out her bottle of pills and slid one under her tongue.

"This whole trip is taking too long," Angelene said when she thought Mama Gran had dropped off to sleep. "What else – "

"No. Don't ask what else can happen," Mama Gran interrupted her by saying.

PART III

BATTLE IN EBENEZER

Now Israel went out against the Philistines to battle,
and pitched beside Ebenezer ...
First Samuel 4:1

Holy Bible
King James Version
set forth 1611

FORTY

They got to Memphis at two in the morning. Highway 70 took them without many turns to Main Street. "This road goes all the way across the state," Angelene had said, examining her map before they left Hosannah's. Then she got out a U.S. map and said, "Looks like it goes from ocean to ocean. We could just keep going ..."

"Do us no good," Mama Gran said.

"Turn left," Shep said as they waited for a light to change to green. To the north, the edge of town wasn't far away. Straight ahead less than a half mile was the Mississippi River. Maybe a mile to the south was another universe, one where the trio he was riding with could be accommodated. No problem. It wouldn't even be a problem that he was with them. They wouldn't assume the whole ensemble belonged to him. He hoped the police were as asleep for the present as this part of town suggested.

Main Street was lined with buildings of several stories, casting darkness in spite of the street lamps. The streetcar tracks in the street were silent. Tomorrow they would be buzzing with power from the electric wires crisscrossing overhead as the streetcars made their way down the middle.

"Where will we go?" Angelene asked. "Do you know someone here?"

"I bet Walter will know where to turn when we get there," he said.

Walter briefly glanced his way and then focused on his watchful driving. In a short while, he said, "I think I see it up ahead."

"That's Beale Street," Shep said. "Ever heard of it?"

"No," said Angelene.

"I was there once," said Mama Gran.

"Heard about it. Thought it was just talk," Walter said.

"Does this part of town never shut down?" Angelene said, as they sat in the car waiting for Walter. They had found a parking space behind a store called Schwab's. "That sounds like, well, it doesn't sound like a name one of us would have," she had said as they pulled in its narrow drive.

"It's Jewish," Shep said.

"Midnight wouldn't have it in his part of town."

Mama Gran said, "You'll find every kind of person here."

In a quarter-hour Walter returned. "I found us a hotel a few blocks from here. Mixed company won't be no trouble."

He drove east on the street with some fronts lit by light escaping from inside and some dark doorways hiding all their secrets. For about three blocks music could be heard, fading at times, more intense at others, horns, piano and bits of voice, as they cruised. They made a turn and a large building stretched before them. "What is this?" Angelene said. "Not a house is it? It doesn't look like a hotel."

One light made a smokey beacon through a window.

"It's a house," Mama Gran said, the two story columns being lit as the headlights flashed across them when Walter made a turn. "I expect it's been here a mighty long time. Like the one I was born in. Somebody still living there. On hard times."

Angelene craned her head as they passed to see the large area of land around it, its long side porch and two story height. "What is that long area at the back built on to it?"

"That's where their people stayed. Their house slaves," said Mama Gran. "Plenty of the big houses as we go down that river road. Probably be out of sight, though."

Shep could hear no bitterness in her voice.

"It's hard for me to understand, to believe."

"Child, you've lived your life, the large of it, under ownership. To a person of your race."

Just as Mama Gran's daughter had done.

Walter parked on the side of the next street. A two-story stone house, obviously a Victorian mansion turned into a hotel, with a clearly utilitarian addition on one side, sat like a peacock among smaller houses of peeling paint on narrow lots. Its large front porch had been enclosed, and a small painted sign in the yard said "Hotel for Negroes."

Inside, Shep barely earned a look from the old man pulling on his coat as he hurried to the desk upon hearing the bell ringing as they entered. "Welcome, welcome," he said. "How many rooms do you be needing?" Shep paused, not feeling he should act as the one in charge here. "Three," Angelene said, "if you have them."

"Yessum, yessum, three rooms for hire," he said, and Angelene half shook her head as if to say is this all there is to it?

"Middle of the week," the deskman answered, alert to nuances from his customers. "Now, Saturday night, the rooms be rockin'."

"Rocking?" she said.

"They'll all be spoke for," he answered with a big smile. "Will you sign here, please?" He turned the book, ready to allow whoever wished to lay claim to a bed for the night. But by now he was watching interestedly, realizing he had an unusual party.

"I'm maid to Mrs. Rivers. I'll share her room," she said, and signed only one name on the line. Then she signed another line with the name Tom Rivers, as Walter watched. "Her son will have a room." Then she handed the pen to Shep with a little uncertainty. They hadn't thought to discuss this.

He signed in as James Kolosky. There'd be trouble if this ever came to light, using another name, but maybe the captain would understand. Only two other rooms were in use, he noticed as he glanced quickly up the page.

"Best rooms here in the main house," the man said, assessing them. "The rooms cheaper in the other part."

"Yes, we'll take these," she said.

"You the only ones so far," he said. "In the house."

Six A.M. He'd programmed himself to wake, in spite of sleeping just a few hours on the decent mattress under a cooling ceiling fan. He went through a routine of stretching his leg and arm, and then sit-ups and push-ups, feeling some help from his injured arm, then to the stairs and down for a walk around the block. But he decided against it in case he attracted attention in this area and decided to walk the stairs instead. But they were squeaky so he didn't do that either, possibly waking the others.

Back in the room he unpacked his shaving gear and clean underwear and socks, which he had laundered at Lionel's. He had refused Mrs. Brighton's offer to do his laundry, saying GI's did their own. But he hadn't washed any outerwear, knowing he couldn't iron. Mrs. Brighton and Angelene had laughed at the army green skivvies and undershirts he pinned on the line, and Mrs. Brighton had mended a hole in a sock.

Hosannah had done a great job on the boiled shirt. He put on what he would wear after his shower and took everything else down to get laundered. He didn't have many spares on this trip, but even the small duffle was almost more than he had been able to manage at first, slung over his shoulder or tied over his back like a pack.

He had heard Walter's shower last night, washing the field dirt and corn cutting off, and knew he had already left to get the car seen to, so he headed to the central bathing room with tub and shower. The Gentlemen's toilet connected on one side of the bathing room and the Ladies toilet connected on the other side, with doors opening to the hall, and there was yet a third door out into the hallway from the central bathing room. Lots of doors to tap on politely and locks to check, but practical, large, and almost opulent, befitting the mansion that it had been.

He took off his clothes and laid them over a chair, smoothing them, hoping steam from the shower would help. It was something like an oversized laundry tub with a ring supporting a shower curtain and a shower spigot dangling from a pipe. He felt like whistling. Getting clean did that to people, didn't it? Before long he wasn't even worrying about using too much hot water. It felt good on his leg, his arm, his back. He thought a long soak in the tub would have been good, but wanted to get through before Angelene and Mama Gran would want the room.

The tub was a big white porcelain one on clawfeet, probably original to the house. He'd heard Memphis had a good water supply far underground. Water and its source always interested him because of its importance and regular scarcity on the farm. He'd had the well that Ulys's boy drowned in – that's how he usually thought of it, sadly, though the boy still breathed – filled in with dirt and had water trucked to the houses while he had a new one dug fifty feet away and had a pump and spigot installed.. Dorthea's daddy had not complained, just said it should have been done long ago, and drove to Memphis for the duration of its installation.

He took the patch off his eye, keeping the eye closed as the water washed all around it. The lid fluttered when he cleaned it daily. But he was careful to only open it to put the drops in, and he held it open with his finger.

What would happen if he let it open? Had the lid been inactive too long? Would it stay open if the eye could see? He pondered that as he dried off, then focused on his injured leg, looking at the indented area made by the missing flesh in the thigh, the skin healing over it in soft red patches. He touched the scar valley just above the knee, moving and flexing his leg with the heat of the shower still penetrating his limbs. His side had healed and stitches been removed and he felt no lasting effects from that first slicing that day when the tank exploded. The steamy room became too much for him so he raised the small window and felt a welcome gust. He arranged a clean patch over his eye.

When Walter learned how long the car repairs would take, if there was time enough he would hire a cab to the army hospital, out on the eastern edge of Memphis, and ask if a doctor was available. His heart quickened, telling him he didn't know if that's what he really wanted to do. Find out. He wanted to put off the knowing if it wasn't going to get him back to double vision.

He rotated his shoulder and stretched his arm, looking for a sign of improving muscle appearance. He would get back on weights, try some of his old football regimen to build himself up, sorry specimen that he had become.

Just as he was about to step into his shorts, the door from the Ladies' opened and Angelene stepped in, carrying a small satchel. "Oh!" she said, stepping back outside as he said, "Sorry!" and wrapped a towel around his waist.

"I thought you were finished."

"You can come in," he said, "I'm halfway decent now." She stepped in, surprising him that she did. She was in creamy colored pajamas and a robe ending at her thighs and tied around her waist, and flat slippers. Unlike the long look he had given her, she looked at anything but him. He slung another towel around his shoulders. "My body's been looked at by a hundred people," he said. "Got used to it. Shot to hell look didn't improve it."

She pulled the towel from his shoulders and looked over his body as if she were on a reconnaissance mission. She stopped at his leg, bending enough to touch the trench with her fingertips. "How you must have suffered. I'm so sorry." She brought her fingers to her lips and then put them back on the scar.

"It's okay," he said, enclosing her. "Suffering is when it's so bad you don't come back." She cared about his hurt body, he had known it. She'd made up her mind to answer her own questions since he hadn't told her. But damn it, how do you tell this without appearing to ask for sympathy? Maybe that's what he would have been doing. He didn't think he was embarrassed to look like this. He couldn't be. He had survived. He felt rather than heard her sob a time or two and stifle them. "Angelene, no." He'd never held a sobbing woman, maybe never had a woman sob over him.

Patsy had cried as he left her in her parents' doorway, but he knew she cried for herself and the damned deal that fate had forced upon her again. He believed Dorthea would not be caught dead sobbing. As far as he knew, she hadn't shed a tear when her grandfather and father died. But whether she would have or not, if she had known the extent of his injuries, he would never know. He had chosen not to tell her those months ago.

"I wish, I don't know. That I was a nurse. That I could have taken care of you."

"No, I'm glad you weren't there."

"Think I wouldn't have been up to it? Run from blood and raw flesh?"

"God. No. That's the last thing I would think about you." What if it had been her instead of Patsy? If she had cared for him. Would he have made himself run from her on this home-bound journey?

"Think I wouldn't be here now if I had seen you as you must have been then? Bet you couldn't even feed yourself. You look skinny."

No. He wouldn't have been unable to hope that she would still look at him as a man who had survived intact. He put his lips on her throat and resisted taking a bite of her flesh. Not even a kiss dared form against her skin. She pulled away.

He tried to keep it lighthearted. "I look that bad?"

"No," she said, pushing a finger against his chest, "not what I expected! Lord, from the way you hobbled about I figured you were half missing!"

He laughed. "Did I play it up or not?"

She wiped at her face and smiled and leaned into him. "I'm happy to see you healing. To see how much better you are than when we met. You make me happy."

He put his arms around her. He felt so lighthearted he wondered if this was what happiness was. He made her happy.

What she must have been through with Midnight. And maybe that was part of her crying a minute ago. For here he was, a man who she realized wanted to do every sweet thing to her that a man could do for a woman, maybe since he saw her step out of that car. And despite that he was war-torn, despite that in plenty of places including where they were, it would be against the law, she had wanted that from him. He couldn't be what she must have pictured herself wanting during the years whenever she had allowed her mind to go with the possibilities. She must have dreamed of another type of man. Someone like Lionel.

His mouth moved to her chin and up her jawline, a brown- butter molasses candy of flesh and bone.

She put her hands on his hips and he stirred. She laughed.

"Hell. Sorry. I'm sorry." Just because she wanted him and he knew it, and he wanted her and she knew it, that didn't mean what they wanted was going to happen.

"I guess men are men," she said.

He smiled at her happy tone and rubbed her back, feeling her bones through her night garments. "Even gentlemen?"

"Even white gentlem – "

He put his finger to her lips, tilting his head toward the men's door. They listened as the door from the hall into that room opened and closed and the lock on that side clicked. She put her hands to her ears when they heard the man's stream start. She shook in his arms with silenced laughter before pulling away to start for the women's door. He grabbed her, his look saying don't go. He leaned over and started the tub faucet, the water drowning out any sounds from next door. In a few minutes he turned the tub water off and tapped on the men's door and listened and unlocked his side and opened it a bit. The guest had returned to his room. "He must have checked in this morning."

"Yes, I know," she said. "I paid the clerk to let me know."

He wasn't surprised. She molded against him, her soft parts against his hard ones, her long hard arms and legs against his soft wounds. Then he kissed her, wanting to and knowing she wanted him to, and so she wouldn't have to be the first. She kissed him back, unhesitatingly, and then as an aggressor.

At first it couldn't be called having sex. Making love, yes. Kissing, touching, feeling, pulling away, back together and doing it all over again, and finally the rush as if another second would be too long to wait for the loving they had tried to avoid these days past. Him bracing against the wall, her leaning against him, knee bent at his hip, her pajama bottoms at her feet, her top still on, hiding her breasts from his hungry eyes, helping each other get connected. And then sounds telling that their mission to be for each other and give to each other at least this one time if never again, was accomplished. Some might have called it simply having sex by the end of the episode. Then nothing but a struggled–for silence for a few minutes with her head against his neck and his head in her hair and his arms holding her so close he finally wondered if her breasts were hurting against him, and he gave her a little more space. They had given to each other, and then taken what they had wanted for themselves, knowing they were welcome to it.

"You know. How I felt from the start."

"Yes. And why you couldn't do anything about it. I'll help you get dressed. Mama Gran will be awake by now," she said, reaching to hold his shirt while he pulled on things. She'll know what we've been up to."

He hated to think that Mama Gran might be disappointed or angry at Angelene. Would she worry about her granddaughter's soul? But wasn't her marriage to Midnight null and void from the day he forced her? Would the old lady absolve her? Even then, would she condemn her for being with a married man? And would she think less of him?

He opened the door to the Women's. "I could swear that I had locked this door," he said.

"It was locked." She flashed a hairpin from her pocket.

It took him a second. "You picked the lock?" He wondered why he was surprised at anything she did. "My Mata Hari. I know an organization that could use a spy like you."

"What was a lady to do?" she said. "You were such the gentleman."

He wished he'd been the first to give in, to hell with all the reasons he couldn't have.

He leaned into her and pulled her close, still as happy as he ever remembered feeling. Her hair, even thicker now from the steamy bathroom, tickled his nose and chin.

"I'm getting my hair done today. Somewhere."

"I like it, liked it every day and every way," he said.

"That's because you like me."

"That I do."

"Too soon to do the heat again. I hate the chemicals," she added.

"Then don't do it." One of the earliest things he remembered was when he was about four, and his mother was still in bed with the door closed and lights off, so Thula took him with her to get her hair done. He didn't like the smells and the heat, so she let him go outside to play with his toy tractor. She looked like a stranger when she came outside to go home. She had to hold his hand to make him go with her. Soon she was back to her old self.

"You probably don't know what I'm talking about."

He smiled and said, "I'm just an ignorant man."

"I expect I'd be surprised at some of the things you know about. No, really, I shouldn't be, considering how we met. Who the hell would hobble out there like you did. But this I know. Women have their secrets. All women." She gave him a look, so he would understand that she was revealing a secret to him.

He nodded. He wondered what secrets she could still have.

She touched her hair. "And we'll go through a lot to look our best."

"You could never look any better than you do now. Just different."

"You mean that?" she said, smiling in rebuke.

He twisted a handful of her hair and put his lips to it.

"I believe you think that," she said, and kissed him. "It needs washing. All this traveling. I'll surprise you."

"Can't wait to see it."

She unlocked the door and they stepped out into the hall.

They heard steps at the bottom of the stairs at the end of the hall.

"I better disappear," he whispered. He stepped to his room. She dashed out the bath door after him and darted inside his room with him and put her back against the closed door.

FORTY-ONE

He kissed her until the door down the hall opened and closed, while he un-wrapped her robe and threw it toward the chair. She stepped out of her flat slippers. He unbuttoned her pajama top and slipped it off her shoulders and threw it toward the chair. His hands wanted to be on her breasts but they went to her shoulders, so he could see the stretched skin over the firm flesh and the tightened centers of darker, almost pink shades that called to his tongue like frosting in a spoon.

She wrapped her leg around his ankle and pulled his mouth against her, then unbuttoned his shirt.

Then she pulled his face to her and kissed him while he guided her toward the bed. He put his hand between her legs and felt moistness in her pajamas from earlier. He slid the silky garment down and sent it to the chair, and put his fingertips against her and felt her welcoming warmth.

His tongue finally let go of hers and he helped her strip his shirt off and ignored the pain as he forgot his arm didn't want to straighten, but she noticed and went more carefully. His mouth found her breast again and he pulled her hips against him. She kissed his ears and rubbed her fingers over his head and neck, then he felt her fingers on his woven belt.

She couldn't manage the buckle. He undid it as she bent and untied his shoes and helped him out of his clothes, then kissed his stomach and shoulders as she straightened. "Never done that before," she said. He knew that was true and hated that he was just barely above being glad of it, instead of wanting her to have enjoyed touching and kissing her husband.

She lay on the bed and reached for him, moving over so he could lie by her side. The sight of her there, lean and bared to him, answered the questions he'd refused to let himself consider. He had not even tried to imagine her body inside her clothes. It would have seemed an invasion of her.

He nibbled her lips and licked them and draw them into his mouth and tried not to think of the rest of what he wanted. But she was in a hurry, too, and moved her hands down his back to his hips and pulled him onto her. He braced on his healing arm without thinking and required his mending leg to do its work without asking it.

She lifted herself to him with freedom and desire that he knew she'd never felt before. "I want you," she said clearly, and raised her mouth against his and he felt she didn't want him to speak. He knew this was her time. The time of making love to a man she wanted, and he was grateful to be the one. He thanked the God of war for sparing him for this. He hoped she would not remember the wounds that same war god had given him that had so recently occupied her

thoughts, for he knew she would want to ease him. She didn't. And in a few
seconds even he didn't feel the effort any longer.

FORTY-TWO

"The car'll be ready by nine or ten tonight," Walter said. "I told them to rush, I'd make it worth their time."

Agnelene nodded then took a sip of her coffee.

Walter held his cup of coffee to his lips and blew on it, then added, "The garage has to get the parts from a white place. Another part of town. Big Ford place they say, but they can get these parts for us. Cost a pretty penny."

Angelene nodded again. She seemed to not even be concerned. He didn't look at her. Walter and Mama Gran could easily see that her mind wasn't on the car.

It was lucky parts were available, with so much going into the war effort. Then again, they were repairing cars to keep them running because new ones were hardly ever available, and rationed out around the country when they were.

"You were right Shep, the hose and clamps got to be replaced, too."

Angelene appeared not to notice that Walter had dropped the "Mr." with Shep. Shep was glad Walter probably hadn't even noticed, and that their friendship had evolved to the point where nothing else would do.

They were alone in the dining room of the hotel. Part of it appeared to be the original dining room of the home. An addition on the outer wall allowed three more tables. Its front window opened to the front porch, showing beyond that the smaller run-down houses of the shotgun type, three rooms lined up behind each other, with small porches and yards, many with hydrangeas blooming in large blue or pink balls. Angelene asked Mama Gran if she would like to sit in the rockers on the porch after breakfast.

"It would be a treat," Mama Gran said after taking a moment to consider, "the front porch of a house like this."

"I'll get a cab to drive me to the Army hospital out on the edge of town," Shep said. "It's about time this scrap got lost," he added, pointing to his eye covering.

"Hmmm. It'll be interesting to see both your eyes. Maybe you won't be as dashing," Angelene said, appraising her coffee cup more than him.

He could tell her heart wasn't in teasing about it. The stakes were too high.

"Tomorrow, I could drive you," Walter said. "If we weren't leaving first thing."

"I could spend a week here," Angelene said. She turned to look out the window.

There wasn't any reason to discuss it.

The doctor came into the small room and introduced himself, Drew Mitchell. "Your records haven't reached us yet, Lieutenant Haddon. It's not surprising, though. So."

Shep didn't say he was two weeks early.

The young doctor was dressed in khaki with a white doctor's coat over. His cordovan shoes were shining like polished stones, just as any new recruit's did. He was probably just out of med school when he got drafted and sent to this huge Army hospital, built since the war started. He'd seen several one-and-two-story buildings in a grid on this huge campus of lawn and shade trees; he had no idea how many acres, but he thought it would sit in a corner of the over three hundred acre complex of Walter Reed in Washington.

They had come in off Park Avenue on the eastern outskirts of Memphis, and gone straight to the administration building. Then he'd been driven in a jeep to this building. Servicemen in uniforms and hospital gowns and robes lounged outside on benches and in wheelchairs, under several kinds of oaks, hardwoods, and some magnolias.

The doctor washed his hands at the small sink, lathering and rinsing them with abandon, probably just as the book said to. Shep thought back to the dirt and blood that must have gotten on the medic's hands when he was first treated. Couldn't be helped there. He thanked God again for the medic's presence.

"Sit on the table," Dr. Mitchell said. "So, tell me about your injury."

"Just your usual. Piece of German tank, through the cornea."

"Through it?"

"Yeah, into something they called the aqueous humor. How's that for fun?"

"Just a little fluid that nourishes the lens and cornea. And helps shape the eye. And keeps the pressure right."

"Oh. Is that all."

"So. It stopped there?"

"Wish I could say so."

"The iris?"

"Scratched it." He couldn't help but notice the little shiver the young man didn't get suppressed.

"That all?" the doctor asked hopefully.

"Seemed to be. They got that handled eventually."

The doctor nodded but appeared puzzled. "Vision returned?"

"Pretty much. But it always felt like something in it. Took a while for them to find it. By then things were looking blurry. They did surgery. Then it got infected."

"We don't specialize in eye injuries here. I'm a GP. Guess we'll eventually get a lot more patients here from this big invasion on the French coast. Heard a lot of them didn't even make it off their landing boats."

He thanked God his cowardly prayer on his battlefield hadn't been answered. He'd lived. And now he was recovering. God, be generous with those boys like Kolasky had been, who would come back men or not at all. "It makes me grateful for my scratches."

"Hell, man, I wasn't saying –"

"Didn't even think you were."

"And here I am in the lap of luxury –"

Shep laughed. "And I wasn't thinking that."

Drew laughed. "Yeah, Army knows where to find me! I'd walk a mile to see your file."

"Wish they had let me bring it."

"And take a chance on you reading it? This is the army," the young doctor said, shaking his head. "Everything top secret. Much less your own files."

Shep managed to smile. This new doctor could not know of some of the secrets they had. "I've been cleaning it as directed." He'd used the last water in his canteen the night he slept on the hay. "Putting the drops in morning and night. Let's do it."

"Might as well. Lie back. I'm going to cover the uninjured eye."

Shep felt the white gauze square settle over his lid.

"Now I'm going to remove your patch. Keep the eye closed. I'm turning the light off and opening the shade a little. See any lightening behind the lid?"

"Not yet," Shep said, refusing to say no.

"May not mean anything. May take a while for it to adjust."

He heard the click as the ceiling light was turned on.

"We may or may not know today. Go ahead and open your eye. See anything now?"

The lid didn't want to open on its own. He hadn't exercised it. Just the fluttering when he took it off for cleaning and drops, the patch padded to keep it closed. Had it atrophied? It felt like it needed a good rubbing with the heel of his hand like when he was a boy waking too early. "Feels like its asleep."

"Don't rub it," he said, reaching for a small bottle on the table. "I'll put some lubricating drops in. The drops may tingle a little. The lid didn't get injured?"

"No." A little tingling might be reassuring about now. It felt dead.

"Lucky. And unusual. Hard for the eye not to blink. I guess it happened in less than the blink of an eye. But I guess real luck would have been not getting hit."

"They said the lid is hard to repair."

"I'm getting myself in deep, here," Drew said.

"No. You are absolutely right. I was lucky in many ways."

The drops brought the lid to life.

"Blink a few times. Roll your eye around to let the drops spread."

In a minute Shep put his palm over his eye and moved it away, then covered it again. "I see more darkness when I put my hand over it." How was that for grabbing at negativity for hope?

"I'd say that's a good sign."

"Now I see more light," he said, moving his hand away, trying not to be hopeful.

"Even better. Blink a few more times. The drops might not be dispersed yet."

The doctor removed the gauze over the other eye and held up his penlight. "Try to follow this," he said, moving it back and forth."

Shep felt his eyes moving, the injured one hurting a little with the strain. Was that a good sign?

He couldn't tell if he saw the light with both eyes or not.

"Good news," Drew said. "Both eyes are following it." He clicked off the light. "Close your good eye. Can you see me? An outline?"

Shep blinked several times. Damn. Wait. "Blurred, but yes."

"I wouldn't have bet on it. Of course, I'm no specialist."

Shep said, "Thank God for Army doctors."

"Yeah. God and your other Army doctors."

"I'll thank you, too."

He walked for an hour on the precise concrete walks that led from building to building at the Kennedy Army Medical Center. He had a quick sandwich at officer's mess and purchased new clothes at the officer's store. Then he went to the exercise room and used the machines and weights and showered. It was good to be back in the army's arms for a while.

He was in a cab heading back downtown, due west. It was still too early for the sun to set. That was good. He wouldn't want to risk watching it. He wondered if young Dr. Drew Mitchell was more daring than the ones at Walter Reed Army Hospital. But their expertise got him through injury and that was their monumental responsibility. Keeping soldiers alive. Rehabbing them was maybe the responsibility of the next crew.

He put his hand in front of his uninjured eye. Drew thought the vision would get back to normal soon. He could see the back of the driver's head. The cap covering it. The murky form of a car ahead. He was to continue to use the drops twice a day until the bottle was empty. Put the patch over it about half the day for a few days if it felt weak. But he wasn't complaining. Not complaining at all that Mama Gran had been right.

FORTY-THREE

"Let's go in here," Angelene said, tugging lightly on his arm and looking at the café as if she saw the musicians beckoning them.

He'd told her that the two of them together wouldn't create a huge stir on this street. Most people would be her color, and some of them would look, but there wouldn't be trouble. Unless a fight broke out in one of the clubs and the police burst in before they could get away. Most everybody here was here for the music, drinking, dancing, and food, or the card playing in the back rooms. Although some looked for cocaine, some looked for somebody to get with for the night or shorter, and didn't care who else was here for their own reasons. There wasn't as much commotion as on a Saturday night, and only a couple of clubs in full swing. A drug store and movie theatre were drawing customers.

He wasn't wearing the patch. It would be dark enough that the eye wouldn't be shocked, as the doctor had said it might be if he went too long without it in the daytime. The skin around it was like a puckered lemon.

Angelene drew many looks, and he did more than he'd expected. He wondered if the street might be off-limits to servicemen as he didn't see any others. He wished he had some civilian clothing. But then again, Second Army Headquarters was in Memphis, and an article about it in a publication he'd read while in the hospital had caught his attention. Its general had commanded all personnel wear uniforms. Just passing through, if MP's showed up, he could plead ignorance. Although that was never an excuse in the army.

Angelene's hair was pulled back and up with some thick braiding. It was perfect and she liked that he told her so. She wore a black dress zigzagged with glittery threads, very short sleeves and thin netting over a neckline that barely missed showing what a jealous man might think was too much for anybody else to see. The skirt swirled just below her knees when she walked in the high-heeled black shoes with straps around her ankles and toes. He was surprised she would have something like this outfit with her, considering her mission. But she'd brought everything she could with her, hadn't she, because she wasn't planning to go back. Dorthea would not have gone on a trip without it, or something like it, at any rate.

"I know you travel prepared," he said. "But how did you know you'd go partying with a lonesome soldier on Beale Street?"

She laughed and studied her newly polished nails. "A girl should never leave home without a party dress."

"I'm glad I'm at your party."

She laughed. "My mission has been accomplished. So are we going in here?"

The bandstand was just a step higher than the floor, not much bigger than a banquet table. The drums drifted out over the side, and the upright piano would crash if it shifted one inch, which it just might from the pounding it was getting. The trumpet man had lungs that Shep would have wished for when he was at the bottom of the well, but his best attribute was maybe that he was so thin he took up little room on the stage. The slide trombone almost jabbed the closest person at the front table. The man with the guitar apparently had done nothing but eat and practice his craft; he hung over the stool like a feather mattress thrown over a chair on the front porch to air in the sun. And they made beautiful music.

"And it's like this in other places on this street?" Angelene asked when the music stopped. "Even the middle of the week. You get the idea they subsist on it here."

He nodded. He and Dorthea had come around here with her college crowd a few times, but they hadn't visited Beale on their honeymoon. She'd said "Thanks, but no," with a shake of her head and a frown when he'd suggested it.

But Angelene looked pretty high-toned sitting there sipping a cocktail, and from time to time keeping the beat with her hand, or tapping air with a foot dangling from a leg across the knee of the other one. There was dancing in an area as small as the stage, but he hadn't asked her. His leg wouldn't do any smooth moves, but he would have made do. He just didn't want to draw any extra attention.

"I notice you don't ask me to dance, Lieutenant," she said, lifting her chin.

"I was waiting for the right music. Real slow."

"Oh," she said, tilting her head down. "You've made me forget your leg."

"Uh huh," he said, smiling. "And just how did I do that?"

"You are no gentleman," she said, laughing. "I won't make you dance. But only because people would stare. Not because you can't."

He woke from a light sleep to sounds from next door. Then a muffled cry, and a sound that might have been a woman being slapped. Just enough to know it was happening, more than hearing it clearly. Someone else had checked in; the gentleman they had almost encountered this morning was down the hall. And he was not gentle. Hopefully Angelene would sleep through it. She'd wonder if they'd also been heard. He reached to check his watch. Little after two. The clerk was napping when they had returned, and she had tiptoed by not to wake him, or they'd have been informed.

Mama Gran knew, as Angelene had said this morning, that Angelene and he had moved to another place in their relationship. Angelene hadn't said that Mama Gran approved, but she didn't seem to object to what they were to each other now. He hadn't seen disappointment when she'd looked at him today. She'd patted his cheek when he arrived from the hospital, and told Angelene to enjoy her evening, that she would rest soundly in the comfortable bed. Angelene had ordered a meal for her to eat in her room.

He and Angelene had ordered a steak and baked potato and green salad at a restaurant next to the music club. "I'll take you to a booth in the back, here, if you don't mind, Suh," said the waiter. "Fah's I know, we off limits to you."

Angelene looked questioningly at Shep, and the waiter added, "You genelmen in uniforms, I'm speakin' about," as he drew the short curtains around the booth.

After listening to the music, they'd drifted back to the hotel, without even discussing going to another club. Nor did they discuss how this was going to end. What the possibilities were. What the choices were. Were there any? Or was there just the inevitable that fate had in store. God. What a wreck it all was.

Angelene had looked in on Mama Gran and then entered his room. Seeing her come to him, and knowing he couldn't fathom what pain and indignities she might have endured, made him want to just hold her. It almost seemed enough knowing she wanted him. But soon, that wasn't what she wanted. She kissed him and moaned in his throat and ran her hands down him and he knew that tonight was her gift to herself. And he was glad he was the one she wanted, although he felt woefully inadequate. Not just because of his physical state. She deserved more than his miserable self. But she thought differently, and he took courage from that.

When he took off his shirt and threw it toward the chair, it slid to the floor, and she picked it up, smoothed it and put it on a hangar. Then she pressed herself against him until he lost balance on his unsteady leg and they let themselves fall with gentle laughter onto the bed, where lying in each other's arms was enough for a few minutes. She stood and pulled him up, turned her back to him so he could unzip her dress. His arms circled her and his hands covered her breasts and she'd said, "Umm. Your hands are gentle."

He had willed her to forget what she might have been made to endure and snuggled against the back of her neck. Soon she moved away enough to step out of her dress. He hadn't realized what a bit of nothing it was until it was at her feet in a puddle. He picked it up and it practically fit in both palms. "I guess this is what you would call a little black dress," he said, laughing, and tossed it in a ball to the chair.

"Thought you'd like it."

He kissed down her throat and she laughed when he grabbed her black straps with his teeth and slid them down over her shoulders, then undid the hooks at her back so he could kiss her breasts. She let the garments slide down to gather at her feet, standing in her shoes, and put her thumbs inside the elastic at her waist and pulled it down. She stepped one leg over them and with her other toe caught the garments and kicked them away as he laughed.

She had buried her face in his shoulder. "Never knew this could be fun."

It was no good letting thoughts of what he would like to do to her husband enter his mind. He'd tried to only remember that this was her night. He wished he knew secrets of lovers that had been passed through the ages, wished he'd read all the books the guys had talked about, but all he had was his wish to be all that she could want or need for this night.

She had stood before him in her black garter belt and stockings as if to show that she knew she could trust him just to look. She crooked her finger at him to come to her and smiled. "Thought you'd never ask," he said, and knelt and unbuckled her shoes and she stepped out of them. He nibbled up one leg and then her stomach and breast and neck and to her lips, and then down the other side to the flesh above her stocking on the other leg. Then he slid the rubber backing up the metal stocking clasp, front and back to free the stocking, and took time to bunch it down and take it off, he hoped, without tearing them. Part of him knew they would be hard to replace on the non-essential list, unless that was another exception she could manage. But she would like it anyway, so he had resisted hurrying and did the other stocking the same way.

"You get officer training in that?"

"Just a natural."

She reached behind her waist and unfastened the garter belt and slung it around her finger. He dodged and laughed. "Hey, we're allies."

She'd pulled him against her and nibbled his lips and down his neck. "Time to get you undressed, too," she had said, her fingers flying.

Either the sounds next door woke her, too, or she was always the light sleeper she had said the night they'd slept so far apart on Arch's not-abandoned land. She got up and clicked on the radio and turned the dial until she found music, and adjusted the volume just loud enough to disguise the intruding sounds. He got up and they moved in a soft dance with their skin against each other until the song went off.

She left the radio on and pulled him back to the bed. They lay down and she rolled over on her side away from him and he turned that way too, glad his recovering arm was on top and over her. What a wreck he still was. And so tired he joined her in sleep.

"A good little soldier," she said, running her hand over him, waking him, feeling that tightening even before he did.

"Little?"

She laughed. "No, my darling man."

That sounded like something Dorthea would say about her piano player, but coming from Angelene, well, she could call him her darling man any time she wanted to. She kissed him and he felt her tongue reaching for his. He put his hand on her braided hair and pulled her to him until he thought she had finished her exploring and then released her.

"And I think you are the best."

He tried to think of a comeback to tease her. "Your vast experience tells you that."

"I thought it was yours."

"I'm a fraud," he said, serious when he meant to be hilarious. "There's only been one with me, too." But that one had taught him where to touch, when to do what she wanted, what not to do. Not how to hold out until she was satisfied. He'd known that was required from the start. He'd never even questioned how Dorthea had come to know just what she wanted. But with Angelene, no, it hadn't been that way. Each time, there'd only been the knowledge that what each did was just what the other wanted, that each was listening to the other without even making it known.

This time they made love as if they had been each other's comfortable mate for years. She on top, using him for her own enjoyment. He couldn't have enjoyed it more.

"I'll have to go back to Mama Gran's room soon," she said, getting up, pouring some water from the pitcher on the dresser into the bowl. She took a cloth from the rod on the wall and wet it, then washed herself between the legs. He couldn't take his eyes away from her. When she noticed him watching, he said, "I won't watch, if it makes you uncomfortable," and she said, "Why shouldn't you watch?" She wet the cloth again and squeezed it and cleaned her legs. For her to do this, let him watch, it seemed almost more intimate than sex. The trust to bare herself, go through so private a ritual. He got up and walked to her and took a towel from the rack and dried her, and told himself if he stiffened up he was the worst kind of man.

"I opened myself to you. You didn't make me. Why would I mind you seeing?"

He wanted to say something to her that would equal what she had just said and trusted him with, but he could think of nothing. "Don't hide anything from me," he said. "I wanted to be with you from the start. You must know."

"Yes. And I know why you couldn't."

He picked her up and carried her back to the bed. Then he tilted her face to him and made a face that he hoped looked like a sulking little boy. "What?" she said. "Is something wrong?" "Yes," he said. "I would have done all that washing up for you."

"You're a devil!" she said, grabbing a pillow and swatting him.

They slept for a while with her face against his shoulder, her leg and arm over him, until the barest of daylight broke through a narrow space between the dark curtains onto their faces and woke them. "No," Angelene whispered, "the night can't be over!" She bounded off the bed to the window to pull the curtains together. With a hand on each curtain panel, in the midst of dragging them together, she froze looking out the window, then came back to life and stepped back with her hands at her throat.

He jumped up and pulled her away, knowing what it must be. "Did he see you?"

"Not him! It's parked out there!" she whispered.

She would be sure, no need to ask.

He made a slit between the curtains and looked out the window, which faced the alley. They must not have wanted him to park it on the street. A white Chrysler hearse. With gold trim instead of chrome. Good God. And was it Midnight in the room next door? Angelene was already pulling on her dress and grabbing up the rest of her things and throwing them into her little bag. He hurried dressing but she was first and helped him with the buttons. "It's him next door," she said softly. "How did I not know that? I think he's finally sleeping. He would request this old part. The best."

They threw things into his duffle.

"Walter'll be getting up about now. He'll look around first thing," he said. "He'll see it."

She nodded.

He considered that he might take her to Mama Gran's room and come back and shoot the bastard in the heart. He'd like to break his neck but he didn't think he could manage that yet. But if he killed him, if a man's body were found here, they would all be suspects, and if a man came up missing, they'd all be suspects. They would easily be tracked down. God. There was only one thing to do, and that was to let things play out as Angelene had planned.

He thought for a moment. Suppose the man was awake and heard them leave the room and looked out his door because of curiosity. He got his gun from his duffle and thought then he would have no choice and the sooner the better.

He slung his bag over his shoulder, and with his hand on the doorknob, she whispered, "Wait." She put her arms around his neck. "I wanted another time."

He kissed her knowing they'd probably never be together like this again. They both knew it. What could he do to make it happen? Nothing. To take care of this? Nothing. The only thing to do was make sure to be there when she met Midnight. Whatever she said or did to try to keep him away, he would be there.

Finally he let her pull away. He put his hand on the doorknob. Again, she said, "Wait. It squeaks." She took a small bottle of lotion that he'd seen her rub into her hands from her handbag. She held it over each door hinge and coaxed a drop out, rubbing it in. What must she have been through, to have to think of doing that? She took her shoes off to carry them.

He opened the silent door and peered into the empty hall. It was carpeted and softened their steps. He followed her past two doors against empty rooms to Mama Gran's room. As she unlocked and opened it a large hand reached out and clamped her mouth and another hand pulled her inside.

Before Shep could drop his bag off his shoulder and at least try to leap in, he saw Walter's face, and ducked inside, too.

"Didn't know if you knew about him being here," Walter said, barely loud enough to understand. "Took all night to get the car finished. I parked at the back door so it would already be there to get it all loaded this morning. Then I looked around the new part, just my habit to check things out, and went through the alley to the front to get in. Saw the chariot."

Angelene had started helping Mama Gran dress the instant they'd gotten inside. She was holding back a cough with a white handkerchief as Angelene slipped shoes on her.

"Does he have traveling companions?" Shep asked.

"The diggers go where he does," Walter said. "But he must have wanted some select time." He glanced at Angelene. "I thought I saw two fit his specs, big, black suits, go in a joint while I was getting a bite to eat before the car was ready. Got shivers. But I didn't recognize them, and he wasn't with them, so I thought I had the heebies."

"He must have hired new help. Left his usual ones there to look after things," said Shep, feeling he was getting to know the man's priorities. "I'll go down and see if anybody's around, see if they've spotted the car." He tucked his gun into his belt.

"No!" Angelene said.

"Maybe they don't know about him yet," Walter said. "Be good to know if they're watching."

In the hall, Shep noticed a pair of men's shoes against the man's door. They'd been spit shined, glowing in the dim bulb's light. What was it about them? They weren't the hulkers he figured needed to fit a man like Midnight. Maybe he was in another room. He went down the back steps hugging the inside wall, giving praise that his leg was working so much better, and thinking that he actually might be feeling more sensation in his arm. He propped open the door to the back alley with a concrete block probably left there for that purpose, so he could get back in. When he came back up, apparently Midnight was still asleep. Angelene had changed clothes and they were waiting.

FORTY-FOUR

Hwy 61 was carrying them down into the land of the legends of Mississippi. The delta cotton farms like the one he ran. The wealth of the ones who owned them, like Dorthea. The poverty of the ones who worked those farms. The music of the men who bemoaned the circumstances. The writers who chronicled it. And anyone else was just a supporting character. Mama Gran watched time fly by as they went down. Angelene from time to time positioned her head to look through the rear view mirrors or turned her head to glance behind.

Finally she said, "He must have returned home earlier than he planned."

"If he got wind of your leaving, he could have come straight down from Chicago. That would be much quicker."

"I told the chef Mama Gran was too sick for me to leave her at home by herself. If Midnight tried to reach me at home, he would have called the restaurant. The chef would have been more afraid of not telling how many days it had been than telling."

"The good Lord decided to look out for us last night," Mama Gran said.

Angelene turned again to her window.

"Knew we was gettin' out early," Walter said, feeling the need to talk, as no one had spoken in some time. "So I went back and got my packing done. Then I went to eat and take in the sights before I picked up the car. Had it gassed up. No trouble."

"Thank God it was still at the garage and not parked at the hotel," Angelene said.

Walter glanced into the rearview mirror to reassure himself. "When I got back and saw the white chariot, I decided I'd just go on in and put a knife in him."

Shep wondered if it would have been that easy. Midnight wouldn't take chances.

"You didn't, though," Angelene said. "Thankfully."

"Yeah. Didn't know if them Memphis police would take to being bought off, specially by out-of-towners like us. If I was caught. Which I figured I would be."

"You thought right," Angelene said. "And it's not for you to do, anyway. That's my privilege."

"Thought that, too."

"He'll settle in there for a day or two. It's too much like he thrives in to leave right away. He thinks everything happens in his own time."

Was she trying to ease Mama Gran? If Shep knew him like he thought he did, he'd pull out of there after getting some sleep, since he'd had his fun.

He turned to look at her to see if she really believed what she was saying, and was surprised to see she was leaning her head back and had a hand over her stomach and the other over her mouth.

"Let's stop for a minute," he told Walter.

He helped her out and she took several deep breaths. "What is it?" he said, taking her arm as she walked several steps. Was all this getting too much for her by now? Last night's close call, and all that was happening between them.

"Just too much riding so early. Up all night." She managed a smile.

Mama Gran and Walter didn't seem overly concerned, so he tried not to be.

"What can I do?" he said.

"A wet cloth for her head will help," Mama Gran said, and Walter fetched one.

In a few minutes she leaned on the fender and said, "I think I'm hungry. Anybody else?"

"I think we all need something," said Mama Gran.

A flatbed truck hauling cages of chickens slowed as it approached but kept going. A tractor pulling a load of hay crawled around them to the other side, almost stopping, and the driver in overalls and wide straw hat yelled, "Need help?" Shep shook his head and called back, "Appreciate the offer, though."

Other traffic would be coming by, maybe someone really curious about a car like this pulled over. A highway patrol. Or even a white hearse. He wanted that. But not in this wide open spot. "I hate to say it, but how about something to snack on while we're driving, until we get to a better place?"

"We won't get out the fine china," she said, and laughed, making sure she brushed against him as she walked to the back. "Soda crackers sound good to me. And oranges. I bought them yesterday."

She smiled up at him while she was rummaging in the trunk. It was as if thinking of yesterday made her happy.

"Walter, can you manage to eat as we go?"

"Can't peel oranges," he said, laughing. "Get me an apple."

"I'll peel your orange," Shep said as Angelene said the same thing.

Angelene laughed and handed him a cup, "And just spit the seeds in this!"

"Turn right at the next road, Walter," he said. "We'll go about ten miles over to Highway One. Closer to the river. Shouldn't be much traffic." He liked it better, too. It took the lay of the land, and followed the river bends in places.

"Cotton blooming pretty," Mama Gran said.

"From here they like white and pink flowers you could put in a bowl," Angelene said.

"Be a good crop this year," Mama Gran said in a little while, breaking the thoughts everyone was keeping inside.

"Now, just what do you know about cotton?" Angelene said. "You never lived on a plantation. Never picked it."

"Just living down south," Mama Gran said, ignoring Angelene's skepticism. "It's part of life if you're here. Yours and everyone's." She looked at Shep. "Is it still the way?"

"I reckon you've got it right."

"Seemed like it was important as air or water when I was here."

"It's at least the food and shelter and clothing for most," he said.

Angelene must have been thinking that over, and they all gave way to their thoughts again.

She wouldn't understand that cotton and how much you had also determined your standing in the community and the daily friends you spoke to and things you bought with or without thought. And it gave you latitude in some personal decisions, and responsibility to those who depended on you and that you depended on to bring that cotton in. The three thousand cotton acres of Dorthea's had been all that to the town of Shepperton.

"That cotton caused a lot of trouble," Mama Gran said at the end of her thoughts.

"It may be different now. Because of this war. The government asked for more food and less cotton." There had been a large cotton surplus a couple of years earlier, and much of it was still in storage. Food from the U.S. was in demand for all the allies. He and Ulys had corresponded about food crops, and it was going well, or at least not bad, because Dorthea had not complained too much about planting carrots and sweet potatoes and green beans instead of her beloved cotton.

He wondered how the farm had fared moneywise. Ulys didn't know accounts, only whether a crop came in good or bad or how many bales to the acre, and he wouldn't ask Ulys, anyway. Money was not something he and Dorthea had written about. God. What had they found to put in their letters? She had done some travelling, and he knew she might prefer to be in Memphis or New Orleans, but she would put the farm first. Wasn't that part of why she'd married him? Since a lot of it had been in his family she knew he'd love it and take care of it like it was his own. Thing is, shouldn't he have done that anyway, because it was hers? Of course. And possibly he did.

The business of the war hadn't changed the road much as far as he could tell. Only a little more traffic, maybe one vehicle a mile. Through little hapless towns before you knew you were in them. A few roadside stands, their vegetables displayed under a canvas stretched on poles, or thrown-together plywood covers leaking sunshine in, and a glass jar for the change, rationing not performed. A lonesome gas station about every fifteen miles. May be a new gas station at the crossroad a way back. Not that it looked new. It had been baked and washed to a state like the other buildings.

He noticed Walter checking the gage as they went past it. "How's the gas?"

"Wouldn't hurt to be looking for a likely place. I don't favor getting below a quarter tank," Walter said.

"Greenville's not too far. Shouldn't be any questions. They'll make their own assumptions about us. I'm an officer coming home from Washington."

"Still living the life," Angelene said, quoting the Kentucky lawman. But bitterness wasn't really in her now. She leaned forward and touched his shoulder.

There would be no sign announcing mileage to his town, as he remembered thinking that day he met Angelene and Mama Gran and Walter. But he was recognizing the signs. To the west the levee was visible. A big curve should be coming up soon where the road followed the bend around an oxbow lake made when the river flooded probably centuries ago. Then the wide drainage ditch with the bridge sign warning no loads over 10 tons. He should be seeing the catfish shack where many went on Saturday nights to eat the cornmeal-battered, fried sweet meat of the big bottom-feeders, and then stayed for music and dancing. The board and tarpaper building should be visible way off on the river side. Damn. That couldn't be it. He covered his bad eye with his hand and focused with the good one. Must be. Burned. Accident? He might never know.

"What was it?" Angelene said.

"Weekend hangout. Catfish. Music, too. Blues."

She waited a time, then said, "Did you ever go there?"

In other words, was it her kind or his? Though it was her color that built and owned and ran and populated it for the most part, his kind had not been turned away if you were willing to take the first few stares. "I've been there. A few times."

It slowly moved past them in the distance, the back view full with trees from the river bank, the cotton fields on three sides having given many of its customers the money to spend there.

The miles were rolling away, but he hoped the man would know about this road and catch up with them so it could be over and done with. He was afraid fate might some way try to keep him from Angelene when the time came.

"My water," said Mama Gran. "I've been drinking more like Lionel said."

"Should be a dirt road a couple of miles ahead. Walter can pull in out of sight of the road and we can take a break. It's just a shady lane. Goes to a good view of the river. Got some open areas, unless it's changed."

Angelene nodded and turned her head to look out the window. "It's time to get the food out, too."

"I wouldn't mind looking at the river again," Mama Gran said.

After their necessity break Walter drove close enough for Mama Gran to see from the car, then got out and joined Angelene and him on the high bank. She stared up and down as far as could be seen. No boat or tugboats were in sight. Just beautiful water reflecting the light, showing no sign of the dirt it carried, and that almost had a bluish tint in some spots, unusual for this big muddy.

"Knew it was big," Walter said. "Don't remember it from when I was a kid. It was night, too, when we crossed." He looked toward the car. "I'll go check on her."

"All the water in the world come through here?" Angelene said, backing away a little. "I thought there was another big river. Amazon. Nile?"

Shep laughed and put his arm around her. "Want to see those?"

"No. This looks like it could wash away the world."

"It's come pretty close."

"This country of yours, and this river. I can see ... I don't know, maybe what's made you. It's powerful. It's given some of that to you."

He liked her saying that. He hoped it was true. "You've got this in your blood, too, from far back."

She looked surprised.

"Mama Gran has this land in her."

"But hers was different. Her power was to survive."

He was sorry that was probably the truth. "That's number one."

"Thank God it gave that to you, too."

Maybe she was right. Hadn't he thought of home when he was dying on that hell of a land?

"Look," she said, looking over his shoulder to the north. "A huge boat. It's so long."

"It's a tugboat pushing barges lashed together."

"It's like this river's just floating on its back, carrying that on its stomach."

He laughed.

"Makes it look easy. Like you do."

"God. Angelene."

He wanted to say a million things to her. At least one. But she said, "Let's go to the car," taking his hand.

They spread a blanket and got out some food. She opened a can of tuna. He sniffed at it. Before the army, he'd never tasted fish directly from a can. His had been from the river or the gulf, old by no more than a day. She laughed and spooned some onto a cracker for him. He tucked it into his mouth and chewed and swallowed quickly. It wasn't something he'd request.

"Now, if I had a little of Hosannah's mayonnaise you'd like it," she said, handing him another.

Probably would, eat it and like it just because she wanted him to. They were acting as if it was a picnic but eating like it was their last meal.

He heard a noise and turned to stare down a dusty path he knew led to a little oxbow between the river's banks and the levee. Four Negro children in overalls with cane poles over their shoulders lolled toward them, kicking a tin can that no doubt had been used to hold their baitworms. When the children saw the group they froze, the one holding the string of fish even dropping it in the dirt. Then they huddled together.

Shep said, "Afternoon," and stood and walked toward them, then stopped and motioned for them to come over. They nodded and said "Yessur," but couldn't get their feet to move. Angelene stood and said, "Hello, children. Won't you come join our picnic?" A cultured schoolteacher again, as he'd speculated what seemed like forever ago. Mama Gran, sitting on the edge of the back seat, motioned them over. The children, unable to resist the intrigue of this group, moved toward her as if she had them caught in a lasso.

"How you do, Mistah Haddon," the oldest boy said when they got near.

Angelene turned her face away from them.

Kids grew so fast. The boy did look familiar. But this was too far from home for the people on his place, even if it was just fifty miles. "Hello, son. I'm doing very well."

"You get hurt in the war? You limpin' little."

That told him the boy wasn't from the farm or he'd have known about his being injured and hospitalized. "I'm about over it now." He took a wild guess. "Didn't you visit over at our place a couple of years ago?"

"Yessur. Come to see my Uncle Ulys and his boy."

"That's right! You helped record the sacks at the weigh station. Hauled the pickers their water, too. You did a good job."

The boy smiled and the others did, too. "I was there last year, too."

"You've grown so it took me a while. But that's what happens in a couple of years, isn't it?"

"Yessur. I'm thirteen, now."

"Guess you'll be back this year."

"Uncle Ulys said so."

Some explanation had to be forthcoming because news about this interlude would travel faster than smoke signals. It would leave these children's parents and be in Dorthea's kitchen helpers' ears by morning, if not tonight. "These are friends," he said, "giving me a ride home," looking back toward Angelene and the others. "You all come have your picnic before you head home."

Things had now changed. He could never live with Dorthea again if he passed her by this close and she knew about it. It wouldn't matter that he came back later. No matter who he was with or why. He could even see it from her point of view. He didn't want to put Angelene in this dilemma nor did he want to put Dorthea in it. But there was only one thing to do.

FORTY-FIVE

They had discussed things as they drove to Memphis from Hosannah's and felt their time together being shortened like a length of thread being wrapped around a spool. They all understood he would not let them face Midnight without him. He had said they would simply pass Shepperton without stopping and he would come back when it was all over. He didn't know for sure yet what he would do when they met Midnight. Helping them this time wouldn't be as astonishingly simple as when he possibly saved them the day they first met. A life would be lost this time. He knew that with certainty. And if Angelene was right about what this land had given him, and unless the war God had saved him to lose his to a man called Midnight, it would be Midnight who would never see the light of day again.

Whether Dorthea would put together what was between Angelene and him, he wasn't sure. For one thing, her self-confidence might not allow credence to his being involved with another woman. Also, she wouldn't easily entertain the idea of his being intrigued by a woman of color.

If Angelene wouldn't go down the road to meet Dorthea, and agree that he tell Dorthea that he had to see them to their destination because of danger they might encounter relating to their color and their car, then he wouldn't go home. It would be the end of his life with Dorthea, but he'd have to live with that. There would be no life with Angelene. She wouldn't have him if he left Dorthea because of her. And she was going back to Lionel and Joyanne, he knew even though she had yet to say it to him because there was no need. After all, he knew her by now, and she couldn't hide anything from him.

Dorthea was pragmatic. She might even decide it was the lesser of two evils to see them out of his life once and for all on his terms. But how would Dorthea react to the group? He couldn't face her again if she was less than polite to them, if they were mistreated in his own home. But Dorthea was a gracious hostess. He thought she would manage to put her best foot forward for Angelene. If only to show her that she was nothing to be the slightest bit concerned with.

Angelene was in no hurry, pulling more food out of her basket. She must have enjoyed shopping while he was getting his sight restored. The children hadn't seen a can of tuna, from their reactions, wrinkling up their noses as she opened another and offered it to them. The little girl who didn't take her eyes off Angelene accepted a taste on a cracker. Even she couldn't help screwing up her face, and Angelene laughed. That put them all at ease and they

~ 209 ~

sat down and tried the fish so different from their crappie and brim and cat. Walter rinsed his cup and gave them water in it. They bent their necks at angles looking up at him like they were looking up a fifty foot pine. Surprisingly to Shep, they liked the green olives she offered. Maybe they had decided to eat whatever this fairy-tale lady gave them, recognizing it as a one-time chance.

The children examined the cheese, crackers, canned pineapple slices, even the apples set before them before tasting. In a little while he looked at his watch, and Mama Gran said, "You are good children. Go along home now, so your mama won't worry."

They were almost packed, and he knew there were things he had to say to Angelene, and she felt it, too.

"Walter, can you finish this?" she said.

"We'll manage it," Mama Gran said. "You go do your talking."

Down the lane a little, she said, "How far are we from your home?"

"Less than two hours."

She put her arm through his. "This is a sweet-feeling place. I'll bet the moon is beautiful through the trees at night."

He gave her a peck on the lips. "It's a lovers' lane."

"A what?"

"Damn. You are a city girl."

"It's where you bring your best girl?"

"If you're lucky enough." They were out of sight of the car by then, and he kissed her and ran his hands up her back and pulled her close and had a mighty fight with himself.

She put her arms around his waist and leaned into him with her hips. "Or maybe not your best one," she said.

"I was only here with one girl."

"And she wanted to and you didn't."

"I was just an innocent kid. Save myself for marriage."

She thought for a minute. "Maybe not so innocent."

Could it be possible? He'd sprung the trap on Dorthea? There was never any doubt they'd marry once she said that was going to happen. But yes, he had done it as much his way as she had hers to insure it.

"We'll take you home. If you've decided it's best. I know she'll hear about this."

"It's the only thing to do. You know the reasons to do it and not to do it, just like I do."

"I may even have reasons you don't know anything about," she said, leaning her head against his cheek.

"And what might they be?" he said, pulling her chin up so they could face each other.

"I want to see what kind of woman she is."

"That right?" Maybe he didn't know all concerning her.

"I know the kind of woman you think she is. Self-sufficient, maybe make eyes at somebody else every once in a while, maybe replace her man if he left for good. But I think I know something about her, too. And I don't believe you're two different men. One with her and another with me. You couldn't be with a woman you didn't love."

She kissed him on the cheek with gentleness and looked into his eyes with no room for argument.

"So, my darling man, I want to look for what you don't see in her. I have to know that she loves you."

After letting that shocking statement sink in, he said, "And I have to put Midnight out of your life."

"I can't let you kill Midnight for me."

FORTY-SIX

He turned around to see Angelene and Mama Gran sitting straight and still against the back seat. But they had camera eyes. They took in the long gravel-rut drive lined on each side with crape myrtles that had grown to thirty foot trees, some maybe planted when the house was built seventy years ago, and ending at a short brick walk. The trees were in wild pink bloom and enough blossoms had drifted down to make the road look like pink gravel. A few of the trees had succumbed and a couple of spots were not replanted yet. Not like Dorthea to let that go.

A few cup oaks gave shade to the house at various times of day. The acorns and their caps were larger than the Elahvale tree. It struck him now they had pineapple looking ridges and grooves much like the grenades he had dropped. One of these trees was a hundred years old, not the beauty the tree in Kentucky was where he'd waked and had first seen Angelene. But it was a survivor. The only one that came through the fire.

The house at the end of the drive and the narrow walk was built tall off the ground on bricks, like the original one had been, to help prevent termites and in case of flood, but it had been flooded anyway in the 1920's, when the Mississippi lost all semblance of having banks. There was a deep porch, which stopped short of the width of the house on each side, and that area was filled in with pink and white azaleas, bloomed out by this time of year. Round columns held up the tall eave, with its inlaid wreath of plaster eyeing their progress.

The single-story house was squared, with ceilings twelve feet, and six-foot windows that could be raised high enough for a man to bend and walk through. Sometimes the cross breeze would try to blow your shirt off in the spring. A wide center hall ended at the dining room, which ran almost the width of the back wall, stopping short enough on the left for what was now family dining area. The kitchen had been moved inside about sixty years ago and had been in that space, but Dorthea had added the new kitchen just behind it several years ago. Two rooms opened off the left side of the hall and three off the right side.

On the right back wall of the dining room was a triple wide door that led down two steps to the large addition, not visible from the front, which Dorthea's mother had added during the 'twenties flood repairs. It was where he spent much of his time. It had large windows, a raised fireplace that covered half a wall with five feet of brick hearth in case of cinders flying. An office, now his, took up a large corner. Double glass doors opened to a bricked patio and pool.

Not far were several buildings, some original and some added as needed in whatever fashion made them functional. There were small houses for the maid and cook. A brick pumphouse behind the kitchen sent water up from the well. The old outside brick kitchen was now a furnace room. Fallen trees were hauled in from the swamp and chopped to burn. A buried pipe sent the heat to other pipes under the house and up into grates in the floors.

The lawn wasn't over a couple of acres, with pastures and fields starting on either side. A statue of Aphrodite was enclosed in the circle drive, and some plantings around it looked to be drying up. It wasn't like Dorthea to allow that, either. It was possible that she was away.

Walter drove slowly, trying not to raise dust. When Dorthea was expecting people, a party, she had the drive sprinkled to hold down the dust; if it looked rainy, she had a white awning stretched over the walk to the porch. "Stop here," Shep said, "at the walk."

"Long way. Steps high. I'll carry Mama Gran," Walter said.

"We'll wait until we're invited," Mama Gran said.

"You are invited," Shep said.

"We'll wait," she answered.

The faint smell of insecticide drifted up from a far cotton field now that the dust was settling.

Dorthea would have been expecting him at some point a week past on into the next few weeks. He'd given her no departure date. He had put his key on the dresser before leaving for training, but if she wasn't at home, it wasn't a problem. Someone would be here. He didn't get the bell pulled before a Negro woman, one he had not seen before, in a floral dress with a huge white apron opened the door and stood in surprise.

"I'm Mr. Haddon," he said.

"Yessur. Lawd. Come on in." But she stood in shock, blocking the door.

"Is my wife at home?"

"Yessur. Lawd."

"Is she in the garden room?"

"Yessur. Come on in." But she continued to stand still, looking past him.

He had never come in the front door as a habit. Usually it was the kitchen door or from the patio area. He stepped in, the maid having no choice other than moving aside. He glanced around trying to see it with a first-time perspective, as he had the outside. It wasn't hard to do. It almost felt like the first time. The front parlor on the left was visible through opened double doors, the second one joined through very wide double pocket doors, both with their large mirrors and dark red velvet settees and dainty chairs. To the right were the bedrooms, where each for several decades now had a bathroom and closet carved out.

"She's with the baby."

That was interesting. It wouldn't be like Dorthea to babysit. He felt his stomach flip-flop. "Would you get her, please?"

"Yessur. Lawd."

"I'm coming, Vernese," he heard Dorthea call in a soft voice as she closed the door from the back. "The baby's asleep."

She was in a yellow sundress, her hair pulled away from her face in barrettes as when she was a little girl. She didn't look as sleekly thin as before.

She stopped when she saw him, her hand moving around her waist. "Shepherd!" she said in a whisper. She hurried to him and put her arms around him, closing his arms inside. "My Shepherd's come home!"

Although his eye was feeling weak from lack of sleep, he had not put his patch back on, and he didn't like himself for it. She stepped back to look him over, but quickly grabbed him and kissed him like he remembered her doing, like she owned him lock, stock, and barrel. He could join in or not. God. She'd never change. Did he want her to? Without bidding, guilt flowed through him about Angelene and, about her concerning Angelene as well.

"Just like I've been thinking about," she said into his uniform collar.

He couldn't help smiling.

"That old smile," she said. "After what you've been through. I didn't want you to lose that smile." Her green and gold eyes glittered like halos.

Her pronouncement was enough for her. She wanted it and it was so, he thought, with a little catch in his throat. God Almighty. He wouldn't ever change, either, would he?

"How are you? You look ..." she looked him up and down, "leaner. But still like my Shepherd."

"You are beautiful," he said, meaning it.

"I guess some things just don't change," she said, flirting already. "But you'll see. How did you get here? I expected that you'd end up on the train and call from Memphis."

"No." He glanced toward the front door. "I've been traveling with some new friends."

"And they're outside? I hope they won't stay long! I want you to myself."

She started to the door.

"I should tell you. They're not anybody who you'd expect." He had ceased to think of them as different from him, and he wouldn't make excuses even to ensure that she accept them. "But I expect you to make them welcome –"

"They brought you home," she interrupted. "They're welcome to my house. To your home."

She moved to where Vernese still looked out the open door, and stepped around her and onto the porch. She took in the three and the car in one glance. If she was shocked, and she must have been, she covered it. As Shep moved to lead her across the porch, she took his hand instead and led him down the steps. Was it for support at the surprise? Or had she already assessed there was something compelling out there. "Good afternoon," she said. "Won't you please come inside?"

Walter got out and helped Angelene out, then went around and lifted Mama Gran. They stood there for just the slightest and then Angelene led the way up the steps. She had on navy shoes with a slingy strap around the heel and a tailored navy dress, and looked like blue midnight against the golden sunshine of Dorthea.

As Dorthea and Angelene stood for what seemed minutes, but what he knew was only a camera exposure time, he got the feeling both recognized something of herself in the other. Some reserve quality that each could use to survive, and more, to thrive. And maybe even an appreciation for each other's beauty. It didn't feel like something that had to do with him. He believed each fleetingly felt they could have been friends in a different world, or enemies if they had been going after the same thing. But he didn't believe Dorthea gave real consideration that Shep might be involved, and he didn't think their involvement entered into Angelene's present thoughts. They were both women who each in her own world was the usual prettiest, smartest, savyest. Neither of them smiled.

Dorthea held out her hand and said, "I'm Mrs. Haddon. Dorthea to our friends."

Angelene took her hand and said, "Hello. I'm Mrs. Midnight."

Dorthea was un-phased.

Angelene added, "Please call me Angelene."

"Dorthea, this is Miss Johnston, Angelene's great-grandmother," Shep said, breaking their reverie. "Mama Gran, this is Dorthea."

He didn't know what Dorthea thought of that familiarity. Maybe she understood a closeness had developed. Maybe she understood everything. She was a quick learner. She did step forward to put her hand on Mama Gran's arm and said, "Hello, Miss Johnston," accepting that Mama Gran wasn't "Mrs.," although that would have been unusual in the delta, having grandchildren and not having been married in some sort of ceremony.

"And this is Walter Smith."

"Hello," she said. "Won't you bring her inside now? The afternoon sun is about to hit us here."

An excuse? Was she slyly using that excuse to invite them in, skillfully letting them wonder if otherwise she wouldn't? He wasn't sure.

Inside, she guided them to the front parlor. Again, he didn't know if she would have done it to let them know she was in her element and they were inside only by her grace, or if she would have made them comfortable in the other room if a baby had not been sleeping in it – that was something he sure as God wanted to hear more about. And he didn't know how they would have felt if they had not been invited into the front parlor. God. It was complicated. Dorthea told Vernese to take Walter to the kitchen to rest and for her to make lemonade.

"While we're waiting for lemonade, would you ladies care to visit the powder room?" she said, leading them, not giving them a chance to refuse.

"Thank you," said Angelene.

When Dorthea returned from showing them across the hall, she walked close to him standing at the side window, looking out and catching the breeze. "What in God's name?" she said, her voice low. "Just what does this mean?"

"We've been traveling together for a few days. I helped them out and then they helped me."

"You probably risked your life getting them out of some situation they and their long car should never have been in!"

He shrugged.

"It didn't occur to you to walk away? She's beautiful ... but that didn't matter!"

He still wondered. He hoped he would have been guilty of that.

"Vernese will tell Ida when she comes and they'll have this all over the farm. And it won't stay here. Floodwater wouldn't spread as fast!"

She sat down to think it over.

FORTY-SEVEN

"That was a reluctant goodbye," she said from the door as he walked up the steps while the dust disappeared.

"We got to know and depend on each other," he said.

"I trust they're staying in New Orleans for good."

He'd seen no reason to tell her their destination of Vicksburg. "Did you say earlier that the baby was sleeping?"

"Well, I wondered if your hearing had been damaged, too!"

"I was supposed to ask about a baby while they were here? I was supposed to ask if we have a baby that you chose not to tell me about?"

She seemed to be thinking that over.

"Are you watching it for a friend?"

As she didn't answer, he said, "Dorthea, is it our baby?"

She put her arm in his. "Come see him," she said, "then answer your own question." She smiled up at him.

He and Dorthea had a child. He had a son!

The baby slept, a blue thin gown scrunched up to his knees. White knit booties lay discarded at the end of the cradle. One of two ceiling fans was going, keeping it comfortable with nearby trees big enough to shade this addition in early afternoon, the windows open. His wispy hair was the color of Dorthea's.

"He has blue eyes," she said.

Shep took off his tie and unbuttoned his top button and bent over the crib. He'd like to pick him up, but instead breathed the baby scent, letting it spread through him just as his blood spread through the baby.

"You know why I didn't tell you," she said.

She'd say it was so he wouldn't worry. But reluctantly, he accepted what he knew, that she had her own reasons. It could have been that if she'd had a miscarriage, and he didn't even like to think of that possibility, she might never have told him.

"It wasn't a hard pregnancy," she said.

He believed her.

"You should have told me. Yes, I would have worried. That would have been my right. My duty. But I should have known, anyway, should have felt it, deep inside. God knows I wondered."

"You had your mind occupied fighting to survive, and then getting mended. I'm glad I didn't tell you."

He didn't say that maybe he would have fought even harder to stay alive and to mend. "How old is he?"

"New York was about a year ago." She put her arm around his waist and he heard the memory of their coming together in her voice.

"It's coming back to me," he said, knowing his voice showed that he remembered what she wanted him to. He and Dorthea had made a child. A son!

"That smile. You never could hide happiness," she said. "Go ahead, pick him up."

He'd held babies before. All the mothers here handed him their new babies to admire. He was glad he had been able to get his shirt laundered.

"Here, put this over your shoulder. He spits up for the fun of it, I think."

"What did you name him?"

"After my daddy and granddaddy, of course."

He spread the cloth printed with little blue bunnies and reached for his son. The name that counted was his.

It was almost supper time. In the land where dinner was at noon. It felt good. He was walking the edge of the west field, avoiding the one sprayed in the afternoon. It looked green and healthy. Ulys had said it was sprayed a couple of weeks earlier. He turned leaves looking for bollworms and found none.

Dorthea'd insisted Shep get out and look around the place for an hour. Go to the houses. Check it out with Ulys. See the new vegetable crops. He could have waited. He hadn't spent enough time with Grayson William Ellis – the Third if the last name of Haddon hadn't been at the end. She called him Willie, but he knew it wouldn't stick. Grayson would win out. He wasn't sad about that. Her father had been called Willie.

Ulys's son had lain still on his bed, eyes moving but not alert, his arms and legs boney and useless under baby blue pajamas with the legs cut off and neatly hemmed above the knees for coolness. He recognized them as some Dorthea had bought him years ago. He still didn't know if it was for the best that he'd gotten the boy out of the well before his last breath. What kind of life was this? How had Ulys and his wife managed? But wasn't that God's choice? Even if he'd known the boy would be this way, could he have done differently? God do what's right for this boy and take care of Grayson.

He headed back to the house in the farm pickup. What a change a child could make. He had never been so glad to come upon Dorthea and his home. He wondered where Angelene was now, and mentally calculated the hours until they were to meet as he rolled up his sleeves and washed his face and hands in the bathroom that connected to his office. Never had having a bathroom, just for that simple purpose – not even considering anything else – seemed to be a luxury.

He walked in and looked at the small round table set for supper in the garden room. A salad of cucumbers and tomatoes on spinach leaves wilted by hot bacon grease waited by their plates. Roast chicken sandwiches with the crusts untrimmed the way he preferred them were piled on a center plate. Thin potato slices which had been fried in bacon fat until they were crisp, then drained on dish towels – he'd snatched them hot from the towel when Thula prepared them for him as a boy – perched in a perfect fan display in a napkin-lined basket with salt and pepper shakers next to it. Whole green beans that had been steamed and sprinkled with the crisp bacon crumbles lay like stacked logs in an oval platter. He tried not to think of Buford's log truck or the green beans that had waited in Hosannah's cooler, already cooling in their glass jars by now. Tall crystal glasses already full of ice waited for the sweet tea to be poured. Condensation ran down their sides onto the padded coasters like his Double Cola had on Mr. White's bench. A bowl of whole fuzzy peaches, he was sure just picked this afternoon in the orchard, waited peeling as wanted. It was exactly what he would have asked for. But a grand dinner would come in a few days, with a dozen neighbors in attendance, he was certain.

A bottle of champagne cooled in a stand full of ice by the table. It was dry country, of course, but that never kept her from having whatever liquor she wanted to serve.

Dorthea had used the hour to do whatever she had previously ordained as necessary for the time of his return. She wore a whipped cream cloud of a dress, that hugged all the right places and floated around her calves. An emerald bracelet and earrings made her eyes greener, and she looked to be walking on air in shoes with barely enough strap to hold them on.

She was expecting him to notice and what kind of man wouldn't? And there was no need to punish her by not letting her know. He swept up and down her with his eyes and helped her twirl, then kissed away her smile and didn't resist when the kiss deepened and her breasts pressed. She pulled away, happy.

"Where's the baby?" he asked, the very word making him happy.

"At this age, they sleep most of the time, you know."

"I know that?" he said, letting his contentment come through in a smile.

"The back bedroom is the nursery. I've had a cot put in there for Vernece."

He heard clanking pans in the kitchen. "I'll just go look in on him," he said.

Grayson was sucking, his tongue's tip going in and out over the bottom lip. He now had on a white gown, his thin long legs curling out of it, the light blanket kicked aside. This room felt cool, but the little fellow ought to know if he was too warm, so he resisted pulling the cover back over his son's legs. He looked around. The large canopied bed was still there, the room being large enough for the old furniture that had graced it for so long, as well as the new nursery requirements. He turned to leave, then turned again and reached for the thin blanket, lightly settling it on his son's legs. Sometimes, he'd have to make decisions he knew to be best. And they might not be just what Grayson would want. So he might as well start now. The little legs accepted the warmth.

Dorthea came in and stepped behind him, putting her arms around him. "Vernece usually comes in and puts her feet up this time of day," she said, and he followed her out.

He popped the cork and poured their champagne. The thought of toasting his son was overpowering anything else he was feeling. He handed Dorthea a glass and tapped it with his. "To our son," he said, and tipped the glass back and drained it, glad of the bubbling liquor to swallow down with the crack of his voice at the sweet words.

"Is there someone else you want to toast?" she said, after sipping hers.

"Of course." He poured more. "To my son's mother."

"Is that who I am now?" she said.

"To my wife," he said, then gulped the still wonderful liquid.

"Oh?" she said. "Wife and mother."

Hell. Some things didn't change. "You are who you are," he said, even managing to add a smile, raising the glass to her. "To Dorthea."

"I'll drink to that," she said, and finished her glass, then held it out for more.

"To my husband," she said, raising the glass to him and then she drained it.

Well, that was that.

FORTY-EIGHT

They were still sipping iced tea.

"Can't eat the last sandwich?" she said. "You've lost weight."

"It'll come back." He selected a peach and examined its perfection before popping it apart in halves and scooping the pit out with a spoon. He peeled each half, the juice dripping onto the plate and his fingers. He cut the halves into slices and handed her the plate, and then peeled another peach and took a bite from it, finally wiping the juice from his fingers and chin with his napkin. She laughed.

"Forgot all your manners in Italy?"

"Didn't need them."

"Didn't they come back to you in the hospital?"

"I just tried to get the spoon to my mouth without spilling it," he said, laughing.

"Didn't you have some help? So much you couldn't do on your own."

He took another bite of peach. Was she getting at something? "I'd say we all got pretty good care, and help when we needed it."

Little Grayson cried and he tilted his head. "I'll go get him," he said, when the crying continued.

"He's all right. Vernece is good with him. She's had four of her own. I couldn't ask Betsy to stay. Not with her son to care for. She recommended Vernece for Grayson."

Didn't ask Ulys's wife because she had her almost comatose son to care for. Had Dorthea crossed a threshold? And his name no longer Willie. Was that for his sake, he wondered.

"Vernese helps in the kitchen, but the baby's her main responsibility."

The crying stopped in a moment.

"It was probably air on his stomach," she said, sliding her fork under a peach slice that she had cut into halves. "We haven't gotten his bottle just right, I expect. We've only put him on it this week. But Vernece says they get air no matter what."

He wanted to ask if the baby was gaining what he should, why she had stopped nursing, but he looked healthy and happy. He nodded. His son.

"You're smiling again," she said, smiling back.

"I'm glad to be home," he said. It came from nowhere. And it came from so deep inside he knew it must be true.

"I was beginning to wonder. It took you long enough to get here."

"Oh?"

"I called the hospital last week. I thought you might have trouble getting train reservations. I was thinking of sending Ulys for you. But you were already checked out."

Maybe he did know her so well that what he thought were his own thoughts were hers. When the idea came to him at the gas station where he saw Angelene and Walter and Mama Gran, it wasn't so farfetched after all, just as he'd speculated then.

"I was worried about you. Can you understand?"

"It was your right." Just as it was his to have been told about the baby. "I should have let you know my plans."

"I've heard some of those army nurses, well, they love their jobs beyond the call of duty."

"If you saw what they have to do, you would have only respect for them."

"Nurse Patsy was certainly helpful."

Why was he surprised that she knew about Patsy?

"How do you know of her?"

"I called her a few days ago."

He leaned back and picked up another peach. It was another one that would have been at home in a still-life painting. Even a shiny green leaf remained on the stem. This he would have expected. But her calling Patsy?

"The nurse I spoke with remembered you two had left together. Or rather, that she was giving you a ride part of the way. I had Cousin William get her number."

Ah. Their Representative in Washington had nothing more important to do with a war going on. But don't blame her. Even he had thought of asking him to intervene back at the Kentucky state line. His leg was getting stiff and he needed to stretch it. He almost wanted her to know. To say, I tried, but I'll never be the way you want me again.

"She was worried that you were walking and hitchhiking, though she said it would be good for your leg if you didn't overdo it."

He put the peach back in the bowl.

"Don't look so concerned. She told me you were friends, that she had given you a ride as far as her family farm in West Virginia. Of course, she was in love with you."

"You're putting something on me. Credit, you think? Discredit, I'd say."

"What nurse wouldn't be? You'd be getting medals. And all polite and embarrassed. Wanting to spare them any unpleasantness you could. And even with bandages and slings and hospital gowns I expect you still looked passable."

He wrinkled his brows and shook his head.

"You don't think I'd marry an ugly man, do you?" she said, appraising him in an exaggerated manner.

"I don't think I'd win a beauty contest. Even before all the damage."

"You appear to be repaired," she said. "Not even a band aid."

He opened his hands palm up, as if to say nothing to it.

"I'm so glad your eye is healed, but I wanted to see you with the eye covered. My very own swashbuckler."

She put her hand to her mouth when he said, "It very nearly didn't come off." Might as well let her know he'd almost come home half blind. God. And he might as well accept he would never be the man he was. Even if he eventually healed physically, he was now a changed man. Would she accept it?

"I guess that's what intrigued Nurse Patsy the most?"

He got up and paced. But it wasn't because of his leg. He couldn't sit still any more and hear Patsy maligned. "I guess I reminded her of her fiancé who was killed in the Pacific. She put her grief to work. Changed it into compassion for her patients."

She sipped her tea and considered. She didn't really consider that she had anything to worry about, he was sure.

"Are you discharged? They don't expect you to go back after all that, do they?"

"I'm still active duty."

"I like you in uniform," she said, running her finger over his shoulder insignia.

"Glad you like it, ma'am."

"Did the people all like it?"

She'd insisted he wear it around to the houses. He smiled. "It scared some of the kids. They thought I was the sheriff."

She laughed, then put her finger to her lips and nodded toward the front of the house. But they both knew it wouldn't penetrate those ten inch walls with the doors now closed.

She poured the last of the champagne and stood by him, rubbing the small of his back. "Aren't you about ready to get out of it?"

They drained their glasses and she undid his tie. Whatever the cause or reason, even if he didn't want to, he did respond to her. To show her he was still good enough, or because she was beautiful and wanted him, or because he was a serviceman home with his wife after so long. Or God help him, because he knew she had been jealous of Patsy and it had somehow given him a feeling of the upper hand that Angelene and Pearl had talked about. He didn't know. But he thought of

Angelene's velvet arms and legs and knew this was going to be more to contend with than he had even thought, whenever it did happen.

"I'm glad to have my husband back."

"I waited until after supper to tell you ... I'm sorry, but I have to go soon."

"When do you report?"

"That's not what I meant. But I report the last of August."

She seemed to think about what to ask. "Where will you be stationed?"

"There's a new organization in Virginia. It's sort of low-key."

"You mean secret operations? Well, you can keep a secret!" She put her arms back around him.

"I'm sorry it's worked out this way," he said, putting his head against hers. "But there's something I have to do for maybe a couple of days. I have to leave in a few minutes."

"What? No! Why would the army expect you to do such a thing!"

"There's nothing I can do differently about it."

She stepped away and looked at him like a horse trader. "Is it army business?"

"No." The possibility of lying was there, but he couldn't.

"What could be so important?"

"The people who brought me, they're in trouble and I owe it to them to help."

"Write them a check."

"Did they look like they need money?"

"Your son is in the other room. And you're not even staying the night? And you wasted time getting here." She kissed him and put her hands on his shirt buttons.

He covered them with his. "It was a healing time. I thought I needed it." If he'd known he had a son here waiting for him, maybe he'd have rushed all battered and torn standing room only on a bus to see him, and the past week would never have happened. And he and Dorthea would have dealt with their running competitions as best they could. But he didn't know for sure. He couldn't blame all his decisions on Dorthea's.

"I have to go."

"Mr. Midnight didn't waste time getting to his wife," she said, unbuttoning his top button. "Just let him help them."

"What are you talking about?"

"He came by while you were out with Ulys looking over the place."

"Why didn't you send for me!"

"For one thing, I only had Vernece here with me. I wouldn't be alone here with someone I'd just met, who looked so pleased with himself, a dark one or not!"

Damn it to Hell. She usually had a half dozen in shouting distance! "You were right on that count!" He pulled her to him. "Why didn't you tell me when I got back!"

"I really didn't think it was important. I assumed he was expected by her."

"I'm sorry I reacted that way. What did he say? What did you tell him?"

"I told him how long they'd been gone."

He checked his watch.

"Are you saying he's dangerous? My God!"

"Not to you." But only God knew what the man had in mind.

"He certainly didn't seem so."

What? "Are you sure it was Mercer Midnight?"

"He claimed to be! And like Mrs. Midnight said, he was a mortician. He wanted to give the appearance of being meek and mild. A little man. If I didn't hate the word, I'd say scrawny. He wore thick glasses."

Must've been his shoes outside the hotel room door after all.

"I thought it was strange. A Negro mortician down here would not be caught dead driving his hearse anywhere except to funeral business. I've never seen anything so gaudy in my life."

The white chariot. It was ahead of him. Between him and Angelene. "How many were with him?"

"Two. And they looked like heavyweight boxers. Not like Mrs. Midnight's driver, Mr. Smith. But as big as Ulys."

"I'm so sorry. He may have learned my name from a newspaper article."

"Do you mean to say you were in the newspaper with them?"

"The Highway Patrol Captain didn't think the reporter knew our names — "

"The Highway Patrol!"

"Or that I was traveling with Angelene." Mercer Midnight must have paid dearly to have him traced in this war age, where information was not easy to get under any circumstances. He wasn't sure he could even have found it from the Kentucky Highway Patrol.

She pulled away, noticing his use of Angelene's first name, but only said, "I asked him. He said he had people looking for his wife, that he didn't like her being away from him. And he didn't let her travel alone. I didn't care for that. He didn't even indicate that it was because of her traveling in the south. Why shouldn't any woman go where she wants?"

Angelene would have been reassured to hear that from Dorthea. "I'm sorry you were involved."

"But you wouldn't have done differently. I might not even have wanted you to."

"Can I tell you that surprises me?"

"It would. You may not like hearing this. I married you for more than one reason. It may sound overly dramatic, but I really can't phrase it differently. One reason was to get my family's bloodline honorable again. If it ever was. For my children."

"Honorable?" It hit him like a fist. What had he done on this trip? Break laws. Break army regulations. And break his oath to his wife, this woman who was standing here believing in his honor. "You must not know me at all."

"You proved it over and over when you were young. Again when you started running the farm. Again when you joined the army. The Ellises didn't even fight for the Confederacy."

Yeah, growing up, he'd heard that about her family. "Maybe they were following their convictions."

"They followed their money to New York for the duration. Great Granddaddy Ellis had his cotton broker arrange it and left the overseer in charge here."

He'd heard that, too, more than once, but never after it became clear that he and Dorthea were an item.

"He went there to 'recover his health.' Far away from it all. I have his diaries."

He thought of putting his arms around her, but she wouldn't take kindly to that. She'd think he was feeling sorry for her. She must have seen sympathy in his eyes, as she stepped back.

"It wasn't Yankee soldiers who burned us down. This place came through the war unharmed, so his neighbors knew he swore allegiance to the Union."

That was news to him. "We can't know what anybody was going through then."

"The Ellises were asked for loans, but instead they bought up the land, so the locals burned them out."

"Some people just aren't strong enough. They can't do what others think is right. They think what's right is what's best for them."

"Some people are strong enough. You are."

He remembered what Angelene said today when they were watching the river. God, he hoped Dorthea and Angelene were right, that he was strong, had power. To do what was right. To do what these two women needed to help them.

"Your people lost a lot doing what they thought was right."

"I like to think if they'd accepted what they actually were fighting for, they'd have done differently." Here they were generations later, her wishing her family had supported the cause for the wrong reasons, and him regretting his family did support the cause for the wrong reasons.

"They were willing to take their medicine for their earlier decisions. That's what I wanted."

"My daddy was a gambler, and I'm half him."

"But he didn't turn his weakness into dishonesty. He paid his debts. You're not ashamed of him."

He'd done one thing he didn't think his daddy had ever done. For what he'd done with Angelene, he took full responsibility. And it was between him and God.

"I still have the diaries," she said. "I hope our son never sees them. But maybe he should know."

"You don't have to keep the diaries. Burn them." He couldn't resist enclosing her. She pushed him away. "My daddy and granddaddy took your daddy's land."

He stepped to her. "And yet, here I am."

She was thrown by that for a second. "What?"

"Maybe I spent all that time while we were growing up being exactly what you would think you need. I don't know."

"Good God. But if you did ... you were what I need."

"I'm not the man you've been describing."

She put her lips against his and he let her still his denials. "It didn't hurt that it was you, that you were the one. You were the one who could give me what I wanted as well as needed."

"You've given me a lot to try to live up to," he said, like a promise, when she was through. But hadn't that always been his mission with her? Now, he acknowledged some new acceptance about Dorthea and him, and wondered, now that he knew what she felt for him, what it might do to their lives. And how what he had done that she could never know might change their lives.

"I tested you enough to know."

"I thought you were just one mean little girl."

"I was."

They looked into each other's eyes and smiled.

Then he was buttoning his shirt, straightening his tie, and headed to his office.

She grabbed his arm. "Why are you going into your office?"

"You know he didn't have to come down here in that white hearse."

"She's run away from him."

He nodded.

"So he's taking her back however he can!" Her hand went to her throat.

He put his hands on her shoulders. "Ulys said he had kept my car tuned. I told him to put gas in it this afternoon."

"You're going back there to get your shotgun," she said, the first sign of loss of control in her voice.

"I won't have to use it."

"Call Sheriff Connor! He can call the police in New Orleans to help you. You don't have to do this all alone, do you?"

He saw no need to tell her the truth of the meeting, Vicksburg. He thought it was for her own good. If something went wrong, the less she knew, the better. Sheriff Connor's brother Roy was sheriff in Vicksburg. Their daddy was district judge; all got campaign contributions from her granddaddy, now from her. It never hurt to have the law on your side, the old man used to say, without thinking of the ramifications of that belief. And that the law was incestuous didn't bother him either. God knew Roy Conner wouldn't hesitate to pick Midnight up. Shep had heard stories. And

Roy Connor would see in a minute that Midnight and the law weren't compatible. Why would he drive an empty hearse from Washington if he didn't plan on taking a body back? Maybe it would be better if the law gave Midnight what he had coming rather than him if he got to him first. Or Angelene, if she saw him first and her confidence was justified, and he hoped to God it was.

But no. Law justice was too good for Midnight. "Probably won't need the law in on it. I expect he just needs to know Angelene's not going back with him."

"Are you coming back?"

He was touched. Her first uncertainty about him. "I'll do my best."

She actually laughed. "I don't mean that. You won't be in that hearse! I meant are you going on with her?"

He was surprised and proud that she believed in his ability so much, even in his recovering state. "So much for honor!" he said, laughing.

"I'm not always sure just what you'll think is the right thing! Sometimes it's not what I think it is."

He pulled her to him and she put her arms around him in a way he'd never felt from her. They weren't circling her possession. Or it simply could be that he had finally taken ownership of himself.

"I was walking half way from Washington, D.C. to give myself time to heal and get strong again, to be the husband you expect."

"All right, then," she said. "Get your pistol, too. I can't help but wonder what's transpired on this journey. But the day you let friends down – someone who has befriended you," she emphasized the friend words, "or someone who needed you, you wouldn't be who I married. And I understand now who you are. Not noble. Just a man who thinks he's got to do the right thing."

He kissed her and she let him do the kissing.

"It doesn't mean I like that you're going. Or that I'll always like what you think is right, any more than I did before."

As he walked out, he told her to send for Ulys to come up to watch the house for the night, and to find work around there until he returned. God help if Midnight came out on top of this thing.

She called out, "There's a coupon book in the glove compartment if you need it."

FORTY-NINE

His car was actually Dorthea's. It was the Cord Speedster she'd driven in college. He said he would like it when she was buying a new one and was thinking of selling it. He'd liked to be reminded of their college days, when he'd had some control over her by not giving in to her, he supposed. Also, the two-seater was wickedly fast on the straight delta roads and could half-circle around a cotton wagon or loaded pickup as soon as he thought of it.

A sign reflecting in his headlights that Vicksburg was thirty miles ahead was behind him almost before he had time to read it. Midnight was probably already there, cruising, but it was his funeral if Shep spotted him. Like most country boys, Shep was expert with guns even before the army re-taught him. He glanced at his shotgun standing on the floorboard leaning against the seat and his army issue pistol on the seat.

After Midnight was put in his own hearse, they would find the restaurant, or the old family Mama Gran's daughter had lived with, or at least the cemetery. He concentrated on the few details Angelene had given him about the restaurant, the house it was in. It had a fine front porch, as it was apparently the one Mama Gran compared the hotel to in Memphis. So would every fine house in Vicksburg. But this one had been made into a fine restaurant. And didn't it have a view of the river? Even if it wasn't still in business, somebody would remember.

He entered town almost at the river. Town had closed for the night. The Delta Bus Station was just south of downtown. He flew by it before he realized. He turned around and pulled up in front. The lights were out. What the hell? The door was padlocked! The sign wasn't even there. Closed down. This was to be their meeting place. He was on time. Why weren't they here? Would they have felt exposed, with the place shut down?

Where would they have gone? The restaurant? Damnation, what was its name! She'd mentioned it that night on the Stones River. LaBelle. Where was it? Then it hit him just who would be up, who would know if anything had happened, and who would know about the restaurant.

He drove west, winding down close to the river, not far. A joint was open, though dimly lit, vibrating with pounding from the piano. Places like this always had someone looking out for whatever. A couple of men were standing outside, watching, cigarettes dangling. They had on open collar print shirts and pants loose in the manner of many pleats at the waist. Some might say it was to have plenty of room to conceal their weapons. Knives or brass knuckles probably. Guns were hard for Mississippi Negroes to come by.

He stopped the car on the narrow hard-packed dirt street. The darkness just behind said the river was there. One of the smokers stepped to the car, making sure to avoid stepping on something with one foot. "What you need, army man? You lookin' to roll roun'?"

"I'm not looking for that."

The men glanced at each other. "You want gamblin'?" the second said, authority in his voice, putting his hand down in his pants pocket. The place must bring in the money.

"No," Shep said. "I'm looking for a particular woman. A beautiful black woman. She's in a black Cadillac – "

The men laughed and slapped their thighs. "We want one of them women, too!"

Shep laughed, too. Opened for that one. "She's real. Got a driver and an old lady with her. From up north."

"What business she be o' yours?"

"She's a friend in trouble. I owe her a favor."

The two men looked at each other and the head one said, "We don't want no trouble here. No trouble. You better be on your way, Mr. Army Man."

"One more question. Have you seen a white hearse around town this evening? Washington D.C. plates?"

They glanced at each other and backed away from him, looking around as if a mortician's wagon would pull up for them.

"How long ago was it here?" Shep said, getting out.

"Go on away from here. I'll go in for the boss, you don't."

"Go get him. I need to talk to him."

The man motioned for the other one to go in and said, "You gonna be sorry you stayed."

But like Angelene, Shep knew money still talked. Only it had to be at a place where its language was understood. He'd opened the office safe and taken out a stack of twenty dollar bills before leaving.

A very dark man in a white suit and white shoes followed the garde du corps out. He was smoking a cigar and brushed ashes from his lapel, all the while focusing on Shep. "What a white man in a army suit doin' here? Black woman in a Cadillac on you mind. Askin' 'bout a white deadman car."

"I came to give you twenty dollars."

"That's more like it." He held out his hand and Shep put it there.

Shep took several bills he had folded together from his pants pocket and flattened them, pulling one off the top. He stood there holding it to be seen.

"Who you want killed? Put in that white wagon?"

"When did you see it?"

"Hour ago. He didn't give me no money. Didn't give me nothin' but threats."

"He's from up north."

"Thinks we give it away free." He held out his hand and Shep put the bill in it.

"He pays up there, buys the law. Hurts anybody else who doesn't cooperate. He doesn't understand our system. We buy information at a fair price."

"He a runt. Two big field hand diggers to back him up."

"What information did you tell him about the woman?"

"Only what I knew." He put the bill in his inside coat pocket and held out his hand. "Whole new set of information you be wantin'."

Shep lifted another bill from his stack and gave it to him.

"I didn't know nothin' bout her to tell. Ain't seen her or no black Cadillac."

Shep knew the system by now. He held out another bill that was quickly tucked away. "Did he ask about an old restaurant?"

"Yeah. He wanted to know about that old lay bell restaurant the black cookin' man had. Where the white folk went to eat their vicious whey. Been closed down since '29. Fallin' in. Don't guess they liked that French food with no liquor to wash it down." He looked at his two men. "Cold potato soup sound good?" He laughed, teeth as white as his suit in the dark.

"Where is it?"

"I guess I can throw that information in," the man said, waving away the bill Shep held out.

It would be easy to find, just a couple of turns.

Shep held out the bill again and said, "Where's the cemetery for Negroes? The well-off ones?"

"Well-off? I'm the only well-off. Ain't dead yet." He laughed long and loud. "I'll tell you where the cemetery is. Only one of them, too, slave times to now." He reached out for the bill.

When Shep was getting in his car, he pulled another bill out. "What happened to the Delta Bus Station?"

"Guess I've made my quota tonight," his informant said, getting the bills out of his pocket, lining them up together, folding and putting them in his inside coat pocket, refusing the one offered. "Not enough riders. Lot of folk rode that bus to north and stayed. Some even got the draft." He moved his hefty white suit close to the car and said, "Do business with you anytime. Won't charge so much next time. Had to make sure what you about."

Shep held out his hand. "Shep Haddon, from up Shepperton."

"Grip Wilson."

As they shook hands, Shep said, "I guess I see where you got your name."

Grip's teeth showed as he said, "That where Ulys Wilson live? Your place?"

Shep nodded.

"We cousins. You the one saved his boy?"

"I pulled him up. Can't decide if I saved him or not."

"Man, that's the business of the Bossman up there."

"Thanks for your help tonight."

"I'm gonna throw in something else, now I know you. The undertaker asked 'bout the graveyard, too. Didn't think nothin' about it, considerin'."

FIFTY

Shep jumped in the car and didn't even feel the bruise coming up on his bad leg from the bump he just gave it. He drove the block up to the river bank and then the half mile north, the wide river visible at times because of its black nothingness. He didn't expect them to be there, but had to make sure. God help them if they had chosen to wait there for him. But Mama Gran would also know where the cemetery was. God don't let them have gone there either. They wouldn't go there. Not tonight. Walter would find somewhere in town for him to find them and wait it out together for the man to show up.

The house was abandoned with gusto. A streetlight showed windows broken, the porch leaning where one of six columns was lying on the ground. Honeysuckle and trumpet vine were having a field day. He knew some of the houses up this bluff had been destroyed by shells from the Northern boats, it was so close to the river. This one had survived to be attacked by time and neglect. From here the boat docks and some industry on the riverside were visible, a few lights still on. He saw something on the wide brick steps that didn't belong there. He lifted himself out and picked it up. Angelene's scarf. Not the one Hosannah had coveted and kept. The one Angelene had draped over Mama Gran's shoulders today. It had been left for him. But had Angelene left it, or had Midnight, to let him know he had them.

He drove the few blocks to downtown and through side streets and alleys for a few minutes. But all the while he knew in his heart where they were. His headlight blasted tunnels in the dark for the car to fly through on the road out of town. Grip had said the turnoff was about three miles south. There'd be no sign. It was supposed to be soon after he would pass a falling-down barn. There was the billboard Grip had talked about. Damn. Missed the turnoff. The barn was already fallen down and he was lucky the lights caught the protruding tin roof. He turned around in the road. No traffic to stop him.

The lane wasn't used much. Not even deeply rutted. An elbow turn almost sent him into a ditch. His truck would not have taken the turn at that speed. His lights caught the bank and total blackness beyond to the other bank. It wasn't a ditch. It was a drop-off into a narrow river heading to the Mississippi. He didn't worry that Walter couldn't have handled it even in the big car.

The cemetery should be about another mile. He thought about turning off his lights, but no moon was showing and he didn't want to end up in the river or against a tree. He slowed, looking for a place to pull over. But the road was squeezed by the river and trees. You didn't meet anyone coming back, or turn around, if you were headed to this resting place. He though about stopping in the road and walking the rest of the way, surprise whoever was already there. But if Midnight wasn't there, they'd know he was if they were behind him. But it was closer than Grip had remembered so he didn't have time to make a choice. The tombstones of the burial ground sprang into his car's lights dead ahead.

He guided the car into the cemetery pull-off, between faded signs spotlighted enough to make out Ebenezer Slave Cemetery on disintegrating wood. On the right, more readable, Ebenezer Cemetery for Negroes. His lights bounced off a white hearse and a shadowy long black car. They looked to be just arrived. Midnight stood behind Angelene.

Shep glanced at his shotgun on the floor and his officer's pistol on the seat. His leg wanted to cramp but he drug it out of the low-slung car's floorboard and climbed out, leaving the lights on.

"Mister," Angelene called out, "you have no business here. Please get in your car and leave."

"Just try it, Lt. Haddon," Mercer Midnight said, pointing a small pistol at him.

"It's true," Angelene said to her husband. "This is none of his concern."

"I'd say he's concerned. Wouldn't be here if he wasn't! Not concerned with much else, I'd say!"

"We only gave him a ride."

"You been together. In the news too. Described down to your high heels! Sonabitch wanted a room to put you in!"

Walter was sitting on a tombstone, the diggers on each side of him, guns pointed, kerosene lanterns hanging from their other hands. "He don't have another gun, boss," one of the men called.

"Get over here," Midnight said, pointing his gun at Shep.

Shep walked closer.

"Ames, you stay there with Goliath. Jeff, you check cripple here for a gun. Check the car."

Jeff patted his pockets and chest and thighs and said, "He ain't decked out with nothing but ribbons." Then he looked in the car. "Left it all in here. Got a long gun and army pistol."

Midnight said, "Give me your pistol, Angel. I know you didn't come here without it."

He reached under her skirt and pulled it out of a band around her leg on the inside just above her knee. He tossed it inside the hearse and then slid his hands all over her, between her upper thighs, even under her arms, looking for another one. "Where's the Derringer?"

"I don't have it. I brought the big one for you."

"So," he said after thinking it over. "You finally respecting me."

A back door of the car was open where Mama Gran lay against the back seat, head on her shoulder, left arm hanging, palm up. He didn't know if she was still drawing breath.

Mercer Midnight walked over and turned on the lights of both vehicles, which they'd probably turned off when they heard his car approach. Then he looked Shep over. "He why you left, Angel?"

"No. I didn't need any reason other than you."

Midnight moved closer to her. She was taller than he, but she seemed to shrink.

"You didn't think I'd go back on my word, did you? Can't give you another chance. My reputation don't allow it."

"I don't want one."

Angelene's voice was firm, just as it was at Mr. White's Kentucky gas station.

Midnight now spoke as if to console a grieving wife, such as a burying man would do. "Everybody wants a second chance."

"I'm having a baby," she said.

Her husband cackled. "Angel try anything! You can't be having a baby!"

A baby! She'd told him the doctor said she couldn't have another baby. Was she lying to Midnight, trying to buy some time? She wouldn't lie to go back to him. She wouldn't go back especially if she was pregnant. That was why she finally left. If the baby survived, and if she did, she wouldn't raise it with Midnight. Yes, women have their secrets.

"He didn't say I couldn't get pregnant. I guess Mama Gran's home remedy failed one more time."

"It his baby?" Mercer Midnight said, turning to look at Shep.

"How could that be possible? I met him a week ago. You had me watched."

"Somebody slipped up there," he said, pointing to Walter. "Be just one more thing you going to regret."

"Only one thing I regret, Mercer. I wanted to take you out and I didn't."

"You and what Army?" he said, then laughed, realizing he'd made a joke. "This one man cripple army? I know about him. Half blind, useless arm, stiff leg."

"I could've put a knife in your back at that hotel on Beale. Unless you now in the habit of havin' the men do the pumpin' for you."

"Ames, hit him upside the head with your gun!"

~ 236 ~

Walter reeled with the blow and his head dribbled dark blood.

"Jeff, you in trouble, big," Midnight said after watching Ames. "I told you to find out who was there."

"I did for sure, Boss. Nobody registered but an old lady from Detroit and a couple of salesmen from here and yon. Alabama. Kansas City. He said wasn't no white man."

"She paid him off. Ain't you learned what to do when you want information?"

Shep wasn't too surprised that she had taken the extra precaution of buying the proprietor. He probably had a double check-in book under the counter.

"Next time, you want to make sure of something."

Mercer Midnight's voice was cold. Shep wondered if Jeff felt he'd have a next time. "You was supposed to be outside my door last night, too."

Jeff backhanded Walter across the chin with his gun barrel.

Walter must have been expecting the retaliation. He grabbed Jeff's arm before it left his face. Before Jeff wrenched free with Ames's help, Walter turned the gun hand toward Ames and was able to force the trigger. Midnight ducked behind Angelene before Shep could make a move.

"You hit, Ames?" Midnight called, pointing his gun at Shep.

"No. Hole in my suit, dam'im. Shoulder pad." He sounded as if he dodged bullets every day. He pointed his gun at Walter but Midnight said, "No. We'll let him help the digging. Got a lot to do. Don't want daylight beatin' us."

Mama Gran moved in the seat. "What was it?" she said. "A cannon?" She tried to get out.

Angelene pulled away and Midnight let her go. "Mama Gran, just rest here."

"Did you find Tillie?"

"Not yet." Then she turned to Midnight. "She paid for a headstone. I'm going to look for it." She walked past Midnight, ignoring him, and picked up her large flashlight lying on the ground.

There must have been a scuffle before he got there, Shep decided.

She swung the light around, spotlighting all varieties of markers. The cemetery covered three or four acres and over a hundred years, but the slave section looked as old as the Ebenezer stone battlefield where the Philistines first slew the Israelites, as littered with graves as the field must have been with ancient soldiers. Piles of petrified wood denoting a burial, a mound or a sunken place, a fallen small concrete marker, dates un-readably old.

"Everybody join the procession," Midnight said. "We'll tour this fine southern city for Nee-grows. The undertaker first. Next, the departed. That'll be you, Angel, then Grandmother Dear. Then the half-dead shepherd who couldn't guard his flock.

"Traitors next. They'll have the firing squad. Ames, you the rear guard. Jeff, get the shovels."

FIFTY-ONE

Midnight enjoyed his devil's twist on God's calling. He led them winding among the graves. Shep helped Mama Gran. Angelene followed Midnight as if in a trance.

Finally Midnight stopped. "Right over there, Ames, next the edge. Away from the tree roots."

"How many you want, Boss?" said Ames.

Midnight didn't hesitate. "Two. I'll take my lovely wife back. People see her, make believers out of any that ain't."

"That's still one short," said Jeff.

"You saying I can't count?" said Midnight. "I bought permits for two graves. Even if I'd knew, raise suspicions buying them by the lot."

"How'd you get permits, boss?"

"You trying to learn the business, Jeff? No harm to tell you. That's what telephones and telegraphs and money transfers can do."

God. He did do things by the book. As far as practical.

Jeff backed away a little.

"Give the traitor a shovel, Jeff."

"You want the general to help, too?" said Jeff.

"I want him to help, I'll say so. You help."

Shep didn't feel too good about Jeff's chances of getting back home with air in his lungs, from Midnight's point of view. He thought Jeff felt the same way from the cautious looks he kept darting toward Ames.

"Angel," Midnight said. "Come on. Little toy soldier can help us. We got to get this taken care of. We'll find that grave if it's here. And it won't be."

"Do you mean you'll help? Why?"

"It's my duty as an undertaker." He actually rubbed his hands together, in spite of holding a gun.

Could there be a man who loved his job better?

"Then we gonna open it up and put her mama in with her. If she's buried here. And if she ain't, won't be no problem. Just dig 'em deeper. Can't leave bodies on top of the ground. Won't put none of mine in the river. Wouldn't be professional."

Angelene stumbled. Shep figured it was all getting the best of her. His good arm still supporting Mama Gran, his healing arm reacted as if it had escaped unharmed and reached out for Angelene.

Midnight said, "You touch her I'll shoot her." Shep put his arm up and stepped back and Midnight put himself in professional mode again.

"Most graveyards have plans. Like maps. Supposed to have plots numbered, filed in the courthouse. Here, it probably ain't so. Do us no good, anyway. Be all over by time court opens! But say it was early 1880's? All right. First ones in front date all the way back to 1840's. What was her name?"

"Tillie. Johnston or DuValle," said Angelene, sounding resigned, as Shep had never heard her.

The undertaker moved around a little. "Jeff, hand me a light. Think I can see in the dark? I ain't no bloodsucker. Let's look over to the edges. Don't guess you'd think of running."

Shep didn't know if Midnight was speaking to him or Angelene. Or possibly Jeff.

"Forget the family sections. They wouldn't put her with the family! I say look at the smallest stones. I'll bet the funeral man took his share of the money if he did put her here."

"She gave him plenty for his share," Angelene said. "I expect some mortuary men are honorable. They might think about their own graves."

He drew back to slap her, but stopped. "Don't want no marks on you," he said. "People got to know in their hearts I gave you what you had coming, but you'll be open casket. They should see what a beautiful woman I had for my wife."

They could not find the stone. Shep glanced at the diggers. Walter and Jeff were over half in the hole, like the mechanic at White's.

"She's not here," Midnight said. He laughed. "Pocket of the Miss'sippi burier too good for money, huh? She's in the river."

"Look for the DuValle family section," said Mama Gran, who had managed to come alive and move away from Shep toward them. "He might have had another reason for not letting her go with me."

"Love?" said Angelene.

"Or possession. They're both powerful," said Mama Gran, looking full at Mercer Midnight.

Midnight flashed his light around.

"Here it is," said Angelene in a few minutes, walking through an opening in a wrought iron fence around a section with several headstones. She went in and out around the headstones with her light like a spirit in unrest. "DuValle. Mira DuValle, 1889. Joshua DuValle, 1922. Heptha Simms DuValle, 1931. Infant DuValle, 1850. Marie Thomas DuValle, 18 something. James DuValle Thomas. 1890 something. Turrell DuValle, 1895. Infant DuValle, 1860, here's another. I can't read it."

Midnight moved to shine his light on it, also.

"Tillie Johnston DuValle," said Angelene, triumph making her voice strong. "Grandmother Tillie," she said, touching the stone, her words bleeding with loss.

Shep helped Mama Gran step to the site. Mama Gran seemed inches smaller than this morning. No movement seemed inside her. Angelene moved to them and stepped with her close to the grave.

This was the opportunity he had been waiting for. Angelene and Mama Gran away from Midnight and the diggers occupied. In the second he was going to act, Mama Gran exhaled a moan like a sad song and collapsed in Angelene's arms, her life gone.

Angelene screamed, "No!" and collapsed with Mama Gran on her. Midnight looked surprised and jumped toward Angelene as if he were afraid of a ghost getting him, but lowering his pistol. Ames looked toward them and said "What is it, Boss?" and just at that time scuffling happened where Walter and Jeff were. They heard a shot and Angelene yelled, "Walter!"

At the same instant Shep lunged toward Midnight, who seemed to forget he had a gun as well as a flashlight. Shep tackled him like in days of old. The wiry man went down like a wide receiver. Shep bent his good leg and pulled out the pistol tucked in his sock, the pistol he had brought from his office at Dorthea's suggestion, and had counted on whoever searched him to miss. He stuck it under Midnight's chin, just as Angelene reached them and Shep heard three shots so close he didn't know who had caught bullets or who had fired. Midnight's gun dropped and Angelene was kneeling on the ground, a two-shot Derringer in her hand. Midnight was on the ground beside him, blood gushing from his temple. And from his mouth.

A shot behind them got their attention. The lanterns had the site lit. Jeff was not to be seen, probably already warming his grave with a broken neck at Walter's hands. Ames was at the grave's edge pointing his gun at Walter's head, the hole now so deep that Walter could not get out of it as quickly as he needed to. But Walter grabbed Ames' feet and the man went down, his pistol arm flailing. As he was bringing it around to fire again, Shep pointed his pistol and fired like he'd never learned to do in combat training. He'd practiced fastdraws and dodging pretend bullets and firing in the woods so much as a boy, he'd never lose the sense of aim without having more than an instant to focus. It wasn't so different aiming to kill a man this time instead of putting a bullet in a tree.

Just when the sound of the shot died, they heard a car coming and saw its lights. God. Who could it be?

"Is it the law?" Walter said, climbing out of the grave.

"Are you all right?" Shep asked Angelene, pulling her to him.

~ 241 ~

He felt her head nodding against him. "No matter what else happens. He's gone."

But where the hell did the Derringer come from? She had known Midnight would search for it. There was only one place. Mama Gran had carried it for her. The first chance she had to get it was when her grandmother collapsed.

"Are you hurt bad, Walter?" she said.

Blood was trickling down his side.

"I think it went in and out."

"I'll get a cloth," she said, just as the car arrived. It was an old black car, definitely not the law. Four Negro men got out, the first three none other than Grip Wilson and his two lookouts.

"Good God!" Shep said. "Man, I'm glad to see you. But what are you doing out here?"

Grip smiled and said, "Came to see the beautiful black woman in the big black car!"

The men with him spread out and took the scene in. "FBI couldn't have done more," one said. "Good place for killing if it needs be done," Grip said. "Handy."

"I guess they're dead," Walter said. "We haven't checked."

"Boys, make sure," Grip said.

"The Yankees lost this battle," said the man who had gone inside to fetch Grip at the riverside joint.

"Wasn't they a Bible battle at Ebenezer?" said the other man.

"Seems like," the first man said.

"Grip, this is the woman this war was fought over," Shep said, putting his arm around Angelene's waist to steady her. "Angelene, this is Grip Wilson. I met him in town. Turns out we're like distant cousins."

Grip laughed.

Angelene said, "I'm glad you kinfolk stick together."

"And this is Walter Smith, Mrs. Midnight's driver and bodyguard. Friend to her and me." Grip shook hands with Walter like he had with him, like city people do. Grip had left the farm.

Angelene's shoulders started heaving with the effort to hold in all that needed to break free.

"Now, what is it we need to be doing?" Grip said to Shep. "I don't know if the shots was heard anywhere, but ain't never no good idea to be around dead folk didn't die of natural cause."

"Would they mind finishing the grave and digging another? He was a legitimate mortician. He got permits," Shep said, pointing at Midnight. "And we might as well use them."

"Kill y'all then bury you in the law!" Grip shook his head.

"If we dig two, like he arranged, maybe there won't be any questions."

"Whatever you say, Cousin," Grip said.

Angelene opened the trunk and poured water over the rag and had Walter take his shirt off. It looked as if he was right about the bullet not lodging in him. She squeezed water over it, then got a small bottle of iodine. "It's going to hurt bad," she said.

"Pour it on," he said. "Won't hurt. Feels too good to be alive."

Then Angelene turned back to where Mama Gran lay, and Shep followed her. He put his arm around Angelene's waist. "I'm glad she was able to know that her daughter has been here all this time, buried with their family," he said.

She knelt by Mama Gran and he went and fetched a blanket from the car. Walter came over and helped him wrap her body which now seemed weightless.

"I'll not put her in Mercer Midnight's hearse," she said. "It's seen too much evil! Tell Grip to take it somewhere and burn it. Then dump it in the river."

"While you were doctoring Walter, I talked to Grip. He says there's a Negro mortuary we can take Mama Gran to down the road a few miles. We'll carry her in the car. Just like we came down here together. Grip can drive mine and lead us there."

"She got her last wish. Maybe God will let her know what else transpired here tonight."

"We got it all ready," Grip called. "We got the midnight man in one, the other two together. Any last words?"

"God forgive them if He wants to," Angelene said. "I can't."

"Shovel it in," Grip said to the men.

FIFTY-TWO

Shep was in his room and Angelene in hers next door. Walter was at home with Grip, as there was not another room in the small home Grip had taken them to that rented room and board to travelers of her kind. Walter wouldn't hear of sharing Shep's room, and Shep wouldn't say I'll be with Angelene, anyway, so my room's available. This was the first time the four of them would not be together in a time that seemed like he was born as an adult to it. Angelene wanted to stay with her grandmother through the night, but had listened to her body's voice of reason.

But the custom in the south was not to leave the casket alone until the burial, so Grip asked an old lady he knew to sit with her. She said she remembered a tale about a woman who had stolen her grandbaby off to the North, away from a slave-owning black-skinned family. Against nature, slaving your own. She would like to sit with her.

Shep went to the small bathroom and showered after he heard Angelene go back to her room. He'd thrown his duffle of clean clothes into the trunk before he left home. He left his dirty clothes in a pile outside his door as the landlady said; she knew a way to get blood out if it wasn't too old. She didn't even seem inquisitive about the blood or his being white and in her hotel. Grip had taken care of it.

"Be some cold roast beef and cornbread," she offered, "if you folk hungry."

"Yes, m'am," he said. "Would you bring our supper to her room?"

She did look surprised at that.

"She's tired," he told Mrs. Grant, to make her more comfortable about it. "And we have several things to discuss."

He knocked on Angelene's door. She opened it and pulled him inside. Her hair was still wrapped in a towel to keep the shower from wetting it. She was in a light short-sleeved robe, down to her ankles, and tied at the waist. She collapsed against him as his arms went around her.

They stood there until Mrs. Grant knocked, bringing the supper. Shep moved a little table so that one could sit on the bed and the other in the room's only chair, and Mrs. Grant arranged the food on it.

"Would you like this dress?" Angelene asked, handing her the midnight blue. "If you can get the spot out. I don't like it any more."

Mrs. Grant said, "I know just the thing."

He pulled the chair out for Angelene, but she said, unwrapping her hair, "I'll take the bed and put my feet up."

He propped pillows against the headboard and she sat against them, and he moved his chair next to the bed so they were facing each other.

They ate the meat and spread the cornbread with butter and tomato preserves, swallowing milk down, not talking, except for Angelene's usual comments on the food. "Down here is where Mama Gran learned to make her cornbread. Never had tomatoes like this. It's good to eat again."

He put the tray outside the door and slipped his shoes off and climbed into the bed with her.

"I don't know who I am now," she said. "But I'm not Angelene. You're lying here with a stranger to herself."

He stretched to reach the lamp and pulled the chain. He heard her sob, as she had when she saw his injuries, and knew she was weeping her old life away. No Angelene any more. Would it be easier to let her go, knowing it, or harder? Either way, he understood that she was someone else now.

He settled next to her, feeling her adjust against him and put her head on his shoulder as he put his arm under her neck.

"Poor Tillie. Tillie's dark life ended at the age my dark life started," she said.

He touched her hair, still pulled up and braided. In a few minutes he said, "Tillie deserved a chance to live. Just as you do. Maybe you could give her a chance to live."

She thought it over. "Yes. I'll be Tillie now, and live for both of us."

Just as Mama Gran had done as her life left her, he felt Angelene exhale the last breath as the woman she had once been.

He lost her brown skin in the darkness. He moved his other hand to find her, and knew that it had come to rest on her stomach. He thought about her baby, knowing they both would have a good life with Lionel and his family.

Would Tillie always remember the first man who loved Angelene? The first man Angelene loved? She snuggled closer against him. In a few minutes she was asleep. Then he closed his eyes and slept, too.

END

GLINDA MCKINNEY

While reading some of the world's great books and teaching them to high school students in Mississippi and Tennessee, Ms. McKinney decided to try her hand at writing about some of the characters she had nurtured in her imagination. She enrolled in creative writing and began her first novel. These days, she continues writing; substitute teaches; teaches four-year-old Sunday School; helps coach the local high school tennis team; "reads 'til her eyes bleed;" revels in her circle of friends; recently bid farewell to Babycakes, her cat of almost 24 years; and most of all spends as much time as possible with her family.

She would like to hear from you at
glindamckinney@att.net
She would also be grateful for a review on Amazon or a shoutout on your Facebook, Twitter, or other favorite media site.

She invites you to read her first novel, **The Ladies of Shallot**, available in paperback through your local bookstore, Amazon.com, or through your Kindle or any E-reader.

Her next novel, **Glory Days**, will be out Spring 2015.

Excerpts from both books follow.

THE LADIES OF SHALLOT

THREE - Heard a Whisper

But it wasn't Lydia Hawkins. A man stood near the rail watching the rain. His shoulders were as wide as Crystal remembered Dad's being. He was not quite as tall as Dad or even the Reverend John Half. He had neat dark brown hair – unlike Dad's which was the very color of hers according to Sarah, until it seemingly turned gray overnight, and which he let grow, the last few years wearing it tied back with a length of twine or strip of rough cloth, befitting his artistic muse, he said.

A dark sweater clung to this man's shoulders like an old friend, like it dawned on her that she'd like to. His jeans had that been washed a million times look with the slim fit of him imbedded in them. His brown boots looked expensive and made for walking over hill and dale and through rain like today's. He wasn't the bigger-than-life image of Dad and the Reverend, but a casual emission of being in charge of his own life. She wondered.

Seeing all that in the instant before he turned to face her was maybe like seeing your life flash in front of you just before you figure to die. But she couldn't bring herself to look into his eyes to see what the man was driven by, as she felt the Reverend Half had wanted to do that evening he stood on her border and looked at her.

This man had a nice nose. She couldn't remember John Half's particularly; his whole face was what you saw. And this man had a neat beard and mustache, like so many men were wearing, except in Shallot. He had a little gray at the temples, so she knew he was at least in her generation, although she had no gray and never would. Sarah would nag her too much to ever allow it when it did come. She would know this man the next time she saw him, all right, if she ever did.

"Miss Bell? I'm Matt Hawkins."

Probably as in Mr. Lydia Hawkins. Was this anger she felt welling up? Because he had come to take her prized possession?

"Come in," she said, leaving the screen door closed as she turned back inside. That wasn't polite. But she could feel him staring at her and that wasn't polite either. Even though she had stared at him, he couldn't have known it. She hadn't even felt stared at by John Half two weeks ago. She'd just felt his considering.

It was hard to reconcile, a man in the house after so many years, since Dad died. Sure, old man Thrasher came inside to do whatever she couldn't manage with the help of her fix-it manual, but it was rare and always while she was at work. Especially unsettling because this man reminded her of Dad, why, she didn't know.

"It's stunning," he said, following her glance away from him to the painting.

She saw him cover up his surprise that the painting wasn't already packaged properly.

"Would you like me to send a professional to wrap it?" he asked.

"No. I can do it."

"If it doesn't stop raining, I'll come another time," he said.

"I wouldn't take a chance on it getting wet," she said, past her first fluttering over him, annoyed now, wondering if it showed.

"No, I'm sure," he said, "it's just that you shouldn't be expected to do it. It's not even your responsibility anymore." He gave a hint of a sarcastic smile. "Already new-owner insured."

"I'll take care of it," she said, leaving him standing there. She went upstairs and unearthed from one of Willette's closets a large box that a mink coat had been delivered in from Levy's up in Memphis, who knew how long ago, the store had been closed for years. The yellowed tissue paper still inside would make good cushioning. She went down the back stairs to the back hall, ran in the kitchen and turned off the burner, then picked her way down the basement steps to get a roll of brown wrapping paper left from Dad's stock of supplies, so old it might disintegrate the minute it saw light. A step fell through as she came back up and dislodged the paint can that was bracing it on the step below. She let out a little surprised yelp and heard the clattering. Sarah had correctly told her the steps weren't for the faint-hearted a few years ago when they went down during a tornado scare. When she came through the doorway in the back hall, Matt Hawkins was there, about to come down, and she almost bumped into him.

"You OK?" he said.

"Just a paint can I knocked over."

He followed her to the front. "Would you like me to take it down for you? The frame looks heavy."

"No, I can do it." Then she remembered long ago instruction. "But thank you." Good grief. Dust was thick on the back of the frame next to the wall. Note to self. Fire the maid. Ha ha. She braced it on the floor and used her soft shirttail to rake it off.

"Even the frame is a work of art," he said.

"It was hand carved by Dad." And it was brushed with what looked like real gold. It occurred to her the frame was probably worth several hundred dollars. She should ask extra from Lydia Hawkins for it. After wrapping the painting on the dining room table with two layers of tissue paper and stuffing the crevices with more tissue, she secured the box with duct tape, then wrapped the entire box in the heavy paper.

"Back in a minute," she said, and went to the storage room on the enclosed back porch for a roll of heavy plastic she kept for gardening needs.

Matt Hawkins let her do it without protest or further offers, not even any small talk.

"This should protect it from the rain," she said with some satisfaction.

He smiled. "It's stopped raining. The sun's been out for a while."

Well, she deserved that. But she ignored it and darted her eyes away. She ran her hands over the plastic, testing the edges of the tape, seeing the painting in her head, knowing she would never touch it or even see it again. She was glad she wasn't the crying type.

GLORY DAYS

ONE

He carried her in like a young bridegroom might, noting only a slight strain in his muscles, strong from years of labor. He stopped just inside the door, letting his eyes adjust to the room cleansed of light by the lateness of the November day, and by the dark coarse curtains pulled together at both windows.

Not even a glow of banked ashes remained in the fireplace. But gradually, light that didn't know how fast it was supposed to travel crept slowly through the half-open door into the aphotic room and hung on the dark air like a spectre.

The soft purse dangling from her arm bounced against his thigh, and the smooth fabric of the scarf around her hair brushed his chin as he shifted to see the room he'd never been in. Thinking of the irony in that, he felt her head jerk from his touch, though he knew she realized the contact had been unintentional.

"Which bed?" he asked. The double bed nearest the fireplace was covered smoothly with patchwork quilts. A crocheted coverlet, similar to the one on his wife's bed, lay haphazardly over rumpled white sheets on the other one, like a voluminous wedding gown tossed aside in haste.

There was no mistaking the impatience in her voice when she said, "The one closest to the fireplace, but put me down here." She was light in his arms, even in her winter wool coat and holding the blanketed baby in her own arms.

"It's the baby sick, not me," she added.

She had told him that already, when he lifted her out of the truck and carried her across the yard so she wouldn't have to slog through the mud. He hadn't wanted to pull the truck next to the porch; likely it would have mired down. It rained again this afternoon on the way back from Goforth, and there was already too much water and mud left over from the rain of the past week.

Why he had not put her down when he reached the porch and then gone back for the other child asleep in the seat he couldn't understand. Why he hadn't set her down when he entered the room, he couldn't say. But he didn't repeat now the excuse that he had soothed himself with, that he was saving her shoes from the mud. Though he knew she was seventeen years younger than his thirty-eight, she succeeded in making him ill at ease almost every time they met.

"It was considerate of you," she said, surprising him and, he thought, herself as well. Maybe she was feeling better about everything, now that she was back home. At any rate, her words were somewhat reassuring to him.

He was glad he'd thought to rake his boots on the edge of the porch planks before stepping into the house. "I'll get the boy," he said as she put the baby on the bed. "William," she said, realizing, of course, that he already knew the boy's name. When he returned with William, still asleep, and with her small package of purchases, she was kneeling at the fireplace trying to start a fire.

He didn't want to ask again which bed, and hoped she would volunteer the information, even if it did appear to be an order like before. Something told him she wouldn't want the boy in bed with the sick baby, but what did he know about children?

"Put him on the bed with Jenny. On the foot. I'll have to get the other bed made up." Her attitude told him he should have known something so simple. "I had to strip it this morning and wash everything. You know how baby puke smells."

He couldn't help smiling a little that she would say that to try to shock him; she knew how to put a man in his place. Then he realized she was embarrassed when she said, "I shouldn't have said that. It was the wrong thing ..."

"It wasn't so bad," he told her. She gave him another one of those looks that said, you really don't know what I'm talking about, do you? then said, "Not just because ... I never call it that ... I shouldn't have said anything like that because it might remind you of your baby."

"That's all right. It didn't." It was so long ago; he sometimes went a few days without thinking about his son.

"See? I said the wrong thing again to you. You hadn't made a connection, but now I've reminded you."

Did what he thought really matter to her? "Don't worry about it." He carefully placed the boy on the bed then stood with the package, holding it as if it were a football in the crook of his arm. It was wrapped in brown paper and tied with string and seemed too small to contain the things she surely needed to buy for two children, even the oldest, at two, still young enough to be called a baby. "Where do you want this?"

"On the table," she said, nodding toward the corner with a small table with two straight-backed chairs and a highchair at it. "Would you get the matches out of the package and light the lamp? I just used the last one here," she added, and blew on the fire as it almost went out.

Trying not to rummage, he looked for the matches. They were under a thin can of talcum powder, a box of baking soda, some spools of thread, a jar of petroleum jelly, a bag of oatmeal and a few cans of evaporated milk. He turned up the wick and struck the match, and after lighting the lamp and carefully replacing the glass chimney, squeaky clean, over the flame so it wouldn't get smoked, he went to the fireplace and held the match to the wood.

"I've never been good at building a fire," she said, and blew on it again. "I'm scar – Grandma or Henry always did it."

He was surprised that she almost admitted she was scared of anything, and wondered why she was afraid of lighting a fire. "You keep it too clean. Let some ashes build up under the grate." He poked at the partially charred logs, knocking off what he could that was burned and with the shovel raked all the ashes from the bed of the fireplace so they were under the wood. He shifted the logs so air could flow and create a draft and then added the splinters and bits from the wood box. He fanned with his hand and the flames lapped and leapt.

She looked at him like he had given her the gift of fire. "Do you know where fire came from?" she asked.

That was a question out of the blue. While he was pondering what to say, she told him.

"I read a legend about it once – a giant animal stole fire from heaven or somewhere and gave it to men, and then … I don't know what, but something awful happened to him because of it," she said.

"Not an animal. A Titan," he said, then seeing her puzzled expression before she removed it, he added, "Sort of an ancient God."

But then she looked at him like she expected to hear the rest of the story. He wasn't sure he remembered it all. Miss Wombold's Latin class was over twenty years ago and seemed longer. And this certainly was an unlikely place and time to recall it. "Prometheus," he said.

He glanced at the Remington on the wall above the mantel. "If you need me, go in the yard and fire it. The sound would carry over the fields to my place."

She nodded, but he didn't think she would ask him for anything unless one of her kids needed something and he was the only alternative, like today, to get the croupy baby to the doctor. She didn't say anything else, so he turned to go. He looked toward the baby girl. "I'll stop by tomorrow and see how she's doing."

"You don't have to do that. I know she'll be fine. Besides, Henry should be here tomorrow."

She said it like she dared him to deny it. But he knew Henry would be back. Bad pennies and seven-year locusts and Henry. They all turned up eventually. "I'm sure he will," he said.

Made in the USA
Coppell, TX
24 January 2023